The fiery brilliance of the Zebra Hologram Heart which you see on the cover is created by "laser holography." This is the revolutionary process in which a powerful laser beam records light waves in diamond-like facets so tiny that 9,000,000 fit in a square inch. No print or photograph can match the vibrant colors and radiant glow of a hologram.

So look for the Zebra Hologram Heart whenever you buy a historical romance. It is a shimmering reflection of our guarantee that you'll find consistent quality between the covers!

MOONLIGHT TRYST

Feeling her way, Rachel moved slowly to the head of the bed where she found the top edge of the covers. He was lying in the center of the bed, but there would be room for her to slip in beside him if she were careful.

She was very careful, lifting the covers just enough to allow her to creep beneath them and lowering herself with infinite care. Her slight shivering eased as she relaxed into the feather mattress and breathed in the musky male scent of the body next to hers.

Her fingers grazed bare flesh and the blood began to race through her veins. Panic surged through her. This was a mistake, a terrible mistake! Her muscles were just coiled to propel her from the bed when the body next to hers moved.

He muttered something that sounded like her name, and his arms went around her. His heat, his scent, were enervating, overwhelming any resistance that she might have made. In the next second his mouth found hers, and all thought of resistance drained away.

"Rachel?" His voice was a mere rasp, but the single word contained a myriad of questions. Every one of them was a question Rachel did not want to answer.

"Yes," she whispered and pressed her mouth to his again . . .

BESTSELLING ROMANCE
from Zebra Books

CAPTIVE SURRENDER   (1986, $3.95)
by Michalann Perry
When both her husband and her father are killed in battle, young
Gentle Fawn vows revenge. Yet once she catches sight of the
piercing blue eyes of her enemy, the Indian maiden knows that
she can never kill him. She must sate the desires he kindled, or
forever be a prisoner of his love.

WILD FLAME   (1671, $3.95)
by Gina Delaney
Although reared as a gentle English lass, once Milly set foot on
the vast Australian farm, she had the Outback in her blood.
When handsome Matthew Aylesbury met Milly, he vowed to have
her, but only when the heat of his passion had melted her pride
into willing submission.

WILD FURY   (1987, $3.95)
by Gina Delaney
Jessica Aylesbury was the beauty of the settled territory in Aus-
tralia's savage Outback, but no one knew that she was an adopted
part-native. Eric, the worshipped friend of her childhood, now
an outlaw, was the only man who made her burn with desire. She
could never let anyone else teach her the pleasures of woman-
hood.

TEXAS TRIUMPH   (2009, $3.95)
by Victoria Thompson
The Circle M was most important to Rachel McKinsey, so she
took her foreman as a husband to scare off rustlers. But now that
Rachel had sworn that they be business partners, she could never
admit that all she really wanted was to consummate their vows
and have Cole release her sensual response.

TEXAS VIXEN   (1823, $3.95)
by Victoria Thompson
It was either accept Jack Sinclair's vile proposal of marriage or
sell the Colson Ranch. Jack swore, if it took till dawn, he'd sub-
due Maggie Colson's honey-sweet lips and watch her sea-green
eyes deepen to emerald with passion.

*Available wherever paperbacks are sold, or order direct from the
Publisher. Send cover price plus 50¢ per copy for mailing and
handling to Zebra Books, Dept. 2009, 475 Park Avenue South,
New York, N.Y. 10016. Residents of New York, New Jersey and
Pennsylvania must include sales tax. DO NOT SEND CASH.*

TEXAS TRIUMPH
VICTORIA THOMPSON

ZEBRA BOOKS
KENSINGTON PUBLISHING CORP.

ZEBRA BOOKS

are published by

Kensington Publishing Corp.
475 Park Avenue South
New York, NY 10016

Copyright © 1987 by Vicki Thompson

All rights reserved. No part of this book may be reproduced
in any form or by any means without the prior written
consent of the Publisher, excepting brief quotes used in
reviews.

First printing: March 1987

Printed in the United States of America

To my mother, Mary Straface,
who taught me how to be a lady,

and

to Nira Herrmann and Phyllis DiFrancesco
who deserve co-author status on this one.

Chapter I

Rachel watched the men riding into the ranchyard. From her post by her father's office window, she could just barely make out their silhouettes in the winter twilight, but still she could easily pick Cole Elliot out of the group. As much as she hated to admit it, the sight of his tall body astride a horse had imprinted itself in her memory during the nine months she had been home from school, and even darkness could not disguise it from her.

Just yesterday she had stood at this very window and watched him ride in, but she had not stood at the window very long. She had flown out the door and down the steps and into the yard, screaming her futile protest at the sight of the blanket-shrouded form draped over the horse Cole Elliot had been leading.

Elliot had vaulted from his saddle and caught her before she could reach her father's lifeless body. Then he had held her while she sobbed out incoherent questions, answering them with a cool deliberation that had calmed her even as it had amazed her.

Looking back, she realized that he had been just as upset as she, but that he had channeled his emotions into anger.

"Papa," she had whispered brokenly as she watched the gentle way the men lowered his body to the ground.

7

"It's not a pretty sight," Elliot had warned her, his voice strange and husky. She had hardly noticed, however, so intent was she on reaching her father's side.

How could anyone who had been so alive just hours earlier suddenly be so cold and white and still? she had wondered then. Even now, more than twenty-four hours later, she could not believe it. Oh, she had suspected the worst when he had not come back from his morning ride at noon. He never missed a meal without telling her ahead of time, and Elliot had been furious, blaming himself for letting her father go alone. Not that he could have prevented it, of course. Rachel had overheard their argument that morning, Elliot telling her father he was a damn fool, and her father telling Elliot he would ride where he damn well pleased on his own ranch.

The scene in the ranch yard blurred as tears flooded her eyes. Impatiently, she drew an already soggy handkerchief from her pocket and dabbed them away. She had cried enough. She could not afford to mourn any more just now. Later, when things were settled, she would indulge herself in an ocean of tears, but for now she must meet with Cole Elliot, and he had already seen her weeping. This time he would find her calm and rational. This time they would talk. And plan.

As she watched him and the other men dismounting down in the yard, she allowed herself a moment of worry, wondering how her meeting with him would go. He was a difficult man to talk to, a difficult man to understand, and now she realized that even after all these months, she really did not know him well enough to judge what his reaction would be to the suggestion she planned to make.

How could he still be such a mystery when he had been so much a part of her daily life since she had returned home? He was, in fact, the first person she had seen when she stepped down from the train the day she returned home from school. She had been scanning the station platform, looking for her father, and her searching gaze had snagged for a brief moment on the tall stranger.

Exactly why he caught her eyes, she had never been quite certain. It could not have been his looks because no one would ever accuse him of being handsome. His features were too sharp, as if the relentless Texas wind had scoured away any excess flesh that might have softened him, leaving only sun-darkened skin stretched sparely over his bones. His nose was a little on the large side and a trifle crooked, as if it had once been broken, and his mouth was too broad. Still, he was quite striking, standing there in his spotless white Stetson and his brand-new clothes, clothes she had then suspected must have been purchased that very morning to impress whomever he was meeting at the train.

Just as she noticed him, he noticed her, too, and she saw a flicker of interest in his eyes, eyes that were as startlingly blue as the broad Texas sky. Gratified, she made a mental note to pursue that interest, but for the moment she had something slightly more important to do.

"Rachel?" a lovingly familiar voice asked.

That was when she found her father. She could tell by the uncertainty in his voice that he could not quite believe it was she, and she was immensely pleased. She was dressed in the height of fashion, from the top of her beribboned bonnet to the pointed toes of her black kid boots. At Miss Isabel Prine's School for Young Ladies, she had learned everything there was to know about being a proper lady, and she had taken great pains to display all her knowledge today.

"Papa!" she cried, rushing into his arms. He hugged her with bone-crushing intensity, and when he finally released her, she kissed his cheek above his mutton-chop whiskers. "Oh, Papa, you're just as handsome as ever," she declared. And he was. He was still the good-looking, "Black Irish" man pictured in her parents' faded wedding photograph. She pretended not to notice that the cares and worries of the last two years had added new lines to his face and a touch of gray

9

to his thick, dark hair.

"And you're all grown up," he exclaimed, his eyes misting suspiciously. "You look just like your mother did the first time I ever saw her."

Rachel laughed in delight, thrilled that she was, at last, the woman her father had always wanted her to be. She could remember nothing of her mother, but she had seen pictures and knew how much her father had loved the woman who had given her life. Her father was paying Rachel the ultimate compliment. Two years ago when she was only an awkward adolescent, Sean McKinsey had seen the potential. Not wanting that potential to be wasted, he had shipped her off to the very same school where her mother had gone twenty years earlier. That he had other far more serious reasons for wanting her temporarily out of Texas, she knew only too well, but now was not the time to consider them.

"Do you think you got your money's worth?" she asked, teasing and turning a very graceful pirouette for his inspection. She knew he would think so. He had, in fact, gotten far more than his money's worth. Rachel had been quite pleasantly surprised with Miss Isabel's school and had taken to the regimentation as if born to it. Miss Isabel always said that Rachel possessed a natural grace, but it was far more than that. She took an absurd pleasure in learning all the intricate rules of decorum and in conducting herself like a Real Lady. If the other girls poured tea properly, then Rachel poured it beautifully and with a flourish. Her excellence became almost a joke in the school, especially because she herself recognized the humor of the situation. There she was, a shining example of everything the Lady of the Manor should be, but all she really wanted out of life was to return to her father's ranch on the Texas prairie where the social event of the season would be feeding bacon and beans to a hungry, saddle-sore roundup crew.

Her dark brown eyes dancing with the secret joke, Rachel waited for her father's verdict. His matching dark eyes took in her stylish, hourglass figure clad in a maroon traveling suit, her raven hair pulled taut into an intricate knot and the face that two years' maturity had sculpted into loveliness. He smiled with satisfaction. "I think I'd better send Miss Isabel a little something extra," he concluded with a wink.

Rachel laughed and kissed him again, delighted that he was so obviously pleased. When she stepped back from the kiss, she noticed her father looking at something over her shoulder.

"There's somebody I want you to meet," he said, prompting her to turn. In that one second she recalled the tall stranger who was probably still somewhere nearby, and she remembered her resolve to follow up on the spark of interest he had exhibited.

Turning with an anticipatory smile, Rachel experienced a small jolt of surprise to discover that the person her father wanted her to meet was none other than that very stranger. He had pulled off his snow-white Stetson to reveal a shock of sun-kissed brown locks which had been hastily finger-combed in preparation for this introduction. Her smile brightened. How convenient. This very interesting man happened to know her father.

"Rachel, this is our foreman, Cole Elliot," her father announced with obvious pride.

Rachel's smile froze in place. Cole Elliot? This man couldn't be Cole Elliot. She knew all about her father's new foreman—well, at least he was new in the two years since she had been gone—and somehow she had pictured a much more mature, much different man. This Cole Elliot could not be ten years older than her nineteen, far too young to have been all the places and done all the things her father had bragged about.

Or was he? Now that she looked closer, now that she met those blue eyes squarely, she saw how old he really was. Not old in years perhaps, but old in experience. Those azure eyes had seen more trouble than Rachel ever wanted to hear about, and the lingering sadness she sensed in him snuffed out her smile.

"Cole, this here is my daughter, Rachel," her father was saying, and he placed one large hand on her back to encourage her to move in Elliot's direction.

Automatically, because such niceties had become automatic with her, she lifted her kid-gloved hand, prepared to offer it to him, and her gaze flickered naturally to where his own hand hung loosely by his side.

By his *gun*. Her gaze locked on the worn wooden grip. A working cowboy seldom wore a sidearm, but sometimes he might strap one on to go to town, just to show off. This weapon was no "show off" gun, however. This weapon had seen serious use, and the tied-down holster gave silent notice that it was always ready.

A thousand thoughts jumbled together in her mind, but the most disturbing one was that her father, her sweet, wonderful father, had come to town with a gunman at his side. Were things so bad that he did not dare to show himself without a bodyguard? Was his life in actual danger?

Swallowing down hard on the panic that surged within her, she lifted her eyes once more to Cole Elliot's. "How do you do, Mr. Elliot?" she recited by rote. The hand she had lifted came to rest against her stomach. She had been away a long time but she still remembered the etiquette of the plains. "I won't offer to shake hands because I know you want to keep your gun hand free, but I'm very pleased to meet you," she said woodenly, knowing that her solemn tone belied that statement but unable to force herself to sound cheerful at that moment, even for the sake of common politeness.

Surely, Mr. Elliot would understand her feelings, she thought, and for a moment, she imagined that she saw comprehension in those clear blue eyes. Then, as if someone had snuffed a candle, they suddenly grew blank of expression. "Miss Rachel," he said in acknowledgment, and nodded curtly.

She had thought then that she and Elliot had understood

each other, but she could not have been more wrong. She had expected that they would enjoy a certain amount of camaraderie since they were both concerned with her father's safety, but from that day forward he had treated her not with friendship but with a deference that was almost onerous. She had tried everything to break through his shell of reserve, knowing as she did now much her father wanted the two of them to get along—and more than get along, if her suspicions on that score were correct. But nothing, not common politeness, not circumspect efforts at flirting, not even outright rudeness had even dented that shell. The intriguing stranger she had glimpsed on the station platform had ceased to exist.

Rachel sometimes wondered if she had imagined the flicker of interest she had seen in those blue eyes that day. It wasn't very flattering to think that simply meeting her had stifled that interest forever, but that did seem to be the case. Oh, he was always unfailingly civil to her, and she supposed they had established a sort of working relationship. Perversely, she could never quite be satisfied with just that, though. Sometimes she was even tempted to do something drastic to get his attention, but as much as she longed for them to be friends, she never quite had the courage. Her one attempt in that direction had failed miserably, and she had since concluded that she would probably have to explode a load of dynamite in his face to get any kind of reaction at all.

Rachel smiled grimly at the thought and stepped away from her vigil at the window. Rubbing her arms to ward off the winter chill that had crept through the glass, she realized that, in a manner of speaking, she really was dealing with dynamite. The suggestion she was planning to make to him would be the emotional equivalent of an explosion. She only hoped it would not do irreparable damage to their already tenuous association.

The horses' hooves made weary plocking sounds on the

packed earth of the ranch yard as the men rode in. Hunched in their jackets with hats pulled down over their ears against the cold, the half-frozen men still made the effort to turn in their saddles and glance up at the ranchhouse where a light burned in the office window to dispel the evening shadows.

She was up there, alone now. Out of respect for her loss, they quickly averted their eyes, even though she could not possibly know that they had been staring up at her house and thinking of her. Such was their sense of place.

Their gazes went, instead, to the man who led them. To him would fall the task of reporting what they had found today, and not one of them envied him the job. As they climbed stiffly from their mounts, they watched him, noting how calmly he bore the burden of his responsibilities.

Cole stretched and then tried to stamp the numbness from his legs. He, too, had seen the light in the ranchhouse office window, and he frowned now, thinking of the message he would have to deliver. After having had to tell her yesterday that her father was dead, he didn't like the thought of bringing her more bad news.

"I don't reckon you found anything either?"

Cole glanced up at the tall, lanky man who had come to meet him. It was his segundo, Miles. The two had split up earlier in the day, each leading half the men in hopes of covering more ground and, perhaps, finding the trail of Mr. McKinsey's killers. Cole could tell from the expression on the older man's gaunt face that his luck had been no better than Cole's.

Cole shook his head grimly, not bothering to hide his disappointment. They hadn't really had much hope, though, not with the ground frozen the way it was.

"Poor kid, it'll be tough on her," Cole muttered, half to himself.

"She's not made of glass, you know. She can take it," Miles contradicted.

Cole glared up at Miles, suddenly and unaccountably

14

furious. "She shouldn't *have* to take it," Cole declared.

Miles's weathered face twisted into a concerned frown. After all these months of very carefully keeping Miss Rachel at arm's length, Cole sure hadn't taken long to slip into the role of her protector. Miles wondered if Cole had even realized it himself yet. And what his reaction would be when he did.

"No, she shouldn't," Miles agreed, and then in a peace-making gesture, offered, "I'll unsaddle your horse for you."

"No," Cole snapped, and then added apologetically, "Thanks, anyway." Turning, he led his gelding into the barn.

Miles shook his head as he watched Cole walk away. Poor Cole. Whether or not he had realized that he was Miss Rachel's protector, he was feeling the burden of it, and he didn't seem too happy about the situation, Miles observed. Cole should have been, though. Any other man would have been thrilled to have a girl like Rachel McKinsey dependent on him, but not Cole Elliot. No, Cole Elliot would have a real problem with that.

Part of the problem, of course, was that the girl was about as pretty as a papoose in a red hat, and that she had the figure to set a man's juices running hot and cold all at the same time. But nobody was complaining about her looks. The trouble was that she was also the kind of girl who made a man feel like he had two left feet, both of which were usually planted squarely in his mouth. Not that she did it on purpose. It was her training, Miles supposed, the things she'd learned at school, and he had long ago decided that she really couldn't help acting so prim and proper. Once you got to know her, she was as sweet as pie.

Of course, Cole made a point of not getting to know her. Miles had never been able to understand exactly why, especially when the pure fact of the matter was that Cole was crazy about her. Not that he had ever admitted it, but Miles knew all the symptoms and Cole had all of them. Sometimes Miles suspected Cole had some fool notion that he just

15

wasn't good enough for a fine lady like Miss Rachel. It didn't make much sense, but it was the only explanation that Miles could come up with.

Poor Cole, Miles thought again. He would be in no hurry to get up to see Miss Rachel. No wonder he wanted to unsaddle his horse himself. He'd probably rub the animal down, too. He would probably even wait until the poor beast shed its winter coat if he could. Shaking his head, Miles drifted over to the cookhouse, leaving Cole to fight his own demons.

Cole did rub the gelding down, but only because putting a horse away wet in this weather was dangerous. At least that was what he told himself. Never for a minute would he admit that he was putting off a very unpleasant confrontation. It was funny when he thought about it, how he and Rachel had been at loggerheads right from the very beginning. What wasn't funny was that he could still remember exactly how he had felt the very first time he had seen her.

It would be a year ago come spring. Her father had sent her off to school someplace back East, and she'd been gone a couple of years. McKinsey had suspected trouble was coming even then, and he'd wanted her out of the way. Cole had often wondered since then how Sean McKinsey had kept his daughter away as long as he had. Two years was about her limit, though, and then one day she had sent a telegram saying she was on her way home.

She had been, too, so they hadn't been able to stop her, and there was nothing for it but to go to the railhead and meet her. Mr. McKinsey insisted that Cole go with him, hinting darkly that the two McKinseys might come to blows over this minor rebellion and that he would need Cole's cool head to maintain order.

Cole always enjoyed a trip to the railhead, and he and Mr. McKinsey went a day early and really tied one on the night before. Luckily, the girl's train was late, so they were feeling almost human by the time it chugged into the station the next afternoon.

Cole didn't expect to be surprised. He knew what Rachel McKinsey looked like. He had seen her picture sitting on Mr. McKinsey's desk a hundred times. Somehow, though, it had never occurred to him that the solemn-eyed ten-year-old with the tidy braids would have grown quite a bit in the succeeding nine years.

He was leaning lazily against the wall of the stationhouse when the train pulled in. Mr. McKinsey had been pacing anxiously for over an hour, and Cole watched in amusement as McKinsey tried to pretend nonchalance when people began to climb down from the train.

There weren't many, and so Cole saw the young woman right away. She was a fine figure of a woman with a mighty well-turned ankle, if the glimpse he caught when she stepped down from the train was any indication. She was wearing some kind of fancy bonnet with a lot of feathers and bows on it, but it sat way back on her head so he got a good look at her face. Her dark eyes were searching and for one heartstopping moment they rested on him. He thought her smile wavered, just a bit, in that second when she looked at him, but he might have been mistaken. Much more than his smile was wavering at that moment. In fact, he almost felt as if he'd had the wind knocked out of him.

She wasn't what you'd call beautiful, so he knew that wasn't what made him feel so strange. Still, she had a wonderful smile, and while he watched, it grew even brighter and more wonderful as she finally spotted the person she was looking for.

"Papa!" she called, and the next thing anyone knew she was hugging and kissing on Sean McKinsey. When Cole finally got over being surprised, he felt a little foolish for not having figured it out sooner, but then he felt better when he realized that Mr. McKinsey hadn't recognized her, either.

"You're all grown up," Mr. McKinsey said, blinking pretty fast. "You look just like your mother did the first time

17

I ever saw her."

She laughed at that, a delighted kind of laugh, and that was when Cole first thought about music boxes. Not that he knew all that much about music boxes, but a girl he'd gone to visit a lot in New Orleans had kept one in her room at Madame LaGrange's, and she'd played it for him a few times. That was the kind of voice Miss Rachel had, all nice and tinkly and sweet.

Mr. McKinsey motioned him over then and introduced him as the foreman of the Circle M. Rachel looked at him for a long time, staring first at his face as if she was trying to see inside his head or something, and then going over the rest of him like she was checking for lice. She spent quite a bit of time on his gun, making him awfully glad he hadn't gone ahead and worn two of them. He sometimes did if he was expecting bad trouble, but luckily he hadn't expected Mr. McKinsey's daughter to give him much of that. Still, he knew she didn't quite approve of the way his one gun was tied down or the way the wooden grip was shiny from use.

"How do you do?" she said. He noticed how the sparkle had died in her dark eyes when she spotted that gun. "I won't offer to shake hands because I know that you'll want to keep your gun hand free, but I'm very pleased to meet you, Mr. Elliot."

From anyone else, Cole might have taken offense, but he sensed that she didn't mean to give any. She was only letting him know that she knew exactly what he was and that she did not approve, of the gun or of the man who carried it. Cole supposed that if he were a girl who had just come home to find a hired gun working for her father, he might have reacted the same way. Still, her rejection stung. For one brief moment he had imagined that he and Rachel might be friends and maybe even more than friends. He must have been crazy to even think such a thing. Rachel McKinsey would never have a relationship with a man who made his living with a gun.

Cole mumbled something, and then her father asked about her luggage. Cole willingly offered to fetch it for her, eager to escape those disdainful eyes. He didn't even mind that she had two very heavy trunks. When he had finished loading them into the wagon, he found the McKinseys sitting on a bench beside the station. Mr. McKinsey was looking mighty uncomfortable, and Miss Rachel was talking to him. From the set of her jaw, she wasn't talking about the weather, either. Cole recognized that expression, having seen it on her old man a time or two.

They didn't hear him approach, and so he overheard a little of what they said. "I knew something was wrong," she was saying. "You should have told me about the rustling. At least I wouldn't have imagined something a lot worse."

"It's going to get a lot worse before it gets any better," McKinsey replied. "That fella Statler isn't going to be satisfied until he runs the whole county, and he ain't too particular about staying inside the law, either."

"How many more men like Mr. Elliot do you have working for you?" she asked. Cole didn't like the way she said "men like Mr. Elliot." Clearly she saw him as just one of her father's hired guns, men whose very existence was an offense to her.

McKinsey shifted in his seat. "Fifteen," he admitted reluctantly, but hearing her murmur of relief, he added gloomily, "Statler has more than twenty."

Knowing that this was exactly the sort of thing McKinsey did not want to discuss with his daughter, Cole took pity on the old man then and cleared his throat to rescue the rancher from his daughter. McKinsey shot him a grateful look that made him smile grimly, and that was the way things had gone for the next twenty-four hours.

They had stayed in town another night so Rachel could rest before the long drive home, and even though Cole knew she couldn't like it, he had hung around so that she didn't have a chance to question her father anymore. Cole knew

19

she'd do it as soon as they got home, but he owed it to Mr. McKinsey to give him as much time as possible to figure out just what he wanted to tell her. Unfortunately for McKinsey, Cole had been sure she'd get the whole story out of him one way or another anyway, no matter how determined the old man was to protect her.

But all of Mr. McKinsey's efforts to protect her had been a waste of time. Now McKinsey was dead and nothing could protect her from that. Nothing stood between her and Statler except . . . Cole stiffened at the realization that he himself filled that role. As little as Rachel would like it, he was all she had left. From now on she would have to depend on her father's hired gunman. Cole's lips stretched into a grin of bitter irony. Cole Elliot was no maiden's idea of a knight in shining armor, but poor Lady Rachel would just have to accept him in that role. She had no other choice.

When he had finished with his horse, Cole took an extra minute or two to wash up before he set out for the house. If his step was a little slow, he put it down to fatigue and not to the fact that he would rather have faced down Will Statler and all two dozen of his hired gunnies than to converse for five minutes with Miss Rachel Anne McKinsey.

Wearily, he climbed the stairs to the ranch house porch and without thinking went to the office door, knowing instinctively that that was where she would be. When he had knocked, he could hear slight scuffling sounds and the scrape of a chair, and then her voice saying, "Come in." Even through two inches of solid wood her voice sounded like a tinkling music box, the one he'd heard that time, so long ago, in New Orleans. Wincing at the thought that Miss Rachel would hardly appreciate such a comparison, Cole followed her command and entered the ranch office.

She was standing in the center of the room. He could see that she had been working at her father's desk. The huge ledger book was open, and she had probably been trying to make some sense of it. Cole could have told her she was wasting her time. Sean McKinsey had never been one for keeping the books.

"Miss Rachel," he said by way of greeting, dragging off his battered Stetson and meeting her eyes. They were beautiful eyes, large and deep brown, and he could see they had been crying. He didn't let himself think about that, though. Instead he reminded himself that she wasn't at all pretty. Her nose was a little too straight, her jaw a little too square, her mouth a little generous to be conventionally pretty. Still, she had a face a man wouldn't mind waking up to.

The room suddenly grew uncomfortably warm for someone who had been working out in the cold all day, but whether the heat came from the stove or from the presence of Rachel McKinsey, Cole took no time to decide. He only knew he'd better get out of his sheepskin jacket before he melted down to tallow.

Rachel waited patiently until he had done so, watching as he hung the jacket and his hat on the row of pegs beside the door. She was trying very hard not to fidget, but it was becoming increasingly difficult. Knowing what she had to discuss with him was making her very uneasy, especially when she noticed the grim set of his jaw. He could be very intimidating when he wanted to be, and he seemed to take great delight in intimidating her. Not that she ever let on that she was the least bit daunted, however. She prided herself on maintaining her cool composure. This was her small vengeance on him for the fact that he seemed impervious to her attempts to make him like her.

"Thank you for coming, Mr. Elliot," she said in a carefully neutral voice.

Cole wondered whether talking like that came naturally to her or whether it was something they'd taught her at that fancy school. There she was, thanking him for coming, as if he were doing her a personal favor instead of just doing his job. He supposed it had to do with being polite to the servants or something. Bristling at the thought, he nodded

21

curtly, biting back the urge to set her straight about his status around here. He had to remember that she'd just lost her pa and that she was in a bad way. He also had to remember that Mr. McKinsey would want him to take care of her. He shifted his weight, physically uncomfortable under the burden of such a responsibility.

"Oh, excuse my manners," Rachel said, noticing his discomfort and silently rejoicing that he was as uncomfortable as she. "Please, sit down."

Cole watched her small hand flutter in the direction of the chairs placed close to the stove. Too close, if you asked his opinion, but since nobody asked him, he sat down, following her lead.

Another minute of silence went by as Rachel fiddled with the material of her skirt, and Cole briskly smoothed down the thighs of his jeans. He watched her delicate hand reach up to check the sleekness of her dark hair and then drift down to touch the immaculate white collar of her dress. He found the fact that she was just as tense as he small comfort. What he had to tell her was not something he felt like blurting right out, but at the same time, he knew she'd have a hard time asking. As it turned out, she didn't need to ask.

"If you'd found anything, I suppose you would have told me by now," Rachel observed. She had known the minute he walked in the door that he had nothing new to tell her. She was getting so she could read him like a book in spite of the way he always tried to keep his face so blank of expression when he was around her. He gave himself away in other things, small things, like the way he moved his hands or the way he stood. She had studied him covertly many evenings while she had sat embroidering and he and her father had talked.

Cole was nodding, grateful for her perception. "The ground was frozen when it happened, and they didn't leave any clear prints, nothing we could follow." A Texas Blue Norther had blown in a few days earlier, freezing all in its

22

path, and covering the trail of the murderer. For the first time in his life, Cole regretted that it had not also snowed, since snow would have made tracking so much easier.

"You're still sure it wasn't an accident?" she asked, testing him, and watched his face grow hard with suppressed anger, as she had guessed it would.

"I've seen a lot of accidents, Miss Rachel, but I've never seen a man get the top of his head bashed in from falling off a horse, and you saw the rope burns on his wrists . . ." Cole let his voice trail off, sorry that he'd brought it all back to her like that when he saw the sheen of tears in her eyes. Watching her cry yesterday when they'd put her father in the ground had been about the hardest thing he'd ever had to do, and he sure didn't want to ever have to do it again.

Rachel was not going to cry though. Resolutely, she dashed the moisture from her eyes and swallowed the lump in her throat. Someone had come upon her father when he had been alone, had tied him up, and when he was helpless, bludgeoned him to death. She didn't need much imagination to figure out who, or why, either, but crying wasn't going to help at all.

Cole watched her regain her composure with some relief and a lot of admiration. Miles had been right, she did have a lot of nerve, for a girl. Still, he owed it to Mr. McKinsey to make this as easy as he could on her. "You're going to have to decide what you're going to do now, Miss Rachel," he told her somewhat apologetically. "I don't expect Will Statler'll give you much time to grieve before he comes poking around, trying to scare you off."

Rachel gave him a sad smile, regretting that she had to tell him and knowing full well what his reaction would be. "Statler was here today."

"Today?" Cole was incredulous. Statler hadn't even waited until McKinsey was cold in his grave.

"Yes," she informed him with amazing calmness, grateful that she knew how a lady conducted herself under trying

23

circumstances. She would have hated for Cole Elliot to witness a demonstration of her true feelings on the matter. "He came while you and the men were out looking for tracks. He was very sorry to hear about my father's accident, he said," she added stiffly.

"I'll just bet," Cole muttered, surging to his feet. The fury he felt made it impossible for him to stay still, and he began to pace the small room.

Rachel watched him, noting, not for the first time, how like a wild animal he was. He never seemed quite comfortable inside a house, as if he hated being confined between four walls. Only when he was outside was he truly himself. She could remember so clearly the first time she had seen him come into the parlor. She had felt almost as if a mountain lion had ventured in, a housebroken mountain lion, to be sure, but a creature that had no business in such genteel surroundings, nevertheless. She had experienced some sort of nameless excitement at the thought, the same excitement she had felt every time she had seen him after that, and the same excitement she would die before letting him know she felt.

"What did he say?" Cole ground out when he had regained some control over his temper. It was just a good thing he hadn't been here today when Statler had shown up. He might have throttled the man with his bare hands.

"He made me an offer for the ranch," she said tentatively, knowing such information would do little to pacify her furious foreman and wondering how to get him to be still. She found his restless movements quite disturbing.

"How much?" he demanded, forgetting that such a thing was most certainly none of his business, even forgetting how Miss Rachel would resent such an intrusion into her privacy.

"A dollar a head," she admitted reluctantly, knowing how insultingly low the offer was. She winced at his violent response.

Cole said a word he had no business saying in front of a

24

lady, but Rachel pretended not to understand. Then he pounded his fist against the wall with a force that made the old house jump and Rachel along with it.

He only hit the wall once, though, before a horrible thought stopped him cold. "You didn't take it, did you?" he asked, blue eyes narrowed to suspicious slits.

Rachel was appalled. "Of course not!" she informed him, haughtily. Did he think she was a fool?

"Thank God," he muttered, pushing the hair off his forehead in an impatient gesture.

There was more, though. "He said some things that disturbed me even more than that," Rachel began, hoping to regain Cole's undivided attention.

She succeeded. "What kind of things?" he asked, his blue eyes narrowing again as his imagination ran swiftly through several very unsavory possibilities.

Rachel sighed as the pacing began again. She found it comforting to know that her problems upset him, but she just couldn't concentrate with him prowling the room like that. "Please, sit down. It's very difficult to talk when you're . . ." she made a wandering motion with her hand.

Chastened, he swiftly returned to his seat, but he knew it would be a struggle to stay there. Every nerve in his body was screaming for action, and he was pretty sure that when she finished telling him what Statler had said, he would want to commit cold-blooded murder. How she could just sit there so calm and cool and tell him all this was beyond Cole Elliot's understanding.

"He said . . ." Rachel paused a moment, searching for the best possible phrasing. She wanted him to understand exactly what she feared, but she didn't want him to guess that fear because she didn't want him to think her weak. "Statler suggested," she began again, choosing her words carefully, "that now that my father is . . . gone, my men will no longer be willing to fight." Seeing Cole's puzzled look, she explained. "He seemed to think that the men wouldn't fight under a woman's command. Is that true?"

An instinctive denial rose to his lips, but died there. He wanted to say no, the men would fight for her to the last man, but when he thought about it, he knew that in all honesty, he could not promise such a thing. She had courage, that much he knew, but she was also a lady. In a fight like Statler would give them, things would get mighty dirty. When they found Sean McKinsey's murderers, they would hang them without waiting for the law, and when they had proof that Statler's men were the ones rustling the Circle M cattle . . . "The men might be afraid that you'd be too soft," Cole hedged. Whether they'd actually leave her, he had no way of knowing, but he thought it foolish to give her false hope.

Rachel did not need an explanation. She could see the doubts on his face, and she had already reached the same conclusion herself. Right now she was angry and hurting and wanted blood to revenge her father's death, but when push came to shove, would her anger be enough to overcome her woman's softness? If she had no answer, how could she expect the men to have one. And how could she expect them to stay with her?

There was a solution, though, or at least she thought there might be. It was something she had been wrestling with all afternoon, and the time had finally come to present it to him. The whole idea went against every bit of training and every natural instinct that she had, but it was her only hope, as well she knew. Twisting her hands in her lap, hoping to hide her apprehension, she asked the question that had been haunting her all day. "What if I were married?"

"Married?" Cole echoed, more than a little surprised at the sudden shift in subject. When he had considered for a moment, however, he realized it was a logical question. If she had a man to stand by her, a man the other men could look up to, she wouldn't have any problem at all. Somehow, though, he couldn't quite bring himself to say that. The thought of Rachel McKinsey being married made him feel

26

slightly sick to his stomach, like somebody'd punched him a good one.

And then there was the question of who. Not that half the men in the county hadn't courted her since she'd come back from school. Any one of them would have jumped at the chance to tie up with her, but which one would she pick? Had she ever shown a preference? A too-handsome face shimmered before his mind's eye, and his lip curled in disgust before she interrupted his musings.

"Not Hank Oliver," she declared. For some reason she knew exactly what Cole was thinking, perhaps because she had thought the same thing herself or perhaps because she had seen the immediate revulsion on Cole's face. As her most ardent suitor, the storekeeper was a logical choice, but not as a man to lead a fight. Even Rachel knew that much. No, she had a much more suitable candidate in mind.

Cole's relief was momentary. If not Oliver, then who? Cole shifted in his chair, rubbing his palms along his thighs. Not that it mattered, he decided. He hated the thought of her marrying anybody. "Who did you have in mind then?" he asked with creditable calmness.

Rachel locked her hands together in a death grip. This was the hard part, but she would not flinch, would not let him see how very difficult it was to admit that she needed a man who cared nothing for her. Choking back the pride that rebelled at such an act and taking a deep, fortifying breath, she blurted, "You."

"Me?" Now he really did feel like somebody'd walloped him a good one, right in the gut. He couldn't have heard her right.

"Listen, before you say no, hear me out," Rachel entreated, hoping her desperation did not show in her voice. "What have you been doing for most of your life?" Without waiting for the answer he was obviously still too stunned to give, she went on. "You've been fighting other people's battles, haven't you? Going from one fight to the next, selling

27

your gun to the highest bidder. But what happens when the fight is over? I'll tell you what happens, they pay you off and send you on your way. Nobody wants a gunfighter hanging around when the fighting is over.

"But this time, if you marry me," she hesitated over the word only slightly, "you won't be fighting somebody else's battle, you'll be fighting for what's rightfully yours. And when it's all over, nobody will send you on your way. This will be your home. That's what you want, isn't it?"

Rachel leaned forward in her eagerness to convince him, to draw the correct answer from him, and she scarcely dared breathe while she waited. That she was right, she never doubted. Too many times had she heard him discussing the Circle M with what could only be called affection, too many times had she seen him look around the ranchhouse parlor with the unmistakable longing of a man who would never belong, braving even her presence to spend time there with her father. She had heard the two men discussing ranch business and knew that Cole ran the place with a devotion to duty that far surpassed whatever loyalty even his generous wages could have inspired. Yes, he loved the Circle M. Her only concern was whether he would take her to get it.

Cole knew he must be dreaming. He had an overwhelming urge to laugh out loud, except he was afraid he'd wake himself up. Instead, he simply stared at Rachel, trying to make some sense out of what she had offered him.

She was right, of course, he did want a home, and he wanted that home to be the Circle M, but how in the blue blazes could she have known that? He'd even thought, a time or two, about maybe getting married someday. Not to Rachel McKinsey, of course, or to anyone like her. He'd never even let himself dream about such a possibility. Rachel McKinsey would want a man with polish and manners and education, all the things Cole didn't have and never would. She wouldn't want to be harnessed up with a bangtail like him. She must be desperate to come up with an idea like that.

But, of course, she *was* desperate. She needed him. Not him exactly, though. She needed his gun. It was the same deal that he'd been making for over ten years now, except that this time the pay was far higher than anyone had ever offered him. Miss Rachel was offering herself, her sweet self, but then, the stakes were higher for her, too, than for anyone else he'd ever worked for. She needed far more than just a hired gun. Hell, she already had a whole bunkhouse full of them, when it came to that. No, she needed a partner, a man who could fight and could lead a fight.

Rachel's eyes never left his face as he considered her offer. Instinct told her that if she gave him too much time, he would talk himself out of it. She could have wept with frustration, but since that wouldn't have helped anything, she refrained. She refrained, also, from enumerating her own considerable charms as an additional argument. What good would that do when the man was obviously immune to them? At least she knew that he liked the ranch well enough. That was her ace in the hole.

"At least say you'll think about it," she said when she had at last given up hope that he would answer her. The words almost choked her, and she only prayed she did not sound as if she were begging.

She did, though, and that did it for him. "No," he said. The word came out louder than he'd intended, but he really couldn't help it. He was irritated, mostly at himself.

Rachel felt her cheeks burn in humiliation. What had she expected, anyway? She, herself, would never have accepted such an outlandish offer. How could she have expected Cole Elliot to do so? "Oh," she managed in a very small voice, and then, gathering the remnants of her pride around her, she straightened her spine and lifted her chin. "I'm sorry if I embarrassed you. I didn't mean . . ."

"Oh, no," he protested, realizing that she had misunderstood him. "I didn't mean that the way it sounded. I meant I will, I'll marry you." He'd be a fool not to, wouldn't he?

Rachel's shoulders sagged in relief. For a moment there things had looked so bleak, but now everything was all right again. She hadn't let herself think about what might happen if he turned her down, but just for a second, she had had to, and the prospect had been awful. How could she ever have faced him again? How could they have worked together? How could she have expected him to stay on? Fortunately, she did not need to answer those questions now. For whatever reason, he had not turned her down. He might not want her, but he would take her to get the ranch, and that was what mattered most. It wasn't very flattering, but she reminded herself that this wasn't a love match. "Thank you," she said softly.

Thank you? Cole couldn't believe this was really happening. Rachel McKinsey had just proposed to him and now she was thanking him for saying yes, like he'd done her a big favor, when the truth was exactly the opposite. She had just done him the biggest favor of his life, and he might even have told her so, except that a brand new and very disturbing thought distracted his attention. Did Miss Rachel have any idea of what marriage was all about? Did she know what married people did? Did she know that she had just committed herself to sharing his bed? Somehow he doubted it.

Knowing he was a fool for doing so, but compelled by some strange, noble impulse that he never would have suspected he possessed, he said, "Miss Rachel, are you sure? I mean, maybe you should take some time to think this over. A lot of things have been happening, and you don't want to do something you might be sorry for later." Even as he said the words, he could have bitten his tongue. What was he trying to do, talk her out of it?

Rachel frowned. What was he trying to do, talk her out of it? Did he think she had made a decision like this lightly? Or maybe he was trying to get out of it by a back door. He was too much of a gentleman to turn her down, so now he was trying to get her to withdraw her offer. "Mr. Elliot," she began stiffly, "if you would rather not, you do not need to feel honor bound to accept my offer." She pressed her hands more tightly together, hoping they would not tremble and betray her, and hating the way her cheeks burned.

"Oh, no," he assured her quickly, realizing instantly what impression he had given. "A man would be a fool to turn down this ranch and . . . and all," he finished lamely. He had almost said, "and you," but he certainly didn't want her to realize that having her was by far the most attractive part of the bargain.

Of course, Rachel thought, he wanted the ranch. "Well, then, there's nothing more to discuss, is there?" she asked, averting her eyes so he would not see her disappointment.

"No," he replied.

An awkward silence fell as they each considered their new relationship. There were still a few details to be worked out, and Rachel hoped he would think of them, but when he didn't speak for several minutes, she decided that she had better.

"There's a preacher in Stillwater," she began.

Cole nodded. He had been thinking the same thing. Stillwater was the closest place, too. "We could go there tomorrow."

"Tomorrow!" Rachel gasped. That was a little sooner than she had expected. Having only decided today that she was going to get married, she wanted a few days to get accustomed to the idea, to get ready.

"Yes, tomorrow," Cole affirmed, understanding her reluctance only too well, but knowing he was right, nevertheless. "There's no use putting it off. The sooner Will Statler finds out about it, the safer you'll be." He didn't add that he was starting to think that maybe he'd better get himself hitched to her before she had another chance to think it over and change her mind.

"I just thought . . . it's so soon . . . my father . . ." she

31

tried, tears threatening again at the thought of her loss.

Cole agreed, it really was much too soon after her father's death, but they had no choice. "Your father would want to know you're being taken care of, don't you think?" he asked.

Rachel had to agree, and she nodded, blinking back her tears.

"Stillwater is quite a ways from here," Cole went on, trying not to notice how close she was to crying. "We'll have to get an early start." It would take half the day just to get there.

Rachel nodded again. "We could stay overnight at the hotel there and come home the next day," she suggested, trying a small smile. One night wouldn't be much of a honeymoon, but they wouldn't be having much of a wedding, either, certainly not the wedding about which she had always dreamed.

Her suggestion caught him by surprise. A vision of the Stillwater Hotel flashed into Cole's mind and then a vision of him and Rachel checking in as man and wife. He almost groaned. If he had had to name the last place on earth he wanted to spend the first night of his married life, the Stillwater Hotel would have been it. Good Lord, the walls were so thin, you could hear a person sweat through them, and when it came to clean . . .

"No," he decided, sounding more gruff than he had intended, "we better not. I don't think it'd be too good for us to be away from the ranch overnight, in case something happened, and besides, that hotel, it's kind of a fleabag . . ."

His voice trailed off, but Rachel got the idea. He didn't want to stay at the hotel. She supposed the idea of a honeymoon would hold no appeal to a man like Cole Elliot, and now that she recalled, the Stillwater Hotel really was a fleabag. For a moment there, she had let some silly romantic notions get the better of her, but there was nothing romantic about bedbugs.

"All right, we'll come back here tomorrow night, then,"

she agreed, slightly disappointed but willing to compromise. There was no need to start out with an argument, anyway. She wasn't going to give him any reason to regret his decision to help her, at least not if she could help it.

Cole wasn't in any condition to appreciate her compromise, though. The thought of coming back here tomorrow night, married, was conjuring up all sorts of images in his brain all of a sudden, and the room was getting hotter by the second. "Well, then, I reckon I'll come by for you in the morning, first thing," he said with a forced heartiness, rising to his feet.

"Won't you stay for supper?" she asked, knowing that she should not let him go, not just like that. Now that things were settled, it seemed only right that they spend a little time together. Tomorrow, marrying a virtual stranger would be painfully awkward. Perhaps if they could be together this evening, they would both begin to feel more comfortable.

The thought of trying to eat supper in front of Miss Rachel was not something likely to make Cole Elliot feel comfortable, however. He knew she would find his table manners on the crude side, and he didn't relish the idea of being judged and found wanting. "I already ate," he lied, moving toward the door.

Rachel rose and followed him. She knew he hadn't eaten. He was lying because he didn't want to eat supper with her. Maybe he didn't even want to be around her. The thought hurt. Was this the way he was planning to treat her after they were married?

She looked disappointed, and it made her eyes all dewy. Suddenly, he wanted to make her feel better, to make her smile. Staying here wouldn't do that, though, he reminded himself. Besides, if he let her see too much of him, she just might change her mind about the whole deal, and he for damn sure didn't want that.

Still, she was tempting. She looked so cute that without warning he began to wonder what she would feel like in his arms. All soft and warm and sweet, he guessed, his arms fairly aching to find out. Unless she pushed him away and slapped his face. But would she? They were getting married, after all. This time tomorrow, he'd have a right to do a lot more than just kiss her.

But they weren't married yet, and there was no use in scaring her off before the deed was done. There'd be time enough for all that later, when he would have a right to her. And when she would have no right to refuse. With a supreme effort of will, he reached for his jacket.

Rachel watched him, annoyance rapidly replacing her hurt. He might have accepted her proposal, but he certainly didn't seem too thrilled at the prospect of marrying her. He couldn't even stand the thought of spending one moment longer with her than absolutely necessary. Why, he hadn't even tried to kiss her! The thought made her tingle.

It wasn't so ridiculous. They were engaged, after all, even if the circumstances were a bit unusual. He might very well try to. Not that she would allow him to, of course. She felt her bosom swell with indignation at the very thought. If he had seemed the slightest bit enthusiastic about becoming her husband, she might have felt differently. A proper gentleman would have at least pretended he wanted her, but then she knew only too well that Cole Elliot was not a proper gentleman.

Cole Elliot was rough and crude and, she suddenly realized, quite a bit larger and stronger than she. If he really did want to kiss her, how on earth could she prevent him from doing so? The tingles she had felt earlier were racing up and down her body now. He could easily force her to his will, and for one awful moment, she wondered if she would mind at all.

For one long minute, Cole allowed himself to imagine what it would be like to hold her in his arms, to feel those breasts straining against him, to taste those luscious lips. Did she know how tempting she was, standing there looking up at him like that, her brown eyes all sparkly, almost as if she were asking for it?

She waited, looking up at him. He was so tall, so straight, and standing close like this, she could even smell him. He smelled fresh like outdoors and musky like male animal. He was looking right back at her, too, his blue eyes intense, as if he were trying to read something on her face.

Her whole body seemed to yearn toward him. It was pride, that's all, she told herself. She only wanted him to want her as much as he wanted the ranch. She only wanted him to reach for her, and then he was reaching . . .

. . . for his hat. Drawing a steadying breath, Cole took his Stetson down from the peg. For one more moment, he stood, fingering the brim. Then he forced himself to say the words he least wanted to say. "Well, good night."

Rachel swallowed her sigh of disappointment. "Good night," she replied. Then, as if it had been an afterthought and not a compromise, she offered him her hand. It seemed only right that they should at least shake on their agreement, even though shaking hands was a far tamer way of sealing their bargain than she had anticipated.

Cole drew another deep breath before accepting the tiny hand she offered. His large hand closed over hers with extreme care, as if he were afraid of breaking it, and when he felt the softness of her delicate skin, he actually was. Glancing down, noting with amazement the contrast between her milk white skin and his own, sun-darkened and callused, he realized once again how unsuited they were, and how little right he had to take advantage of her desperation. That wasn't going to stop him from marrying her, though.

"See you in the morning," he said, his voice only slightly husky.

"In the morning," she echoed, but he had already turned and was going out the door.

Rachel stood where he had left her for a long time, letting the frustration drain slowly out of her.

"What he say?"

Rachel jumped slightly at the familiar voice, and then turned to face the tiny old woman who had entered the office through the door which led into the ranch house. "He said yes, sort of," she replied, a hint of irony in her voice.

The old woman smiled, creasing even more deeply the thousands of wrinkles that lined her face and revealing toothless gums. "I tell you he would," she gloated, her voice scratchy from decades of use.

Rachel sighed and walked over to the chair he had just vacated and slumped down into it. "Oh, Lupe, am I doing the right thing?" she asked. Now that she had seen how reluctant he was to make the bargain, a whole new set of doubts had begun to assail her.

"You have no choice," Lupe reminded her, taking the opposite chair. She moved slowly, in deference to her advanced years, and when she had seated herself, she added, "You need a man. You tell me that yourself."

Rachel nodded absently, noting that the chair still bore faint traces of his scent, that enticing mixture of horses and leather and tobacco and sweat and some mysterious something else.

"You need a man and he is the one you pick, no?" Lupe prodded her, impatient with Rachel's wandering attention.

"No, he is the one *you* pick," Rachel corrected mockingly, glaring reproachfully at the woman who had raised her since her mother's death. She could not even remember her mother's face, but Lupe had filled the dead woman's place admirably. Still, Rachel realized, she was awfully old. How old exactly, Rachel could not even guess. For all the eighteen years Rachel had known her, Lupe had always looked exactly as she did now, withered and wizened and frail, as if a good wind might carry her away. Could she even remember what it was like to be a young woman, to have dreams about life and love?

Rachel had always thought of arranged marriages as something reserved for royalty, but here she was, arranging one of her very own, and suddenly she wasn't at all certain she was being very wise. Lupe had made it sound so logical when they had discussed the whole thing just this morning, but Lupe might have forgotten about the more intimate aspects of marriage. Rachel frowned at the thought.

"Why you pick him?" Lupe demanded sharply.

"Because you told me to," Rachel snapped, irritated at Lupe's habit of commanding her, as if she were still a recalcitrant child.

Lupe cackled delightedly. "Then why you agree?" she insisted, folding her gnarled hands in her lap as if she were prepared to wait until doomsday, if necessary, for Rachel's cooperation.

"Because," Rachel began with long suffering, preparing to enumerate the reasons for her decision for Lupe's benefit, but when she saw the twinkle in those sunken black eyes, she stopped. Those eyes, the only part of Lupe that betrayed any spark of the life that still burned within the old woman, were laughing at her.

"Because," Rachel began again, a resigned smile teasing at her mouth, "he's good with a gun, but he takes no pleasure in killing. He's a hard man, but when he breaks a horse, he doesn't kill its spirit. He's a fiddle-footed drifter, but once he gives his loyalty, he'll stick till hell freezes over." Rachel gave her foster mother an impish grin. "All right, you've convinced me again," she conceded, but then her grin faded as she remembered the kiss that hadn't happened. "I just wish he liked me a little bit."

Lupe made a rude noise. "He like you fine," she declared.

"Lupe," Rachel argued with some exasperation, "he never even looks at me!"

37

"He look at you sometime when he think nobody see him," Lupe reported. "He will look at you plenty when you are marry, you see." Rachel's expression betrayed her lack of conviction. "He is young. His blood is hot. When he come to your bed, he will love you. You will see," Lupe predicted with annoying confidence.

Rachel almost groaned. Life was always so simple for Lupe. It always came down to a few natural functions, eating, sleeping, eliminating, and *that*. If those areas of a person's life were running smoothly, then everything else would be fine, too. Well, Rachel already knew everything there was to know about eating, and sleeping and eliminating. It was the other that she was getting worried about.

"But I don't even know what I'm supposed to do," Rachel pointed out, certain that her ignorance would be a cause for humiliation. Cole Elliot did not seem to be the kind of man who would be very patient with maidenly protestations, and the thought of appearing anything less than confident in front of him horrified her.

Not that she was totally ignorant. Lupe had long ago filled her in on the basics of what went where and the fact that babies resulted, believing a young girl needed to be armed with that information before being sent to some heathen school way off in a place Lupe had never even heard of. She had not felt it necessary to give Rachel any information on technique, however, since the point of informing her at all had been to prevent her participation in such things and not to encourage it. Now, however, the situation was completely different.

"I will tell you what to do," Lupe announced, and promptly began to do so.

Rachel listened raptly, with mingled fascination and horror, wondering where on earth Lupe had learned of such things. The old woman must have had a very full and interesting life at some time in the distant past to know so much, Rachel decided at long last, when Lupe had finished her very detailed instructions.

"And he'll like that?" Rachel asked weakly, not at all certain that she would.

Lupe nodded sagely. "He is good man. You will like it, too. You will see."

Rachel wasn't exactly sure she wanted to.

Chapter II

When Cole got to the cookhouse, the rest of the men had already finished their supper and gone. The cook grumbled at having to fix Cole a plate when his work should have been finished, but Cole ignored him, granting him his right to complain. Anyone who slaved over a hot stove all day to feed a bunch of ungrateful cowboys deserved to grouse if he felt like it. Cole had more important things to worry about.

He was going to marry Rachel McKinsey. Tomorrow. He turned the thought over and over in his mind, examining it from every angle. The implications were awesome.

For one thing, his station in life was going to change drastically. He would go, overnight, from being a hired gun who owned little more than a bedroll and the clothes on his back to being one of the largest ranchers in Texas. He wasn't too worried about the responsibility. He'd already been running the Circle M for almost two years now. That part of it would be no problem. The problem would come in getting other people to accept him in his new role.

And the most important of those other people would be Miss Rachel Anne McKinsey. Cole still wasn't certain that she had any idea what she'd gotten herself into by proposing to him, but he'd given her a chance to back out and she hadn't taken it. As far as he was concerned, that settled things. She was going to be his wife, whether or not she had a clue about the things that went on in the marriage bed.

Tomorrow night when they came back here, sweet little Rachel would be all his. The thought sent an unnatural heat coursing through his body. He knew exactly how it would be, too. Having Rachel McKinsey was something he had imagined too many times to have any doubts about. She would be the best. For one exquisite moment he closed his eyes and pictured what she would be like.

The sounds of an argument taking place in the kitchen interrupted Cole's fantasies. The cook was informing someone else about how much he disapproved of people who came late for meals. In another minute Miles emerged from the kitchen carrying a cup of coffee.

Miles gave Cole a puzzled shrug and then sat down opposite him at the table. "You'd think I wanted him to cook a steak dinner," he remarked.

Cole grinned in sympathy.

"How's Miss Rachel holding up?" Miles asked, growing more solemn. Cole noticed how his friend's natural dignity seemed to increase whenever he was discussing Rachel, making him look almost out of place in the simple range clothes he wore.

"She's doing all right," Cole said, trying not to think about what he knew of Miles's past, about how he once had worn a frock coat instead of these range clothes and how his now-spectral eyes had once held a smile. "She's got a lot of nerve, for a girl," Cole admitted with a hint of self-mockery.

Miles slanted him a grin, remembering their conversation in the ranch yard earlier. "She's got a lot of nerve for anybody," he corrected before taking a sip of his coffee. He was glad to see that Cole's mood had improved enough to allow for a little bantering.

While Cole was mentally agreeing with Miles's assessment of Rachel's courage, he couldn't help but wonder what Miles would say if he told him that she'd just had the boldness to propose to him. Deciding he, himself, wasn't quite ready to say it out loud yet, he chose instead to feel Miles out on the subject. "Statler came by today while we were gone," he said mildly.

Miles swore softly. "Did he try to scare her off?"

Cole nodded. "Offered her a dollar a head for the cattle and told her the men wouldn't fight for a woman." He waited then, watching Miles chew this up and swallow it. He was having a hard time.

"That bastard," he said at last, his voice tight with anger.

"You think he's right?" Cole had already reached his own conclusion in the matter, but he respected Miles's opinion. Miles was second in command after the foreman, and besides, he was a good bit older than Cole.

"I don't know," Miles replied quite honestly. "The Kid will do whatever you tell him and a few of the others probably will, too. As for the rest," he considered a moment longer, "they're a tough bunch. I can't see them working for a woman." He shook his head in regret.

That was pretty much what Cole had thought, too. What he didn't know, and what he had no intention of asking was what they would do if he married Rachel. "I'm taking Miss Rachel into Stillwater tomorrow," he remarked with elaborate casualness. "She's . . . ah . . . got some business to attend to."

"Some legal stuff about the ranch, I guess," Miles supposed.

That was pretty close, Cole decided and nodded. "Wonder could I get Cookie to heat me some water for a bath," he said, casting a cautious eye toward the kitchen.

Miles choked on his coffee. "A bath?" he asked after his fit of coughing was over. "In this weather? You'll catch pneumonia," he predicted.

Privately, Cole thought it was probably worth the risk. A man only got married once, after all, and he didn't want to stink. On the other hand, it would be a little hard to explain such reasoning without revealing the true reason for his trip to Stillwater. "We'll be together in the buggy all day, there and back."

"You'll have your coat on," Miles pointed out, amusement twitching at his mouth.

"Not all the time," Cole grumbled, rising from the table. He for sure wouldn't have it on tomorrow night after they got home.

Dumping his dirty dishes into the wreck pan, he ignored Miles's bray of laughter and marched into the kitchen to request one more favor of the cranky cook.

While he soaked in the hot water, Cole tried to imagine how he'd feel about one of the other men marrying Rachel, about how his own attitude would change toward that man, but he couldn't. Just thinking about her marrying somebody else filled him with a nameless dread that might almost have been jealousy. He had wanted her for too long to even think about her with someone else. That didn't help him guess what the reaction of the other men would be, though. He could only hope that all of them didn't have the same possessive attitude toward his future bride that he did.

Rachel found it very difficult to sleep that night. She tossed and turned, changing her mind a hundred times about going through with the wedding. Marriage under the best of circumstances was frightening enough, but to marry a virtual stranger—a stranger who didn't even like her—was terrifying. To fill those long dark hours until he came for her in the morning, Rachel tried to recall everything she knew about Cole Elliot.

She knew, she realized with increasing dismay, very little. Before coming to the Circle M, he had been a drifter, a man whose reputation with a gun had gotten him jobs in places where he would need to use that gun. He had been at the Circle M almost two years now, the longest he had ever

44

stayed in any one place, or at least that was the impression Rachel had gotten from what her father had told her about him. Her father had liked him, too, she remembered with a bittersweet pang. Sean McKinsey had even hinted, quite broadly, that he couldn't understand why Elliot hadn't tried to court her and that he probably would if she would only give him the slightest encouragement. What her father didn't know was that she had once tried to encourage him and had been humiliatingly rebuffed.

The truth was that, until today, Cole Elliot had never been the least bit interested in her as a woman. And he still wasn't, she admitted reluctantly. She had won him not with her charms but by offering him the Circle M. Try as she might, she couldn't recall one time when he had so much as smiled at her.

In fact, she had only seen him smile, *really* smile, one time and that had been in an unguarded moment when he had not even known she was around. The men had been breaking horses in the corral one evening, and Rachel had been sitting on the front porch pretending to read so that she could watch. She would have preferred a seat on the corral fence, but that would have been scandalously improper and extremely dusty, too, so she contented herself with simply observing from afar.

The men were taking turns and, she suspected, betting on each other's prowess with the wild mustangs. There was a lot of good-natured hooting and hollering going on, but Rachel ignored the profanity and found herself grinning more than once at the colorful insults being passed back and forth.

Then a stallion was brought out. He wasn't majestic by any stretch of the imagination. Quite the contrary, he was just a scruffy bangtail, small and wiry and still shaggy from shedding his winter coat. Still, she sensed a vitality in the animal, a strength of will that would never quite be mastered.

When the stallion had thrown three different riders,

Rachel gave up all pretense of reading and watched with unabashed interest as Cole Elliot slid down from the fence to take a turn. That was when she realized what it was about the animal that fascinated her. His brown coat was almost the same color as Cole Elliot's hair, but more than that, she somehow knew that the man possessed the same indomitable streak she had sensed in the animal. They would be a good match for each other.

"I got a hundred dollars says you can't stick, Cole," one of the men yelled.

"You're on," Cole replied without even looking up. He was circling the blindfolded horse, his tall, slender body moving with the natural grace that had always intrigued Rachel. After a minute she realized that he was talking to the animal, soothing it. His hands reached out and stroked the horse's heaving sides in what might almost have been a caress, and she watched in amazement as the horse shuddered and ceased to struggle against the man who held his head. Then Cole took that man's place, holding the animal himself, letting it breathe in his scent, and all the time still talking in that quiet way, still stroking, stroking.

Mesmerized, Rachel left the porch and walked halfway across the ranch yard where she would have a closer view of what was happening. From her new vantage point, she could hear the low timbre of Cole's voice and even feel the intensity of the confrontation. Her hands clenched into fists as his tension vibrated through her.

Then, in one smooth motion, Cole mounted and called out for the blindfold to be removed. The stallion started bucking immediately, twisting and turning, contorting into impossible configurations, and doing everything in its power to dislodge the alien human presence on its back. But the rider clung tenaciously, his long legs gripping the animal's sides so that Rachel could see every corded muscle outlined beneath the heavy denim of his jeans. The thinner fabric of his shirt stretched taut as his shoulders and arms strained for

46

domination and his well-made hands clutched the reins, granting no mercy.

For what seemed like hours, the battle continued, but still Cole held on amid the cries of "Stay with him!" that came from the watchers.

Sensing failure, the beast made one last frantic attempt to brush aside his tormentor, racing for the side corral fence at a curious angle. Rachel was slow to guess its intent, but Cole was quicker and managed to kick free of the stirrups and jump to safety before the horse could crack the rider's leg against the wooden post.

Rachel's cry of alarm was lost in the men's howl of outrage at such treachery, but before she had time to take more than a few anxious steps toward where Cole lay in the dust, he was up again.

"Son of a bitch!" she heard him say as he scrubbed blood from his face with his sleeve, and then his expression suddenly altered from fury to delight, splitting into an utterly brilliant smile. Rachel's breath caught at the transformation, but almost before she had a chance to register the unexpected indentation the change had produced in his cheek, he vaulted back into the saddle. Using the quirt and his spurs in a way that might have seemed savage to one unused to such things, he soon brought the stallion into complete submission.

When the horse was standing still and docile, quivering from his exertions, Cole wearily swung down from the saddle. Once more he spoke to the stallion, words lost in the rumble of other voices but which Rachel imagined were words of comfort from the victor to the vanquished. Again he reached up to touch the animal, and gently, almost lovingly, stroked its shaggy neck. But the stallion shook him off and tossed his head and whinnied, almost as if to say he might be subdued but would never be conquered.

"Son of a bitch," Cole said again, grinning hugely. In the raucous laughter that followed, someone handed him a rag with which to wipe the blood and sweat and grime from his face. The blood, Rachel now saw, came from a bloody nose, a common consequence of such an experience, and she felt the tension drain from her body.

As if suddenly sensing her eyes on him, Cole looked up and caught her staring. So in tune was she with him at that moment that even from across the corral Rachel could feel the intensity of those blue eyes. "Something wrong, Miss Rachel?" he asked gruffly. Plainly, he did not like the idea that she had been watching.

"No," she replied, ignoring the scowl of disapproval he was giving her and trying to ignore how very much that scowl and all she had just witnessed disturbed her. "I was just enjoying the show."

She had turned then, breaking contact with those startlingly blue eyes and breaking the spell that had drawn her to the corral. Only then had she remembered that they were not alone, that the other men were standing around, watching and listening to this curious exchange. Giving them what she hoped was a cool little smile, she had started walking back to the house. Still, she had heard one of the men ask Cole what he was going to name the stallion.

"Hundred Dollars" had been his reply.

Reliving this incident now, months later, in the haven of her bed in the dead of night, Rachel was astounded to discover that her heart was pounding much as it had been that day. She shouldn't have been surprised, though. Encounters with Cole Elliot, even imaginary ones, always left her curiously disturbed. Once they were married, she suddenly realized, such encounters would occur on a daily basis.

And would be of a much more intimate nature.

Groaning at that thought, Rachel rolled over and clutched her pillow to her bosom in an unconscious attempt at comforting herself. If only he liked her. If only she could be certain that Lupe was right and that once they were married, he would love her. Rachel would even be satisfied if he would only smile at her, just once, the way he had smiled at that awful stallion.

Sighing, she hugged her pillow tighter. Well, whatever happened, she was going to make the best of it. She needed Cole Elliot, and she was going to marry him. And, she decided, smiling into the darkness, she was going to make him smile at her.

As he had promised, Cole came for her first thing. Dawn was still making only feeble headway into the darkness when he knocked on the front door. Rachel, who had already been up for hours, wondered whether he, too, had found it difficult to sleep.

He didn't smile when Rachel let him in. He only nodded and mumbled, "'Mornin'," dragging off his almost-new Stetson.

"Good morning," she replied, suppressing a sigh of disappointment at his less-than-enthusiastic greeting. A long, uncomfortable silence fell as they looked each other over.

Rachel supposed that Cole didn't own a suit. At least, she had never seen him in one and he wasn't wearing one now. Underneath his sheepskin jacket he had on a pair of brown, nankeen trousers and a brown checked shirt, and he was sporting a white Stetson. With some surprise, she realized these were the same clothes he had been wearing the very first time she ever saw him, the clothes she had guessed he had purchased to impress her that day. And they were, she now remembered, the ones he saved for special occasions. He was even wearing his good, handmade boots, and they looked as if they'd been spit-shined for the occasion. He might not be dressed like the bridegroom of her dreams, but he had taken great pains to make himself presentable. His hair was even laying flat, carefully slicked down with macasser oil which changed its normally light brown color to a deeper, richer shade. Nothing he did would keep it from falling into his face for very long, Rachel knew, and she liked it much better that way, the way she was used to seeing it. She resisted an almost overwhelming urge to muss it up a bit, knowing instinctively that would not be the best way to earn the smile she coveted.

Cole looked her over with what he hoped was discreet interest. He thought she had never looked prettier, even though it never would have occurred to him to say so. She was wearing a blue wool dress that was more like something you'd see in a picture book than something a real, live person would wear. It hugged her in all the right places, showing off her breasts and the way her waist curved in to almost nothing. She looked just about good enough to eat. Cole cleared the huskiness out of his voice and asked, "You about ready?" Suddenly, he was in a big hurry to get started.

Once again Rachel resisted the urge to sigh in disappointment. He hadn't said a word about how she looked. He probably hadn't even noticed. "I just need to get my coat," she replied. She had chosen her outfit so carefully, too, hoping to please him. She was wearing her pale blue wool, knowing how it clung to the upper curves of her body and fell away into an elaborately draped bustle and a bell-shaped skirt to show off her fashionable figure. Delicate lace threaded with satin ribbon trimmed the collar and cuffs and edged the placket where the gown buttoned down the front, adding softness and femininity. She had only wanted to look pretty for him, but had he paid any attention?

"I'll go fetch the buggy, then," he said, oblivious to her displeasure. He was thinking how funny it was that he always forgot from one time to the next how much he liked the sound of her voice. He guessed he'd get to hear it every day from now on. It was a very pleasant thought.

He had already turned to go when a harsh, unintelligible command stopped him. The voice made him jump a little, and he turned back in irritation to see Lupe's shriveled form lurking at the far side of the room. "What did she say?" he asked Rachel, trying not to let his annoyance show.

In spite of her nervousness and disappointment, Rachel had to bite back a smile. For some reason Lupe took great pleasure in refusing to speak English when Cole was around, and although he prided himself on his ability to "talk Mexican," he had never been able to make heads or tails of Lupe's unique dialect. Their feud had become a standing joke around the ranch. "She said she has some hot bricks for us to put under our feet," Rachel interpreted, wishing he were at least as aware of her as he was of Lupe.

"Good," he grunted, eying Lupe suspiciously. He had never cared much for the old crone. Not only did she look exactly like everybody's idea of a witch, but she acted like one, too, always sneaking around as silent as an Injun and watching him with those beady black eyes, like she expected him to spit in the beans or something. The old bat was positively spooky, and Cole did not enjoy being spooked. "I'll go fetch the buggy," he repeated firmly, and went to do so.

On the way, he couldn't help glancing around to see if their departure was attracting any undue attention. He had taken a little ribbing down at the bunkhouse for getting all duded up, but he didn't think anyone suspected anything. The fact was that any one of them would have gotten dressed up for a trip to Stillwater with Miss Rachel, so there was nothing suspicious in that. The bath had aroused some comment the evening before, but he figured that was normal. No, nobody suspected anything, he determined.

Rachel waited on the porch steps for him to pull up in the buggy, noting how skillfully and confidently he handled the reins. She wished she felt half that confident. Fortunately, she knew exactly how to conceal her true state of agitation. Pinning a small smile to her lips, she adjusted the collar of her coat while he climbed down from the small hooded vehicle and came around to help her up.

His hand on her arm was impersonal, as impersonal as the

way he accepted the bricks from Lupe, and she experienced a slight irritation at his aloofness. Even when he tucked the buffalo robe around her legs, smoothing the thick fur as she had seen him smooth around the heaving sides of the stallion, he did not deign to meet her eyes. She might almost have been a total stranger to him, she realized with growing annoyance. Only the fact that Lupe was standing right there, watching her every move, prevented Rachel from telling Cole she had changed her mind. Somehow Rachel sensed that even going with a man who cared nothing for her would be a far lesser evil than facing Lupe if she called off the wedding.

Busily adjusting the buffalo robe around her in an attempt to distract herself from her second thoughts, Rachel had not had time to notice just how confining the interior of the buggy would be until Cole took his seat once more beside her. Suddenly, all the space and all the air evaporated, consumed by his overwhelming presence. She found herself mysteriously short of breath as she hastily scooted over in an attempt to make some room, but there simply was no place left to scoot. Caught between the side of the buggy and Cole Elliot, she froze in place, painfully aware of every move he made as he pulled the buffalo robe over his own lap. His elbow bumped her arm and then his thigh grazed her knee, sending the oddest sensations slithering across her body.

How could she be having so much trouble breathing when the wind was whipping through the buggy with the force of a gale? And why was her heart pounding as if she had run a mile? And why was she so sensitive to his presence, so literally unnerved, when he seemed unaware of her? She was a fool. What had ever made her think that she could marry a man who cared nothing for her? Lupe or no Lupe, Rachel was not going to give herself to such an unfeeling . . .

"You warm enough?" Cole asked, hazarding a glance in her direction. She looked so small and delicate under the heavy lap robe, like a little china doll, but he knew she was very real. He was having a difficult time getting his breath to come evenly, and he felt like a complete fool. All he had done so far was help her into the buggy, and already he couldn't think about anything except getting his hands on her again. He had needed every bit of his self-control to just spread the lap robe over her without hauling her into his arms.

Rachel blinked under the intensity of his blue eyes as they gazed down at her. They held the strangest expression. "Y— yes, I'm warm enough," she replied quite truthfully. In point of fact, she was quite warm and growing warmer by the second, although the Texas wind continued to howl and its nippy bite still stung her cheeks.

"Good," he said, trying not to inhale too deeply because even in this wind he could smell the scent of roses that always surrounded her. He would be surrounded by it, too, when he took her in his arms, he thought, and then he reached for the reins so he wouldn't reach for her.

Fascinated, Rachel watched him slap the horse into motion. They were out of the ranch yard before she recalled that she had just been about to call off the wedding when he spoke to her. Oddly, that idea no longer held any appeal. Settling back into the seat, she shifted the heavy lap robe and glanced at him again.

He wasn't exactly handsome. He was awfully big and strong, though, and she felt strangely safe here with him. He wasn't quite as indifferent as she had believed, either, if the expression in his eyes just now was any indication. If only she could get him to smile at her . . .

For an instant she recalled the way he had smiled at the stallion, the way the dimple had creased his cheek, and she imagined what it would be like to have that smile directed at her. Another warm glow suffused her. Along with the memory of his smile came memories of the other things she had seen that day, the way he had gentled the stallion and the way he had used his body to conquer it.

Once more Rachel let her gaze stray over to where Cole sat

53

driving the buggy. Underneath the heavy coat he was wearing were the sinewy muscles that had mastered that stallion, hard and corded and strong enough to overpower even the fury of a massive animal. They would be firm and hard to the touch. To her touch. Underneath his gloves were the fine hands that had so gently stroked. Rough, callused hands that could yet be tender. Would they be rough or gentle when they stroked her naked flesh? Rachel squirmed uncomfortably in her seat, recalling that soon he would have the right to do just that.

"It's getting warm," Cole commented, shifting his long legs to push the buffalo robe off his lap.

"Yes," Rachel quickly agreed, knowing the outside temperature had nothing to do with the heat coursing through her body. She tried not to notice the way the brown nankeen of his trousers molded his thighs, but her eyes seemed irresistibly drawn to the sight. She was being ridiculous, she knew. She had seen the man's legs a thousand times. Why was the sight of them suddenly so fascinating?

For the same reason the rest of him was so fascinating, she admitted reluctantly. Because soon he would be her husband, and because not too long after that he would take her to his bed.

Rachel firmly resisted the urge to fan her burning cheeks, and, with what she hoped was nonchalance, she let the buffalo robe slide off her own lap and onto the floor of the buggy. She hoped the weather had warmed up quite a bit, because for some reason she was suddenly stifling under the heavy robe.

In silent acknowledgment of her action, Cole slipped off his gloves and stuffed them into a coat pocket. Now Rachel was totally unable to keep her eyes from him. The sight of those hands, the hands she had just been wondering about, drew her gaze like a magnet. Browned by countless hours in the sun, callused by years of hard work, still they moved with a finesse that belied their roughness. Rachel remembered how his palm had felt against hers last night when he had taken her hand, and she had no trouble at all imagining exactly how it would feel against her.

Beneath her corset and her myriad petticoats, that flesh tingled in a perfectly shocking manner. Startled by her reaction, Rachel glanced up guiltily to see if her companion might have guessed what was happening to her or, worse, if he knew he was the cause. Fortunately, he seemed unaware of the strange emotions stirring inside her, and she forced herself to look away from him, to admire the passing scenery. Think about something else, anything else, she told herself sternly, locking her gloved hands together in her lap.

Unfortunately, the passing scenery was not much of a distraction. The broad prairie stretched for monotonous miles in every direction, marred only by an occasional clump of mesquite or grove of cottonwoods clustered around a bit of water. Even the grass was brown now, dormant under winter's frigid onslaught, and the wildflowers that would adorn the plains with a primitive beauty were still several months away from blooming. No, the scenery did nothing to take her mind off her companion, and every now and then some part of Cole Elliot would bump against her, sending all her emotions skittering wildly once again and reminding her of what was going to happen during the night to come.

Cole glanced over at her for what seemed like the hundredth time. Also for the hundredth time, he tried to think of something to talk to her about. He didn't want to remind her of her troubles, so talking about her father or the ranch was out of the question. Outside of that, Cole couldn't think of anything else they had in common. He'd already asked her if she were warm enough, and since she'd just removed the buffalo robe, he had to conclude that she was.

What made it bad was that he could tell she was getting fidgety. The way her hands were clenched in her lap and the way she hardly looked at him were making him uneasy. She might very well be having second thoughts about getting married like this. If only he could see her face, he'd be able to tell for sure, but she had turned away from him. Because the hood of her coat was pulled up to protect her from the cold, about all he could see of her was the end of her nose. It was cute, but it wasn't telling him much about her mood.

He guessed he'd have to wait and see. There was no use trying to talk her back into anything until he knew for sure that she wanted out. There was also no sense in giving her any ideas up front. Instead, he distracted himself by wondering whether she would wear a nightdress tonight or not, and if she did, whether she'd let him take it off. He tried to imagine those big brown eyes laughing and teasing, flirting the way other girls he knew flirted. He had a little trouble with that, but he didn't have any trouble at all imagining what she would feel like in his arms. She would be all soft and warm and she would smell of roses. His whole bed would smell of roses. Roses and Rachel. Cole shifted uneasily in his seat to ease a sudden constriction and forced himself to concentrate on his driving.

Rachel peeked at him around the edge of her hood. He still wasn't paying a bit of attention to her, she noticed with some irritation. How could he be oblivious to her when he was just about all she could think about? The silence was becoming oppressive, too, but for the life of her, she hadn't been able to think of a single thing to talk to him about. Fortunately, Stillwater was very close now, less than an hour away. When they got there, they would find the church and . . . Suddenly Rachel remembered something they needed to discuss before they found the church.

"There's something we have to do as soon as we get to town," she ventured, watching his reaction carefully.

Caught by surprise, Cole slowly turned toward her and eyed her cautiously. "What?" he asked, wondering if she was about to call the whole thing off.

Rachel took a deep breath and plunged in. "We'll need a ring. There's a store in town . . ." She hastened to explain

56

but he interrupted her.

"I've got a ring," he informed her, not nearly as relieved as he should have been that she was still planning to go through with the wedding. He had been hoping that she wouldn't think of the ring so he could just spring it on her during the ceremony. He didn't want her to object to the ring he had provided, and knowing how fashionable Rachel always was, he had a sneaking suspicion that she wouldn't think it was good enough for her.

Rachel couldn't help staring in amazement. She had never dreamed that he would have even thought about getting a ring, much less that he would have obtained one. And where could he have gotten it on such short notice? Several very unsatisfactory theories occurred to her, but before she could explore them very thoroughly, he glanced down at her again.

Misreading her look, he began to regret the impulse that had prompted him to bring the ring. "It's old," he hedged. "If you want a new one, we can stop at the store."

She was silly to just sit there wondering, she told herself. "Where did you get it?" she asked.

"It was my mother's," he told her gruffly. "But if you want a new one . . ."

"No!" she protested a little too loudly. She wanted his mother's ring very much. "No, your mother's ring will be fine," she added more calmly. The fact that he had kept his mother's wedding ring was almost overwhelming her. This was a side of Cole Elliot she had never suspected existed. Who would have imagined that he would be sentimental? Then she thought of something else. "Maybe I'd better try it on . . . just to see if it fits." The fact that she was inordinately curious also played a large part in her suggestion.

"Oh, yeah," he said, digging down into a pocket to retrieve the ring. He hadn't even thought about it not fitting.

Rachel took the tiny circlet from his outstretched palm and turned it over in her hand. The ring was of fine quality gold, embossed with a patina of age that gave it an aura of worth no newly purchased ring could ever have. She slipped it on her finger. "It's perfect," she declared, holding out her hand to admire the way the gold glittered in the morning sun.

Cole watched her through narrowed eyes. She actually seemed pleased. He had expected her to insist on something brand new. He never would have guessed she would be excited about getting a hand-me-down ring. Not that he really cared how she felt about it, of course. The ring meant a lot to him, and he had intended to marry her with it whether she liked it or not.

He could so clearly remember the night he had found it. He had been twelve years old and still aching from the beating his father had given him. The old man had lain in a drunken stupor while Cole, having decided that he had taken his last beating, made a roll of his spare shirt and a moth-eaten blanket. Then he had pulled up the loose floorboard and found the small wooden box where his father kept any spare cash he happened to have. Cole was leaving, and he would need anything the box might contain. That the box contained little of value was not surprising, but he took what coins were there. He had picked up the ring thinking it was a coin, too, at first, and then he had realized what it was. Fond memories of his long-dead mother had come flooding back, and he thrust the ring into his pocket along with the coins, thinking he could always sell it if times got tough. Times had indeed gotten mighty tough on occasion, but for some reason he had never been able to bring himself to part with the ring. Now he was glad that he hadn't.

Rachel couldn't seem to take her eyes off the ring. Not that it was so spectacular, of course. It was just a simple gold band. What fascinated her was what it stood for. Cole Elliot had saved his mother's wedding ring. Cole Elliot had remembered to bring it with him today. Cole Elliot had *cared* enough to bring it with him today. Maybe he wasn't quite as indifferent about her as she thought.

She looked up at him through her lashes. He was watching

her with what could only be called suspicion, as if he did not quite trust her enthusiasm. "The ring is very nice," she assured him, but he did not look very reassured. Her delight faded, and the ring began to feel very heavy on her finger. "I suppose you'd better keep it . . . until the ceremony, I mean," she said, slipping it off her finger and reluctantly handing it back to him. She had the oddest feeling that he simply did not believe that she liked the ring.

Cole took the ring without comment and tucked it back into his pocket. He still couldn't tell for sure how she felt about it. She had all those pretty manners and always knew the correct thing to say. Maybe she was only being polite, making the best of a bad situation, or trying not to hurt his feelings. Proper ladies did that sort of thing, and Rachel was the most proper lady he knew. Well, like it or not, she would wear it. Maybe later he'd buy her a new one, but for now that was all she was going to get. Setting his jaw stubbornly, he turned his full attention to his driving, squinting into the distance to see if he could yet spot their destination.

Seeing the tensing of his jaw, Rachel sighed. What did a person have to do, anyway? she wondered in disgust. All she had been trying to do was please him but she had failed miserably. Maybe, she thought with a naughty grin, she should take a lesson from that stallion. Maybe she should toss him on his head.

The town of Stillwater perched presumptuously out in the middle of the prairie, and Cole and Rachel could see the large cluster of buildings long before they reached them. When at last they approached the outskirts of the town, Cole was the first to speak.

"What do you say we find the preacher first and then go get something to eat?" Cole asked, anxious to get the knot tied good and tight before Rachel had a chance to change her mind.

"Fine," Rachel agreed readily. Even though it was getting on toward noon and she hadn't been able to eat any breakfast, food was the last thing she wanted to face right now. She was also thinking that once the ceremony was out of the way, maybe some of this awkwardness she felt with him would vanish. Cole was beginning to think he was going to have to ask someone where the preacher's house was, but then he spotted the church steeple on the far side of town. Figuring the preacher would live nearby, he headed the buggy toward it.

The preacher lived in a small clapboard house next to the church. Cole pulled the buggy to a halt in front of it, and they both sat staring at it for a moment. Smoke was coming from the chimney, so someone was obviously home. "Well," Cole said, apropos of nothing.

Rachel gave a nervous little laugh and fought down a wild urge to run away.

"Well," Cole said again, "Guess we better go in."

Rachel nodded, wondering how so many butterflies could have been set loose inside her stomach. Cole seemed to take forever to climb out of the buggy and tie the horses up to the hitching rail outside the church. Finally, he came to hand Rachel out. She thought for a moment that his fingers lingered on her waist, but she might have been mistaken. Side by side, but not touching, they went up the walk to the front door of the little house. Cole twisted the bell and they waited, not looking at each other.

After a moment, a short, bald-headed man opened the door and stared at them curiously. Cole cleared his throat importantly and asked, "Are you the reverend?"

"Yes," he said, his pale blue eyes darting from Cole to Rachel and back again. "Yes, I am. What can I do for you?"

"We came to get married," Cole informed him.

Rachel concentrated on keeping her hands from fidgeting.

The little man brightened at the information, giving them an understanding smile. "Come in, come in," he invited, stepping back to allow them to enter.

The minister's parlor was a tiny, immaculate room

resplendent with crocheted doilies and bric-a-brac. If Cole had looked out of place in the ranchhouse parlor, he looked positively alien in this place. Rachel had to bite her lip to keep from smiling at the cautious way he moved to keep from bumping into anything.

Cole glanced around the room in irritation. This was just the kind of place he hated, the kind of place where a man had to watch every move he made. He breathed a silent prayer of thanks that the ranch house wasn't anything like this, although he had to admit that Rachel seemed much more at home here than she did at the ranch. Standing there in her neat, blue dress and her tidy little coat, she looked like she had been made especially for a room like this. That didn't matter, though, he thought with an almost savage possessiveness. From now on, she would be with him, wherever that was.

"Who was at the door, Papa?" A tiny lady bustled into the room. She was round and jolly-looking, her face wreathed in what Rachel came to realize was a perpetual smile, and when she saw the two strangers, she stopped, giving them an inquiring glance.

"These two young people have come wanting to get married, Mama," the minister explained. "I would introduce you, but we haven't gotten as far as names yet," he added with an apologetic smile at his wife.

Cole quickly remembered his manners. "I'm Cole Elliot," he said, stretching out his hand to the minister, "and this here is Miss Rachel McKinsey."

The minister shook hands with Cole and nodded at Rachel, who was afraid to offer her hand for fear it might be trembling.

"I'm Reverend Hollister and this is Mrs. Hollister." Everyone nodded all around and a brief silence fell. The Reverend Hollister was sizing up the young couple and Mrs. Hollister was doing the same. Cole was wondering if he was going to have to repeat the reason for their visit even though the man had just told his wife why they had come. Rachel was examining the pattern on the carpet.

"So you want to get married, do you?" Reverend Hollister asked. He had done a lot of weddings in his time, and in his opinion this couple looked more anxious than eager and not very happy at all. He wondered if the girl were in a family way or running away from an unhappy home.

"My, my, you've come a long way to do it, too, haven't you?" Mrs. Hollister observed with her usual cheerfulness. She hadn't missed the wind-rouged cheeks or the travel dust on their clothes.

Rachel glanced up at that. "Yes, all the way from Canaan," she replied, naming the tiny town nearest the ranch.

"What a long way," Mrs. Hollister remarked and then added, "McKinsey, did you say? Are you any kin to the McKinseys of the Circle M ranch?" She, too, had noticed the couple's odd behavior, but unlike her husband, she was not averse to discovering the reason for it.

Rachel gave the kind little lady a sad smile. "I guess I am the McKinseys of the Circle M ranch."

"But your father . . ." Reverend Hollister began.

"Passed away," Rachel concluded.

Mrs. Hollister murmured something sympathetic, and Reverend Hollister said, "I'm so sorry. We hadn't heard."

"It was very recent," Rachel explained, her voice quivering slightly.

Cole had had just about all of this he could stand. Instinctively, he stepped forward and put a protective arm around Rachel's shoulders. "Excuse me, but we're in kind of a hurry. We've got to get back to the ranch tonight." This was his voice of command, and Reverend Hollister would have obeyed, judging from the way he started stuttering and looking around for his Bible, but Mrs. Hollister was not so easily intimidated.

"Nonsense," she scolded. "You're not in that much of a

hurry. At least take your coats off. I imagine Miss McKinsey wants to freshen up a little, too, before the ceremony."

Miss McKinsey almost didn't hear this last suggestion. The room suddenly felt quite a bit warmer just because his arm was around her.

Cole glanced down at her then and caught the strange expression on her face. It took another second for him to realize that his arm was still around her, and he dropped it instantly. He bit back an ironic smile, thinking what her reaction would be if she knew all the other things he'd thought about doing to her.

"Miss McKinsey, would you like to freshen up?" Mrs. Hollister asked again.

Rachel nodded, unwilling to trust her tongue but suddenly recalling the fact that she probably would not make it through the ceremony if she didn't take a trip out back first. Mrs. Hollister hustled her off to the rear of the house, leaving Cole and the minister alone.

"Let me take your coat," Reverend Hollister said, and when he had, he added, "She's a lovely girl."

Lovely. Now that was a good word for her, all right, Cole decided. He rubbed his palms along his pant legs and glanced toward the door through which Rachel had disappeared and wondered how long it took to "freshen up." Cole wished the preacher would offer him something, but since what he needed was a good stiff drink, he doubted that wish would be granted.

As if she had sensed Rachel's disappointment at such a hasty, cheerless wedding, Mrs. Hollister did everything in her power to make amends. Rachel felt a little silly in the tiny, white-veiled hat the old lady had given her, but at least she felt much better for a visit to the outhouse and having had a chance to wash the travel dirt from her hands and face.

Just as they were about to rejoin the men, Mrs. Hollister handed her a small bouquet of dried flowers arranged in a crocheted doily. "I keep these 'specially for weddings," the preacher's wife explained.

Cole was just starting to wonder if maybe Rachel could have decided to back out at the last minute when she suddenly appeared in the doorway. He couldn't help staring at her. She looked beautiful, all done up in blue like that with that lacy white thing hanging down over her face. He couldn't quite make out her expression, but he thought she was smiling a little.

"Your bride, Mr. Elliot," Mrs. Hollister announced, jarring Cole back into reality.

"Join hands, please," Reverend Hollister said, taking charge of the situation. He had the feeling that if he waited for these lovers to do so, he would grow old in the process.

Rachel came forward then, pleased that she had finally gotten some reaction from her groom and a little surprised that she was actually beginning to feel a bit like a bride.

Cole's hand closed around hers. His skin was hot to the touch, but that might just have been because hers was stone cold. His palm was rough, the way she remembered it, but comforting, as was the strength she sensed in him, and she felt good standing beside him. She really had made the right choice, she decided, glancing up at his somber profile. This was the right man, the man who would take care of her. She would take care of him, too. He was, she noticed, painfully thin, thin the way a man who works hard and eats only because he is hungry is thin. Fattening him up would be her second challenge. Making him smile at her would be her first.

Cole promised to have and to hold and to love and to cherish Rachel. Last night he had spent a lot of time thinking about how good it would be to have and to hold her. Now, quite suddenly, he was realizing that having her brought some serious responsibilities. He would have to take care of her, protect her and make sure she was happy. He could take care of her easily enough, and protect her. He could use his gun for that. But how on earth was he going to make her happy?

Rachel repeated her vows more quietly but just as steadily as Cole had. She wasn't about to let the fact that she was nervous daunt her in any way. Feeling strangely detached, she watched Cole's hand slip the golden ring onto her finger, and then it was over.

"I now pronounce you man and wife. You may kiss the bride."

Turning to Rachel, Cole lifted the delicate veil with great care, placed his hands on the points of her shoulders, and lowered his face to hers.

He felt the tiny explosion of her breath against his lips, and scented the sweetness of her breath as it enveloped his senses. She yielded gently under his hands as he drew her to him. Her mouth was exquisitely tender, pliant, and luscious, a sensual treat that made him think simultaneously of warm honey and warm feather beds. Desire thrummed through him, heating his blood, singing siren songs inside his brain, and tightening his hands to draw her closer still.

Rachel's world had suddenly tilted dangerously. When his face had closed in on hers, she had known a small measure of relief that in spite of that moment of hesitation, he was going to seal their marriage in the traditional way. The taste of his mouth had obliterated that relief in an avalanche of pure sensation. Instinctively, she had moved closer.

Reverend Hollister cleared his throat rather loudly, finally breaking the spell that held the two newly-weds. With great interest he watched them jump guiltily apart. He would have staked his eternal soul on the fact that this girl was not with child. If she were, he knew beyond question that this man had had nothing whatsoever to do with it. No, that kiss had been the first time they had ever touched flesh to flesh, but if Reverend Hollister was any judge, it wouldn't be the last. Sighing mentally, he wondered what his chances were of convincing Mrs. Hollister to take a nap with him this afternoon.

Rachel didn't think she'd ever seen eyes as blue as Cole's had been just now. The sight of them had made her blood run hot and cold all at once. Still trembling with reaction, her cheeks burning from the intensity of her emotions, she turned a quivering smile on the Hollisters.

"Thank you, both, very much. You've been so kind," she said, trying not to notice their knowing looks.

"Not so fast, young lady," Reverend Hollister chided. "It's not legal until you sign the paper, you know." While Cole and Rachel waited uneasily, Reverend Hollister located a blank marriage certificate, filled it out, and offered them the pen.

Rachel took it and scratched out, "Rachel Anne McKinsey" with finishing school neatness. Cole very gingerly accepted the pen from her and scrawled "Coleman T. Elliot" in barely legible script. Reverend Hollister carefully blotted the ink and presented the paper to Rachel with a flourish.

"Best wishes to you, Mrs. Elliot, and congratulations, Mr. Elliot," he said, offering his hand to Cole once again.

Rachel murmured a "thank you" around the smile that curved her lips. Mrs. Elliot. She liked the sound of her new name.

Mrs. Hollister bustled up and planted a kiss on Rachel's cheek, effusing wishes for happiness for them both. "You'll stay and have dinner with us, won't you? I've got a nice fat chicken and it's just about done," she insisted.

"Oh, no, thank you . . ."

"No, ma'am, we have to . . ."

Cole and Rachel spoke at once, their gazes meeting for one startled second at the coincidence and then careening off again to look at something, anything, else.

"Well, if you have other plans . . ." Mrs. Hollister surrendered in the face of their obvious reluctance.

Deciding it was safe to speak for Rachel since she had already expressed her opinion on the matter, Cole said, "I promised Rachel dinner at the hotel. It's all the honeymoon we're likely to get."

Rachel almost choked at his lie, recalling the horror with which he had greeted her suggestion that they spend the night in that same hotel, but she managed to keep a straight face. Smiling blandly at the preacher and his wife, she thanked them again, and then primly removed her borrowed veil while Mrs. Hollister fetched their coats.

Out of the corner of her eye, she saw Cole shake hands with the preacher one last time, and from the flash of gold, she concluded that he had passed the man a twenty-dollar gold piece. Twenty dollars! she marveled. He must set more store by her than she had suspected to pay such a princely sum. A secret smile curved her lips, a smile that might have made Cole wonder what she was thinking about if he hadn't been so concerned with getting them away from the preacher and his grinning wife.

Cole dropped Rachel off at the hotel before taking the horses and buggy to the livery for a well-earned rest and feeding. She waited impatiently in the dingy lobby until he returned, unconscious of the curious looks she was receiving from the regular noontime diners, but very conscious of the heavy gold band on her finger. Twisting it nervously, she wondered again about the fact that he had kept it and tried to picture in her mind the woman who had worn it before her. What had she been like? How had she died? Did Cole look like her?

It was odd, now that she thought of it, to realize that she had started thinking of him as "Cole" instead of "Mr. Elliot" or simply as "him." Now she would have to start thinking of herself as "Mrs. Elliot." The thought made her smile, and then she remembered his kiss. Cole Elliot wasn't a bit shy, at least not once he got started. She shivered slightly as she recalled the way his mouth had sought hers. She was still smiling at the memory when Cole returned.

Rachel rose when he approached, her brown eyes searching his blue ones for a hint that he, too, remembered their kiss. He wasn't smiling, but for the first time that day he actually looked pleased.

He came right up to her and stopped, staring down as if he couldn't quite get enough of looking at her.

"Hello," she said inanely, unable to think of anything more profound. Had he always been so tall?

"Hello," he replied, not noticing how ridiculous their exchange was. Had she always been so pretty?

For a long moment neither of them moved. Rachel studied the way his hair had tumbled down onto his forehead from under his hat. The sun had bleached that particular shock until it was almost gold, even in the dim light of the hotel lobby. Rachel wondered if it would feel as soft as it looked. "Do you like onions?" she heard herself ask.

His forehead creased in puzzlement. "Onions?" he repeated.

"It smells like they're serving steak and onions today," she explained. How strange. She could hear her voice but she seemed to hear it from far away. She wasn't consciously saying anything. Her mind was on something else entirely.

His brow smoothed. "Yeah, onions are fine," he said, but then he frowned again, remembering something else. "Do you like them?" If one of them did and one of them didn't, that could make things unpleasant later in the day.

Rachel, blissfully unaware of the problems onions might cause, simply nodded, hoping to erase that frown once more. She succeeded.

"Good. Then let's go eat," he said, a little relieved.

After only the slightest hesitation, Rachel moved toward the hotel dining room which was located just off the lobby. She had already removed her coat and hung it on the row of pegs beside the dining-room door, and she paused while Cole did the same. Then, side by side, they entered the room, found a table and sat down.

Cole leaned back in his chair and crossed his arms over his chest. What had happened to her eyes? They were even darker than usual, dark and soft and deep, with an expression in them he'd never seen before.

"Cole Elliot, is that you?" Startled, Cole looked up into a vaguely familiar female face. It was the waitress. She had paused on her way to another table, and even though she was balancing three plates of steaming food, she sashayed her way over to their table.

"Well, now, when did you blow in, honey?" she inquired with an overly friendly smile.

Cole saw Rachel stiffen at the familiar way the girl addressed him, but he was preoccupied with trying to remember who the girl was. She was only vaguely familiar to him and for the life of him, he couldn't even remember her name. "Just now," he replied, trying to recall the exact circumstances of their meeting and whether anything more than a little friendly conversation had ensued.

The girl was delighted. "Then you'll be around for a while?" she asked eagerly.

Cole shook his head. "No, we'll be leaving this afternoon," he said, wondering how on earth to get rid of the girl. He simply could not remember how well he knew her, and God only knew what she might say in front of Rachel.

"Aw, that's rough," the waitress complained, and then seemed to notice Cole's companion for the first time. She gave Rachel a dismissing once-over and then turned her attention back to Cole.

Rachel was seething. Wasn't he even going to introduce her to his . . . his *friend?* Was he going to flirt with another woman right in front of her when they'd been married for less than an hour? He'd never flirted with Rachel at all, ever, and that made her angrier than anything. Why, this girl wasn't even pretty! Unless you counted her more-than-ample bosom, that is. And maybe Cole Elliot did count it, Rachel thought bitterly, feeling underendowed for the first time in her life. He certainly seemed to be on friendly terms with this woman, friendlier than Rachel could ever imagine him being with her.

Cole glanced uneasily at Rachel, wishing the waitress to kingdom come and wondering what Rachel would think if this girl were to allude to some wild escapade in which he had been involved. As it was, Rachel already looked far from pleased.

Seeing Cole's look, the girl seemed to catch on that she was causing some sort of problem with him. "Well now, what can I get you?" she asked, suddenly all business.

Cole waited a second in case Rachel wanted to express a preference, and when she didn't, he said, "We'll take two dinners when you get a chance."

"Here you go, then," she replied helpfully, setting down two of the plates she held, trying to make amends with promptness. "I'll be back in a minute with your coffee," she added, swishing off before either of them could protest such preferential treatment.

Rachel stared down at her plate with a decided lack of interest, and reflected bitterly that Cole certainly knew how to get fast service in a restaurant. "You didn't introduce me to your friend," she observed. Her voice had a disgruntled ring to it that she immediately regretted, but since it was too late to remedy that, she tried forcing an artificial smile.

Cole stared at her. The smile didn't fool him. She was mad and he knew it. Although why she should be mad, he didn't know, since the girl hadn't revealed anything. "I don't remember her name," he replied, deciding the truth couldn't hurt anything.

"Oh," she said, feeling foolish but no less angry. He might not remember the girl, but she remembered him well enough. Apparently, he wasn't quite so standoffish with all women as he was with Rachel. Picking up her knife and fork, she attacked her steak with vigor, despite the fact that her appetite had yet to return.

Cole followed her example, still intrigued by her obvious displeasure. She didn't have a single thing to be mad about unless . . . The idea was too preposterous to even consider, but as the minutes passed and Rachel still refused to look up at him, he began to imagine that it might be true. She was jealous!

The more he thought about it, the more he believed he was right. Not that he imagined she was in love with him or anything, but after all, they were married now. Cole knew he wouldn't want some strange man coming up and flirting with Rachel. The idea that she might feel the same way about him made him grin.

They ate for a while in silence before the waitress returned bearing two cups of coffee. "Everything all right?" she asked solicitously, her too-friendly smile still firmly in place.

Cole decided to find out if his theory was true. "Well, now," he said, pretending to consider the question, "I reckon I've got a pair of old boots that would make a better steak than this," he allowed, grinning up at the waitress.

Nancy—that was her name, Cole suddenly remembered—threw back her head and laughed. From the corner of his eye, he studied Rachel's reaction.

Rachel did not believe she had ever heard Cole make a joke before, but apparently, he was quite accustomed to doing so. The knowledge disturbed her, but what disturbed her more was the fact that he was making jokes for the benefit of this girl. If he wanted to entertain someone, he could very well entertain his own wife. Rachel decided to get rid of the girl once and for all. "Yes," Rachel remarked, batting her eyes innocently and smiling sweetly, "I only wish I could remember why I made you promise to bring me here."

Nancy's laugh ceased abruptly, but Cole didn't notice. He was too busy watching Rachel smile at him, knowing she was teasing him for the lie he had told the preacher, and also knowing that she was flirting with him. Her brown eyes sparkled as if she were laughing inside.

What Cole missed, but what Nancy didn't, was the way

Rachel had propped her chin onto the fist of her left hand, so that her wedding band was clearly visible. The girl's eyes darted first to Cole and then back to Rachel, catching every nuance of meaning in the look that was passing between them, and knowing full well that although Rachel wasn't even looking at her, she was staging this whole little scene for Nancy's benefit. Nancy got the message. "Well," she said, wiping her hands on her apron, but neither of them seemed to notice her at all. With a shrug of defeat, she slipped away.

When she was gone, Rachel slowly lowered her left hand, feeling a little guilty for being so catty but not at all guilty for getting rid of the girl. Maybe Cole didn't like Rachel all that much—yet—but he was her husband, and no one was going to get the idea they could flirt with him right under her nose. She picked up her fork again and resumed her meal.

After another second, Cole did, too, although he could have been eating that old pair of boots for all the difference it made to him. Rachel had been flirting with him. It wasn't the bold, brazen kind of flirting he was used to from the girls who worked in the saloons and the brothels or from girls like Nancy who were maybe just a little friendlier with men than they should be, but it was flirting just the same.

"Is there anything else you want to do while we're in town?" he asked after a few minutes.

Rachel glanced up. "No, I can't think of anything," she replied, certain that she wanted to get out of Stillwater as fast as possible. She couldn't help but wonder what sort of things Cole might do in town if he didn't have her along. Would he go off somewhere with that girl? Would he kiss her the way he had kissed Rachel that morning? Rachel found that thought more than a little disturbing. Yes, she wanted to get out of Stillwater right away.

Cole sipped the last of his coffee and watched Rachel cut her steak into tiny little pieces. Tiny little pieces that she didn't even eat. He studied her thoughtfully. She really was upset, and just because he had talked to another woman.

Biting back a triumphant grin, he waited until she finally put down her knife and fork and blotted her lips carefully with her napkin.

"Are you ready to go?" he asked, trying not to sound quite as eager as he felt. Suddenly, he couldn't wait to get out of Stillwater and back to the ranch. Tonight was his wedding night.

"Yes," she said, gladly rising to her feet. But if she had thought that putting Stillwater behind her would make things easier, she had been wrong. Once again trapped within the confines of the buggy with Cole, Rachel discovered that her irritation over the girl was intensified by the growing attraction she felt for the man beside her.

In spite of her efforts to ignore his very disturbing presence, she was forcibly reminded of it every time either of them made the slightest move. No matter how carefully she kept to her side of the seat, she could not avoid the very frequent brush of his arm or leg against her and the strange sensations such contact produced. Although she would have thought it impossible, she was even more aware of his physical nearness now than she had been on the trip to town. And though she tried desperately not to, she found herself reviewing all the things that Lupe had told her would happen on her wedding night.

When Lupe had first explained these things to her, Rachel had simply not been able to imagine being locked in a passionate embrace with this man she hardly knew. Now she could. The kiss they had shared had given her fancy quite a bit of inspiration. Now she knew what his mouth felt like on hers and the sensation had been far more than pleasant and quite exciting. She wasn't too certain the rest of it would be, though. The very idea of opening herself up to a man, of allowing him to touch the most private parts of her body was positively frightening.

On the other hand, Lupe had said that Cole was a good man and that Rachel would enjoy it. Perhaps it wouldn't be quite as awful as she had feared. He could be gentle. She had seen him that way with the stallion. If he touched her like that, she wouldn't mind a bit. In fact, she realized, noticing the way her body warmed just from the thought, she would like it very much. And she would love more of his kisses.

On top of that, Lupe had also promised that when he came to her bed, he would love her. Remembering how she had felt when Cole flirted with that trollop at the hotel, Rachel decided that she very much wanted him to fall in love with her. In fact, she wanted him to worship the very ground she walked on. The thought made her smile.

She was still smiling a little later when Cole pulled the buggy off to the side of the road near a clump of bushes. He was ostensibly resting the horses, but she knew he was also providing her with a little privacy, just in case she needed to do anything.

Cole climbed down from the seat and stretched wearily, mentally berating himself for his decision to make this round trip in one day. If he hadn't been so pigheaded, he might have Rachel alone in a hotel room right now. This way, he'd have to wait hours for her. Slowly, he made his way around the buggy to help Rachel down, reminding himself with every step to be careful. Every time he touched her made it that much harder to take his hands off of her again. If he didn't watch himself, he might just drag her off behind those bushes. Smiling grimly at what her reaction might be to such manhandling, he sucked in a fortifying breath and stepped up to where she sat.

"You can take a little walk and stretch your l—yourself, if you want," he suggested, reaching up to take her arm. Mentally cursing himself, he realized he'd have to watch his tongue, too, or he'd give away what he was thinking.

Rachel glanced up, noting the slow flush that rose on his neck and biting back the smile that threatened. Did he think her such a ninny that she would be shocked to discover that he knew she had legs? Pianos had legs, of course, and chairs

74

and horses and cows. Men even had them, but not women. No, women had limbs. It was a little silly, and the girls at Miss Isabel's school had giggled over it more than once. Rachel might have giggled over it now, except that a new thought occurred to her: before the night was over, Cole Elliot would know all about her legs, and the rest of her, too.

As soon as her feet touched the ground, she stepped out of his very disturbing grasp and headed for the bushes, welcoming their privacy for more than one reason. She really had to get control of her emotions. She knew instinctively that to let him see how attracted she was to him would be a tactical mistake, at least until he had displayed an equal attraction. There was nothing more pathetic than unrequited love. Rachel had entertained enough suitors for whom she cared nothing to know that. She would just have to be careful not to make her feelings too obvious. There was no use in giving him the idea she was chasing him.

When Rachel finally felt that she was in complete control of herself, she schooled her expression to hide her thoughts and strolled back to where Cole was waiting for her at the buggy.

When Cole handed her back into her seat, he noticed that she looked a little strange. She must be getting tired, he reasoned. God knew, he was, so she must be exhausted. Sure enough, they hadn't been on the road again very long when he noticed her nodding off.

Rachel was indeed tired. Her day had started early, and she had hardly slept the night before. In spite of all the disquieting thoughts running through her head, she couldn't seem to keep her eyes open. Still, it was difficult to fall asleep because just when she would drop off, the buggy would bounce and jerk her awake again. There was just no way to get comfortable, but when she was about to give up hope, a bounce of the buggy brought her smack up against Cole. He felt awfully warm and solid. As drowsy as she was, Rachel smiled. They were married, after all, so there was nothing improper in her snuggling up to him if she wanted to, and she did want to. She snuggled closer and closed her eyes.

At first Cole didn't move, expecting her to straighten up again immediately. When she did not, he hazarded a quick glance down at her face and realized she was fast asleep. Gradually, he allowed his tense muscles to relax, and after a while he shifted his arm until he was cradling her, just to make her more comfortable, of course.

The scent of roses that always surrounded her was faint in the chilling wind, but he could still smell it. There was something about her that always smelled so fresh and clean and exciting. He took a deep breath and imagined how it would be to hold her like this in the middle of the night.

Soon, very soon, he told himself. He had made the right decision not to spend the night at the Stillwater Hotel. Even the suggestion still had the power to make him feel slightly ill. Far better that they wait and have their first night at the ranch.

Cole frowned at the thought. He should have been very happy, but as much as he wanted her, he could not help the niggling little doubts that teased at him. The problem was that he kept remembering that look of fear in her eyes when he had kissed her at the preacher's house. In all the times he had imagined the two of them together, he had never once imagined her afraid of him.

Not that he expected her to like it or anything. Everybody knew that women didn't enjoy it, not the way men did. Whores pretended to, of course, because that's what they got paid for, and decent women put up with it because it was their duty. He understood all that and accepted it. Still he couldn't stand the thought of scaring her, readily acknowledging the fact that something like that would probably be terrifying to a sweet, innocent girl like Rachel. She'd probably never even heard of such a thing, and if she had, she would have been completely shocked, as anyone with any sense would expect her to be.

Cole guessed he should know how to handle the situation. He'd been with more women than he cared to remember, but most of his experience had been on a pay-as-you-leave basis. Although he had lost his own virginity at the age of fifteen, he had never knowingly taken a woman's, and he had certainly never been with anyone as innocent as Rachel.

Wedding-night stories he had heard around numberless campfires came unbidden to his mind. There was the fellow who had told how his wife had screamed bloody murder, crying and calling for her mother and then crawling under the bed. He hadn't been able to coax her out, either, and she'd stayed under there all night. Another one had said his wife had fainted dead away at the sight of *IT,* and ever after had insisted on total darkness to protect her delicate sensibilities. Still another had locked herself in the bedroom and refused to come out. Even the stories that hadn't been quite so awful were bad enough. The men in general had agreed that breaking in a virgin was a risky business, at best, and something to be avoided at all costs unless forced on a man, especially if he had been foolish enough to get himself married to a nice girl.

Cole let out his breath in a long sigh, only to have it strangle in his throat when Rachel suddenly grabbed his thigh.

Glancing down quickly, he saw what had happened. She hadn't done it intentionally, of course. How could he even have thought such a thing? She was sound asleep and her hand had fallen from where she had wrapped it around his waist. That's all it was.

Cole grinned, thinking how flustered little Miss Rachel would be when she woke up.

Glancing down at where Rachel's head rested against him, he sighed again. Part of him was wondering how all that shiny black hair would look spread out across his bed. The other part of him was wondering how he could make her glad to be lying on that bed.

77

Chapter III

Lupe had fixed them a wedding supper complete with a cake. Rachel made the discovery when she entered the house alone and found that a small table had been pulled over in front of the fire, covered with a clean white cloth and set for two with her mother's good china. Lupe had even dug up one of the silk roses Rachel had made at school and put it on the table as a decoration.

Rachel entered the house alone when Cole dropped her off. He suggested that she go on inside and get warm while he took care of the horses. With a sigh of regret, Rachel went in, supposing that he had never heard of the custom of carrying a bride across the threshold.

Lupe fussed over her, calling Rachel her little *chata,* something she hadn't done in a long time, not since Rachel had gotten back from school. Beginning to feel more like a bride again, Rachel told her briefly about the ceremony and dinner at the hotel. She left out the part about the waitress, which really wasn't all that important anyway. And besides, there was no use in dwelling on the fact that her husband had known other women before he married her.

Lupe was an appreciative listener, and Rachel warmed to the topic. In the retelling, her wedding sounded almost like an adventure. It was, she realized when she heard Cole's footsteps on the porch, an adventure that was just beginning. Her heart did a funny little lurch in her chest as she lifted her gaze to the door.

Cole came in then. To Rachel's eyes, he seemed even taller than ever. He had washed his hands and face at the outside pump, and they were red. He was chaffing his hands together to warm them as he came through the door, and Rachel waited for the slight hesitation he always made when he came into this room. His blue eyes would narrow, and he would stand there expectantly in the doorway until someone—it had always been her father—acknowledged his presence and welcomed him. Except that this time Cole did not hesitate. This time he came fully into the room, glancing around until his restless gaze found her.

Rachel felt the impact of that gaze clear to the soles of her feet, and she had to consciously take a breath to restore the air that had whooshed unexpectedly from her lungs. She had been prepared to welcome him into her home, but he no longer seemed to need such a welcome. Instead, his very commanding physical presence actually dominated that home. Rachel knew she should have resented such an invasion, but oddly, she did not.

"Hello," she said inanely into the silence that had followed his entrance.

Cole nodded in response to her greeting, dragging off his Stetson. He knew he should say or do something, and he would in just a minute, but for now he couldn't seem to stop looking at her. She was standing silhouetted by the fire, her every curve outlined to perfection, and for just a second he could almost feel those curves under his hands.

Drawing a ragged breath, he mechanically lifted one of those hands and began to release the buttons of his coat. That was when he noticed something else about her, the way she was fiddling with the material of her skirt. She was nervous. And why shouldn't she be? he wondered. If she had any idea of what was coming, she would be frightened too.

As much as he wanted to simply carry her off to the bedroom, he would take things slow and easy.

The first thing he would have to do is stop looking at her. Reluctantly, he forced his gaze from her and that was when he noticed the table. He frowned.

He knew it was for them, for a celebration. He hadn't had any trouble figuring that out. The old woman had really gone to a lot of trouble. She'd dug up a silver candlestick from somewhere and a lot of fancy dishes. And where on earth had she gotten a flower in the dead of winter? It was there, though, right alongside the single candle, stuck in a fancy little glass holder. He tried to remember if he'd ever eaten at a table with a flower on it. He didn't think he had.

"Doesn't the table look nice?" Rachel asked, not liking the way he was scowling at it. Lupe had worked very hard to set a romantic mood, but evidently she had wasted her time. Rachel very carefully concealed her disappointment as those blue eyes lifted to her again.

"Yeah, real . . . nice," he agreed, although "nice" was not the word he was thinking. He wondered if Rachel realized that the old bat had set things up for Rachel's seduction. Judging from the way his bride was smoothing down her already-smooth collar and fingering the lace on her dress, she must have a pretty good idea that something was going to happen.

Before he could explore that idea, Lupe distracted him, buzzing around him, mumbling about something, reaching out that claw of a hand and almost touching his sleeve and then pulling it back again as if she didn't quite dare to, mumbling all the time. He glared at her in irritation. "What's she saying?" he asked Rachel.

Rachel noted that the top of Lupe's head scarcely reached the third button on his shirt, that she barely weighed one-half what he did, and that he could probably squash her like a bug with a mere flick of his wrist. The fact that he would never even consider doing such a thing, no matter how much the old woman annoyed him, gave Lupe a power over him that she delighted in using and which amused Rachel no end. In spite of her anxieties, Rachel could not help but smile at seeing the new boss of the Circle M at a momentary disadvantage. "She says she made us a special meal and a cake, too. A wedding cake," Rachel reported.

"Great," he replied without much enthusiasm, using the excuse that he needed more room to remove his coat to step away from the tiny woman who was grinning her toothless grin at him. Lupe watched him, nodding some sort of approval, and then slipped silently away to bring out the meal.

The big front room was warm from the fire that had burned all day, heating the hearth stones to a pleasant glow. Cole had always liked this room, liked the way it was big enough so a man didn't feel hemmed in but still felt homey. The furniture was rough, most of it homemade and scarred by countless spurs, but Lupe kept it polished up bright and shiny. The curtains on the window let you know that you were in a fancy place, but they weren't so frilly that a man felt foolish.

Cole walked over to where Rachel stood by the fire. He carefully skirted the table and deliberately did not look at Rachel.

"Are you cold?" he asked. He might not have been looking at her, but he was painfully aware of her nonetheless. He moved over to make more room for her at the hearth.

Rachel stepped closer, only too glad to be near the warmth that had nothing whatsoever to do with the fireplace. She studied his somber profile and fought the urge to reach up and trace his craggy features with her fingers. Holding her hands to the fire as he was doing, she reflected that she would be ever so much warmer if he would put his arm around her as he had this afternoon in the buggy when she had been asleep.

She had thoroughly enjoyed awakening in his arms, or

practically in his arms. For the first few seconds when she had not quite been awake, she had reveled in the solid warmth of his body. Then as full consciousness had returned, she had grown a little embarrassed at the unseemly way she was draped across him. Why, her hand was even on his leg! Such behavior was probably indecent even if they *were* married.

She had sat up quickly, apologizing for being so inconsiderate and wondering what on earth he must think of her. Only then had she noticed that his arm had been around her, holding her close. She thought he removed it rather slowly, but that might have only been because it was stiff. The wind had felt much colder then. Of course the day had been growing old and the sun had been setting, but Rachel was certain that being robbed of Cole's warmth had a lot ot do with the drop in the temperature.

He had said, "That's all right. I didn't mind," and flexed his arm to work out the stiffness. She had been sure that he meant it.

Unconsciously, Rachel moved a little closer to Cole, hugging her arms in silent invitation. "I guess I got a chill. I can't seem to get warmed up," she commented, lifting her gaze tentatively to his face to see his reaction. She encountered blue eyes full of concern, but as she watched, that concern evaporated in the blaze of another expression entirely.

Cole looked down into eyes grown fathomless in the flickering firelight. Mesmerized, he watched her lips—those luscious lips—part slightly in invitation, an invitation he could not refuse. If she was cold, he knew just how to warm her up. His arms lifted to enfold her.

Rachel's blood was pounding in her ears as she saw him reaching for her. Needs she had never dreamed she possessed flared to life, searing her very soul. The sensation startled her, and she gave a tiny cry at the raw desire that was almost physical pain.

83

The sound startled him, shocking him back to reality. Instantly, he dropped his arms and took a step back. Just a moment ago he had vowed to take it slow and easy and here he was about to grab her right in the parlor, in front of God and everybody. And in front of Lupe, he noticed with disgust as the old woman made a disapproving noise and sidled past them carrying two plates of food. Where in the hell had she come from? No wonder Rachel had yelled. He'd probably scared her to death.

Rachel's body sagged with disappointment. Why had Lupe chosen that particular moment to come in with their supper? When Rachel looked up at Cole again, he had turned away and was running a hand through the shock of golden hair that had fallen down on his forehead. Now he was embarrassed, Rachel realized in dismay. The only thing more awkward than having a reluctant husband would be to have a reluctant, embarrassed husband. Rachel could have wept in frustration.

"Supper," Lupe announced to no one in particular and then slipped silently from the room.

"Well," Rachel said with forced cheerfulness to Cole's taut back, "it certainly smells good. Shall we eat?" Eating, of course, was the very last thing Rachel wanted to do at the moment. She placed a hand on her quivering stomach and prayed that she would at least be able to choke down a few bites. Somehow she had to bring some normalcy to their situation to ease his discomfort and restore the closeness she had sensed was developing between them.

"Yeah, it does smell good. At least the old woman can cook," he allowed, unable to keep the sarcasm from his voice.

His barb brought a reluctant smile to Rachel's lips, and she gave a silent sigh of relief. He couldn't be too embarrassed if he was up to insulting Lupe.

Her smile still firmly in place, Rachel took her seat at the table and waited for Cole to do the same. They began their meal in silence, neither being perfectly sure what might be an appropriate topic of conversation.

Rachel took advantage of the silence to surreptitiously study her new husband. Why had she once thought that he wasn't handsome? She loved the rugged planes of his face, even the way his nose was slightly crooked, and she thought he had the most wonderful eyes. Rachel's stomach did a flip-flop just thinking about the way his eyes had glittered down at her a few moments ago. Bluer than blue, they held the clarity, and the mystery, of the broad Texas sky. And when he smiled, laugh lines crinkled outward from their corners. He would be smiling more, now that they were married. She would see to that.

As she peered at him over her coffee cup, the shock of sunbleached hair tumbled down onto his forehead. Fascinated, she stared as one of his finely made hands lifted to brush it back, and her own fingers itched to help him, to touch his golden brown locks and caress his bronzed cheek and trace the spot where his dimple would appear.

Her heart racing at such wild fantasies, Rachel quickly lowered her eyes to the table, but there she saw his hands. He had such wonderful hands, long and slender. Perfect hands for handling a gun, but she did not allow herself to dwell on that. Instead she remembered how they had stroked the stallion. Soon they would be stroking her. Rachel's body quivered in the oddest places at the thought. She took another sip of coffee to moisten a suddenly dry mouth and hoped the subdued lighting would hide her burning cheeks.

Frantically, she ransacked her brain for something light and frivolous to say to break what was rapidly becoming a dangerous silence. "How does this steak compare to your old boots?" she asked with what she hoped was playfulness.

Cole lifted his head in surprise. He wasn't used to making polite conversation at meals, and to tell the truth, he could not have actually said whether he liked the steak or not. He was only eating out of pure habit, that and a need to occupy himself with something besides noticing how lovely Rachel looked in the soft light. He slowly chewed the bite he had just taken and then swallowed it. "It's pretty good," he allowed. "Like I said, Lupe can cook."

Their gazes held for one long moment, and then Lupe appeared beside them, startling them both. Rachel quickly lowered her eyes and took a deep breath to regain her splintering composure before looking back up at Lupe. The old woman had brought in the cake and now she cut each of them a large piece. When she placed one of the slices before Rachel, she gave the girl a sly grin that made her blush.

Then, still grinning, Lupe turned and handed Cole his plate. As he was drinking down the last of his coffee, she leaned over and muttered, "Eat so you be strong tonight." Cole choked on his coffee.

Rachel half rose from her chair, anxious to help him in some way, but he recovered quickly. After giving Rachel one extremely concerned look, he turned on Lupe the most murderous glare Rachel had ever seen. Sinking back into her chair, Rachel watched in amazement as Lupe cackled delightedly and then padded silently from the room. Rachel had not caught exactly what Lupe had said, but from Cole's reaction, it must have been very interesting. Not quite bold enough to inquire, she started eating her cake instead.

Cole stabbed his fork into the cake, and reflected that it really was a good thing Lupe was such a good cook. Otherwise he would be sorely tempted to toss the old witch down the well. Wouldn't you know that the one time he was able to understand her, she would be saying a thing like that. Thank God, Rachel hadn't heard her. But then, maybe she wouldn't have known what Lupe was talking about even if she had heard.

Covertly studying Rachel from across the table, he determined that she didn't seem to be the least bit nervous about what was going to happen, which confirmed his suspicions that she didn't have a clue. When he saw the dainty way she laid her fork aside and used her napkin to delicately blot her lips, he was sure she couldn't. Uneasily, Cole wondered what her reaction was going to be when she found out.

Not liking the unpleasant visions that teased at his imagination, Cole decided now would be a good time to take care of a little business that he had been putting off.

Abruptly, he stood, startling Rachel. "I better go get my gear from the bunkhouse," he said.

"Yes, of course," Rachel agreed, rising also, acutely aware of how late it was getting and the fact that when he came back, it would be time for bed. She hoped he couldn't tell how eager she was. Or how nervous.

He lingered a moment, studying the way she still looked so perfect even after the grueling day they had had. Not a hair on her head was out of place, and the blue dress was as immaculate as it had been that morning. She was like that china doll he had thought of earlier, too flawless to be real. He wondered vaguely if, like the doll, she would also be fragile. At least he knew she would not be cold, not if their earlier kiss was anything to go by. He'd just have to be careful not to scare her, he reminded himself, reaching for his coat.

Hunching down inside his jacket, Cole cursed the chill wind that whipped across the empty ranch yard. Still, he walked as slowly as he could toward the bunkhouse. Lights were blazing from the windows, and he knew that on a night like this all the men would be there. He didn't relish the thought of packing up in front of them, but couldn't think of another alternative.

Every man in the room looked up when he entered, and he nodded stiffly in response to the friendly greetings. Instinctively, he sought out Miles who was seated on a far bunk mending a harness. The older man smiled. "Did Miss Rachel get all her business done?" he called.

Cole felt the heat crawling up his neck, but he kept his face expressionless. "Yeah," he replied.

"Don't suppose you had time to kick up your heels any?" This inquiry came from the other end of the room, and this time Cole sought out and found another man.

"We weren't hardly in town long enough to spit on the sidewalk," Cole explained, unable to suppress a grin in response to the laughing eyes that met his.

"Too bad," the Kid said, but no trace of sympathy marred the beatific smile on his pretty face. Pretty was the only word that could describe the Kid. The fact that he stood over six feet tall and had shoulders as broad as a barn door were all that prevented him from being taken for a girl. He wore his corn yellow hair long and curling to his shoulders, but instead of making him look effeminate, the style somehow made him seem even more masculine. Heavy-lidded azure eyes that always held a mischievous twinkle stared out from beneath ridiculously long lashes, but it was the smile, the smile that revealed teeth too straight and white to be believable, that made him so irresistible.

Women found him so, at least, and most men were glad to call him "friend." If they were unlucky enough to see the speed with which he could draw a pistol, they were even grateful for the honor. For some reason that Cole had never been able to fathom, the Kid had chosen him to be more than a friend. Miles teased Cole about it sometimes, about how the Kid looked up to him with a sort of hero worship and followed him with almost puppylike devotion. When Miles had said the evening before that the Kid would do anything Cole said, he had not been exaggerating.

Suddenly, Cole remembered where he had met Nancy. "Remember that girl in Stillwater? Nancy, I think her name was," he said.

The Kid shrugged noncommittally. "That depends on if she's knocked up or not," he said innocently, drawing a burst of raucous laughter from the rest of the men.

Cole couldn't help laughing, too. "Well, she didn't

mention it, but she's slinging hash at the Stillwater Hotel now. I saw her today."

"Lucky you," the Kid remarked, his smile never fading, his blue eyes dancing.

Yeah, lucky me, Cole thought, even as he grinned back at the Kid and shook his head in wonder at the boy's easy attitude. He guessed the Kid had never really cared about a girl before. If he had, he wouldn't be able to joke about one that way. Cole's headshake suddenly changed, becoming a gesture of wonder over his very own change of attitude. Yesterday he would have been as unconcerned as the Kid.

Quickly, before anyone else could engage him in conversation, he moved on into his room. As foreman, he had his own private quarters, a room all to himself with a door he could close, although he rarely did.

Looking around that room now, he was struck by how bare it seemed compared with the coziness of the big house. He certainly wouldn't need much time to pack, he reflected. Aside from a few changes of clothes, his leather leggings, his guns, and his bedroll, he owned only a shaving kit and a few odds and ends. He had several pictures of some scantily clad ladies that he had torn out of *The Police Gazette* and tacked up on the bare walls to brighten the place up a bit, but he reckoned he could leave those here for the next resident. Smiling grimly at what Rachel's reaction would be to such pictures, he began to pluck his clothes from their pegs and toss them onto the bed.

He only needed a minute or two to gather up everything else, and when he was done, he rolled it all into a bundle and tied it with a length of twine. They'd want to know where he was going, and he'd have to tell them, no matter how much he preferred not to. Not knowing what their reaction was going to be was the hard part. He could deal with anything, anger, disapproval, even hostility, but this business of not knowing what to expect was really getting to him. He probably should have told Miles last night and let him break it to the men today while he was gone. That would have been the coward's way out, he knew, but at the moment it held a certain amount of appeal.

Bracing himself, he picked up his bedroll and went out into the other room.

"You ain't leaving, are you, Boss?" The note of alarm in the Kid's usually careless voice surprised Cole, catching him off guard. The Kid's habitual smile was a little crooked.

"No, I'm just moving up to the big house is all," Cole explained in an effort to reassure him.

Somehow his statement had the opposite effect. The Kid's crooked smile faltered and then faded, curling into a sneer as he rose to his feet. Suddenly, Cole was aware of the fact that all sound in the noisy bunkhouse had ceased at the Kid's question. The formerly friendly atmosphere had evaporated. The air crackled with hostility. The enmity was so real, so palpable that Cole could feel it swirl around him like a swift, malevolent fog. Automatically, every nerve in his body came to attention.

He hadn't expected them to like it, but he had never expected anything like this. The Kid's eyes had turned cold, the way they did when he was ready to kill. Too startled to even realize the implications of that fact, Cole could only stare at his friend for the space of several heartbeats.

"You're moving in on Miss Rachel then?" the Kid asked, contempt curling his beautiful lips. His hand dropped to his side where a silver Colt Peacemaker hung low on his hip.

From the corner of his eye, Cole caught the flexing motion of the Kid's fingers. The boy wanted to kill him! And all because he'd married Miss Rachel. His own fingers tensed in an instinctive response.

That was when the truth of what the Kid—and probably the rest of them—were thinking finally dawned on him. "Not exactly," he said with a small smile of self-mockery, forcing his hand to relax. "You see, we got married today in Stillwater."

It took a minute for his words to penetrate, to crack the killing wall of ice that had formed over the Kid, and when they did, the boy blinked several times. "Married?" he asked, as if he had never heard the word before. "*Married?* You and Miss Rachel?"

"That's right," Cole affirmed, listening to the buzz of conversation that had started around him. They wouldn't like the truth, but the truth was a whole lot better than what they had been thinking. He was a little insulted that they could have thought such a thing about him, but before he had time to dwell on that, Miles stepped forward.

"Now just how in the hell did you manage that?" he inquired. His voice was a little too calm, a little too soft, and those spectral eyes were trying to burn twin holes through Cole's face. As always, Miles was ready to protect the lady. Miles seemed to have made protecting ladies his mission in life and at very great cost to himself, too.

Cole's glance darted between Miles's outrage and the Kid's astonishment. This couldn't really be happening, he decided. He must be having a nightmare. First the Kid thought he was going up to the house to rape Rachel and now Miles thought he'd somehow seduced or coerced her into marrying him. Didn't these people know him at all? "It wasn't like that," he said, the coldness of his voice matching Miles's.

"What was it like, then?" Miles challenged.

Cole winced inwardly. A gentleman shouldn't tell it. He knew that, but he couldn't have the men thinking he was a dirty skunk who'd taken advantage of Miss Rachel's time of trouble to get ahold of her ranch, either. If they thought that, they'd never follow him, and if he was going to protect Rachel, he would need every one of them. "She asked me," he said.

Miles gaped. He knew Cole well, knew how he felt about Miss Rachel, how they all felt about her. She was somebody very special to them, and now that her father was gone, they knew that they had to protect her. Marrying her, though, was another matter entirely. He hadn't really thought that Cole would ever have been so presumptuous, but for a minute there, the evidence seemed overwhelming. Now it seemed that the truth was even more so. *"She* asked *you?"* he repeated incredulously.

"That's right," Cole affirmed. He saw that Miles was accepting that fact, so he allowed his gaze to drift over to the Kid. The Kid still looked like somebody'd dropped a hammer on his toe, but he wasn't mad anymore. Cole glanced around the room. The other men were watching Miles, waiting for his reaction. If Miles believed it, then they would.

"Does this have anything to do with Statler?" Miles asked, suddenly remembering the conversation he had had with Cole the night before.

Cole felt the tension start to drain out of him. He was beginning to think that he might not have to shoot his way out of the bunkhouse tonight after all. He nodded. For the benefit of the rest of the men, he explained. "Statler showed up here yesterday and told her that you men wouldn't fight for a woman. She was afraid if she didn't have a man to lead the fight, Statler would beat her." He shrugged with unfeigned modesty. "She picked me."

Miles shook his head in wonder and the rest of the men had much the same reaction. Then Miles's face hardened again. "You better be good to her, or you'll have to answer to every man on this place," he warned. A murmur from the other men confirmed his statement.

Cole felt his hackles rise. Miles might consider himself God's appointed protector of women, but Cole didn't need to be told how to treat his own wife. "And the men on this place better fight to the last man for her, or you'll have to answer to me," he warned right back.

For a long moment, Cole exchanged glares with the other men, and then, as if they were satisfied with what they saw, the men, starting with Miles, relaxed visibly. A small smile twitched Miles's thin lips. "Well, now, I reckon that's fair," he allowed. Then he said, "By the way, congratulations."

"Thanks," Cole replied grudgingly.

The Kid glanced at Miles, as if for approval. Miles nodded. "Congratulations," the Kid said, his smile returning.

The other men muttered their own good wishes. They were still not totally approving, but they weren't going to stop him from leaving, either. He nodded stiffly in acknowledgment, knowing that he would still have to prove himself before they would accept him as the owner of the Circle M.

Miles grinned at the determined glint in Cole's eye and guessed his thoughts. Then he glanced down at Cole's bedroll, and seeing that he was all ready to go, he said, "I reckon you've had enough of us for now. You'd better get on up to the house before your bride gets worried."

Cole ignored Miles's knowing smirk. The man was getting as bad as that old witch Lupe with all those secret grins and broad insinuations. Hitching the bundle up under his arm, Cole nodded his good night and left, knowing that Miles would serve as his advocate with any man who might still have misgivings about the new arrangements.

Glancing back at the brightly lit bunkhouse, he decided that he'd gotten out of there pretty easily. The men would come around in time, and he knew he could trust them to fight. Now all he had to worry about was dealing with Rachel.

Rachel wasn't exactly sure what she should be doing. Lupe had cleared the table, and then disappeared. She would not be back tonight. On that, Rachel would have bet money. That left Rachel all alone to face Cole when he returned, and Rachel had just made a rather disconcerting discovery: while Lupe had given her detailed instruction about what was expected of her once they were in bed, she had neglected to mention exactly how they were to make the rather awkward transition from being fully clothed and out of bed to being only very partially clothed and in bed.

Now that she thought of it, she could very well have taken advantage of the fact that he had been gone for a few minutes to make that transition herself, except that now it was too late, and besides, they had neglected to discuss which bedroom they were going to occupy.

There were only two possibilities, of course, her room and her father's. Her father's room was the logical choice since it contained the large, oversize marriage bed that her parents had shared. Having peeked inside as soon as Cole left, Rachel knew that Lupe had made up the room for them. Still, her bedroom contained a double bed and all her things were there, making it a more comfortable, familiar choice, although how comfortable it might be for Cole, she had no idea.

Whichever room they chose, she could ask him to give her a few minutes to get into her nightdress. That would be a reasonable request. She would do so as soon as they had decided which room to use. Nervously, she touched her hand to her hair. It was still smooth, still pulled tightly back into a prim chignon. In a few minutes she would have to decide whether to braid it for the night or leave it loose.

"Oh, dear," she whispered, hearing his footsteps on the porch outside. Frantically, she darted over to a chair and sat down but then stood up again immediately, knowing she could not possibly stay seated. Locking her hands in front of her, she drew a deep breath and determined not to let on how very flustered she was. The whole situation was awkward enough without sacrificing her pride. She would never let him guess just how flustered she had become. She would carry this off with aplomb, if it killed her. With a curious sense of dread, she watched the door.

She was standing when he came into the room, her hands folded primly in front of her, her face devoid of expression.

94

Cole noticed once again how neat she was, the picture of perfection from head to toe.

He set down his bundle with elaborate care and shrugged out of his coat, hanging it on a peg by the door, and then removed his hat and hung it alongside the coat.

Rachel forced her hands to be still, clenching them in front of her to maintain discipline, and tried to smile. She was, after all, a bride. Brides were supposed to be happy, weren't they? The remnants of a question she had decided to ask drifted across her consciousness, but she could not for the life of her recall the very first word. Since that was the most important one, she did not say anything at all, but simply stood, staring at him expectantly instead.

Cole waited, chafing his hands together to warm them from the nighttime chill outside. She hadn't said anything, and she didn't look like she was going to. He guessed it was up to him to get things started. "Where should I put my stuff?" He made a small gesture toward the bundle resting at his feet.

Oh, dear, Rachel thought again. This wasn't working out at all the way she had planned. She had wanted him to choose, and he was awaiting her instructions instead. Impulsively, she decided that it really didn't matter, did it? Which room they chose was irrelevant, and they could always un-choose it if things didn't work out.

With an uncertain glance at the two doors that opened off the front room, she made a hasty decision. "Well, that room is mine," she said, indicating the left-hand door.

Cole didn't move, not quite certain exactly what she was telling him.

He wasn't moving. She had been right: he wouldn't feel comfortable in a girl's room. "And that one is . . . was . . . my father's. You'll probably be more comfortable in there," she added, as if it had been her original intention to choose that one all along.

Cole's eyes narrowed. He had suspected that she didn't

know much about marriage, but how ignorant could she be? Did she really expect him to sleep in a different room? Didn't she know that married people slept together? "You want me to sleep in your father's room then?" he asked suspiciously.

"Yes," Rachel replied firmly so he wouldn't sense the agonies underlying her decision.

Cole frowned at her impassive expression. He hadn't misunderstood her. She really did intend for him to sleep in a separate room. Well, he would just have to set her straight. "Rachel . . ." he began with infinite patience.

"What?" she snapped, instantly regretting the way she had betrayed herself, but somehow unable to regain the same tight grip on her emotions that she had had a moment ago.

Cole saw the fear flicker across her face in that second when she had lost her self-control. It was the same fear he had seen just after he had kissed her this afternoon and when he had almost kissed her a while ago. Suddenly, he realized that he had misjudged her poise. She was scared. What he had taken for calm serenity was really tightly leashed tension. She must not be nearly as ignorant as he had suspected, and she was absolutely horrified at the prospect of sharing a bed with him.

It would be a natural reaction for somebody as sheltered as Rachel, and he guessed that he couldn't blame her. When she had proposed to him, she had been looking for a protector, not a man to share her bed. He had agreed to protect her, too, and even if he hadn't married her, he would owe her that protection for Mr. McKinsey's sake.

Cole wasn't certain if his responsibilities extended to protecting her from himself, but judging by the panic he sensed in her, he figured he'd better do so, at least tonight. Besides, he'd never taken an unwilling woman, and he had no desire to tangle with one right now, no matter how delectable she might be. He was a grown man. He could wait. A day or two wouldn't make that much difference. When they knew each other a little better, nature would take its course. With resignation, he scooped up his bundle of possessions and started for the second door she had indicated. "I'll put my stuff in here, then," he said.

Rachel made a small sound that stopped him in his tracks, but when he turned back to look at her, she stood silent, looking almost unnerved.

Finally, she asked, very faintly, "Are you going to bed, now?" He would never know how much it had cost her to ask that question. She had been debating on how to request the few moments alone she would need to undress, but had decided to begin by determining whether or not he intended to come back out or not. If he did, she could simply go in ahead of him the next time and ask him to wait. If not, she had a slightly more difficult problem.

Cole studied her face. She looked exhausted in addition to everything else. There was no use in dragging things out any more this evening, anyway. If he spent too much more time with her, he might forget all his noble intentions. "Yeah, I guess I will." He gave her a curt nod. "Reckon I'll say 'good night,' then." He turned abruptly on his heel and strode the rest of the way across the room, entered her father's old bedroom and closed the door.

Rachel stared at the closed door for a long moment, aware that her mouth was hanging open but too stunned to really care. All her planning, all her worry was for nothing! He had never intended to sleep with her! He didn't want her! Fury and humiliation warred for dominance, and fury won. With an angry swish of skirts, she marched across to her own room and went inside, slamming the door behind her.

Cole winced when he heard her door close. It had almost sounded as if she had slammed it, but he must have imagined that. Dropping the bundle of his belongings, he slumped back against the door with a weary sigh and surveyed the room. Somebody, probably the old witch, had fixed the place up for him. The bed was made and a lamp burned on the bedside table. All trace of Mr. McKinsey's belongings had been removed, all except for a picture of Rachel which sat by the lamp. She was smiling at him from across the room, a sweet, teasing smile, and he could almost see her brown eyes mocking him. A day or two. Suddenly, it seemed like a very long time.

Rachel gave her waist-length black hair a full five hundred strokes that night with the silver brush that had belonged to her mother. They were swift, angry strokes, and she reflected later that it was a wonder she hadn't brushed herself bald-headed.

Damn Cole Elliot, anyway, she thought more than once. In between damning him, she tried to be reasonable, and reminded herself that she had forced him into this marriage. Even when she tried to argue that he could have turned her down if he hadn't really wanted to go through with it, she had to admit that she really had not given him any choice. No man of honor would have insulted a lady by refusing the offer she had made him, and one reason she had chosen Cole was that she knew him to be a man of honor.

She could only wonder if a man of honor would insult a lady by refusing to share her bed. He didn't have to do anything, of course, not if he didn't want to, but married people slept in the same bed. Everybody knew that.

Of course, she knew that he was reserved with women. No, not with all women, just with her, she corrected, remembering the friendly waitress with whom he had obviously not been reserved at some past time. Lupe had insisted, however, that no man would refuse his husbandly rights, that his natural urges would overcome any reluctance he might otherwise feel. Well, so much for Lupe and her theories. Whatever the reason, Cole Elliot had managed to refuse those rights, and he hadn't looked as if he had regretted it in the least, either.

With that thought burning in her brain, Rachel climbed into bed, clad in her very best nightdress, and pulled the covers up to her chin. The worst part was that she was all alone. The last two nights had been awful, knowing that her father no longer slept in the next room and that he never would again. Tonight, at least, she had thought that she would have someone to hold her and comfort her. He wouldn't have to do anything else as long as he held her.

"Damn you, Cole Elliot," she said again, but this time her words became a sob as grief and loneliness overwhelmed her. Pride forced her to bury her face in her pillow so the man who slept in the next room would not hear.

The next morning Cole was up first, the habits of a lifetime waking him at dawn even though he had slept fitfully, haunted by dreams of Rachel. After what he had been doing to her all night, the prospect of meeting her at the breakfast table was a little disconcerting. Would she be able to guess what was going on in his mind? He briefly entertained thoughts of taking his morning meal with the men, but he didn't relish seeing the knowing looks that were bound to be in their eyes any more than he looked forward to pretending indifference in front of Rachel. Besides, they would wonder why he wasn't having breakfast with his bride. Finally, he chose the lesser of two evils and made his way to the ranch house dining room. Maybe she would sleep late.

But Rachel had been up almost as early as he. She, too, had had some difficulty sleeping. Nightmares of her father being murdered had haunted her, reminding her that she had problems much more serious than an uncooperative husband. The fact that that husband had appeared in some of those nightmares, and had repeatedly turned his back and walked away from her, had not improved her sleep.

To make up for her haggard appearance, Rachel spent more time than usual on her toilette. She dressed carefully in one of her favorite dresses, a pink water-floral print spangled with rosebuds. The color gave an artificial blush to her cheeks, something she sorely needed this morning. Then she patiently plaited her hair into an intricate coiffure. When she had held cold cloths to her eyes and reduced the puffiness her sleepless night had produced, she pronounced herself ready to face the day. And Cole Elliot.

She found him sipping coffee at the huge dining-room table, and to her dismay he did not look anything like the uncaring brute who had haunted her dreams. Instead he looked rugged and handsome and strong and ever so appealing. Rachel could have moaned in despair at the way her stomach fluttered and her knees grew weak at the very sight of him.

"Good morning," she ventured, forcing herself to smile at him. There was no point in letting him know how he affected her, and she would never let him guess how hurt and angry she still was at his rejection. Her best course of action would be to treat him as nicely as she could manage and thereby make him regret that rejection. Carefully resisting the urge to empty the coffeepot over his head, she poured herself a cup and sat down at the place that had been set for her at his right, although she would have preferred to sit at the opposite end of the huge table.

"'Mornin'," he mumbled. Morning wasn't his best time of day, at least not until he'd had about three cups of coffee and this was only the second. Seeing her looking so fresh and cheerful wasn't helping his mood, either. His tired eyes couldn't seem to focus on anything except the way her pink dress molded over her breasts, and even his sleep-deprived brain still had the energy to calculate how long it would take to undo all the buttons on her bodice. Cole drained his cup and got up to pour himself another.

Lupe came in then, slipping silently through the door and carrying two heaping plates. She set them down in front of Cole and Rachel, clucking and muttering in disapproval.

As he took his seat again, Cole ignored her, or pretended to. He didn't have to understand the words to know what she was clucking about, and he certainly didn't care about

100

her disapproval.

Rachel glared up at the tiny old woman, her large brown eyes daring Lupe to say one word, just one word. Lupe glared back, her sunken black eyes replying that it had been all Rachel's fault that nothing had happened last night and that Lupe was very disappointed in her.

Sighing in defeat, Rachel picked up her fork and began to toy halfheartedly with the pile of fluffy scrambled eggs on her plate.

Cole ate mechanically, chewing and swallowing without really tasting, because eating gave him an excuse not to look at Rachel. He had been right. Just seeing her brought back the dreams he had had the night before with crystal clarity. He had dreamed about her before, of course, lots of times. Even when he had forced himself not to think about her while he was awake, he hadn't been able to control the dreams. None of them had been as bad as last night, though. He guessed that was because until yesterday he had never kissed her before. That cursed kiss had set off a whole string of explosive images in the back of his mind, all of which had blown up last night. Just remembering was making him feel hot all over. He shifted uneasily in his chair.

Rachel reluctantly swallowed a mouthful of eggs and stole a glance at her new husband. The awkwardness of their situation certainly hadn't affected his appetite any, she noticed disgustedly. How on earth could she possibly keep up the pretense that she was as unaffected as he? And how on earth would she ever make him as aware of her as she was of him if she couldn't?

But maybe there was another way. The thought teased at her, making her consider other possibilities. Maybe she should just talk to him, tell him how insulted she had been, tell him they had to have a real marriage. Of course he might just come right out and tell her he didn't want a real marriage, didn't want *her*. Suspecting it was one thing; hearing it from his own lips was quite another. No, she had already been humiliated enough. She wasn't going to give him another crack at it. Viciously, she stabbed at another forkful of eggs.

The third or fourth time her gaze strayed over to him, Rachel noticed that he had shaved this morning. She was a little surprised. He usually only shaved once a week, on Saturday. She guessed that was so he would look nice when he went to town. Why, exactly, she had ever made note of the frequency of his shaves, she could not have said. Perhaps it was because she liked the way several days' growth of whiskers gave him such a sinister air, especially when he had that huge, hog leg pistol of his tied down to his thigh. He always looked like a very dangerous man when he hadn't shaved in a while.

Unfortunately, Rachel realized, even now when he was neatly groomed, he was very dangerous to her peace of mind. For just one second she allowed herself the luxury of glaring at him, and that was when she noticed he was wearing another new shirt, brown just like the one he had been married in, but a little different. He was dressed up. Rachel blinked and stared. Something warm stirred in her breast, something she quickly recognized as pleasure. He had gotten dressed up for her! She was beginning to feel very flattered and not quite as furious with him when he raised his eyes and met her gaze.

"I think we ought to go to town today," he said.

Rachel blinked again. His tone surprised her. He wasn't exactly giving her an order, but she didn't think he was going to consider any discussion on the matter either. She knew a momentary urge to challenge him, but realized that if she started acting like a shrew, she would only make him glad they weren't sharing a bed. No, she would be calm and cool and ever so poised. He would never guess her true feelings. She would make him regret rejecting her if it killed her. Still, since it was only Thursday and not the day one usually went to town, she thought she could at least inquire into his reasoning.

"Why are we going to town today?" she asked primly.

Cole wasn't used to explaining his decisions, and his head came up in surprise. It took him a minute to put his reasons into words. "Because, I figure the sooner Will Statler finds out we're married, the better. We can go to town and spread the word," he said at last.

This was the very last thing she had expected him to say. Spreading the word about his marriage seemed like something Cole Elliot would have little inclination for, considering his behavior the night before. To her horror, Rachel found herself blushing furiously. "Of course," she agreed with as much dignity as she could muster with her face on fire. Honestly, he was the most disturbing man. Then a fresh realization sent the color rushing to her face once more. His neat appearance was in honor of the trip to town and not for her at all. Disappointment overwhelmed her.

Cole watched her expression, unable to fathom the depths of those brown eyes. "I'll go down and tell the men. We'll want to take some of them with us in case there's any trouble," he said, knowing that he was only using this as a convenient excuse to end the conversation. He didn't think he could sit here with her much longer and not at least touch her. Swallowing the last of his coffee, he rose, gave her a quick nod, and left.

Rachel watched him go and struggled with her chagrin. Now that he was gone, now that her traitorous body was no longer reacting to his physical presence, she found that she could think more clearly. What she thought gave her some little comfort. At least she hadn't commented on the fact that he was so nicely dressed. At least she hadn't let him know she thought he was trying to impress her. At least she hadn't made a fool of herself.

And at least it was some comfort to know that if she had ever doubted Cole's ability to handle Statler, she could put those doubts to rest. Her husband had obviously been making plans already, and as much as it galled her, she had to agree with his reasoning that announcing their marriage as soon as possible was a wise move.

Rachel stabbed her fork into her eggs and left it there.

"What happen?"

Rachel's head jerked up in surprise to discover Lupe looming over her. There was no use pretending not to understand the question. She had understood Lupe's disgruntled mumblings earlier even if Cole hadn't, thank heaven. "I gave him his choice and he chose not to sleep with me, that's what happened," Rachel replied more than a little testily.

Lupe's eyes narrowed thoughtfully. "You are sure you did not . . ."

"I don't want to discuss it," Rachel insisted, rising from her chair and tossing her head haughtily. "We are going to town today and will not be here for dinner," she added, refusing to meet Lupe's eyes again, knowing the disapproval she would see there. It was so difficult to be firm with a servant who had also been your mother since the time you had been two years old.

Rachel was all ready to go when Cole pulled the spring wagon up in front of the house. She had managed to regain her poise, and noted gratefully that since they would be using the open, flatbed vehicle to carry their supplies home from town, she would not have to suffer being cooped up with him in the confines of the closed buggy again. That should help.

What did not help was the fact that Cole still had to assist her up onto the wagon seat, and by the time he had stopped the wagon and came around to her, she was actually breathless with anticipation. Even though her coat and gloves protected her from any direct contact with his skin, she could still feel the heat of his hands where he touched her arm and briefly encircled her waist through all those layers of fabric. When she was at last settled on the seat, she had to gasp for every breath. Surely, she had laced her corset too tightly.

Cole circled the wagon and took his own seat with grim determination. He was going to have to get hold of himself, or he was liable to stop the wagon at some secluded spot, drag her over the seat and take her right there on the wooden boards. That would, he noted with ironic amusement, certainly shock their outriders, to say nothing of how it would affect Rachel. He slapped the team into motion.

After a few minutes, when her breath was coming normally again, Rachel turned to him and remarked, "It's a beautiful day, isn't it?" There, that seemed like a safe enough topic, and Rachel desperately needed a safe topic to take her mind off other, far-from-safe topics.

"Yeah," he replied, not really having noticed and certainly not caring.

Undaunted, she continued. "Maybe if this keeps up, we'll have an early spring."

"Maybe," he allowed, not daring to look at her lest she guess his mind wasn't on spring at all.

Rachel opened her mouth to say something else, some other, inconsequential remark, but then snapped it shut in annoyance, surrendering to his stubborn refusal to converse. So much for polite conversation, she reflected. She would just ignore him.

Still, as hard as she fought against it, she was excruciatingly aware of his nearness on the wagon seat, even though she had much more room in the open wagon than she had in the buggy. Quite against her will, she found her gaze straying over in his direction time and again. He really needed a new coat, she noticed after a time, eyeing the ragged sheepskin jacket he always wore. Recognizing that thought as suspiciously wifely, Rachel wrenched her gaze from him and stared off determinedly into the distance.

But she found the barren plains scant distraction. He did need a coat he could wear for special occasions, the voice of reason argued against her express permission. Maybe he would even be pleased if she gave him a gift. It wouldn't exactly be a gift, of course, just something practical that a wife did for her husband. She smiled at the thought. She could take care of that easily enough while they were in town today. Hank was bound to have something at the Mercantile.

Hank! Rachel almost gasped aloud at the thought of him. In all that had happened during the past few days, she had completely forgotten about Hank. With a pang of guilt, she realized that Will Statler was not the only person who needed to hear of her marriage. Breaking the news to Hank was going to be unpleasant, to say the least, and he was bound to be hurt. She knew how he felt about her, even if he hadn't actually come right out and said anything yet, and although she did not feel the same way, she was still very fond of him. He certainly did not deserve to be treated so shabbily, but unfortunately there was nothing she could do about that now. Sighing aloud, Rachel began to dread the inevitable encounter.

The town of Canaan, the town closest to the ranch, was a sleepy little collection of businesses and houses that marked a crossroads on the wide Texas prairie. Not many people actually lived there, but many relied upon its existence for supplies and entertainment, making the Mercantile and the Silver Dollar Saloon very successful enterprises. Several other businesses managed to thrive, too, giving the residents of the town an excuse for a rather excessive civic pride.

Rachel scanned the familiar row of buildings as they rode down the one and only street in Canaan, her gaze coming to rest on the Mercantile. Hank obviously hadn't seen them yet because he hadn't come out to greet her. Since it was a weekday and hardly anyone was around, Cole easily found a place right in front of the store to stop the wagon.

Because she was so preoccupied with trying to guess what Hank's reaction was going to be, Rachel almost forgot to dread the moment when Cole would have to help her down from her seat. The sight of his strong, bronzed hands reaching for her quickly reminded her, though, and her breath once again lodged in her chest.

She tried to pretend it wasn't exciting to have his hands at her waist as he lifted her down, and that it wasn't unnerving to be held so close to him for however brief a time. But before she even had a chance to wonder if her act had fooled him, he pulled away. Obviously, he did not find the encounter as pleasant as she did.

He didn't either. He found it sheer torture. He had been dreading it every single second since they had left the ranch, wondering how he would carry it off without giving himself away. Thank God, he had managed to, even though every nerve in his body was tingling as if he were about to be struck by lightning. Backing up a step, he cleared the huskiness out of his voice and said, "I'll leave you here. I've got some business to attend to, and then I'll come back for you."

Rachel stared up at him, her brown eyes wide in disbelief. Surely he knew that she would have to tell Hank about her marriage. Cole was well aware that Hank had been her most attentive suitor for the past six months, and hadn't Hank been the first one Cole thought of when Rachel told him her plans to marry? How could he desert her knowing all that?

Pride prevented her from asking him to stay, however. "You're just going to leave me here?" she asked coldly, letting him see her displeasure.

Cole cast a quick glance at the store. Oliver was already looking out the window. He must have seen them drive up and was waiting to meet Rachel at the door. Fighting down a surge of irritation that he refused to call jealousy, he forced himself to look back at Rachel. "If it was me, I'd want to get the news alone, without the fellow who married you standing around gloating," he explained tersely. He certainly didn't want her to go in there alone. But he figured the poor fellow deserved a little privacy when he heard the news. But maybe not too much privacy. "Miles will stay with you," he decided suddenly, catching Miles's eye and acknowledging Miles's nod of agreement.

Rachel's gaze had followed Cole's, and she had seen Hank standing at the window watching them. He looked awfully small and vulnerable from here. Grudgingly, she admitted that Cole was probably right, that it would be cruel to tell Hank with Cole standing right there, although she could not quite picture Cole gloating. "All right," she reluctantly agreed, waiting until Miles had swung down from his horse before starting up the stairs.

Pausing halfway up, she turned back to find Cole still watching her, waiting until she was safely inside before going about his own business. "How long will you be?" she asked, hoping he could not guess how very much his answer mattered to her.

"Not long," he promised. That's for damn sure, he added mentally, seeing Oliver's eager smile of greeting when he opened the door to welcome her. The storekeeper had a smile that looked like he'd gotten it off an ivory trader, Cole reflected bitterly.

Hank Oliver was, Rachel noted, everything that Cole Elliot was not. That Hank was handsome, she had long ago decided. He had the kind of face that is formed only from centuries of breeding between aristocratic families who marry for financial considerations. The tradition of financial considerations had long ago been broken in Hank's case, but the bone structure remained, giving him a look of elegance quite at odds with the mundane surroundings of the Mercantile.

He wasn't tall. He was much shorter than Cole but still tall enough to look down at Rachel's five feet three inches. He stood slim and straight, giving the illusion of greater height than he possessed, and he chose his clothes to accentuate that slimness. Holding out his fine, well-tended hands to her, he smiled, showing teeth that were almost too white and too straight.

"Rachel," he said, grasping her by the elbows when she

108

failed to place her hands in his as he had expected. Drawing her inside, he looked down at her carefully, his brilliant smile fading just a bit. She didn't look particularly happy to see him, but that was understandable under the circumstances, he concluded, schooling his face to gravity. "I'm so sorry to hear about your father's accident. It must have been awful for you," he said with genuine concern.

Rachel had been too busy wondering how she was going to break the news of her marriage to really listen very carefully to what he was saying, but his tone made an impression and then the word "accident" cut through her thoughts like a knife. "Accident? Is that people are saying?" she demanded, sudden fury making her forget everything else.

Hank gave her a puzzled look. Anger was the last emotion he had expected from her in her grief. "Yes, of course. We heard that your father fell from his horse and struck his head . . ."

"My father never fell off a horse in his life," she informed him, brown eyes blazing, "and even if he had, he wouldn't have landed on the top of his head or tied his hands together before he did it."

Hank's pale blue eyes softened in understanding. The poor thing, she was so upset that she wasn't even being rational. "Where on earth did you get such wild ideas, Rachel dear? You make it sound like someone murdered your father." His hands moved comfortingly on her arms, and he gave her a small, reassuring smile.

Suddenly aware of his hands on her and of the impropriety of it, Rachel shrugged away from him. "Someone did murder my father, Hank Oliver, and it's not just a 'wild idea.'"

Hank refused to be offended and his smile never wavered. "Rachel dear," he began, but Miles cut him off.

"Anything wrong, Mrs. Elliot?" he asked. He had slipped in the door just behind her, and had stood by unnoticed until

109

now. He was just about fed up with Oliver's sympathy, and he figured Miss Rachel was, too.

Rachel glanced up in surprise, having forgotten that Miles was there. She had responded instinctively to her new name and felt a flush of pleasure at hearing it spoken, even if it was only Miles speaking it. He really was the strangest man. He always looked so grave and so, well, so almost haunted, and she had heard so many hints about his coldbloodedness that she was a little startled now to see the warmth in his usually expressionless brown eyes. Cole had sent him along to take care of her, and he was doing just that. She flashed him a grateful smile. "No, thank you, Miles," she assured him before turning back to Hank.

Oliver was glaring at the cowboy, irritated at the interruption and especially at the intimation that he had been causing her trouble. He had just turned back to her when something else Miles had said hit him. "What did he call you?" Hank demanded, certain that he must have misunderstood.

Rachel felt the heat crawling up her face. Thanks a lot, Miles, she thought to herself, feeling all her former gratitude evaporate. She had hoped to do this gently, but now that was impossible. "He called me 'Mrs. Elliot,'" she said as calmly as she could.

This information was impossible for Hank to assimilate quickly, and he could only stare at her in confusion for a moment. "Why did he call you that?" he asked.

Rachel took a fortifying breath. "Because Cole Elliot and I were married yesterday in Stillwater." There, that was it, the whole story in one brief sentence. She waited, watching the emotions play across his face.

Simply hearing the words did not immediately make the truth plain to Hank, and he continued to stare at her, first in puzzlement and then in incredulity and then in growing fury. "You . . . you married that . . . that *killer?*" His handsome face twisted in disgust.

Rachel felt her own fury rising. "Cole is not a killer," she said, instinctively defending her husband without bothering to ask herself why she felt such loyalty. "The men who murdered my father are killers."

Hank wasn't really listening, though. He was too busy thinking of all the implications of her act, and his disgust was rapidly turning to horror. "You gave yourself to . . . to him?" he asked. Images of his beautiful, delicate Rachel submitting to Cole Elliot danced obscenely across his mind, and he barely suppressed a shudder. Looking at her now, he marveled that she still looked so pure, so untouched, after that man had . . .

Rachel did not like being reminded of her as-yet unfulfilled marital obligations, but with a great effort, she took control of her temper and tried to consider how Hank must be feeling. "I'm sorry if I hurt you, Hank, but in all fairness, you didn't have any claims on me. We weren't engaged or anything like that," she pointed out, hoping to make him feel some responsibility for this whole thing. If he had wanted her so badly himself, he should have said so, long ago.

Hank's gentle blue eyes fogged with pain. He was hurting, and for more reasons than just his broken heart. In losing Rachel he had lost more than just a lovely girl. He had lost everything he had been working toward ever since he had first met her. "You knew how I felt," he defended himself. "I've been calling on you almost since the day I first met you. That should have made my intentions clear."

Rachel sniffed disdainfully, recalling only too clearly the countless times Hank had come to call, and had sat in her parlor making small talk without even so much as trying to hold her hand. Still, in spite of his reticence, she knew that he genuinely cared about her, perhaps even loved her, in his own way. Unfortunately, she would never love him back, no matter if he courted her every day for the rest of their natural lives. "A lady never takes anything like that for granted, Hank," she informed him.

Hank's impulse was to argue, and he had to remind himself that it was already too late for that. She was married now, married to that . . . that gunfighter, and there was nothing he could do about it. He couldn't help wanting to defend himself, though. "If I'd known about the competition, I would have . . ." he began bitterly, but Rachel had had enough of his whining.

"Please, Hank, what's done is done. I don't want to talk about it anymore."

"But Rachel . . ."

"Don't you have a list of things you want to get, Mrs. Elliot?" Miles asked blandly from his post by the door.

Rachel glanced up in mild surprise, suddenly remembering his presence again and grateful for it once more. "Yes, yes, I do," she recalled, and began to dig in her reticule for it.

Hank glared at him, but Miles never even blinked. The cowboy must have heard everything they had said, and Hank did not like the idea one bit, but he had completely forgotten about him in the shock of hearing Rachel's news. The fellow was obviously guarding Rachel, too, probably on Elliot's orders, and that knowledge did not sit well at all with Hank.

"Here it is," Rachel said, producing the crumpled piece of paper. "Would you fill this order for me, please, and charge it to the ranch account? Our wagon is outside."

Hank automatically took the offered list, but his gaze had drifted back to her face. How could she be so cold and businesslike? he wondered sadly. They had been so close for so long. Didn't she even regret her decision a little bit?

"I'll just look around the store while you're getting my order ready," she added when he made no move to do so.

Hank nodded and reluctantly turned away, casting one

last glare in Miles's direction before stalking off toward the storeroom.

After leaving the buggy and their horses at the livery, Cole and the Kid and the other men made their way to the Silver Dollar Saloon. It was a little early in the day for drinking, but Cole figured there'd be somebody hanging around who could pass the word along to Statler's crew as soon as he made his big announcement.

The front doors of the saloon were closed against the cold, and the Kid made a small show of opening them for Cole to pass on through. Feeling slightly conspicuous, Cole stepped inside and glanced around quickly.

It was even better than he'd hoped. Two men who worked for Statler were sitting at a far table, nursing a couple of beers. Statler would have the word before the day was out.

"Hey, Sam, you got any champagne? We're here to celebrate!" the Kid called out to the bartender. Any qualms Cole might have had about announcing his own marriage had been wasted. He should have known the Kid would do it for him and do a much better job of it than anyone else could.

"Where do you think you are, Paris, France?" the bartender inquired with a good-natured growl. "What in the hell's so important that you got to have champagne for, anyways?"

As Cole and his men strolled over to the bar, Sam called out toward the back room, "Hey Lettie, come see who's here!"

Lettie. Cole winced at the sound of her name. How could he have forgotten her? Forgotten her so completely that until this very moment, he had not even considered how the news of his marriage would affect her. All the time he had been so concerned about Hank Oliver, he hadn't once thought of Lettie.

A woman appeared in the doorway of the tiny, back-room office, an inquisitive look on her face. That look instantly became a smile when she saw Cole standing at the bar, and she moved toward him immediately. She wasn't exactly a pretty woman, but she was attractive enough to liven up the Silver Dollar Saloon, which was her job. Although her hair had once been blond, it had now faded to a mousy brown, but she kept it styled and curled around her face and some thought it her best feature. She was wearing a flashy dress that barely concealed her plump curves and revealed a goodly length of well-turned ankle. Long pale eyelashes flirted around her large hazel eyes as she moved sinuously across the room and took Cole's arm in a possessive grasp.

Before Cole could even think to pull away, the Kid stepped in. "Oh no you don't, Lettie," he cautioned, pulling her clasping hands from Cole's arm. "You can't mess with Cole now."

Lettie laughed good-naturedly. She was used to the Kid's teasing. "Why is that?" she asked, playing along. "And what's this about champagne and celebrating?"

The Kid's smile never wavered, but he glanced at Cole, knowing this was his secret to tell. The boy's bright blue eyes asked a question, but Cole couldn't let him do this job.

Hating the flush he knew was crawling up his neck, Cole said, "I got married yesterday."

Lettie's smile wobbled and then died. "Married?" she echoed, unbelieving. She knew Cole Elliot very well, better than almost anyone, and married was the last thing she had ever expected him to be. She tried a nervous little laugh. "This is a joke, right?" she asked hopefully.

The bartender forced a laugh, too. "It must be. Who'd have an ugly plug like Cole?" he inquired.

The Kid was still grinning, but no one else was, and Lettie's small hope died.

"It's no joke," Cole confirmed, his eyes saying how sorry

114

he was to be telling her like this.

No one spoke for a long minute until the silence grew oppressive. All the men felt Lettie's humiliation. Until now she had been Cole's girl, or as much his girl as a woman who worked in a saloon could be. Not that she was a whore. No, Lettie did not sell her favors. She did not need to. She made a good living by shilling drinks and earning tips by laughing it up with the cowboy customers and singing occasionally when there was a good crowd. Her favors were reserved for the men whom she personally chose, and lately that man had been Cole Elliot.

That choice had made Cole the object of many men's envy, but even they could not know how serious the relationship had become to Lettie. While Cole was good to her, he held much more important attraction for her in that she sensed his need to settle down, to put an end to the wild, reckless life he had been living. Lettie had the same need, and she had seen Cole as her ticket out of the Silver Dollar Saloon. Now those hopes had been dashed. What she could not figure out for the life of her, however, was whom he could have married.

Sam saved her the trouble of inquiring. "Who'd you marry, Cole?" the bartender asked, breaking the tense silence.

Cole hesitated. An unwritten rule said that you did not mention a lady's name in a place where men were drinking, and he certainly didn't want to call out Rachel's name in a saloon.

The Kid saved him. "He married his boss," he reported with that same triumphant smile he continued to wear.

Sam couldn't have been more shocked if he had said, "The Queen of England." "Miss McKinsey?" he gasped incredulously.

"The very same," the Kid cheerfully confirmed. Putting his arm around an equally stunned Lettie, he added, "Now how about that champagne? You'll join us in a toast, won't you, Lettie?"

Lettie was just about to refuse, but the Kid's arm tightened around her, and he gave her a warning glance which she read easily. He was telling her to be a good sport and not to let anyone know how much this news hurt her. People would feel sorry enough for her as it was, and if she wanted to salvage any pride at all, she'd have to pretend it didn't matter.

"Sure, I'll join you," she agreed with a forced smile, "but from the look on Sam's face, I think we'll have to settle for whiskey."

"Whiskey all around, then," the Kid ordered. The other men concurred, joining in the artificial merriment now that the awkward moment had passed.

Cole, however, simply nodded, his clear blue eyes still watching Lettie closely. She wasn't looking at him now, wouldn't meet his eyes no matter how hard he tried to get her attention. She was flirting with the Kid just as if she didn't care a fig for Cole, and maybe, he thought with a slight shock, maybe she didn't. It was something to consider, and he'd certainly consider it, but not right now. Right now he was too concerned with the fact that Statler's men had just left the bar and were moving very quickly to where their horses had been tied. That much, at least, had been taken care of. Now all he had to worry about was Rachel back at the store with Oliver.

They toasted to Cole's long and happy marriage, and then Cole bought a round of beer chasers. By then everyone had loosened up and was pretending that Lettie had every reason to be just as happy as everyone else was about the wedding.

The Kid was hanging on to her pretty close, which was to be expected, now that Cole thought of it. The boy had always liked Lettie more than a little, and the only reason he hadn't done something about it before now was because Cole had been there first.

Cole watched the way Lettie leaned against the Kid,

letting her full, round bosom brush against his arm in that provocative way she had. Then she looked up and laughed at something the Kid said, and Cole had to turn his face away. He knew her well enough to know that she was pretending, but she was doing a good job of it, and he doubted that anyone else could tell. He felt bad watching her, and so he pretended to himself that that was the reason he wanted to hurry back to the store. The truth was that as badly as he felt watching Lettie and the Kid, he felt positively murderous when he thought about Rachel and Oliver alone together over at the Mercantile.

Chapter IV

When Cole walked into the store, he found Miles still at his post by the door. His friend gave him a nod of greeting, but Miles's expression betrayed nothing of what had taken place earlier. Cole's anxious glance scanned the store, but he saw no one. When he turned back to Miles, more than a little worried, Miles pointed toward the back of the store. "She's down there," he remarked.

Cole found her at the end of a long aisle. Alone, thank God. And looking as calm and serene as if nothing in the world had happened. He fought down an urge to kiss that placid look off her face as he closed the distance between them.

Rachel was holding up a man's jacket, wondering if it would fit Cole when he suddenly stomped into view. The sight of his rugged features brought an involuntary smile to her lips, but it froze there when she saw his set expression. "Did you finish your business?" she inquired, wondering what had happened to displease him.

"Yeah," he said absently, dismissing his business with a small wave of his hand. "What happened with Oliver?" That was all he really wanted to know.

Rachel's smile widened. Was he a little jealous? He was certainly acting like it, and wouldn't that be nice? She shrugged noncommittally. "I told him," she said offhandedly. Then she held up the jacket. "Do you think this will fit you?"

Cole cast an irritated glance at the jacket and then looked back at Rachel's complacent smile. "What did he say?" he asked, knowing that by doing so he was revealing how much it mattered to him but unable to stop himself.

Rachel pretended to consider. "Well, he didn't like it much," she allowed, and then held the jacket to measure it against his shoulders. "It looks like it will fit."

She was playing with him and the knowledge infuriated him. Angrily snatching the jacket from her grasp, he held it away from her and asked as calmly as he could through gritted teeth, "What, exactly, did he say?"

Expelling a long-suffering sigh, Rachel gave him a disapproving look. "He said something to the effect of, 'Oh, Rachel, I thought we had an understanding,' and 'How could you?' That sort of thing," she told him, mimicking Oliver's injured tone of voice almost perfectly.

"Did you?" Cole demanded, his anger stirred afresh by this new bit of information.

"Did I what?" she asked, puzzled.

"Did you have an understanding?"

Rachel almost laughed with delight. He was furious! He really must be jealous, a little bit, anyway, but she knew instinctively she had pushed him as far as she dared. "Of course not," she assured him with just the right amount of outrage in her voice. "If we'd had an understanding, do you think I would have married you?"

Cole thought it over while managing to get control of his temper. "No, I guess not," he admitted at last. She wasn't that kind of woman, or at least he didn't think she was. Now that he thought about it, though, he really had no way of knowing for sure.

"Do you like that jacket?" she asked in an attempt to divert his attention and lighten his mood. She kept a straight face but her eyes were dancing impishly.

Cole looked at the jacket in his hand as if he had never seen it before, having completely forgotten about it. Did he like it? How ridiculous. It was identical to the one he was wearing except that it was new and clean. "Yeah, it's all right," he said absently.

"Good, then I'll buy it for you," she said, trying a flirtatious smile on him.

It bounced right off. His expression had suddenly turned to stone. "You'll buy it for me?" he echoed, obviously displeased. His blue eyes narrowed down to suspicious slits. "I've already got a coat."

"Yes, but . . ." Rachel began but caught herself. She had intended to point out that the one he was wearing was rather disreputable-looking, but something in his eyes warned her not to. For some reason he did not like the idea of her buying him a new coat.

Cole glowered at her. He should have known. They hadn't even been married twenty-four hours yet, and here she was, letting him know that he wasn't quite good enough, that he was a "hired husband," the same way he'd always been a "hired gun." "I'll buy it for you," she had said, reminding him that he now lived off her largess. "I don't need it," he said tightly.

From the way his eyes glittered, Rachel knew the subject was closed. "Fine," she agreed a little apprehensively, wondering what on earth had so offended him. She had only wanted to do something nice for him. Obviously, he was a man you couldn't be nice to.

"Rachel, your order is ready," Hank called from the front of the store.

Cole stiffened at the sound of that voice, his anger at Rachel forgotten momentarily as his protective instincts took over. "Let's go," he said to her, laying the jacket back on the shelf and stepping aside to allow her to precede him.

Rachel was feeling pretty stiff herself as she marched up

the aisle toward where Hank stood, and Hank was looking pretty much like a ramrod by the time he had noticed Cole's presence in the store.

"Oliver," Cole muttered by way of greeting, the expression on his face betraying no emotion whatsoever.

"Elliot," Hank replied, his distaste evident in his tone. He'd be damned before he'd congratulate the man, and so he simply stood waiting.

Cole reached inside his coat and drew a crumpled piece of paper from his vest pocket. "Here's some things I'll be needing," he told the storekeeper.

Hank took the paper grudgingly and scanned it with a practiced eye. "That's an awful lot of ammunition," he commented caustically. "Are you planning to start a war?"

Cole grinned a mirthless grin. So the fellow was itching for a fight, was he? "No, I'm planning to finish one."

Hank's pale face turned scarlet. "Have you thought about what will happen to Rachel while you're out shooting up the countryside?"

Cole's grin never wavered. "I've thought about what'll happen to her if she doesn't have a man to protect her."

The implication was clear that Cole felt Hank was not man enough for the job, and the storekeeper's well-formed lips thinned in fury as his body tensed for attack. For one awful moment, Rachel thought he might actually come over the counter after Cole, but he thought better of it in time to stop himself. Instead he just stood there, quivering with rage, Cole's list crackling as Hank's fist closed over it.

Only when she was sure Hank had control of himself did Rachel dare a glance at Cole. He was still smiling, or at least his lips were pulled back from his teeth in a sort of wolfish grin, but his hands had clenched into fists. He was waiting, every muscle poised, for the attack that would not come.

"Cole?" she said, hoping to avert any further unpleasantness. She placed one hand tentatively on his arm, and even through his heavy coat, she could feel his tension. "We can come back later for our stuff," she suggested.

For the space of several heartbeats, she thought that maybe he hadn't heard her, but then she felt him relax beneath her touch. "Yeah," he agreed at last. "We'll be back later."

"Yes, later," Hank repeated, as if the phrase had been a challenge that he accepted.

Rachel could only stare in amazement. They reminded her of two stallions circling each other, getting ready to fight it out over a mare. As the mare in question, she wasn't sure if she were pleased or angry or simply frightened. When Cole made no move to leave, she gave a little tug at his sleeve. "Cole?" she asked again, and this time he glanced down at her.

He read the uncertainty in her eyes and understood her natural distaste for such a display of male aggression. He wouldn't expect a lady like Rachel to like the idea of two men fighting over her. He didn't regret putting Oliver in his place, though. He only wished he'd had to use a little physical force to do it. The damn little pansy had given in much too easily for Cole's taste. "Let's go," he said a little gruffly.

Rachel only too willingly headed for the door once she was satisfied that Cole was right behind her. Miles slanted her a grin as he held the door open for her, but she shot him a black look that wiped it clean off his face. Honestly, she thought as she paused outside on the wooden sidewalk to rebutton her coat, men were impossible. Or at least Cole Elliot was. One minute he was acting like a jealous lover, and the next he was furious because she wanted to give him a gift. Then he'd almost come to blows over her with a rival when he wasn't even interested enough in her to take her to bed.

Grateful for the chilling wind that would provide excuse for her reddened cheeks, Rachel started down the sidewalk at a brisk pace, her heels clicking a staccato beat on the wood beneath her feet. She wasn't even going to try to understand him. Nothing he did made any sense at all. Besides, she didn't care what he did or why he did it. If he didn't love her, she wouldn't love him either. She wouldn't try to figure him out, she wouldn't try to please him, and she wouldn't let his indifference bother her in the least. In fact, she was quite relieved that he didn't want to share her bed.

"Rachel, where are you going?" Cole demanded when he had finally caught up with her. Honestly, women were impossible. He knew she was upset because he'd almost gotten into a fight with Oliver, but what did she want him to do, pretend he didn't mind that Oliver had insulted him? And her, too, when it came right down to it.

Rachel's step faltered at his question. Come to think of it, she didn't know where she was going, only that she wanted to get away from that little scene in the Mercantile. "No place special," she replied, looking up at him. Irritation crackled in her large brown eyes, but he needn't know she was as irritated with herself as she was with him. "Was there someplace you wanted to go?"

Now she was mad. Whatever was going on inside that pretty little head was sure a mystery to him. "Well, yeah," he said, determined not to let on how much her anger disturbed him. "It's a little early yet, but I thought we might as well eat dinner and then head on back," he told her, ignoring the way those dark eyes were glaring up at him.

"That sounds fine to me," she agreed testily, continuing her march down the sidewalk.

"Uh . . . Rachel?" he called after her.

"Yes?" she asked.

"You're going the wrong way," he told her blandly.

Rachel blinked in surprise. "What?"

"You're going the wrong way. Ma's place is down there," he added, jerking his thumb over his shoulder in the opposite direction from which they were heading.

"Oh," she whispered in embarrassment, looking around to get her bearings. "Oh, yes," she decided, turning on her heel and setting out in the proper direction. Her cheeks were burning, but she would die before she'd give him the satisfaction of seeing her chagrin. Romance, indeed. All he cared about was his stomach.

Things might not have been too bad if they hadn't run into Widow Johnson and her sister, Mrs. Siddons. The two old busybodies were on their way somewhere when they had spotted Rachel and made a point of crossing the street to accost her.

"Rachel, dear, we were so sorry to hear about your father's accident," Mrs. Siddons began while Widow Johnson was muttering something about how awful of her not to have a big funeral and invite everyone.

"It was not an accident," Rachel said, not for the first time today and with renewed irritation. Perhaps she had been wrong not to invite the neighbors for a big funeral. She had been ashamed for people to see her father all broken like that, but if they had, she would not now be listening to all this talk about "accidents."

"What on earth do you mean, not an accident," Mrs. Siddons chided. "We all heard . . ."

"I don't care what you heard," Rachel interrupted, not really caring that she was being inexcusably rude to the older woman. "My father was murdered."

The two sisters exchanged knowing glances. "Of course, dear," Widow Johnson agreed insincerely. They thought she was upset amd were humoring her. "Have you made any plans yet?" the widow inquired.

"Plans?" Rachel echoed, her angry eyes darting from one woman to the other. She really didn't know what they meant by "plans."

"About what you're going to do now, dear," Mrs. Siddons explained patiently.

"Yes," Widow Johnson added, "we were just talking about it this morning, saying how we both thought you'd go back East now. You've got some family back there, don't you?"

125

Rachel glared at the two women. Of all the snoopy-nosed, gossipy . . . They didn't care about her father and they really didn't care what she was going to do. They just wanted to be the first ones to hear about it. Well, she'd give them a bee to put in their bonnets.

Smiling with saccharine sweetness, Rachel gave a false little laugh. "Well, I doubt that I'll be going back East. My husband certainly wouldn't like that one little bit, now would he?"

Cole had been hanging back from the encounter, obviously unwilling to tangle with these two old biddies, but Rachel reached out and clamped onto his arm and dragged him into the little group.

"Husband?" the two women murmured in unison, looking askance at the addition to their gathering.

"Yes, my husband. You ladies know Cole Elliot, don't you?" Rachel asked wickedly, knowing full well the good ladies would never have met such a man, although they more than likely knew plenty about him.

Well, Cole thought, they had come to town to announce their wedding, and he couldn't think of a more efficient way of spreading the news than to tell these two chatterboxes. With a grim smile, he reached up and tipped his hat. "Howdy do, ladies," he said.

"Oh my," said Widow Johnson.

"Rachel, dear," protested Mrs. Siddons.

But Rachel wasn't interested. "I know you'll excuse us now. We were just on our way to dinner. Good day, ladies." Without waiting for their reply, Rachel brushed by them, dragging Cole in her wake.

She was muttering something that sounded like "damn busybodies," but Cole was pretty sure he must have misunderstood. Rachel would never talk like that, although the condemnation certainly fit. He allowed himself one last glance over his shoulder to savor the ladies' popeyed expressions before letting Rachel drag him on down the street.

Rachel was more than a little annoyed. How dare those women presume to judge her on her choice of a husband? Hank Oliver's opinion had infuriated her, but at the time she had not realized that most of the respectable people in town would share it. They were bound to be surprised at her choice, of course. As far as anyone knew, Cole had never courted her at all. Fortunately, only Rachel knew how very true that was and how much she had compromised her pride by proposing marriage to him in the first place.

She supposed, now that she considered the matter, that people would assume Cole had taken advantage of her situation. Those two old biddies had looked at her with pity, as if she had been victimized by someone clever and ruthless. Rachel couldn't help wondering how they would react to the news that Cole Elliot was the one who had been victimized. By the time she reached the restaurant, she was almost smiling at the thought.

The restaurant was a small building adorned with a sign that said simply, EATS. Canaan's answer to the Stillwater Hotel's restaurant was run by a buxom widow whom everyone called "Ma," and whose real name had been lost to memory. What the place lacked in style, it made up for in good cooking.

The place was empty now, since, as Cole had said, it was a little early yet, but Ma bustled out of the kitchen to greet them. She promised their food would be ready in two shakes and promptly disappeared again.

They took a seat at an empty table away from the door, Cole being careful to take the chair against the wall from which he commanded a view of the entire room. Rachel noticed, but she pretended that it didn't disturb her.

Her anger at the two women had faded now, and even though she remembered that she still had a few things to be angry at Cole Elliot for, she hated the idea that he didn't dare sit with his back to the door. "Did you see anyone at the saloon?" she asked, suddenly recalling that he might be aware of some very real danger.

Cole was surprised. Now how in the blue blazes had she known that's where he had been? Recovering quickly, he shrugged one shoulder nonchalantly and replied, "Two of Statler's men were there. They sneaked out as soon as they heard the news."

Rachel nodded with slight enthusiasm. "That's good," she supposed, wondering if it really were. She had known immediately that Cole had been at the saloon because she had smelled it on his breath. That was also the logical place for him to go to spread the word, although she couldn't help feeling a little strange at being talked about in a saloon. Not that it would do her any good to complain about it, though, she guessed.

They sat there in silence for quite a while until Ma brought out their meal. As usual, Cole didn't talk while he ate, and Rachel couldn't think of anything to say either. She was just starting to wonder what they would do when they had finished eating when the front door flew open with a bang that brought her head up.

People had started coming in just after they had arrived. The place was about half full with townsfolk, and Miles and the other men had come in a few moments before. The man who came in now was no casual diner, however. After taking a quick look around the room, he strode purposefully toward Cole and Rachel's table.

The noise of Cole's chair scraping across the floor as he rose was loud in the suddenly silent room. No one had missed the angry set of Will Statler's face. Statler paused a few feet from where Rachel sat and looked down at her with sneering contempt.

"It won't do you no good, missy," he told her.

She didn't need to ask what he meant. Staring up into his slate-gray eyes, she communicated easily with him. He was telling her that her marriage made no difference to his plans. Glaring down at her, he would see that she disagreed completely.

For a moment, Rachel concentrated on not letting the fear she felt show. She was not afraid for herself, of course, although maybe there was a little of that mixed in. She was afraid for Cole. Statler was furious and there was no telling what he might do.

"You got something to say, you say it to me."

It was Cole's voice, but it was a tone she had never heard, never dreamed of hearing from him. When her startled eyes found him, looming over the table with a kind of subdued menace, she could only stare in wonder at the change in him. Gone was the silent man who had married her in Stillwater. Gone was the indifferent man who had left her last night. Gone even was the territorial stallion who had tried to goad Hank Oliver into a fight. In his place was someone else entirely.

The long, lean body stood poised and ready, arms loosely hanging so that the fingers of one hand almost brushed the polished wood grip of his Colt. His eyes, those blue eyes she had so often admired, were narrowed down to dangerous slits, the color that glinted out reminding her now not so much of blue skies but of icicles glittering in the winter sun.

Statler's sneer curled into a parody of a smile. "I got nothing to say to you, Elliot," he assured Cole. "I ain't no gunfighter, and I sure don't like the odds," he added with a meaningful look at the Circle M men seated at a nearby table. "I ain't in no hurry to meet my maker, not yet. I got things I want to do first." He glanced at Rachel a moment, and then back to Cole. "I don't plan on giving you an excuse to gun me down, and if your fingers start to get itchy, just remember your little lady is right here in the line of fire."

That, Rachel saw, was the perfect argument. Cole's lips whitened with the strain of holding his temper in check, but she knew however he might feel about her on a personal level, he would never draw his gun with her sitting there. Statler knew it, too, and his stocky body straightened with the knowledge.

"I got other ways to deal with you, Elliot," the rancher bragged, and then shifted his gaze to Rachel. "Your little trick won't even slow me down, missy. You'll see."

At Cole's outraged growl, Statler smiled, displaying a brace of yellowed teeth. "Congratulations to you both," he said cheerfully. "You'll understand if I don't wish you a long and happy life, too."

With that, he turned abruptly and strolled to the door, nodding pleasantly to the rest of the still-silent customers who had heard every word.

As Rachel watched his retreating back, she tried to decide what it was about him that made her skin crawl, that had made her dislike him from the very beginning, back when she had only suspected his part in the missing Circle M cattle. He wasn't really that bad looking. Neither tall nor short, he was a powerfully built man who might run to fat if he led a more sedentary life. His face was plain, but not ugly enough to inspire the revulsion she had always felt. Maybe it was his hair, which was dark, almost black, and always seemed a little greasy. No, she mentally corrected, if wasn't only his hair that was greasy. It was his whole personality.

And those eyes, those cold, gray eyes. Shuddering slightly, she turned back to where Cole still stood, watching Statler the way he might have watched a retreating rattler which could yet turn and strike without warning. Only when the man was gone, the door slammed behind him and the echo of his bootheels on the wooden sidewalk no longer audible, did Cole relax his vigil. After another moment, he stiffly sat back down.

"Are you all right?" he inquired, the concern on his face a little startling to Rachel. Once again he had changed into a completely different person. This time he was the kind friend who had comforted her after her father's death. She really was having a hard time dealing with his lightning changes of mood.

"Yes, I'm fine," she assured him faintly. Now he was acting

130

as if he really cared about her well-being. She stared at him a long moment trying to read the expression in the depths of those blue eyes. It almost looked like . . . But it couldn't be, she reminded herself sternly. He didn't care for her. If he did, he wouldn't have left her alone last night. If he was willing to fight Statler, he was doing it for the ranch and not for her.

For one awful moment, Rachel was afraid she might do something totally foolish, like burst into tears. She was so lonely. She missed her father so much, needed him so much, and the man she had chosen to take his place was an unfeeling . . . But she wouldn't cry. She wouldn't give him the satisfaction. She would never let him know how vulnerable she was.

Setting her jaw, she glared at him across the table. "Let's get out of this town," she snapped, rising abruptly from her chair.

Cole had to stay a minute to pay the bill, so he could only watch her stalk out the door. Now what was eating her? He could have understood it if she had burst into tears. He wouldn't have liked it, but at least it would have made sense. She had every right to be mad, of course, but why was she taking it out on him? Swearing under his breath, he left some coins on the table and hurried to catch up with her.

Miles paused in the doorway and gave a silent sigh. From where he stood, he could see Mr. and Mrs. Elliot eating their breakfast in the ranch house dining room. Or rather, he could see Cole sipping his coffee and Miss Rachel pushing her food around her plate. They weren't even looking at each other. He sighed again.

Five days had passed since their wedding, and at least things outside the house had been going well. It had taken a little time, but the men were coming around. At first they had been wary of Cole, but when they saw that his new station in life had not changed him or his way of dealing with

131

them, they had relaxed. They were much more likely to call him "Boss" than "Cole," now, but other than that, things were pretty much back to normal.

If they had known what was going on inside the house, though, they might not have been so content. Miles had puzzled over it more than once, and for the life of him, he couldn't figure out what was wrong.

As he entered the room, Miles had the funniest feeling that he would have to be very careful about what he said and did around this pair. It was almost as if the very air around them were charged. He had the strangest notion that if he so much as lit a match, the whole place would go up in a puff of smoke.

"Good morning," he said with forced cheerfulness, the tension in the room making it almost hard to breathe.

Rachel glanced up with what could only have been described as irritation, and Cole grunted some sort of greeting. Apparently, it wasn't a good morning as far as they were concerned.

Miles waited until Cole had drained his cup. "Hardy and Stevens are at it again," Miles announced blandly.

Cole scowled up at him. The two men had been quarreling since the day they had met in the Circle M bunkhouse, and although they had never actually come to blows, the possibility was always there. "Did you straighten them out?" he asked.

Miles lifted his eyebrows in mild surprise. "You're still top screw around here, aren't you?" he asked. "Besides, you're about the only one who can break them up without getting himself killed."

That was true enough, and with a smothered oath, Cole got up from the table and headed out the door. Without so much as a by-your-leave to his wife, either, Miles noticed. Weren't they even speaking? Good God, what could have happened?

Fighting back an overwhelming urge to inquire into what

was clearly none of his business, Miles made a move to follow Cole. Rachel's voice stopped him.

"I never got a chance to thank you for helping me deal with Mr. Oliver the other day, Miles," she said, laying down her fork and rising gracefully to her feet. She wasn't exactly smiling, but she was looking far more pleasant than she had when Cole had been in the room.

"There's nothing to thank me for, ma'am," he assured her. "I was just doing what Cole would have if he'd been there," he added, hoping to put in a good word for his friend.

Rachel's instant frown told him that he had wasted his time. She was certainly mad at Cole about something. Suddenly, Miles recalled what Cole had discussed with him yesterday. It was a hairbrained scheme if he'd ever heard one. Could Cole have told her about it? No wonder she was mad. Maybe he could smooth things over a little, though.

"It's just like that idea he had about selling off all the cattle," he began, plunging in with both feet. "He's only looking out for your best interests."

"Selling off all the cattle?" Rachel echoed incredulously. This was the first she'd heard about any such plan. "What's this about selling off all the cattle?" she demanded, coming around the table toward him.

Miles could have groaned. He'd guessed wrong, and from the look in her eye, he'd gotten Cole into even more trouble. "It's nothing, Mrs. Elliot," he tried, but she was having none of it.

"Tell me," she ordered, advancing on him menacingly, her dark eyes blazing.

He wasn't worried about himself. He knew she wasn't mad at him, but he still cringed a little under her fury. "Cole was thinking that if we round up all the cattle and drive it north and sell it, there won't be anything left for Statler to steal."

"All the cattle? We must have ten thousand head out there," she pointed out in utter amazement. "You couldn't drive them all at once." She planted her hands on her hips in

133

silent challenge.

"We'd have to divide it up into three, maybe four herds," he explained weakly, knowing only too well how ridiculous it sounded. The logistics of such an undertaking were horrendous.

Rachel was too mad to speak for a minute, which gave Miles just the opportunity he needed to escape. "Well, I'll see you later, Mrs. Elliot," he said, backing out the door.

Rachel couldn't have cared less that he was leaving. Making an exasperated noise, she stormed out of the room by the opposite door and stomped into the kitchen.

"Do you know what he's doing now?" she demanded of a very startled Lupe.

The old woman went back to kneading her bread dough. "Not what he should be," she guessed with a lascivious cackle.

Rachel ignored the cackle. "He's going to sell off all my cattle. *My* cattle! Without asking me! Without even consulting me!"

Lupe continued to knead her bread as Rachel swished around the kitchen, waving her hands in agitation as she raved about Cole's treachery. When she had finally run down and plopped into a chair, Lupe looked up again, eyeing her carefully.

"How long you let him sleep alone?" Lupe inquired.

Rachel's outraged gasp was ignored. "Until hell freezes over," she finally vowed, when Lupe's silence insisted on a reply.

Lupe shook her head, making a disapproving sound. "You get no babies, you sleep alone."

"Babies!" Babies were the least of Rachel's worries at the moment, and since it was obvious she was not going to get any sympathy from her foster mother, she stalked back out of the kitchen in much the same way as she had stormed into it.

That day was one of the longest that Rachel had ever lived

through. The thaw had caused a lot of problems for the cattle, and the men were quite busy pulling cows out of bog holes. They did not return to the ranch for their noon meal that day, and it was late when they finally came back for supper.

Cole was tired and hungry and as grouchy as a bear with a sore paw when he sat down to eat that evening. One look at Rachel told him that no matter how good she might look, she was still just about as disagreeable as she'd been ever since they'd come back from town the other day. He'd thought that after they'd been married for a few days, they'd start to get along easier, get to know each other better. When that happened, it would be natural to suggest that he move into her bedroom.

It hadn't worked out that way, though. Instead of things getting better, they had somehow gotten worse, and Cole didn't have any earthly idea why or how. For some reason Rachel always acted as if she had some kind of a burr under her saddle, sort of prickly-like. Cole had a feeling that approaching her would be like trying to snuggle up to a cactus.

Not that he would have minded a few needles. The truth was, he would have wrestled a grizzly bear single-handed for the chance to snuggle up to Rachel. Every time he saw her, she got prettier, almost like she was doing it for spite. Even with her clothes so neat and her hair so perfect, she was the most delicious little piece he had ever seen. He couldn't help wanting to mess her up a little just to see what she'd do. And after he'd messed her up, he'd start in to tasting her to see if she was as delicious as she looked.

Evenings were the worst times, he decided, glancing up at her from across the dining-room table. At least in the morning he could leave, but once he came back to the house, he was stuck with her all evening. They didn't really have anything to talk about, and with one forbidden exception, nothing to do, either. Tonight promised to be pure hell, too, because underneath that plain white shirt, she wasn't wearing a corset. He would have all he could do to keep from staring at the way her body moved under her clothes, and he couldn't keep from imagining how those soft, round curves would feel pressed up against him.

Unfortunately, he was also very aware of the fact that she shared none of his feelings. She had made it abundantly clear that she'd already let him come just about as close as she ever wanted him to be. When he was lying alone in his bed at night, sweating from the strain of staying where he was, he could almost forget why he had decided to give her time to adjust to him. He couldn't forget now, though, sitting across from her and seeing that cool, haughty expression which he knew would change in a second to mortal fear if he so much as touched her.

Cole sighed inwardly. How had he ever gotten himself into such a mess?

Rachel gave him every chance to tell her about the cattle. She waited patiently through supper, chafing over the fact that he barely glanced at her but trying not to let it bother her. She also tried not to let his physical presence affect her as it usually did, but she found it impossible to ignore his scent, which seemed to permeate the room. Even though he'd washed up and changed clothes when he'd come in from the range, he still smelled of outdoors and tobacco and leather and something else that was him alone. She found it very difficult to maintain her fury over his treachery when her breath was growing shallow and her heart was doing strange things inside her chest. This time she could not even blame her corset because she wasn't wearing one.

After supper, they moved into the parlor and sat down in front of the fire, he in an easy chair and she on the settee. She waited while he smoked two cigarettes, but when he got up to leave, she stopped him. For the last several evenings, he had locked himself in the office with the ranch ledgers, and she didn't intend to let him get away from her tonight.

"Isn't there something you want to tell me?" she asked, unable to keep the sharp edge completely from her voice.

More than a little surprised, Cole thought this over, sitting back down in his chair by the fire. Now what was all this about? Had she figured out a new way to drive him crazy? It wasn't bad enough that the whole place smelled like roses and that she looked good enough to eat. Oh, no. Now she was going to torture him mentally as well as physically. What on earth could she want him to tell her? He'd already casually mentioned the few, uninteresting things he had done that day, and nothing else came immediately to mind. "I don't think so," he said cautiously.

Rachel stretched her eyes wide in mock amazement. "Then you aren't even going to tell me before you sell off all my cattle?" she inquired acidly.

Cole frowned. Now where in the hell had she heard a thing like that? He'd thought about it, sure. He'd even mentioned it to Miles . . . Miles! Damn him, he must have been the one who'd told her. Cole's frown became a scowl. Why on earth would he have told her that? It was such a rotten idea. It had sounded pretty good inside his head, but as soon as he'd told Miles, he'd known the whole thing was impossible. He'd known even before he'd seen the look on Miles's face.

"Don't worry about it. It's not your look-out," he said, hoping to soothe her. No wonder she was so upset.

"It most certainly is my 'look-out,'" she informed him, springing to her feet and planting her hands firmly on her hips. "Or have you forgotten that this is *my* ranch?"

For a minute the only thing Cole could remember for sure was how much he liked the way Rachel's breasts jutted out when she stood like that. Then the true meaning of her words hit him, and he, too, came surging to his feet. "You aren't likely to let me forget it, are you?" he accused.

Rachel flew at him then, knowing even as she did so that her reaction was way out of proportion but yet unable to stop herself. In a wild flurry, she swung at him and missed or he ducked and caught her hands or she clawed at him and he warded her off or she stumbled and he caught her or she knocked him off balance and fell with him. However it happened, in the next instant they were both on the floor in a tangle of arms and legs, first struggling and then clinging.

This was it, she knew. This was what she had been craving for days, this overpowering, overwhelming physical contact. She had literally thrown herself at him to achieve it without even understanding why until now, this very instant. His lips found hers with a devouring hunger that was nothing like the gentleness of his first kiss, and she answered him with equal greed. Her mouth opened under his demand, surrendering her honeyed depths to his ravishment.

At first the sensation was strange, foreign, and she resisted the invasion, using her own tongue to force his out. The moist duel had barely begun before she yielded, marveling at the unique sensations, savoring the mixed flavor of tobacco and his essence. She sighed with pleasure when he, sensing her acquiescence, tightened his embrace, crushing her against his solid strength.

Her own hands moved, having somehow snaked around him, and roved over his back and shoulders, exploring him, learning him. She reveled in her discoveries, how the muscles corded his body, how they tensed and rippled beneath the soft material of his shirt.

Meanwhile his own hands were busy, sliding over her curves, molding her to him in a grip that was at once both fierce and tender. The first time his fingers brushed her breast, she gasped and he withdrew, but a few moments later, when it happened again, she thrust herself willingly into his palm, her heightening senses screaming for the contact. How such gentle, tentative kneading could produce such searing pleasure, she had no idea, but she shifted restlessly, freeing his other hand so that he could capture both globes in his tantalizing embrace.

And the kisses just went on and on. Even when they broke

138

to breathe, the air rasping in their throats, their lips still clung moistly, both of them unwilling to break the sweet contact.

Rachel earned his moan of pleasure when her roaming hand found the spot where his shirttail had come loose and her fingers stroked bare flesh. Emboldened, she delved in with her other hand, too, discovering the odd combination of silk and steel that made a man. At first she was so busy that she did not notice what he was doing, but when his mouth left hers to trail down her throat, she suddenly realized that his hands had worked loose the buttons of her shirtwaist.

A small protest died on her lips as his marauding mouth warmed the opening, covering the satiny skin of her exposed bosom with a myriad of tiny kisses. She made no protest at all when he moved aside the silk of her chemise and could only moan with pleasure when his mouth caught one taut nipple.

Cole thought he must be dreaming, except that this was better, far better, then any dream could be. She was here, right here, in his arms, all warm and soft and willing. More than willing. Dear Lord, she was kissing him back, and her soft little hands were doing wicked little things up under his shirt.

And her skin. Had anything ever felt so good? Or tasted so sweet? He could not seem to get enough of the feel or the taste of her, and he muttered a curse at the clothes that barred his access.

Their legs were tangled in her skirts, but he worked one thigh in between her legs, seeking her heat, stroking against it. Instinctively, she answered his rhythm, moving her hips in time to the ancient cadence. She was ready. He knew she was.

It felt so good, Rachel thought. It all felt wonderful, just like Lupe had said. And there was more, too, so much more. She strained to get closer, closer to his warmth, his strength. They'd have to stop soon, she knew. They couldn't do much more than just this luscious kissing and touching out here in the parlor. Soon they would have to move into the bedroom to have the privacy they would need.

For now, though, this was fine, and more than fine. She shivered at the delicious tingles that his hand was sending up her leg, up under her skirt and up and up . . .

She cried out when he cupped her center. So great was the shock, so shocking was the violation, she could not help it. "No, wait!" she gasped, recoiling instinctively from his sudden invasion. It was too soon, too quick.

She had only wanted him to slow down a little, but he jerked away as if she'd burned him.

Cole stared down at her startled face. She looked absolutely terrified. Good God, what had gotten into him? he wondered as he struggled free of the tangle her clothes had created and lurched to his feet. Was he going to tumble her right here on the floor like some two-bit whore?

He released her. She looked so helpless, lying there on the floor with her hair all tousled and her clothes all mussed and her breasts . . . Forcing himself to look away from her exposed bosom, he turned and headed for the front door. If he didn't get away, and quick, he *would* tumble her, right there on the floor, willing or not.

Rachel scrambled up to a sitting position. "Where are you going?" she demanded breathlessly, only remembering at the last moment to clutch the edges of her shirtwaist together over her nakedness.

"Out. I'll be back in a little while," he called over his shoulder, almost forgetting to grab his jacket in his haste to get out the door.

"Cole, wait!" she called, but it was too late. He was gone. She sat staring stupidly at the closed door for a long time, until she heard a horse clattering out of the ranch yard. The sound mobilized her, and she raced to the window in time to see him ride past on his way out to the road.

Shame and outrage burned her face, and she stamped her

foot in frustration while she damned Cole Elliot to the fires of perdition. What in the world was wrong with the man, anyway? She'd literally thrown herself at him, and then she'd wallowed on the floor with him like a bitch in heat, and at the last minute he'd gotten up and walked out.

Suddenly aware of the cool air on her heated skin, she angrily began to do up the buttons of her shirtwaist, trying not to remember how they had happened to become undone. Then she began to wonder if there might not be something wrong with her.

For a minute there, she'd been so sure that he wanted her. He'd done a very good imitation, anyway, before he'd suddenly changed his mind. What was it about her that repulsed him so much that he could not bring himself to do what Lupe had assured her was virtually second nature to all men?

Plunking herself down in the easy chair in which he had sat earlier, she stared into the fire. Well, she had known from the beginning that he did not like her. Her father and even Lupe had told her that it was her imagination, but she had had proof of it long before tonight. She had known ever since that night at the dance.

Just a few weeks after she had arrived home, her father had thrown a party to celebrate her return. Folks had come from miles around. They had barbecued two steers and the festivities had lasted all day and most of the night. After supper the dancing had started, and Rachel had, of course, been the belle of the ball.

Every man there had vied for a dance with her, and she had danced until her feet were more than numb. Every man had danced with her. Every man except one.

Cole Elliot had stood on the fringes of the crowd, watching and watching, with that funny, hard look on his face, his blue eyes narrowed disapprovingly. He was being subtle about it, but she had known that he was watching her and not liking what he saw. Resenting his judgment, she feigned even more gaiety than she felt, smiling and laughing and flirting until her face actually ached from the effort.

Finally, near dawn, in a fit of perversity, she marched right up and challenged him. "Mr. Elliot," she chastened, "you haven't asked me to dance."

Her boldness was rewarded. He looked remarkably uncomfortable, knowing that everyone was watching and listening to the exchange. "I can't dance," he said.

A lame excuse if she had ever heard one. "Why, Mr. Elliot," she said coyly, batting her eyes furiously, "there isn't a man here who *can* dance. That hasn't stopped any one of them from dragging me around to the music, however." She sidled up closer to him, enjoying his discomfiture. "I'll think you don't like me," she coaxed.

Just then the band struck up a waltz, and she tipped her head expectantly.

He cleared his throat and asked, "May I have this dance?" She had left him with no alternative.

With a small, triumphant smile, she led him back to the dance floor and allowed him to take her in his arms. The stiff way he held her, as if afraid to get too close, was almost insulting, but she smiled as if nothing in the world were amiss.

At least he hadn't been lying. He really couldn't dance, not a step. She thought it strange that a man with such natural grace should be unable to do a simple thing like dance, but she hadn't said anything about it. In fact, she hadn't said anything much at all. She'd been too busy trying to follow him as he walked her around the floor. And too breathless. She hadn't wanted to talk, anyway. Simply being in his arms had been enough. Enough for what, she could not have said at the time, but looking back, she wondered if her attraction to him had not begun even then.

Because, as little as she liked admitting it, she was very attracted to Cole Elliot. If she were completely honest, she was more than attracted to him, but she didn't care to be completely honest, not even with herself, not yet. All she was willing to admit was that she liked his kisses and the other things that went with them. She thought she might even like the rest of it, if she ever got the chance to find out what that was.

Sighing, she remembered Lupe's careful instructions, and winced at the thought of what Lupe would say if she had seen the little scene that had just been played out here in the parlor. No doubt the old woman would insist that it was all Rachel's fault, that she had driven her husband away somehow. Rachel felt the weight of some nameless emotion settle on her as she stared into the dying fire, and her chin firmed in determination.

Lupe was not going to find out. Not only that, but not one more day was going to go by before she and Cole Elliot set a few things straight, number one being their marriage and all that that implied.

Reaching for the Indian blanket that adorned the back of the settee, she spread it across her lap and snuggled down under it to ward off the growing chill. He couldn't stay away forever. He'd have to come back sooner or later, and when he did, they were going to have things out, once and for all.

Cole was well away from the ranch before he stopped to think things over. He just couldn't seem to come to grips with the fact that he had almost raped Rachel right there on the parlor floor.

In one more minute, he would have had her drawers off, and it would have been all over but the shouting. If she hadn't hollered when she did . . .

The only thing he didn't know was how she would ever be able to trust him again. He'd behaved like an animal, throwing her down on the floor and attacking her. All those days of being a gentleman, not demanding anything of her, holding all his own feelings on a short rein, were wasted now.

Now she'd be scared to death of him, of the very sight of him, and rightly so. He was a little scared himself. He'd never felt that way before, so out-of-control, so wild. Then again, he'd never been with anybody like Rachel, either.

He'd even thought at first that she was enjoying it. She must have been so scared that she hadn't even been able to fight him off or tell him to get away from her. He must have been pretty far gone to imagine that she'd wanted it. A lady would never act like that. Now that the cold night air had cleared his head and he could think clearly, he remembered that.

He should have known that things would get out of hand if he ever touched her, though. That one time he'd danced with her should have been proof enough.

It had been one hell of a wingding, a whole day of partying and carrying on, and then a dance to top things off. Of course, Cole never danced. It was one thing he'd never learned to do. The other men liked to go to the dance houses and pay to dance with the pretty girls as sort of a warm up for what came later. Cole had never felt that he needed a warm up, and he couldn't see any point in wasting time and money on holding a girl in your arms when you couldn't do anything more about it than just jog around to some God-awful music.

So dancing had never held much attraction for him. Until he'd met Rachel, that is. That night at the dance, watching her with man after man, Cole had known a bitter envy. Not that he couldn't have done as good a job as any of them of pushing her around the floor, but his pride rebelled at such a thing. If he couldn't do it right, he wasn't about to get out there and make a fool of himself in front of her.

Still, he hadn't been able to stop watching her, no matter how much it galled him. He guessed that she had known he was watching, too, even though he'd tried not to be too obvious. That was probably why she had come up to him and shamed him into dancing with her.

144

Even then, he hadn't dared to hold her close. Not that he hadn't wanted to, of course. He'd wanted to do a lot more than hold her, too, and he had needed all his iron control to keep from carrying her off somewhere and doing it. By the time that dance was over, he'd actually been sweating from the strain.

The way he was sweating right now just from thinking about her.

Without really planning to, without even being consciously aware of where he was going or why, Cole found himself, after a long, cold ride, in front of Lettie's cabin. He told himself that he shouldn't be there, that he was a married man, that Lettie wouldn't want him there. Still, he climbed down and tied the gelding in the shelter of the lean-to beside her house and went up and knocked on the door.

The house was dark. It wasn't really late, but late enough that the town had closed down for the night, and Lettie, having been on her feet all day, had gone to bed.

Cole heard a scuffling inside and then a light flared as she struck a match and lighted a lamp.

"Who's there?" her muffled voice asked through the door.

He was starting to feel a little foolish. He'd never come to her place like this before. Always they'd come together, after she got off work. He'd never had to stand at the door and announce himself.

"It's Cole," he finally said.

The door immediately swung open, and Lettie stood there silhouetted against the lamp that sat on a center table. Cole could see the outline of her body through her thin nightdress. It should have been a welcome sight.

Wordlessly, she stepped back from the door, allowing him to enter. No sooner was he in the room than he knew he had made a mistake in coming here. This was not where he should have come to find comfort after the scene with Rachel. The fact that until very recently, this house had been a sort of haven for him was what had drawn him, but now he knew that those days were gone for good.

"Well, now, if it isn't the bridegroom," Lettie was saying, sarcasm thick in her voice. "It sure didn't take long for your fancy lady to get tired of spreading her legs for you, did it?"

His hand was raised, fingers spread, half a breath away from striking her when he caught himself. Lettie had raised her arm and cringed away instinctively to ward off the blow, and for a moment they both stood poised like that, unable to move. Cole stared in horror at his hand and then looked back at Lettie who had finally moved. She was stepping away from him, her face white, her body trembling. That was when he realized the truth. He had almost hit her. At last he drew his hand back, staring at it in amazement and unable to believe that he could have done such a thing. He had never struck a woman in his life, and here he had almost struck Lettie for no reason at all. Or almost no reason. This business with Rachel was making him crazy.

"Lettie, I'm sorry," he said hoarsely, reaching out instinctively to comfort her. Appalled at the way she shrank from him, he dropped his hands to his sides and shook his head to clear it. No doubt about it, Rachel had driven him over the edge. "I never meant to hit you, Lettie. It's just . . . you shouldn't have said anything about her."

Lettie knew that much, and behind her shocked face, her mind was clicking away over that fact. Cole, gentle as he had always been with her, had threatened her physically. Now that she had had a chance to watch him for a moment, she saw that he was truly upset, upset enough that he could do something so completely out of character that he had horrified even himself.

That woman had driven him to it. Lettie was sure of it. For days Lettie had been eaten with jealousy, had been obsessed with wondering how a fine lady like Miss McKinsey had managed to trap Cole. That Cole was ready to settle down, Lettie had suspected for a long time. She had played on it, too, making herself and her home as comfortable for him as she could. She hadn't dared mention marriage, not yet, anyway, knowing how that would scare him off, but she had been confident that with just a little more time, she could have planted the idea in his mind.

That little bitch had beaten her to it, though. For days, and just now, Lettie had let her bitterness get in the way of her usually good judgment. Now that she thought about it, now that she studied Cole and read his mood, she knew that she was being given a second chance. He might have struck out at Lettie, but she would have bet money that it was really his little wife that he wanted to hit. They had had a fight. They must have or why would he be here, with her?

Cole was apologizing again. "I shouldn't have come here, Lettie. I'm sorry. I'll leave now," he offered, heading for the still-opened door.

"No, wait," Lettie said, quickly moving to close the door and stand in his way. She even managed a small smile. "There's no need for you to go, not yet."

Cole couldn't believe that she had forgiven him so quickly or so easily, and he stared at her suspiciously. He was starting to feel more than a little disgusted with himself. This was the second woman he had had to apologize to tonight, and it was a very unpleasant experience.

Seeing his uncertainty, Lettie played on it. "I know why you came, and it's all right. I've missed you, too," she assured him. She reached over and began to release the buttons of his coat. He did not resist, and when the jacket hung open, she slipped inside it, molding herself to him. "We'll do all the things you like," she promised.

Cole felt his blood stir. After what had happened earlier, he needed a woman, needed one badly. His arms went around her. She wasn't as pretty as Rachel, but she'd do. He buried his face in the curve of her neck. The cloying scent of her cheap perfume almost gagged him. It wasn't like the fresh smell of roses at all. In desperation, he lifted his head and ground his mouth against hers.

Rachel started awake. For a moment she could not remember why she was sleeping in the chair, and then it all came back to her. She was waiting for Cole.

She glanced up at the clock, but it had run down and she had no idea what the true time was. From the total silence around her, though, she knew that it was late. The lamp had long since guttered out, and the fire had burned down to coals.

If she sat here much longer, she would get stiff, but something within her rebelled at giving up her vigil. The night was cold. He wouldn't be gone much longer. If she waited here, she would be certain to hear him come in, and then she would confront him.

Just a little longer, she decided, struggling to find a more comfortable position. He'd be home soon.

Chapter V

"Cole, don't go!" Lettie sat bolt upright in bed, not even bothering to cover her nakedness when she realized his intentions.

"I just can't do it, Lettie," he said flatly, rebuttoning his shirt with a brutal swiftness before he could change his mind. This was wrong, more than wrong. For the second time in ten minutes, his own behavior appalled him.

"You're just tired. You need a drink. I've got a bottle in the cupboard. I'll get it," she offered frantically, snatching up the nightdress she had discarded moments ago in an effort to arouse him.

"It's not that!" he ground out, averting his eyes from the sight of her pale body. And it wasn't. It was something far different. There had been a time, and not so very long ago, when the sight of Lettie's body had been more than enough to keep him going for hours. Now his loyalties lay elsewhere. The memory of another body, one more delicately made, one more slender and graceful, claimed his desire, and anything else was just obscene.

He didn't know when or how it had happened, but Rachel had put the Indian sign on him. First he'd wanted her so bad that he'd almost raped her, and then he'd made the very startling discovery that no other woman could ease his

149

longing. It was Rachel or nothing, and if he remembered the look on Rachel's face correctly, it might very well be nothing.

Muttering a curse, he scooped up his jacket from where Lettie had dropped it on the floor.

"Cole, wait," Lettie begged, grabbing him by the arm. Cole couldn't bring himself to even look at her until he realized she had slipped her nightdress back on. "She'll never make you happy, honey. Don't you know that?"

Cole already had a pretty good idea of it, but right now Lettie wasn't making him very happy either. "Yeah, well, we all have our private little hells, don't we?" he asked, shaking loose of her grip.

"You'll be back," Lettie predicted with a sort of desperate smugness. "And when you come, I'll be waiting."

Cole winced at the promise. He paused with his hand on the doorknob and then turned slowly to face her. "Don't wait for me, Lettie. I won't be back, not ever."

Something in his voice, some air of finality, convinced her, and he saw her shoulders sag in defeat. "I'm sorry," he said, and then he was gone.

The ranch yard was dark and quiet when he rode in, and no light shone from the house. Well, what had he expected? he asked himself in annoyance as he rode up to the barn and dismounted. Did he think she would be waiting up for him? He should probably be glad she wasn't. She might've been waiting with a shotgun.

Sometime later, after caring for his horse, he quietly climbed the stairs to the front porch and carefully opened the front door. He didn't want to wake her, and he was pretty sure she didn't want to be awakened. He cast a quick glance at her bedroom door and was a little surprised to see it ajar. Using even more care, he removed his hat and coat and hung them by the door.

He was just beginning to wonder how he was going to cross the room quietly when he suddenly sensed another presence. His swiftly darting glance missed her the first time, but the second time he found her, sitting curled in the big arm chair, all but hidden in the deep shadows.

He felt the stab of an emotion that was equal parts concern, guilt, and desire, and for a minute all he could do was stand there and stare. She had waited up for him, or at least she had tried to. Why, he could only guess, and he didn't feel like wrestling with those possibilities right now. Briefly he considered letting her stay there, pretending that he hadn't seen her, and thus avoiding a confrontation. The temptation certainly had its attractions.

He couldn't do that, though. As little as he wanted to see the fear in her eyes again, as painful as it would be to have her flinch away from him the way Lettie had done, he couldn't leave her sitting there all night. It was getting colder and the room was freezing now that the fire had gone out. She'd be stiff and sore by morning, and she'd probably catch pneumonia if she didn't go on to bed. No, whatever his personal preferences, he had to wake her up and send her to her room.

Telling himself that he didn't want to startle her, he tiptoed across the room and squatted next to the chair. The faint scent of roses teased at him, and he felt the renewed stir of desire. "Rachel," he whispered, knowing that he should not touch her but allowing himself the luxury of brushing a stray lock of hair off her forehead.

She stirred but did not waken. "Rachel," he repeated, a little more loudly. She looked so small and helpless snuggled down under the heavy blanket that he wanted nothing so much as to take her in his arms, to protect her from all the unknown evils. He did not surrender to that urge, however, knowing full well that he himself was one of those evils.

"Rachel," he called a third time, forced at last to shake her slightly. He only touched her for a second, just long enough to jar her awake, and then swiftly removed his hand.

Rachel had been having the nicest dream. Cole had come

151

home, and he had kissed her awake and held her so gently. He was calling her name over and over, his warm breath fanning her face, teasing her with his scent. Her eyes flickered open and there he was, only inches away.

"Cole," she whispered, and reached for him. It was the most natural thing to do, to go where she most wanted to be, to rest against his warmth and his strength. After just a heartbeat's hesitation, his arms closed around her, too, and she slid from the chair into his embrace.

She buried her face in his shirt and inhaled deeply, trying to drink in the smell of him. Suddenly, she came fully awake. Something was wrong. Terribly wrong. She sniffed again. Her body stiffened and she pulled away. "Where have you been?" she demanded furiously.

Cole blinked in surprise. First he'd been so stunned at the way she'd melted into his arms that he almost hadn't caught her when she came, and now, no sooner did he have her than she was fighting clear. In another second he registered the accusation in her voice, and he had to fight down his instinctive guilt. There was no way she could possibly know where he had been. "Nowhere," he lied. "I just rode for a while . . ."

"Don't lie to me," she raged, jerking herself upright and struggling to her feet. "You've been with a woman!" She had been almost sure, and when she saw his face, she knew for certain. It was the perfume. Cheap perfume. And he reeked of it.

"You son of a bitch!" she cried, and then she ran, terrified that he would see her tears.

She sought the refuge of her room, but once inside, the door safely closed behind her, she still did not feel secure. Groping in the darkness, she found a chair and wedged it beneath the doorknob just as she heard the clatter of his bootheels outside.

"Rachel, listen, it wasn't like that!" he was saying. It had taken him a minute to recover from hearing such a foul name from Rachel's sweet lips, but he had recovered now. He knocked politely. "Come out of there. We need to talk," he urged. Cole had just made the very startling discovery that he might have been entirely wrong about Miss Rachel Anne McKinsey. He'd almost convinced himself that he'd only imagined her response to him before, but just now there could be no doubt that she had come very willingly to his arms. If she hadn't somehow guessed he'd been with Lettie, she'd very probably still be there.

"Go away!" she screamed, scrubbing frantically at the tears that scalded down her cheeks. How dare he come to her straight from another woman's arms? How dare he try to lie to her about it?

She was getting hysterical. He could hear it in her voice. "Rachel," he coaxed, quietly trying the door. The knob turned but the door wouldn't budge. He jiggled the knob and pushed harder. Something was holding it. "Open the door, Rachel," he ordered.

"No! Get away from there. I've got a gun! I'll kill you if you try to come in here!" she cried, sincerely wishing that she did have a gun. At the moment, nothing would have given her greater pleasure than to put a hole in the faithless Cole Elliot.

That desire was evident in her voice, and Cole's nerves prickled instinctively. He was pretty sure she was bluffing, but there was nothing more dangerous than a hysterical woman. "We have to talk about this," he insisted. He felt a desperate need to explain things to her, but only silence greeted his request. He pictured her standing on the other side of the door, crying and trying not to. Her pride would never let her open the door, and if he tried to force it, he'd probably only make things worse, even if she didn't have a gun. She was already scared enough of him. There was no use in frightening her anymore. Maybe it was better to let things simmer for a while and then go at it again when they were both feeling better.

"All right. We won't talk tonight, but we *will* talk tomorrow," he told her in an attempt to be reasonable. It was quite a sacrifice to make when what he really wanted to do was break down the door.

Rachel made a furious noise deep in her throat and stamped her foot in frustration. Casting around for something on which to vent her anger, her hand fell on her silver brush. Clutching it gratefully, she called out, "The hell we will! If you want to talk to someone, you can go back to your whore!" Then she flung the brush at the door with all her strength.

Cole kicked the tiny table that stood nearby, shattering it into kindling. "She's not a whore!" he called back, realizing too late that he had thus condemned himself. Cursing viciously, he strode into his room and slammed the door.

Trembling at the sound of smashing wood, Rachel waited, expecting that at any moment her door would meet the same fate. When he stomped away, she trembled more, listening for the sounds of his return. Seconds passed and then minutes. He was not going to return. She had won. Drawing an unsteady breath, Rachel allowed herself to savor her victory. Unfortunately, the taste of that victory was bitter, and the tears that had momentarily slowed began again in earnest. Just when she'd thought that things were as bad as they could get, they'd gotten immeasurably worse. Not only did her husband not want her, he did want someone else. It was so humiliating.

Without even bothering to light a candle or even to undress, Rachel stumbled to her bed and crawled under the covers, seeking a haven. She found only a place to muffle the sound of her sobs, but that was enough, and she accepted that carrion comfort.

"Oh, Papa," she cried into her pillow, "you were wrong about him, and so was I." For a few hours there, as she had sat huddled in the chair awaiting his return, she had imagined that she was beginning to care for the man. Now he had made a mockery of her tender feelings, choosing to scorn what she had offered him for the favors of a common trollop. The shame of it was terrible. So bad, in fact, that she could almost forget how her heart was breaking.

Cole took Rachel at her word, and didn't even try to speak to her the next morning. After a nearly sleepless night, he took his breakfast in the cookhouse with the men. If anyone thought that peculiar, no one dared mention it. After one look at the expression on Cole's face, the men all trod very lightly around him. Miles had the temerity to ask if everything was all right and nearly got his head bitten off for his trouble. After that, no one even thought about speaking to him.

Rachel had finally fallen asleep along about dawn, and when she awoke, she felt even more miserable than she had before, if that were possible. For a few minutes, she wondered if she might be able to get away with simply staying in her room all day, but she quickly dismissed that idea as too cowardly. If she hid from him, he would soon guess how much he had hurt her and she would rather die than admit such a thing. Besides, she reasoned, it was already late in the morning, and Cole would have left the ranch for the day. After splashing some frigid water on her face from the pitcher in her room to ease the swelling of her eyes, she redid her hair and changed into fresh clothes. Feeling the confidence of her restored appearance, she boldly stepped into the parlor.

The sight of the shattered table stopped her cold. She stared at it for a long time, remembering in great detail what had happened to cause its current condition. Lupe's disapproving grunt broke into her reflections.

"He has bad temper," the old woman observed, casting a baleful eye at the splintered mess. "What you do this time?"

Rachel straightened indignantly. "I did nothing," she

informed Lupe.

Lupe nodded with great comprehension. "Ah, that is why he break the furniture."

Rachel gave an outraged gasp. "It isn't my fault!" she insisted, closing in on the smaller woman. "I did everything I could! We were . . . kissing . . . right there," she gestured vaguely, "and then, all of a sudden, for no reason, he just up and leaves." Her face crumpled. "Lupe, he has another woman. He went to her last night." The wound was still raw, and Lupe saw the pain in Rachel's eyes.

Clucking sympathetically, Lupe took her hand and led her to the settee and pushed her gently down onto it. "Tell me," Lupe ordered. "Tell me everything."

Reluctantly, Rachel did so.

Lupe nodded sagely throughout the whole recitation. She wasn't pretending, either. She really did understand, and things were starting to make perfect sense. Lupe had the advantage over Rachel in that she had seen Cole before he left this morning. He did not look like a man who had spent an enjoyable night with his mistress. Instead, he looked like a man wound as tight as an eight-day clock. If Rachel's suspicions were correct and he had gone to see another woman last night, his luck with her hadn't been any better than it had been with Rachel. Of that, Lupe was certain.

"What you think?" she demanded of Rachel when the story was finished. "You think he will wait until he is old for you? He is a man, that one. He needs a woman."

Rachel glared at Lupe, furious that once again she had put the blame on Rachel. "He's *got* a woman," she pointed out bitterly.

Lupe's wrinkled face squinched up thoughtfully. "Is that what you want? You want him to have another woman?"

"Of course not!" Rachel declared quite honestly. Even if she no longer cared for Cole Elliot—and how could she, after what he'd done?—her pride rebelled at the thought of him with someone else.

"Then you must go to his bed," Lupe said.

"Never!" Rachel gasped, bolting to her feet. "I'd die first!" How could Lupe, the closest thing she had to a mother, even suggest such a thing to her? Didn't she have any self-respect?

Lupe folded her hands in resignation. "Then you will die with no babies," she pointed out.

Babies! Was that all Lupe ever thought about? Of course it was, Rachel decided in exasperation. One of the natural functions of life. After marriage came babies. Not that Rachel didn't want babies. She did, very much. She'd even allowed herself to wonder once or twice what her children would look like with Cole Elliot as their father. They would have his clear blue eyes and her dark hair and his dimple. What she hadn't allowed herself to wonder was what it would be like to have children with a man who didn't care a straw about her.

Lupe had no trouble reading Rachel's thoughts as the girl paced around the room in silence. "Do you want to keep him?" Lupe asked after a while.

The question stopped Rachel in her tracks. Did she? It should have been a difficult question, but Rachel found it surprisingly easy to answer. She did want to keep him. He was her husband, after all. She would never be able to hold her head up again if she lost him to some cheap floozy after less than a week of marriage. There was more to it, though, she admitted reluctantly after another moment's consideration. There was him.

She had told herself that she had very good reasons for choosing him, the fact that he was a born leader and good with a gun and brave and all those other things. Those reasons were valid, but they did not fully explain her decision to marry him. Her motivations went deeper than the obvious ones and they touched her woman's heart. Last night she had admitted to herself that she was attracted to him, and had been almost from the very beginning. Her feelings went even deeper than that, though, if she allowed herself to admit it.

Whether she could actually call it love, she did not know. All she knew was that she felt a strange compulsion to have him feel the same attraction for her that she felt for him, to have him seek her out the way he had sought out that woman last night. Even more than that, she wanted him in her power, wanted him to be crazy for her. Only then would she dare to truly give him her heart. Would sharing his bed win her that power?

Lupe watched Rachel's face carefully and at last grinned her toothless grin, pleased with what she saw going through the girl's mind. "It is easy," Lupe explained. "Tonight, you go to his bed. No talking. No fighting. Be quiet and let him do what he wants. Tomorrow he will love you."

Rachel's mouth dropped open in horror. "I couldn't do anything so . . . so brazen!"

Lupe shrugged regretfully. "Too bad," she said sadly, rising to her feet. With another shrug, she glided silently from the room.

Cole slumped wearily into the kitchen and went straight to the sink, where he worked the pump vigorously for a minute before ducking his head under it. The frigid water sluiced through his hair and around his ears and over his face in a refreshing stream. When he felt fully revived, he released the pump handle, waited until the last of the water had drained off, and then shook like a dog, dashing the moisture from his eyes with his fingers. Before he even had a chance to wonder where he was going to find a towel, someone pressed one into his hands and he patted his face gratefully. Only then did he wonder who had given it to him.

Looking up warily, he found Lupe's tiny form standing not three feet away, her beady little eyes watching him in that sly way she had. Stifling an oath, he wrapped the towel over his head and dried his hair vigorously before finally straightening to face her.

"Is supper ready?" he asked gruffly in an attempt to remind her that he was the master here.

The old woman muttered some gibberish, but Cole caught enough to know that she was complaining about the broken table. Although he felt like a fool about the incident, he would not let her know it. He stared her down, never batting an eye. Two could play this game, he decided, glaring at her. If he wanted to break every bit of furniture in the place, it wasn't any of her business.

"What's for supper?" he asked again, making it plain that the subject of breaking things was closed.

Lupe grunted in disapproval and for a moment Cole almost imagined a gleam of amusement in those dark eyes. "Food is cold. You are late," she informed him, bustling around to dish him up a plate.

Cole watched in amazement. So she could talk American when she wanted to, he realized with annoyance. She just never seemed to want to when he was around. Raking his fingers through his still-damp hair, he snapped, "Is there hot water in my room?"

Lupe muttered something under her breath. "It cold, too, now," she said.

Cole spun on his heel and marched out of the kitchen. He was halfway through the dining room before he thought to slow his pace, remembering suddenly that if he kept going he was bound to run into Rachel sooner or later. Not only was she going to be mad about last night, but now she would be mad that he was late and had missed dinner. Thinking back, he seemed to remember that she'd been mad ever since they'd gotten married and for no good reason that he could figure out. He'd been walking on egg shells every minute, trying to be kind, trying to remember that she'd just lost her pa and that her whole world had been turned upside down, and most of all trying not to frighten her. For all the good it had done him. He sighed in exasperation.

Cole raked his fingers through his hair again, smoothing it as well as he could, and then cautiously continued on his way. If she was mad, there was nothing he could do about it anyway. He might as well get it over with.

She was sitting in the parlor on the settee, her back to him. If she heard his approach, she gave no indication, but merely continued with her embroidery. She was always sewing on one damn thing or another, or else she was reading some book.

Now that he was closer, he could see that she had heard him all right. Her shoulders were much too stiff, her fingers worked the needle too swiftly, and when he came far enough into the room to see her face, he saw that her lips were pressed too tightly together. How the woman who had been so soft and feminine last night in his arms could look so mean, he had no idea.

Rachel had known the moment he had returned to the ranch. At first, when he was so late, she had suspected that he had gone to see that woman again, except that none of the other men had come back either. When they had finally ridden in, she had watched from behind the curtains, easily picking Cole out from the group, and she could tell from the way he dismounted that he had been in the saddle most of the day.

Seeing him again, even at a distance, stirred something within her, something she hesitated to label "excitement," but which answered to no other name. She watched him for a long time while he unsaddled his horse and cared for it, enjoying the smooth, effortless way he moved. Her body remembered the way he had moved last night, and her nipples puckered at the memory of his touch. When she realized that her breath was coming more quickly, that her heart was pattering more rapidly, and that little shivers were dancing up her legs, she jerked her gaze away, forcing her feet to carry her from the window. She sat down, determined to appear calm and collected.

160

She had waited then, posing on the settee, ready for his entrance, but he had fooled her by going around to the kitchen door instead. The waiting had annoyed her, cracking the shell of coolness she had so carefully constructed, and now she felt ready for a good fight. She glanced up. "You're late," she informed him.

Cole watched her head come up. He thought she was mighty pretty with her dark eyes flashing like that, even if the look she was giving him would have drawn blood on a rawhide boot. "Yeah," he agreed blandly. "We had some trouble today."

He had said the one word, the one magic word, that had the power to distract her. "Trouble?" she echoed. "What kind of trouble?"

Cole could tell from the way that she put her embroidery down and shifted forward on her seat and the way the fire had died in her eyes that he was off the hook, at least for the moment. "We lost some cattle," he told her, trying not to look at her hand which rested on the base of her throat, perilously close to her breasts. "Twenty, maybe thirty head. We found the tracks this morning where somebody's run them off. We trailed them, but they split up and then we lost them. They were clever, running them in small bunches into places where there were lots of tracks already so we couldn't follow."

Rachel watched his long fingers curl into fists, and she shared his frustration. This wasn't the first time this had happened, and there didn't seem to be anything they could do to stop it, short of catching the thieves in the act, and that was bound to be quite dangerous. Rachel was actually amazed at how frightened she suddenly felt. For some reason she had imagined that marrying Cole would solve her problems. Now she realized that not only did she still have to worry about the rustlers robbing her blind, but she had to worry about Cole's being in danger from them, too.

For a long moment she stared at him, unable to tear her

161

eyes away. What would she do if something happened to him? Rachel watched one of his hands reach up to massage the weariness from the back of his neck, and she noticed for the first time the lines fatigue had etched into his face and the way his broad shoulders sagged. He was tired, and he'd be hungry, too. She knew a twinge of remorse for planning an argument after all he had been through today for her. "You'd better go eat," she suggested. There'd be time enough later for their discussion.

Sensing her change of mood, he was almost reluctant to leave, but his stomach was gnawing on his backbone and he felt as if he didn't sit down soon, he was going to fall down. He nodded his agreement, giving her a sort of half smile which she did not return, and then headed for his room to clean up.

Lupe had been right, the water was cold, but he washed anyway after stripping off his dirty clothes. When he was clean and feeling more like a human, he dressed in fresh clothes, something that had become a habit since he had moved into the big house. He knew that Mr. McKinsey had done so ever since Rachel had come home, and Cole thought he should carry on the tradition. Besides, he hated sitting around smelling like he belonged in a barn with Rachel in the same room.

While he dressed, he considered how, exactly, he was going to explain about Lettie and what had happened, or rather what hadn't happened. Anything he said would sound bad because he had purposely gone to Lettie's house, and Rachel had already figured out what he had gone for, too. Somehow he was going to have to convince her that it simply didn't matter. Unfortunately, he didn't have the foggiest idea how he could do that. Complicating his dilemma was the knowledge that he only wanted to explain everything so that Rachel would be willing to go to bed with him.

Said outright like that, it sounded pretty sleazy and maybe even a little immoral. Rachel was always so neat and clean and proper, it seemed almost indecent for him to want to slake his lust on her. But he did want to. God, how he wanted to.

So he had no choice. He'd have to talk to her, tell her how the cow ate the cabbage. She was his wife, after all. A man had certain rights, and a wife had certain duties. That was the way things were, and the sooner Miss Rachel Anne McKinsey found that out, the better off they'd all be, he decided, giving his hair one last swipe and heading back to the parlor.

Unfortunately for his resolve, Rachel was no longer in the parlor or anywhere in sight. Mentally shrugging off the sense of relief he felt at this momentary reprieve, he made his way into the dining room where he was surprised to find Rachel waiting for him at the large table.

Rachel looked up when he appeared in the doorway. He was tall and neat and freshly shaven, and she thought he hesitated for a moment before coming in and taking his seat at the end of the table where Lupe had laid out his dinner. Rachel was sitting at his right, nursing a cup of coffee. She had decided that they had best discuss their problems before any more time passed, and so she had chosen to keep him company while he ate. Such a domestic setting would certainly be conducive to a domestic discussion.

Or at least she hoped it would. After all that had happened, she no longer trusted her own judgment. She was even starting to suspect that Lupe had been right, after all, and Rachel was at least partially responsible for his walking out on her last night. As angry and as hurt as she was at the thought that he had gone to another woman, maybe she had put him off with her ladylike ways. That was what Lupe had suggested, anyway.

And it seemed reasonable, considering how he always treated her with such excruciating politeness. Even thinking back to last night when they had been kissing there on the floor—Rachel blushed at the memory—she had told him to

163

stop or something like that. He had stopped, too, instantly. That couldn't have been easy for him, either, not if he'd felt the way she had, and she had a pretty good idea he had. Yes, Lupe was right. If he'd gone to another woman, Rachel was to blame, although how she could have kept him here last night she had no idea. He'd run out before she'd had a chance to explain or even to call him back.

Rachel lowered her eyes to her coffee cup, but she could still see Cole's hand out of the corner of her eye. It was holding the fork and moving up and down as it carried the food to his mouth. She tried not to remember how that hand had felt on her body, on places where no one had ever touched her before. Her body remembered, though, and those places warmed and tingled. Rachel squirmed uneasily in her chair.

Cole saw the movement but pretended not to notice. He knew what was coming. She was fairly itching for a fight, could hardly wait until he was through eating to get started. Why she didn't just go ahead and light into him, he had no idea. Probably because she considered it bad manners or something, he decided sardonically. Well, bad manners or not, he wouldn't mind a fight. That's how they'd gotten started last night. With any luck at all, that's how they'd end up tonight, only this time he wasn't going anywhere.

In fact, that's how they were going to end up even if she didn't pick a fight. They'd been married almost a week now, and that was more than enough time for her to get used to the idea. He glanced over at her. She was sipping on her coffee, daintily lifting the china cup to her lips. As usual, she looked perfect, every hair in place, her dress fresh and crisp even though she'd probably been wearing it all day long. For one instant a vision of her as she had been last night flashed across his mind. That hair hadn't been so neat last night and her clothes had been . . .

Cole shook his head to clear it. If he started thinking about that, he'd forget all about talking and take her right here on

164

the table. No, he had to be patient. He had to talk to her first. He would, too, in just a minute, he decided, scooping up the last mouthful of beans on his plate.

Rachel couldn't seem to keep her wayward eyes off him. His hands were not the only part of him that triggered pleasant memories, and when she raised her eyes and saw his mouth, she recalled how much pleasure his kisses had brought. She shivered, but told herself she was only shaking off that thought. After all, that wasn't the only reason she wanted to consummate her marriage. There were other considerations, too. Will Statler, for one. What would happen if he found out she and Cole did not have a real marriage? What if her own men found out? She would be mortified to have them know she could not keep her own husband at home. The prospect of losing their respect and of being the object of Statler's contempt was horrifying.

But not as horrifying as the prospect of explaining her reasoning to Cole Elliot, she suddenly realized, sneaking a peek at his impassive face. How was one supposed to explain to one's husband that she preferred he ease his male urges at home? On her? Just thinking about it made Rachel's face burn. Actually doing it would be difficult enough, but having to talk about it first was simply unthinkable. But what choice did she have?

Cole drained his coffee cup and set it down on his empty plate and pushed the whole thing away from him. He was finished eating and he was ready to talk. He turned to Rachel. For one second he thought she was blushing, but maybe it was just the reflection from the lamp overhead. He opened his mouth to speak, but just then she met his gaze. For one instant he saw the frightened look of a trapped animal in her dark brown eyes, and the words lodged in his throat. How could he talk to her when she looked like that? How was he going to convince her that she didn't have anything to be afraid of when he knew she did? And how in the hell was he going to explain what he wanted to do to her

165

when—as he suddenly realized—he didn't even know a nice word for it?

"Rachel . . ." he began tentatively and soothingly, hoping to ease her fears.

Oh, Dear Lord, she thought, he's going to talk about it! She couldn't, she just couldn't! Panic surged through her. What could she do? Suddenly, she remembered exactly what she could do. She would simply do what Lupe had suggested. Rachel jumped to her feet. "Well, it's late," she said, aware that her voice was high and breathless, but praying he wouldn't notice, "and I know you're tired, so I'll say 'good night' now." Turning with a swish of her skirt, she made her escape.

Cole watched her go in stunned surprise for just a moment before he thought to follow her. "Rachel," he called, rising swiftly and hurrying after her. "Rachel, we have to talk," he called just as she was about to disappear inside her bedroom.

Rachel turned back, her heart beating frantically against her ribs. She saw him standing there, not ten feet away, his hands on his hips, his expression both puzzled and determined. She should, she knew she should. But she couldn't. She simply couldn't. "I'm very tired. I know you'll excuse me." This was not a request but a statement, and before he had time to argue, she was in her room with the door shut. She leaned wearily back against the solid wood of the door and listened. Would he follow her? Would he insist as he had done last night?

Rachel knew that if she wanted to keep him out, she need only grab the chair and press it under the knob as she had before. But she made no move to do so. Instead she listened with hammering heart for him to come for her.

Cole stared after her beginning to feel angry. What in the hell had gotten into her? A few minutes ago he would have bet his boots with his saddle thrown in that she was just spoiling for a fight. Then all of a sudden she had turned tail and run, like he'd scared her or something. Had he? He didn't think so, but then again, who knew about women? Cole Elliot certainly didn't.

He glared at the closed door. Who did she think she was to slam doors in his face? He'd had just about enough of all this, and Little Miss Rachel was going to get told a few things right now, even if he had to go over there and break the damn door down.

Cole was at the door, his hand raised to pound, his mouth open to yell, when common sense caught up with him and a new fury overtook him. What was he doing, banging on her door like some smitten schoolboy? he asked himself furiously, lowering his hand. He'd made a big enough fool of himself last night, begging her to let him in. He'd be damned before he'd make an idiot of himself twice in a row over some fool woman. If she wanted to sleep alone, he'd let her. In fact, he'd let her rot in there before he'd ever humble himself in front of her again. He didn't need her that bad. Cole Elliot didn't need anyone.

With that thought, he turned on his heel and strode into the sanctity and privacy of his own room. Damn her, he thought as he shut the door with just a little more force than was absolutely necessary. Damn her to hell.

Rachel fought off a wave of disappointment when she heard him going into his own room. How simple it would have been if he had forced his way in here and forced her to submit. Then she would have been spared this nerve-wracking waiting. And she did have to wait. She wanted to be sure he was asleep. Nothing would be more awful than having him hear her come in and having him demand to know what she was doing in his room.

So Rachel took her time getting ready. Lupe had washed and ironed her best nightdress, the one with the embroidery on the yoke, and laid it out for her. That irritated Rachel just a bit. The old woman had known Rachel would do what she had suggested even before Rachel had known herself. Still, she stripped out of her clothes and put the delicate garment

167

on, covering it with her warmest wrapper against the evening chill.

After that, she gave her waist-length hair five hundred leisurely brush strokes and then braided it into a long rope, tying a ribbon on the end. The temptation to leave her hair loose was great, but Rachel knew what a mess it would be in the morning if she did, and resisted. Then she took her bottle of rose water and touched some to the inside of her wrists and behind her ears.

After a moment's thoughts, she swiftly unbuttoned her nightdress and applied some under each arm, and as an afterthought, remembering how he had kissed her last night, she let one drop slither down the hollow between her breasts. The sensation was so sensual that she shivered, wickedly noting the way her nipples pursed before rebuttoning her gown.

When she glanced up again and saw her own reflection in the mirror, she almost groaned aloud. Was it only her imagination or did she really look different? Softer, more vulnerable, her brown eyes almost twice their normal size? She tried adjusting the lacy collar of her gown, but that didn't help a bit. Would he notice? No, she reassured herself, the room would be dark. He would see nothing unusual in her expression because he wouldn't see her expression at all. Turning away with some relief, she got up and began to pace the room.

How long should she wait? How long until she could be sure he was asleep? She had not heard any sounds of movement from the room next door in quite a while, and when she paused to listen once more, she still heard nothing. Just a few more minutes to be certain, she decided, hugging herself and pretending that the shivering she was trying to control was caused by the cold.

It probably wouldn't be too very awful, she told herself, remembering the few blissful moments she had spent in his arms. His hands had been warm and strong, and had given her a lot of pleasure. His mouth had been sweet and tender and delicious on hers and gently teasing on the rest of her. A strange sensation spread over her when she remembered, almost as if her blood had turned to honey, warm honey, as it went oozing through her veins, and suddenly she felt very lonely and bereft. Logical reasons no longer seemed very important, but she knew instinctively that she needed to be with him. It no longer even mattered whether going to him was wise or not. She simply had to go.

Without another conscious thought, she put out the lamp, stole from her room and across the short space to his door. The knob turned easily and silently under her hand, and then she was inside. The darkness was thick around her, like a cool satin quilt enveloping her, and she stood there for a long time with her back pressed against the door. The air smelled faintly of cigarette smoke and Cole Elliot's own special scent. She inhaled deeply and then moved on silent feet toward where she knew the bed to be.

Although she could see nothing in the blackness, she still stopped just short of the bed. Reaching out her hand, she found one of the four posters, the one at the foot of the bed nearest her. Quickly, before she could lose her nerve, she slipped out of her wrapper and hung it on the bed post, stepping out of her slippers at the same time.

The room was cold, and she blamed that for the goosebumps that stole up under her nightdress. She could hear him breathing. He wasn't snoring exactly, just breathing the heavy, sonorous breath of deep sleep, and so she knew exactly where he was, her other senses sharpened because she could see nothing.

Feeling her way, she moved slowly to the head of the bed where she found the top edge of the covers. He was lying in the center of the bed, but there would be room for her to slip in beside him if she were careful.

She was very careful, lifting the covers just enough to allow her to creep beneath them, and lowering herself with infinite care. Her first sensation was one of warmth, deep, comforting warmth. Rachel had never shared a bed with anyone and so had never experienced the delicious solace another human body could afford. Her slight shivering eased as she relaxed into the feather mattress and breathed in the musky male scent of the body next to hers.

That scent made her feel slightly faint, and she was almost glad that she was lying down until she shifted a bit and her fingers grazed bare flesh. The blood that had been slowly oozing through her veins suddenly began to race, and she gasped aloud. Moving her hand once more, very tentatively, she touched again and knew for certain: he was naked!

Panic surged through her. This was a mistake, a terrible mistake! Her muscles had just coiled to propel her from the bed and from the room when the body next to hers moved.

He muttered something that sounded like her name, and his arms went around her. His heat, his scent, were enervating, overwhelming any resistance that she might have made. In the next second his mouth found hers, and all thought of resistance drained away.

This was just the way she remembered only better and better. Her lips parted at his gentle insistence, allowing him entrance, and once again she tasted his essence. Her memory had been imperfect, blurring at the edges so that she had no clear recollection of the sharp surge of emotion she was now reexperiencing.

She no longer even regretted his nudity as her hands explored the expanse of his back and shoulders, rediscovering the sinewy strength of him. Not even thinking to question his response but simply acknowledging in some distant part of her brain that Lupe had been right, she molded herself to him, submitting willingly when his weight pressed her into the bed.

One of his hands cupped her breast, and she arched to him, melting under the scorching heat of his body, her hips matching his rhythm as he rocked against her with mounting urgency. A groan rumbled from deep in his chest, and no sooner did she hear the sound than she felt the change in him. It was a slight change, but a perceptible one, altering everything from the texture of his skin to the tempo of his breathing in one swift second.

When she felt his body go rigid, she knew instantly that until this very moment he had been asleep, locked in some erotic dream in which she had been but a phantasm. Now, though, he had awakened, awakened to find her there and real and in his arms.

"Rachel?" His voice was a mere rasp, but the single word contained a myriad of questions. Every one of them was a question Rachel did not want to answer.

"Yes," she whispered and pressed her mouth to his again. She felt his slight hesitation and knew he was wondering, but she couldn't talk, not now, not even in the dark. Wrapping her arms around his neck, she pulled him close, moving against him with the same urgency he had felt just moments ago.

If she had hoped to distract him, she succeeded far beyond even those hopes. The seductive motion of her body wiped every other thought from his mind. He had been asleep, dreaming the all-too-familiar dream that Rachel was in his arms. He was still not quite sure, not quite awake enough to be certain that she really was here, but he wasn't going to let that stop him. If this was a dream, he never wanted to wake up.

Cole's hands moved over her body, learning her curves, and soon even the thin barrier of her nightdress was too much. As he had the night before, he released the buttons at her throat, and this time he found not even a silk chemise to bar his way. With hands and lips he caressed the smooth globes of her breasts, stroking and kneading, tasting and suckling. Inhaling the intoxicating fragrance of roses and her own sweet scent, he grew dizzy with the headiness of the aroma.

171

Fascinated with both the feel of her and her response to his touch, he continued his explorations. His fingers glided over her, stopping here and there when he sensed or heard her breath quicken, and then following with his lips to those spots until he drew a moan from her. Like a blind musician playing an unfamiliar instrument, he groped in the dark, strumming until he chanced upon the magical movement that produced the dulcet tone of her voice.

Soon her nightdress became an intolerable hindrance, and in his besotted state he did what he never otherwise would have dared. He stripped the garment from her, tossing it carelessly aside before continuing his play. Her startled gasp barely penetrated the passionate fog that surrounded him, and he ignored it as he returned to the task of learning her body.

This was something he had never done, something he had never had the leisure or the inclination for. Ordinarily, he simply used a woman's body for his own purpose, the mere sight of it usually being enough to satisfy any curiosity. This, however, was different. This was Rachel, and her body was as different from the many others as she was different, more special, than any other woman.

She was soft, softer than anything else he had ever touched, and she almost seemed to melt under his touch, her skin yielding into a delicious pliancy that drove him on to explore new territory. Her occasional moans had become a steady purr that came not so much from her throat as from her whole body. Like a sleek cat, she undulated against him, the aroma of her arousal rising up under the covers like an incense.

As he had last night, he finally found her center, but this time he approached with cautious, teasing strokes so that when the final invasion came, it would not shock. This time, she did not protest, but welcomed his intrusion, opening for him. This time he was the one who was shocked because she was so hot, so moist, so ready for him, as no other woman

172

had ever been. His control snapped. No longer curious about anything save how she would feel wrapped around him, he levered himself over her.

Rachel welcomed him, taking his weight gladly because it satisfied her compulsion to be close to him and closer still, to fulfill some aching need. Wrapping her arms around him, she caught one of his legs with hers, and chafed her calf against his, reveling in the difference between her silkiness and his hair-roughened flesh. His mouth was doing wonderful things to her neck, and she threw her head back in abandon, exposing herself to his assault.

She was only vaguely aware that he was doing something else, something down below, but she obeyed his urgings nonetheless, spreading her legs, lifting to his coaxing fingers. The pain was as swift as it was unexpected, stabbing into her with such force that she cried out, but then it faded just as quickly. After the initial reluctance, her body accepted him, absorbed him into her depths.

Her cry of pain pierced his consciousness. He lifted his head in a vain attempt to see her face, but her expression was hidden by the darkness. "Rachel?" he rasped, compelled to ask, to know how badly he had hurt her. In his desperate need, he had forgotten to take care.

She did not speak. He only heard the unevenness of her breath and felt the tiny shudder that went through her and then tasted the small sigh that escaped her sweet lips. Irresistibly drawn, he sought the source of that tiny wisp of air, claiming her lips in a kiss that began with tenderness but suddenly changed completely.

The pain was gone now, and when his lips touched hers, she kissed him back with newborn fervor. It was all so different from what she had imagined, not embarrassing at all but uplifting in a sublime sense of the word. He was moving against her, back and forth, and soon she caught the rhythm and began to move with him. They rocked together, suspended in some timeless moment, aware only of themselves and of each other and of the pleasure that grew more intense with each passing second.

Cole hadn't intended to go on with it. He knew he shouldn't hurt her any more than he already had, but when his lips touched hers, his body passed beyond his control. Her warmth held him, inside and out, and he could not have withdrawn to save his very life. Once he started, he could not stop. Driven by a power he had no will to resist, he went deeper and deeper still in the ancient, futile quest for the ultimate union.

Rachel knew something was happening, but it was happening too fast for her to think. Besides, it was wonderful, and she didn't care. She gasped when the tingles began, and again when they spread outward with the scorching speed of wildfire and then came rushing back upon themselves to consume her in incandescence. At last her gasp became a contented sigh while her whole body melted down into the golden glow of fruition.

Seconds later, her contentment shattered when she once again sensed a change in Cole. His body tensed, his breath rasped, and his skin grew moist beneath her touch. Before she could even begin to wonder, a cry of anguish began deep in his chest and rumbled out while his body stiffened and convulsed, pumping, pumping, spilling his life force into her.

Rachel clung to him, guessing that he was in the grip of the same fury that had shaken her. Tears of joy stung her eyes at the thought that she had caused him such pleasure. She had once wanted power over him, but now she understood that that would never be. Now she knew the power would hold them both, but she didn't mind. Smiling into the darkness as she lovingly stroked the glorious body whose weight now bore down on her, she decided that yes, that was just fine. She would gladly trade a little power for such bliss.

After a few moments, Cole moved, instinctively freeing her of the burden of his weight but not quite able to completely fight the lethargy that claimed him. He wanted to ask her if he had hurt her, tell her he hadn't meant to, and tell her something else, something very important, something about how wonderful she was. He couldn't remember exactly, though, and when he tried to speak, nothing came out. He'd tell her in a minute, he decided, after he'd rested.

He was asleep. Rachel wasn't sure how long they had lain there before she knew, but it had not been long. She felt mildly insulted, but simply did not have the energy to work up any indignation.

There would be some blood. Lupe had warned her about that, just as she had warned her about the pain. Lupe had been dead right about the pain, so Rachel imagined that she should probably get up and wash. Not that she wanted to or anything, but she really should. Her halfhearted attempt to move met with rather forcible resistance, however. Cole's arms were wrapped around her, and when she tried to slip out of them, they tightened. He muttered something that she took for a protest, and only when she settled back down against him did he relax again. She experienced a warm glow at the thought that he was not about to let her go even though he was sound asleep.

She should sleep, too. She knew she should, but too many thoughts were jangling around in her head to allow her to do so just yet. Tentatively, she reached out a hand and touched his cheek, testing the scrape of his whiskers. Something in her chest, she guessed it was her heart, swelled with a new and nameless emotion. Lupe had promised that if she came to her husband's bed, he would love her. Although it was much too soon to make a judgment, Rachel was certain that the possessive way he was holding her now was a very good sign that Lupe had been right.

What Lupe had not warned her of, however, was that in surrendering her body, Rachel would also be surrendering her heart. The nameless emotion was not nameless at all, and Rachel knew it. It was love that now curled inside her, all sweet and warm and delicious. She loved Cole Elliot.

When had her love begun? Long before tonight, Rachel was certain. She also knew that it had not happened right away, as soon as she met him. At first she had been wary of him, but that hadn't lasted long. Had it been at the dance? No, she must have loved him by then because she now realized that her perversity in making him dance with her had been caused by her resentment that her feelings for him were not returned.

Her feelings then had been mild compared to the way she felt now. She was certain of that because she had never felt quite this wonderful before. The dance had been just the beginning, the bare beginning, the tiny seed that had sprouted and grown without her even being aware of it. She smiled into his shoulder and snuggled down into a more comfortable position. She was aware of it now, though, and come morning, Cole Elliot would be aware of it, too. On that thought, she fell asleep.

The room was still dark when Cole came awake. His arm was asleep, but when he tried to move it, he couldn't. There was something holding him. He tugged again and Rachel murmured a complaint and then he remembered. He remembered everything.

Easing his arms from around her, he fell back against his pillow in confusion. He clearly recalled what had happened. He had awakened earlier to find Rachel in his arms. She had been so willing, and he had made love to her in a way he had never made love to another woman.

He didn't have any trouble understanding why he had done what he had done. Any man would have, under the circumstances, and she was his wife, after all. The fact that she was the best he had ever had was equally understandable. She was Rachel McKinsey. That made everything different, special. He vaguely recalled thinking something very similar at the time.

No, none of that bothered him. What disturbed him, and disturbed him greatly, was wondering why she had come in here in the first place. God knew, she couldn't have wanted it, and if she had, she had certainly been keeping it a secret. How she had even known to come in here was a mystery, although after a moment's thought, he realized the old woman had probably put her up to it. The two of them were in cahoots, that was certain. A lady like Rachel never would have come up with an idea like that.

The really baffling part, though, was the way she had pretended she liked it. Such behavior wouldn't come naturally to her, and he knew the old bat had put her up to that, too. He felt like a fool for even questioning her response, knowing how any man in his right mind would get down on his knees and give thanks. But he also knew Rachel McKinsey wouldn't come to a man's bed, wouldn't give herself with such abandon, without a very good reason.

Not for one minute did he think she cared about him or anything. He'd seen the way she looked at the men she liked, Hank Oliver and the rest of his kind, and she'd never looked at him that way. No, her reason had nothing to do with any tender feelings for him, and although he couldn't really be certain without actually asking her, he had a pretty good idea just what that reason was.

She wanted to control him. It was that simple and that complicated, and it was a method as old as time itself. Ever since Adam and Eve, women had been using their bodies to keep men in line. The arrangement was only fair, he guessed. Since women didn't get the same pleasure out of sex that men did, they got something else, the security of knowing the man would be back for more. They also had a weapon they could use, could hold over his head, to gain his cooperation outside of bed. He wanted to think Rachel was so special that she would never think of such a thing, but evidently, she had. For some reason, she had decided his loyalty to the brand would not be quite enough to hold him, so she had chosen the only other sure way of tying him to her—by putting her own personal half-hitch around his tallywhacker.

Judging from the way he was feeling right now, she had succeeded, too. He wasn't touching her, couldn't even see her, and the only way he could be sure she was still there was from the scent of roses and the sound of her breathing, but he still wanted her so much he couldn't even make a fist. Considering he'd just had her a little while ago, that realization was doubly startling. Having her once hadn't even begun to scratch the itch he'd developed. In fact, having her had only made it worse.

Well, she had him now, right where she wanted him. If that had been her intention, she had succeeded admirably. If only she'd come to him openly, laid her cards on the table, he might have been able to forgive her. But this sneaking around, coming in when his guard was down, bothered the hell out of him. He felt almost betrayed somehow.

He also felt as weak and helpless as a baby, unable to understand or even name the emotions swirling inside him. Now he'd never be able to leave her, and although he had never intended to, he'd wanted that to be his own free choice, not something coerced from him by one wild night in the sack.

Anger at the way she had manipulated him helped him overcome his lustier feelings so he was able to lay there at her side without reaching for her. He lay for a long time, staring up into the darkness and marveling at the power women had. That was his last thought before exhaustion forced him to sleep again.

Rachel stirred drowsily. She didn't need to open her eyes to know it was morning, nor did she need to see to know where she was. She was in Cole's arms, exactly where she wanted to be. Smiling, she realized he was still holding her exactly as he had been when she had fallen asleep.

Unfortunately, she also realized quite suddenly that she had never gotten back up last night, and most importantly, never retrieved her discarded nightdress. Her eyes flew open at the thought, and she discovered to her relief that Cole was still sleeping soundly. She knew he wouldn't be for long, though, since he usually rose before dawn and the sun was already high in the sky. In a few more minutes she would be face to face with him, and she was certain their meeting would be a lot more comfortable for her if her face were all of her that he could see. She had to find her nightdress.

As near as she could remember, he had pulled it off over her head and tossed it aside. Slipping regretfully but ever so carefully from his very warm embrace, she glanced quickly around. The garment was nowhere on the bed. Clutching the blankets to her bosom, she sat up slowly and looked down at the floor beside the bed. The gown wasn't on her side. That meant it was either at the foot or on his side, and both possibilities put it well out of her reach. She gazed longingly at the wrapper she had hung on the bedpost last night. The wrapper would do the trick, but it was a long way away. To get to it, she would have to practically stand up, exposing her entire rear side, and if he woke up . . .

"Is this what you're looking for?"

Rachel jumped at the sound of Cole's voice, and turned ever so slowly to face him. He was awake, all right. Her movements had pulled the blankets down to his waist, and she blinked once at the sight of his bare chest. The hairs that she had felt last night chafing against her swollen nipples were golden brown, a shade lighter than the hair on his head. Her nipples started to swell again at the memories, and she clutched the blanket more tightly against her.

His arm was outstretched, hanging over the side of the bed, and when he lifted it slightly, she noticed that he held her nightdress. He'd realized what she was looking for and was offering it to her. Smiling gratefully, she reached for the gown, but he held the garment away, just beyond her grasp.

"Don't I get a kiss for it?" he asked.

Rachel frowned. This was the kind of remark a bridegroom might playfully make to his bride, except that Cole didn't look or sound a bit playful. In fact, he seemed almost angry. Maybe that was part of the game, though. If so, she'd play along. She certainly didn't mind giving him a kiss.

Her smile was a little forced because she felt so uncomfortable under the intensity of those steely blue eyes, and then she gave up the smile completely, puckering for the kiss as she leaned toward him.

He moved so quickly that she didn't even know what was happening. In the next instant, she found herself lying flat on the bed, pinned there by his weight, his hands holding her wrists in a bruising grip.

"What . . . ?" she managed to gasp into his furious face, but he wasn't interested in her questions. He had one of his own.

"Why did you come in here last night?" he asked through gritted teeth. He had tried not to ask, but he seemed to have lost all control over himself. He'd been awake since the instant she had pulled herself from his arms, and had been arguing with himself every second of that time. The sight of her with her hair tousled by sleep, the long black braid glistening like a raven's wing against the alabaster of her back, had disturbed him far more than he would have thought possible. He had tried not to think about the fact that the rest of her would be just as white, with a few very important exceptions. He had tried not to wonder if the nipples he had kissed last night would be pink or coral and if the curls on her belly were as dark as her braid.

The desire that had swelled in him had swelled his anger, too, reminding him of his suspicions about her. Without meaning to, and certainly without intending to, he had suddenly succumbed to his need to know for certain.

Rachel felt the anger emanating from every pore in the long body that was pressing against hers. The blanket had caught between them, mercifully protecting her from intimate contact with his bare skin, but she could still sense his tension. He wanted to know why she had come to him, but from all appearances, he was not at all pleased that she had. So much for Lupe's promises that he would love her.

Tears stung the backs of her eyes, but she would not weep. She had given this man everything, her body and her heart, but she would not let him strip her pride from her, force her to admit her weakness. Besides, how could she say such tender words to a man who was fairly snarling at her? How could she tell him that she had simply wanted to be his wife, his true wife, because she loved him?

"Why do you think I came?" she snapped back at him, gratified to note his slight start at her vehemence. "What was I supposed to do when you went tomcatting around after another woman? What do you think would happen if Will Statler ever got wind of that? Or our own men, for that matter?"

She was right and he knew it, but it certainly didn't make him feel any better to have all his suspicions confirmed. She did have a good reason for coming to him, and as he had known, that reason had nothing to do with how she felt about him as a man.

Suddenly, he realized that he was still holding her, still lying on her, and he felt his body stir. With a muttered curse of self-disgust, he heaved himself up and off. Throwing his legs over the side of the bed, he made a grab for the jeans he had worn the night before, and hastily stepped into them. He made for the door as he did up the buttons, knowing he had to get out of the room before he made a complete jackass out of himself and tried to make love to her again. The way she'd been glaring at him, he didn't think she'd be as cooperative as she had been last night, and he didn't want to have to add rape to his list of idiocies.

Rachel stared after him in wide-eyed amazement. What was wrong with him? How could he have changed so much between last night and this morning? What had happened to the man who had so lovingly lifted her to the heights of ecstasy? She simply could not believe that she had failed to please him, not when she remembered the violence of his response and how he had held her all night. The way he was acting, though, was as if she had hurt him in some way.

That thought teased at her. Perhaps she had made a mistake in not telling him the truth. Perhaps she should have taken the chance and revealed her feelings for him. A picture of a smug and gloating Cole Elliot flashed briefly through her mind, but she dismissed it. No, he wasn't like that, wouldn't be like that. He might not love her back, but he wouldn't mock her own tender feelings.

Would telling him change anything, though? She wasn't certain, but considering their present situation and the threat from Statler, she knew that they did not need one more problem to deal with. She had hoped to solve that problem by coming to her husband's bed, but somehow she had only compounded her troubles. If telling him the truth could smooth things over, then she would tell him.

Hastily snatching up the nightdress he had dropped beside the bed for a second time, she slipped it over her head, and scrambled from the bed. Tiptoeing to the door that he had left ajar, she peeked out.

He was standing in the front room by one of the windows, arms braced on the frame. He looked quite striking, bathed as he was in morning's golden glow. It gilded his hair and glittered off the corded muscles of his body. Her breath caught at the sight of him, and she imagined being held against that body once more. On legs that were slightly quivery, she walked softly toward him.

Sensing her presence, he raised his head. She was so beautiful standing there in the rumpled gown that it hurt his eyes to look at her. It hurt his heart, too, especially knowing that all her passion had been feigned just to salvage her pride, just to keep people from laughing at her behind her back.

"Cole?" she said, reaching out a tentative hand toward him.

182

"Don't worry," he assured her bitterly, straightening from the window to face her, "I'm not going to shame you anymore. Like they say, you've made your bed and I'll gladly lie in it. From now on, I'll do my 'tomcatting' at home, with my loving little wife."

Had she been one step closer, she might have slapped the insolence off his face, but she chose instead to run. Gasping with the unexpected pain his ugly promise inflicted, she spun on her heel and raced for the sanctuary of her room. She was developing an unpleasant habit of hiding away from the man like this, but she simply couldn't stand to be near him another minute.

Especially when she was crying, which she was, before she was even safely inside her room. Clamping both hands over her mouth to muffle the sound, she threw herself on the bed and buried her head in the pillows. Thanking God that she had not told him, had not given him another weapon to use against her, she convulsed with searing agony, sobbing out her pain into the bedclothes.

She didn't cry long, though. After a very few minutes, she suddenly sat bolt upright on the bed, scrubbing the tears from her face with the sleeve of her nightdress. So he thought she'd let him do his "tomcatting" at home, did he? Well, Mr. Cole Elliot, she thought, stiffening her spine, you've just got another think coming. Just let him try to share her bed again. He'd think he'd crawled in with a wildcat, and she'd make him wish he had! Never, *never* would he know how she really felt, that for a few brief hours she had loved him. Thank heaven she no longer did, she thought, ignoring the dull ache in the region of her heart.

Cole watched her go with very mixed emotions. He should have felt some satisfaction that his barb had struck home and that he had given her back a little of the pain she had given him, but for some reason he felt none of that. Instead, he felt a few notches lower than a cow pod. He even knew that his threat to do his tomcatting at home was hollow. He couldn't do that, and even if he could have, he wouldn't. He would never let her know how much he wanted her, never let her know the hold she had on him. Hating his weakness and wishing he could hate her, too, he returned to his room, threw on the rest of his clothes and stormed out without even bothering with breakfast.

Miles was waiting for him down by the barn. The older man was sitting on the corral fence whittling. He watched Cole's approach with mild interest.

Cole scowled up at Miles. "What in the hell are you hanging around here for? Why aren't you working?"

Miles lifted his eyebrows in mild surprise. "Did you forget? Your orders were that nobody goes out alone. I was waiting for you." He gave Cole a conspiratorial grin. "I figured you wouldn't want anyone else to know how late you slept in."

Cole squinted into the sun. Good Lord, it was the middle of the morning, almost nine o'clock. The other men would have left hours ago. He could feel the flush creeping up his neck.

"That's all right," Miles was saying, a teasing note in his voice, "I know how it can be with newlyweds."

"Back off!" Cole snarled, turning on his friend with sudden fury.

So startled that he dropped his penknife, Miles lifted his hands in mock surrender. "Sorry, *amigo.*" Exactly what he was sorry for, he wasn't quite sure, but as he watched Cole stalk over to the corral to catch a horse, he made a mental note not to tease Cole about his sex life anymore.

The two men rode out of the ranch yard in silence. After a while Miles ventured to ask, "Where are we heading?"

Unwilling to admit that he really had had no specific destination in mind, Cole quickly made one up. "I thought we'd take another look at where they split up yesterday, see if we missed anything."

Miles muttered his approval, and the two men kicked their

mounts into a lope.

Cole soon regretted skipping breakfast. His stomach was growling ferociously, and he would have killed for a cup of coffee. To top things off, he was getting a splitting headache. It was like having a hangover without the fun of the night before. Wincing at the comparison, he had to admit that he'd had the "night before" all right. Whether he could call what had happened "fun," however, he wasn't certain.

Later he blamed his rotten physical condition for the fact that he had been caught completely unawares. The first inkling he had of danger was Mile's shouted warning, "Hit the dirt!" Obeying instinctively, he threw himself from his saddle as the whine of a bullet echoed in his ears.

Chapter VI

The only cover was the small clump of mesquite from which the shots were being fired, so Cole and Miles fell flat to the ground to make themselves as small a target as possible. Their terrified horses took off.

"Are you hit?" Cole called above the roar of firing.

"No, are you?" Miles answered.

Cole took a moment to sight and fire off a shot with his Winchester, grateful that he had at least had the presence of mind to bring it along this morning. "Not yet," he replied as a bullet thudded into the ground beside him. "How many do you figure there are?"

Miles snapped off a shot with his own rifle. "I've heard two different guns," he called back.

That was what Cole had thought. At least they weren't outnumbered, even though they had been horribly outmaneuvered.

Suddenly, the return firing stopped. Cole and Miles ceased firing, too, and waited for what seemed like endless minutes.

"What do you figure they're up to?" Miles asked.

Before Cole could even think to answer, the two bushwhackers emerged from the mesquite grove on horseback, each galloping full tilt in opposite directions and firing back over their shoulders to discourage pursuit. In unspoken agreement, Miles and Cole stood and took aim, each firing a round of shots at one of the fleeing gunmen. If any of Miles's shots hit, they never knew, but the man at whom Cole was firing slumped in the saddle, and after a valiant effort to keep his seat, fell to the ground as his mount thundered away in a frantic rush.

They spent a few precious minutes catching up their own horses which had mercifully stopped their headlong flight not too far away. When they had calmed the animals enough to be able to follow, they cautiously approached the man Cole had shot, wary of some trick. Their caution was unnecessary, though. The man was dead. Cole's bullet had caught him squarely in the back and blown a hole straight through him. He had been dead before he hit the ground.

Miles swore as he slid from his saddle and stood staring down at the dead man. "You want to go after the other one?"

Cole dismounted more slowly, and when Miles looked over, the younger man was grinning. "We don't need to. We've got all the proof we need right here," he said, nodding at the dead man. "I know this fella. He works for Statler."

Miles returned his grin. "Too bad we didn't catch them rustling, too. That would cinch it."

"Let's see if we can find his horse. With any luck, he'll have a running iron on him," Cole suggested, making reference to the tool that rustlers used to change a brand.

Miles nodded. "You'd better stay here. We don't want anyone to come along and steal our friend, now do we?"

Miles took almost an hour to retrieve the frightened horse and bring it back. Then it took them some time to load the body. They decided to take the dead man directly to town, even though they had little hope that the town marshal would do anything. They would have to wire the sheriff at the county seat and wait for him to come, but at least they could set the wheels of justice in motion.

Marshal Aldrich certainly did not want to do anything.

He seemed almost frightened when Cole told his story and made his accusations against Statler.

"What makes you think this man worked for Statler?" Aldrich asked when Cole had finished. The marshal was a part-time employee who also ran the livery stable and whose main function was to round up drunks on Saturday night. Crime in Canaan seldom got more dastardly than a few rowdy cowboys.

Cole glared impatiently at the marshal. The man was small and sort of weaselly-looking, and Cole had the impression he was trying to weasel out of something now. "I've seen him before, around town. You know he works for Statler, too. What are you trying to pull, Aldrich?"

"Pull? Me? Nothing," the marshal assured him, glancing nervously out the window. Something he saw outside afforded him instant relief, however. "Well, now, here's Mr. Statler himself. He'll be able to clear all this up."

Cole and Miles exchanged a look. They both knew that it was no coincidence that Statler had been in town today.

Statler threw open the door to the marshal's office and scanned the room haughtily. "What's this I hear about you killing one of my men, Elliot?" he demanded.

"Are you going to admit that the man who ambushed me was one of your men?" Cole demanded in return.

"Ambushed?" Statler repeated with feigned surprise. "Is that the story you're giving out?"

Cole made a sound of outrage deep in his throat, but Miles placed a restraining hand on his arm. "Did this man work for you or not, Statler?" Miles asked, jerking his head toward where the body lay at the end of the room.

Statler gave the body a cursory glance. "Yeah, he worked for me," he admitted calmly.

Cole and Miles could not mask their surprise at this careless admission, and even the marshal was shocked. "He did? Are you sure, Mr. Statler?"

Statler snorted. "Of course I'm sure. I know my own men.

This fella's name was Kirk. He worked for me for almost a year." Statler paused a moment, giving a small sigh of regret. "I had to let him go last week, though. I thought he was working with the rustlers," he added with a smirk.

Miles swore softly, and the marshal sighed with relief.

"Is that the story you're giving out?" Cole mimicked acidly.

Statler seemed slightly amazed. "Are you calling me a liar, Elliot?" he inquired blandly. "You can check with any of my men. They'll all tell you the same story."

"I'll just bet they will," Cole said. Miles's hand tightened warningly on his arm, reminding him to keep his temper in check.

"Well, now, I'll wire the sheriff and let him know what happened," Aldrich was saying. "He'll want to get all the facts, I guess, ask you some questions and all that. You did say that you didn't get a good look at the other man, didn't you, Mr. Elliot?"

"That's right, Cole grudgingly admitted, cursing himself for not having gone after him when he'd had the chance. He'd been so sure that he had Statler dead to rights. They'd even found a running iron on the dead man's saddle, just as he'd suspected. He should have known that it wouldn't be over so easily.

"Sorry about all the trouble, Marshal," Statler said. "Give Kirk here a decent burial and send me the bill. He may have been a crook, but I hate to see him buried like a pauper."

"That's very Christian of you, Statler," Cole pointed out, the sarcasm thick in his voice.

Statler smiled smugly. "Yes, isn't it?" he agreed. With a nod to the marshal and one last, regretful look at the dead man, he turned and left.

Cole swore in exasperation.

"I just knew there was some explanation," the marshal said, his gratitude only too obvious. He certainly didn't want to be the one to have to arrest one of the leading ranchers in the community, especially not when it would mean taking him away from his two dozen hired guns. "I'll take care of wiring the sheriff and all that," he added magnanimously. "He'll want to ask some questions, I'm sure."

Cole muttered another curse and strode out of the office, Miles close behind him.

"Do you want to get a drink?" Miles asked when they had gone a few dozen feet down the wooden sidewalk.

Cole did want a drink, but he figured that Statler would be over at the saloon and he didn't trust himself to see the rancher again just yet. Besides, he reasoned, if he took a drink on an empty stomach, there was no telling what kind of foolishness he might get into. "Let's go to Ma's for some grub first," he suggested.

After the food and four cups of coffee, Cole was feeling much better, good enough for the reaction to set in. It always happened this way when he'd killed a man. At first he felt nothing but anger, since he had only ever killed in self-defense. The anger protected him for a time, but it never lasted long, or at least not long enough. Sooner or later he would start to remember how the man had looked, so lost and helpless in death. Other faces would swarm into his memory, the faces of the other men whose lives he had ended. Fortunately, there were not many, but there were certainly more than enough as far as Cole was concerned. He tried to remind himself that if he had failed to kill any one of them, he might not be alive today, but the older he got, the more difficult it became to convince himself that anything justified taking another human life. Sometimes he almost thought he'd rather die himself.

"I'll take that drink now," he told Miles.

They made their way in silence to the saloon, neither man feeling the necessity for discussion. They understood each other, understood what the other was feeling, having experienced it more times than either cared to remember.

Statler was in the saloon, holding court at a corner table.

Cole recognized several townsmen at the table with him. What really annoyed Cole, though, was seeing Lettie at their table. Everyone glanced up when he and Miles entered, and all conversation ceased.

"I was just telling everybody about your close call today, Elliot," Statler called out. "It's a miracle you weren't killed," he added with false sympathy.

The townsmen echoed the sympathy but with more sincerity. Cole ignored them. He was interested only in Lettie's response. The girl wouldn't look at him, though. She seemed to have eyes only for Statler. In disgust, he turned to the bar and ordered two whiskeys.

"Lettie, honey, get us another round of drinks," he heard Statler say. As Cole downed his whiskey in one gulp, he sensed her approach, smelling her perfume even before he could hear her footsteps.

She stopped at the bar beside him and ordered the drinks. Cole hazarded a glance at her, but she was staring straight ahead, as if he didn't exist. Some demon or some urge for self-destruction prompted him. "Hello, Lettie," he said.

Her head snapped around with feigned surprise. Her hazel eyes grew large and then narrowed down to sly slits. "Oh, hello, *Mr. McKinsey,*" she hissed.

Cole felt his face burn even though her taunt was uttered so softly that only he and Miles had heard it. In calling him by Rachel's name, Lettie had struck a stunning blow to his pride and simultaneously reminded him of the disastrous scene the other night in her cabin. "Lettie . . ." he began, not even sure what he was going to say.

"I wish they had killed you, you son of a bitch," she whispered vehemently.

The bartender set the tray of drinks down with a bang. "Your drinks are ready, Lettie," he said with a note of warning in his voice. He had seen enough to know trouble was brewing.

With a haughty sniff, Lettie picked up the tray. "Thank

192

you, Sam," she said and swished off.

"You can't blame her," Miles said when she was gone. "You hurt her pretty bad."

Cole sighed inwardly. Poor Miles didn't even know the half of it. "Yeah, but I'd of thought she had better taste than to take up with a skunk like that," he replied, watching Lettie's retreating back with some disgust. The girl was swinging her hips like she wanted to create a draft, and now that he noticed, she didn't have enough on to even pad a crutch. She had always dressed provocatively but never quite so scantily. She obviously didn't have a thing on under that dress, and it was equally obvious that the other men had noticed it, too. Cole felt slightly sick to think he might have inspired such behavior. He felt even sicker to think of Lettie with Statler.

After a second drink, Cole and Miles left the saloon and headed back to the ranch. Cole was determined to try to track the bushwhacker who had gotten away. He was also only too glad to get away from the saloon and the sight of Lettie flirting with Will Statler.

Lettie watched him go with regret. She'd hated herself for the things she had said to him, but at the same time, she felt certain he deserved that and much more for the way he had treated her. Now she was stuck with Statler, having attached herself to him for the discomfort she knew it would cause Cole. Not that she intended for that attachment to last, however. She knew enough about Statler to know that she didn't want to get involved with him. Unfortunately, she was afraid she might have given him the wrong idea, the idea that she was willing to do a lot more than flirt with him to make Cole Elliot mad. Now she had to disabuse him of that idea somehow.

Her rescuer appeared later in the evening in a very unlikely form. After supper, Hank Oliver strolled into the saloon. He only came in occasionally, and then seldom drank more than one or two beers "just to be sociable." He never flirted with

193

Lettie, although she had tried a time or two to tease him out of his shyness.

At Statler's insistence, Oliver sat down at their table and allowed Statler to buy him a drink. "Well, now," Statler said, looking around at Lettie and Oliver, the only two people left at his table, "looks like everybody here has got a good reason to hate Cole Elliot."

Oliver turned beet red, to Statler's booming delight, and Lettie comforted him as best she could with a surreptitious pat on his knee. He flashed her a grateful look before grinning with false bravado in the face of Statler's mirth. Lettie and Oliver sat in strained silence during most of the rest of the evening, listening to Statler discuss the way Cole had usurped control of the Circle M from poor Miss McKinsey, using the trouble with the rustlers as a smokescreen to justify his own ambitions.

If such accusations had come from any other source, Lettie and Oliver might have chimed right in, but as if they both sensed the irony of Statler pointing a finger at anyone else's misdeeds, neither could manage to make so much as a comment. Statler, however, did not even seem to notice. As if already assured of his audience's sympathies, he made no effort to elicit their response.

It was quite late when Sam announced, "Closing time, gents." The few people remaining in the bar began to shuffle out, and Statler downed the last of his drink, preparing to rise.

"I'll walk you home, Lettie," he said. It wasn't even a polite request, but more like an order.

Lettie felt a small surge of panic. Statler was the last person in the world she wanted to walk her home. She was fairly certain that he would not be content to leave her at her door, but would force his way inside. She didn't imagine for one minute that she could refuse to go to bed with him, either. If she resisted, she knew he would simply rape her. Nervously casting about for an escape, her eyes fell on

Oliver. "I'm sorry, Mr. Statler, but I've already promised Mr. Oliver that he could walk me home."

Hank was a bit startled, but he recovered quickly. Lettie had gambled on the theory that Oliver was too much of a gentleman to make her out a liar, and she had been correct. Rising to his feet, he said, "Thanks for the drinks, Will. Lettie, if you're ready?"

"I just have to get my coat," she replied, not daring to look at Statler, able to sense his rage without having to see it. Mercifully, Statler chose not to make a scene, probably having decided that fighting for the attentions of a saloon girl was beneath his dignity.

It was only a short walk from the saloon to Lettie's door. About halfway there, Lettie looked up at Oliver and smiled. "Thanks for walking me home."

He smiled back. "I really would have asked you, but I thought that you and Will Statler . . ." He let his voice trail off suggestively.

Lettie shuddered. "No, never. That man gives me the willies." Their eyes met and then they both laughed at her unintended pun. Lettie noticed once again how very handsome Hank Oliver was and wondered, not for the first time, why the McKinsey girl had passed him over for Cole. She gave him a coquettish smile, basking in the glow of his attention. It felt good to have a man look at her with pleasure. For days she had been flaunting herself in the saloon, drawing that look from every man who came in, but finding none at whom she could look back with equal pleasure. Now she had Hank Oliver.

The fact that he had courted the McKinsey girl didn't hurt, either. Lettie had lost one man to that prissy little lady, but here was her chance to get back some of her own. When they reached her front door, Lettie paused a moment before opening it, waiting to see if he would ask. He didn't.

"Would you like to come in for a while?" she inquired in her sultry voice. The shadows were too dark for him to see the look on her face, so she didn't bother to change to her sultry expression.

He hesitated a long moment and then drew a ragged breath. "Y—yes, I would," he said huskily.

Reveling in the desire she heard in his voice, Lettie enjoyed her little moment of triumph. "Good," she said, opening the door. Taking his arm, she led him inside.

Cole climbed the ranch house porch with weary steps. They'd lost the trail, which was no more than he had expected. Still, he was disappointed. One man dead and they were not a bit closer to proving Statler's connection to the rustling. The man had been smart from the very beginning. He, too, had lost cattle to the rustlers, or so he claimed. Of course, if he were the one behind it, such losses weren't very costly, and they served well to win him community sympathy. Cole should have guessed that he'd have an answer for what had happened today, too.

Not that things weren't bad enough, but now he had to face Rachel. After what had happened this morning, he had a feeling that she wasn't going to be very happy to see him. For a fleeting instant, he recalled Lettie's words and wondered if Rachel, too, would like to see him dead, if she, too, would be sorry that Kirk and his bushwacking friend had missed this morning. He stepped into the parlor and, as if he'd conjured her, he saw her standing there in the middle of the room, waiting for him.

He marveled at the joy that surged through him at the sight of her, even the sight of her glaring at him, and he wondered what it would be like to have her smile and rush into his arms to greet him with a kiss. His arms fairly ached to hold her, but he knew that wasn't going to happen, so he quashed his feelings as best he could. "Hello," he managed in a neutral voice.

Rachel knew that she should hate the sight of him, but she

196

could not seem to help feeling happy to see him nonetheless. Unwanted emotions stirred in her as she watched him remove his jacket and hat and hang them up. In spite of her anger and humiliation, she had not been able to stop herself from remembering the night before and the way he had made love to her in the darkness. The memories had assailed her all day, attacking at the most inopportune times, catching her unawares and turning her knees to jelly. Each time she had pulled herself up short, reminding herself of the rest of it. Lupe had been right about one thing: if they were ever going to get together, they'd just have to do it in the dark with no talking and no fighting. Everytime they faced each other in the light of day, they ended up quarreling.

Right now was a perfect example. He was watching her as if she were a rattler getting ready to strike, and she was wishing that she had a pair of poisonous fangs with which to do him in. How dare he look so appealing when she wanted him to look like the cad that he was?

The silence stretched between them, almost as if it were a contest of wills to avoid being the next to speak. Finally, Rachel could stand it no longer. "Did we lose any more cattle today?" she asked, knowing the answer would probably be "no," that the rustlers would probably not risk striking two days in a row.

Cole almost replied, "No, but you almost lost a husband." But that sounded too much like whining, and besides, he suspected that she wouldn't care quite enough to suit him. Instead he said, "No, but somebody took some potshots at me and Miles."

Rachel's gasp startled him. Her hand flew to her throat and her face actually paled. Something stirred in the region of his heart and he felt suddenly warmed. She did care about him just a little. At least she didn't want to see him dead.

Rachel couldn't believe the pain his news caused her. If she had had any reason to doubt the depths of her feelings for him before, those doubts were gone now. She loved him. No matter what he did or said, no matter how he treated her, she still loved him, and the thought of losing him as she had lost her father tore through her with an unbearable agony. She had an irrational urge to ask if he'd been hurt, but resisted it. If he had been hurt, he wouldn't be standing here right now, would he? she asked herself sternly, trying to get control over her faltering emotions. She didn't want him to know how his news had affected her. "Was Miles hurt?" she asked instead.

He fought down his minor irritation at the fact that she had inquired about Miles's welfare instead of his own. "No, neither one of us was," he said. There, now she didn't have to ask about him, and he'd never know whether she would have or not. "We got one of the men who ambushed us, though," he added, coming farther into the room.

"Got? You mean you captured him?" Rachel drew closer to him, too, her eyes wide with anguish in spite of her efforts to disguise her fear.

"No," he admitted reluctantly, "I mean I killed him."

Responding instinctively to the pain she sensed in him, she reached out to him, one slender hand going to his arm in a comforting gesture. But no sooner did she touch him, then she felt him flinch, felt his muscles bunch beneath her hand, and she withdrew it immediately. Did he not even want her to touch him? He hadn't found her touch so repugnant last night, she recalled bitterly. "I . . . Wh—what happened?" she stammered in an effort to cover her chagrin at being rejected.

Cole could hardly believe the surge of heat he had felt at just the simple brush of her hand. For a moment he had imagined that she was reaching out to him, that she had sensed his anguish over taking a human life. It had only been a natural reaction, though, something she would have done for anyone, and she'd certainly pulled back quick enough when she'd realized what she was doing. "Me and Miles were riding along, and two men started shooting at us. They missed. I guess they weren't expecting any trouble, so when we started shooting back, they took off. One got away. The other didn't."

Rachel blinked at the stark simplicity of his words. How briefly he managed to tell her how he had almost lost his life. How carefully he refrained from casting himself in any heroic role. She longed to throw her arms around him, to murmur the words that would dispel the clouds that shadowed his eyes. She would have, too, if she thought for one minute he would allow it. Remembering his reaction to her earlier overture, however, she held back, crossing her arms over her waist to help her fight the temptation. "Did you know him? The man you shot, I mean?" she asked.

To her surprise, Cole gave a bark of mirthless laughter. "Yeah, I knew him all right. He worked for Statler." Seeing the hope flare in her eyes, he quenched it. "It didn't do any good though. We took him to town, and Statler claimed that he'd fired the man last week because he thought he was working with the rustlers."

"And the sheriff believed him?" Rachel asked incredulously.

"The sheriff wasn't there," he informed her. "But Marshal Aldrich was only too happy to believe him. The sheriff probably will, too, when he gets here, especially after all Statler's men swear to it."

Rachel's shoulders sagged in defeat. No wonder Cole looked so discouraged. "I'm sorry," she murmured, wishing she could find the words to make it right.

They stood looking at each other for long seconds, neither of them able to think of another thing to say. Cole inhaled her delicate fragrance, and suddenly recalled what his own scent must be like after a day in the saddle. "I'll go get cleaned up for supper," he said at last.

Rachel watched him go, wishing she could follow, wishing she could close the door behind them and thus close out the outside world and all its evil. Then he would hold her and kiss her and before long nothing else would matter except the two of them, together. Rachel sighed, feeling more than a little foolish. Why should she long so for a man who had said such awful things to her just this very morning? She had no answer. She only knew that she ached for him.

Supper was an ordeal. Cole brooded and Rachel watched him, unable to find appropriate words to break the awful silence. For once even Lupe had nothing to say as she bustled about serving them. She had not even inquired about the events of the night before, although Rachel knew that she had changed the sheets on Cole's bed, so she must have seen the bloodstains. Rachel was very much afraid that Lupe had overheard their argument this morning and therefore did not need to ask any questions. Rachel should have been thankful to escape Lupe's interrogation, but at the moment she would have welcomed the distraction.

After supper, Rachel sat down before the fire and picked up some embroidery. She felt a little ridiculous, stitching bouquets of flowers onto pillowcases while her husband paced the floor smoking cigarette after cigarette and fighting whatever demons assailed him on a night like this, but Rachel needed something to do with her hands. Hoping he would, at last, turn to her, she sat there for a long time.

Finally, she could endure it no longer and excused herself. She paused at her door, looking back just in case. He had been watching her, but when she turned, he looked away, tossed the butt of his latest cigarette into the fire with a careless gesture, and began to roll another one. Sighing with regret, Rachel entered her room and closed the door.

A good hour later she was still wide awake and reflecting grimly on the vow she had made earlier about not allowing him into her bed. She shouldn't, she knew. She was a fool to even think about it, but she hadn't suspected how large and empty and cold her bed would seem after having slept with Cole, or how very much she would want him there with her.

He might yet come to her, she reasoned. He had promised, or rather, threatened that he would come to her whenever he felt the urge. What Rachel could not guess was how soon he would again feel that urge. She tried to figure out what a man's needs might be. She knew, although no one had actually told her, that the men made monthly trips to the nearest bawdy house. What she did not know was whether they went monthly because that was as often as they wanted to go or because that was as often as they could afford to go. After all, they always went on payday and never in between times. If a man had a wife, though, a wife he could go to whenever he wanted, how often would he want to?

Rachel's mind boggled at calculating such a thing. All she knew was what Lupe had told her about men and their urges and that their urges were stronger than women's. If Cole's were stronger than hers, she couldn't imagine why he hadn't come storming into her room long ago. As much as she hated to admit it, she certainly wished he would have. She wanted him more than she would have thought it possible to want anything.

She wondered if she were demented or something. After all, less than twenty-four hours had passed since her first experience. Besides which, she well knew that no self-respecting woman should desire a man who had said the things Cole Elliot had said to her. She considered herself self-respecting in the extreme and yet she did feel that desire. The more she tried to deny it, the stronger it got, until the aching and the wanting were almost painful. Cursing Cole Elliot, she snatched up a pillow and clutched it to her to ease the emptiness.

Cole glanced toward Rachel's closed door and lit yet another cigarette. Then, snarling an obscenity, he threw it, unsmoked, into the fire. It wasn't right. He knew it wasn't right. He shouldn't take advantage of Rachel. She wouldn't like it, couldn't like it. Lord only knew how she had stood all the things he had done to her last night. She wouldn't be too anxious for a repeat performance, certainly not this soon.

But he needed her. God, how he needed her. He needed to

hold her, to bury his face in the soft curve of her neck, to lose himself in her sweet body, to let her absorb the pain and the horror. Even just to hold her would almost be enough.

Almost.

Angrily he paced from the fireplace to the window where he stared out sightlessly into the darkness. Damn it, she was his wife. If he wanted her, he had every right to take her. He ought to just march right in there and climb in bed with her.

But what if she said no, what if she refused? a tiny voice whispered inside his head. What if she told you to get out and never come back? Cole's lip curled in contempt. Just let her try, he argued. She was his and he'd take her if he wanted her. Seizing the lamp, he strode up to Rachel's door.

The door flew open and Cole was there, holding a lamp and looking almost angry. His abrupt entrance startled her upright, and under his intense gaze she guiltily snatched up the pillow and clutched it to her bosom.

"What do you want?" she demanded, although her voice sounded a little too breathless to her own ears. She would have to be careful. She couldn't reveal how very glad she was he had come.

Cole closed the door behind him. "You know what I want," he said, moving toward her. In the flickering lamplight he looked almost sinister, but Rachel wasn't afraid. She felt a tingle go through her.

Knowing she shouldn't appear too eager, she surrendered to a perverse desire to goad him. "Do you think you can just come in here anytime you want and . . ."

"Yes," he said, setting the lamp on the bedside table with an authoritative clunk.

The tingle spread down her legs and up her belly. She clutched the pillow more tightly to her breast. Briefly, she entertained the thought of ordering him out, just to see what his reaction would be, just to make him angry. She did not do it, though. Too risky, she decided. He might really leave. Instead she pouted prettily as she watched his long slender fingers release the buttons of his shirt. "You could at least have . . ." she began, but the words died on a startled gasp as he peeled the shirt from his body.

Rachel went weak at the sight of that broad chest. Tearing her eyes from the sight lest she betray herself, she made a little show of putting aside the pillow she was clutching and positioning it for his arrival. If she looked at him one more second, she was going to make an absolute fool of herself and fling herself at him. Nervously, she adjusted the covers across her lap. "You could at least have knocked," she reproached him, remembering to maintain her pout.

"I didn't want to wake you," Cole replied sarcastically, and ignored her outraged cry. Turning abruptly, he sat down on the edge of the bed and began to remove his boots.

Rachel watched the play of his muscles beneath his smooth skin. Because she longed to run her hand over those muscles and feel the smoothness of that skin, she clutched the bedclothes more tightly against her. Soon enough, she told herself. Don't act too anxious or he'll know. She took a steadying breath and inhaled the odor of tobacco that clung to him. She recalled that smell from their first night, and it triggered all sorts of delicious memories.

Cole pulled off his first boot. This time he'd do it differently. This time he wouldn't shame her, wouldn't strip her, wouldn't fondle her like he had done before. He'd be quick. He'd lift her nightdress just far enough and no more, and then he'd do it. He'd just do it, that was all, he decided as he pulled off his other boot. She'd probably appreciate that, and she'd never guess how very much he wanted her. Setting his boot very carefully on the floor beside the bed, he stood and blew out the lamp.

Rachel felt a small pang of disappointment as she heard him removing the rest of his clothes in the darkness. She wanted to see all of him, to find out if the rest of him were so beautifully formed, and she especially wanted to see the desire burning in those blue eyes. There was time, though.

They would have the rest of their lives together for such discoveries. For now she would take what she could get.

Swiftly she released the tiny buttons of her nightdress and slipped it over her head. Now that she knew how these things were done, she would be ready. Besides, this time she would know exactly where her nightdress was when she wanted to retrieve it. She let it fall silently to the floor and then lay back down against the pillow, tingling with anticipation.

Naked now, Cole slipped into the warmth of the bed. She was there, her heat radiating toward him, the scent of roses enveloping him, drawing him. Still, he hesitated one moment before reaching for her. "It won't hurt this time," he said into the darkness. There, he had done what little he could to ease her fears.

Rachel's heart lurched in her chest and tears stung her eyes. Oh, how she loved him! He thought she would be afraid. She wasn't, though. She wasn't afraid of this. No, she was afraid of many things concerning Cole Elliot, but not this. "I know," she told him in a husky whisper.

Rachel turned toward him eagerly. More eagerly than was proper, perhaps. More eagerly than she wanted to, certainly.

He reached for her, desperate for the comfort she could give. She came willingly into his arms, all molten softness, molding her silken body to his. The shock of skin against skin wrenched an agonized groan from his throat. He had expected fabric and gotten flesh instead. Velvet, vital flesh. Rachel's flesh. He called her name. Or thought he did.

She heard him whisper her name as his mouth came down on hers. Her arms went around him, touching him at last, holding him at last. His skin was cool, but she would warm him. Even as she thought it, she could feel the heat that burned within him rising to the surface, coaxed there by her teasing fingers. Her own body, too, had caught fire, and it seemed that her very blood sizzled in her veins. She moved against him sinuously, stoking the fire and spreading it, teasing herself against all the hair-roughened places that teased back.

His hands were everywhere, smoothing along her back, kneading over her buttocks, drawing her against the cradle of his hips, and then sliding down to stroke her quivering thighs. His mouth was busy, too. When he had devoured all the sweetness that her lips had to offer, he moved lower, sampling of her throat, her shoulders, and then nuzzling into the tender valley between her breasts. When she could stand it no more, she shifted under his weight, forcing her aching nipple into the haven of his mouth. He soothed it eagerly and then its mate, until Rachel was panting with want.

Cole wondered vaguely how he ever could have thought that simply holding her would be enough. His questing fingers sought out her center as he told himself he only wanted to know if she was wet. He was lying, and he knew it. He wanted to touch her, wanted to feel her shiver, wanted to feel the velvet folds swell beneath his teasing touch.

When she could stand it no longer, she called out his name, not knowing the words to use to tell him of her need. He understood, and he came to her. This time it did not hurt, unless the soul-rending pleasure that she felt could have been called pain.

She enfolded him into that sweet oblivion that comes when the world narrows down to hold only two people, two people who are striving to become one. They strained together, moving in that ancient rhythm, as if by sheer determination they could break the bonds that held them separate and join their very souls.

It was different this time. No golden glow, no peaceful drifting. This time the ending was shooting stars and soaring ecstasy that made her cry out and cling to him to keep from falling into that dark void where she would be lost forever. Cole's shudders shook her then, the groan that rumbled from his chest vibrating in her own and making her cling more fiercely still. She would not let him fall either.

After a while his glorious weight became uncomfortable,

and Rachel stirred beneath him. With a small grunt of protest, he rolled off her but kept her precious body in his tight embrace. She snuggled up against him, and their sighs of contentment mingled.

And Rachel was content, desperately so. He hadn't said the words, and perhaps he did not actually love her yet, but he had come to her. On some level, at least, he needed her, just as she needed him. Knowing that would help her break through the protective shell she now realized he had built around himself. He had not been able to confide his feelings to her earlier in the evening, but he had bared his soul to her here in the dark. She would not forget, and she would use this insight to make him love her. The step from need to love was short, as she well knew, and Cole Elliot would soon take it. That was her last thought as sleep claimed her.

Cole wasn't quite asleep, and he was smiling in the darkness. He had been right to come. All those faces, those haunting faces were gone. When he closed his eyes, all he could see was Rachel.

Cole's eyes flew open. For a minute he couldn't think where he was, but then he remembered. He was with Rachel. Cautiously, he turned his head and looked at her. She was still sleeping soundly, her face peaceful in the dawn light, and he realized all over again just how really beautiful she was. He studied her face, admiring the way her dark hair framed it, the way her lashes fanned out on her cheeks, the way her nose turned up on end, the way her lips curved into a perfect cupid's bow.

He entertained a small fantasy about what would happen if he kissed that perfect cupid's bow. Her eyes would fly open in surprise and then she would smile and kiss him back. One thing would lead to another and they'd be making love again.

He didn't kiss her, though, certain that he would be a fool

206

to do so. It was bad enough that he'd come in here at all last night. Now she knew for certain just how weak he was, just how much he wanted her. And needed her. Cole Elliot, who had always prided himself on needing nothing and nobody, needed her, Rachel McKinsey, a woman.

Long ago he had determined that to need was to be weak, and so he had learned to be self-sufficient. He kept people at arm's length, knowing too well that trusting the wrong person could be fatal. Only at the Circle M had he finally felt free to bend that rule a little. First Sean McKinsey had chipped away at his barriers, winning first his respect and then his loyalty. Miles, too, had broken through. Wary at first, as wary as Cole, Miles had slowly revealed parts of himself, secret parts, as Cole did the same, until they could truthfully say that they knew each other. With that knowledge had come friendship, the first Cole had ever really known.

Finally there was the Kid. Cole hadn't asked for that, had even tried to avoid it, but the Kid was too much like him, too much like the boy Cole himself had been. He couldn't let the Kid make the same mistakes he had made, and so he had helped him along as best he could. The Kid had sort of wormed his way under the barriers, but he too had joined the small group of men whom Cole cared about, and whom he had, finally, learned to trust.

The problem was that now Rachel was in there, too. Unfortunately, Rachel was not someone Cole could trust. First of all, she was a woman. That was a mark against her right there. A person never knew what was going on inside a woman's brain, and women never did what you expected them to. One minute they'd be sweet as pie and the next they'd turn on you like a rattler. Rachel had already shown her colors, purring at him one minute and snarling the next and for no good reason that he could see.

Now, he'd made things even worse by crawling back to her after swearing that he never would. At least he hadn't made that promise to her. In fact, he was covered there, because he'd actually promised her that he would come to her. She shouldn't have been surprised.

He'd been surprised, though. He'd never suspected how uncontrolled his own response would become when he had a naked Rachel in his arms. She'd played her part well, too, almost making him believe that she liked it as much as he did. It only proved how devious women could be. There was just no telling how far a woman would go to get what she wanted, and Rachel had gone pretty far, indeed, to insure that her new husband stayed home where he belonged.

Well, she needed him, too, he reasoned. Without Cole Elliot she didn't stand a chance of winning out over Will Statler. That sort of evened the score, so he'd let her go on pretending, go on keeping him in line. He deserved it, and he had a sneaking suspicion that before he was finished with Statler, he would have earned it. He'd have to be careful, though. He couldn't come in here every night or then she'd know the truth, that he just couldn't keep his hands off her. No, he'd have to be more careful in the future. He'd discipline himself.

Starting now, he decided, slipping silently from the bed. He watched her carefully, but she did not move. Quickly, he retrieved his jeans from the floor and pulled them on. Glancing back at her to make sure she was still asleep, he tried not to notice the bare shoulder peeking out from under the covers, tried not to remember that the rest of her would be just as bare, and tried not to think about the way she felt pressed up against him.

With a silent moan, he scooped up the rest of his clothes and padded barefoot to the door. Turning the knob with care, he opened the door, and risked one last look back before closing it behind him. God, she looked just like an angel lying there.

"Bueno."

Cole jumped a foot at the sound of that voice. Spinning

around, he confronted a very smug-looking Lupe.

The old bat looked him up and down real careful like, and he felt naked as a scalded dog. He didn't like being examined as if he were a stallion she was considering for stud. "What the hell are you looking at?" he snarled, still remembering to keep his voice low so he wouldn't wake Rachel.

Lupe grinned up into his scowling face. *"Mucho hombre,"* she replied, flashing her gums at him again.

Cole hated the flush that he knew colored his face. He only hoped that he wasn't red all the way down to where the heat started. "Is my breakfast ready?" he tried, to cover his chagrin. She hadn't walked in and caught them doing it, for heaven's sake. And he had every right in the world to be in Rachel's room. There was absolutely no reason for him to feel guilty.

"Sî," Lupe said with a knowing look. "You are hungry. Riding all night make a man hungry." With a fiendish cackle, she turned away and moved toward the kitchen, her shoulders shaking in silent laughter.

Muttering a curse at the old witch, Cole strode into his own room and slammed the door, remembering too late about the still-sleeping Rachel.

Miles had filled the rest of the men in on what had happened the day before. After a solitary breakfast, Cole found them lounging around the bunkhouse porch, waiting for their orders. Cole changed his instructions slightly this time, telling the men to travel in threes from now on, instead of in pairs, and to be on the lookout for ambushes. Cole thought that the one he and Miles had run into had not been an accident, but rather something Statler had planned to demoralize his men. There was nothing that made men more skittish than to know somebody might be waiting over the next rise to take a shot at them.

He also told them the first step in his master plan.

Everyone knew that the Circle M would have to make a cattle drive this spring, rustlers or no rustlers, in order to have enough working capital to get them through the coming year. They would start the roundup and the branding now. It was a little early, but Cole knew that they'd have to take it slow, work the cattle in small bunches so they would have enough extra men to serve as guards while they worked. Then they would have to scatter each bunch, not daring to hold a whole big herd for fear the rustlers would overpower them and drive the whole shebang off to kingdom come. When they'd finished scouring the whole range, they would have to redo all their work, rounding up all the cattle again for the drive.

That would be the most dangerous part, and that's what Cole was counting on. He figured that Statler was just greedy enough to hold out for the one big steal and that he'd wait until he could get the whole herd at once. Oh, he expected Statler would badger them some, just to keep them on their toes, but he was betting all his chips on the one, final showdown. This part of the plan he didn't share with the men, however. There was no telling who might be a spy.

"Kid, I've got a special job for you," Cole said when he had given the other men their assignments. The Kid stepped forward eagerly, his ever-present smile even brighter at being singled out by his hero. "I want you to go to town today and wait for the sheriff to come. As soon as he gets there, hightail it back and let me know. Meanwhile, I want you to hang around the saloon and socialize. Let it slip that we're starting our roundup early, that we're planning a drive, but that we're being careful. Let Statler know we'll be watching for trouble, so it won't be easy to hit us until we've got the whole herd together."

The Kid's handsome brow furrowed. "You can't mean you want him to hit the whole herd? That's when we'll be the weakest. We can't protect the whole herd."

"Don't worry, I've got a plan," Cole soothed, clapping the

210

Kid on the shoulder. "And don't let on to the other men about your job. They're likely to bushwhack you when they hear you get to go to town while they'll be beating the bushes for strays."

Cole mounted up and joined the rest of the men as they rode out of the yard. He cast one last look back toward the ranch house just before it disappeared from view. Was Rachel up yet? And what had she thought when she awakened to an empty bed? Had she even thought of him at all? Feeling foolish for even wondering, he turned his attention back to the job at hand. At least he would have enough to keep him occupied today. Maybe the work would help him not to think about Rachel.

Maybe.

The Kid looked down to where Lettie walked beside him on the dark street. Impulsively, he reached out an arm, encircled her waist and drew her to him. God, she felt good. He'd wanted her for a long time, and he'd waited for her for a long time, longer than he'd ever waited for any other woman. If it had been any other man but Cole, he would simply have shot the bastard and taken Lettie for himself. Unfortunately, it *had* been Cole, the one man he had ever called "friend."

How that friendship had begun, he couldn't even remember anymore. It just seemed that from the very first day he'd come to work at the Circle M, he'd hit if off with Cole Elliot. Of course, he'd heard of him long before he'd ever come to Canaan. Everybody's heard of Cole Elliot. Then again, everybody'd heard of Kid Collins, too, when it came to that. You never judged a man on his reputation alone, though, and so the two of them had sized each other up pretty careful before making a decision.

Looking back, the Kid now knew that the two of them had a lot in common. Both had lost their mothers when they'd been still in shirttails. Both had fathers who weren't worth the powder it would have taken to blow their brains out. Both had been on their own for far too long. They hadn't known all that in the beginning, but somehow they'd still felt some kind of kinship that had drawn them together. Cole had taken the Kid under his wing, had shown him that it took a lot more than a fast gun to be a man. The Kid had repaid him by granting his undying loyalty. Now Cole knew that no matter what happened, the Kid would back his play.

All that was why the Kid had never bothered Lettie before. Many nights he had watched with burning jealousy as Cole and Lettie had gone off together into the darkness, knowing that Cole would spend the night in Lettie's arms while the Kid would ride back to the ranch alone, to his cold, lonely bed in the bunkhouse.

But things were different now. He was still a little mad about the way Cole had married Miss McKinsey without so much as a word to Lettie, but Miles had explained all that to him. Cole hadn't had any choice. Hell, if Miss McKinsey had asked him, he would have done the same thing. Any man would have. And the Kid couldn't be too mad about Lettie's being free, now, either.

Smiling to himself, he pulled her closer to his side, blessing Cole yet again for sending him to town. He had done his job well, pretending to drink too much and then getting a little free with his tongue. He had announced that he was in town to await the sheriff and bragged that while he got to sit on his duff, the other men were out working up a good case of saddle galls getting started on the roundup.

Lettie had watched him curiously all evening. The Kid figured she knew him too well to buy his act, but she was too straight to let on. She'd played along with him, pouring him drinks and listening. She'd even acted like it was the most natural thing in the world for him to walk her home, too. Of course, she'd need a new man to protect her now that she'd lost Cole. That was common sense. The possibility that she might pick him was pretty exciting. She hadn't picked him yet, though, he reminded himself as they approached her tiny cabin.

Lettie snuggled a little closer to the Kid and thought that he, at least, was honest about what he wanted from her. Not like Hank Oliver who'd walked along pretending to be a gentleman when all he wanted was to get under her skirt. The Kid would ask for what he wanted, too, not wait for an invitation. He was young, but he was a man.

Lettie sighed, her breath making a cloud of vapor in the chill night air. She was getting tired, too tired to play the game anymore. There had been too many men on too many nights and too many of them had turned out to be bastards. She wondered idly if the Kid would also turn out to be one. No, she decided. He would be one worth keeping. At least she would be safe with him. No one would dare bother Kid Collins's girl, not even Will Statler. Hank Oliver had provided her with protection for one night, but a man like Statler wouldn't be scared off by a storekeeper for long. If she wanted to be really safe, she'd have to tie up with somebody like the Kid, and she knew it.

They paused on the front stoop. Lettie turned, lifting her face to him, waiting. She did not have to wait long. His face came down to hers, and he took her mouth in a hungry kiss. After a long time, he lifted his head and asked huskily, "You're going to let me come in, aren't you?"

Lettie shifted her body suggestively against his. "Sure," she agreed coyly. "I'll fix some nice hot cocoa to warm you up."

His chuckle vibrated through her body, too. "Is that the only way you know to warm a man up?"

"Oh, I know a few others," she allowed, and then added thoughtfully, "In fact, I'll bet I can do you up so good, your ears'll melt."

The noise he made was half groan, half laugh. "You're on, lady."

"I'm *on?*" she teased, opening the door. "Is that the way

213

you like to do it?"

"That way or any way at all," he replied agreeably, and followed her inside. He closed the door behind them, and reached for her.

"Let me light the fire first," she protested, laughing.

"I know a better way to keep warm," he said, burrowing beneath her coat with both hands.

"Don't you even want the light?" she asked, working the buttons of his coat.

"The light? Mmmmm . . . yeah, that sounds nice," he murmured into the curve of her neck.

Laughing again, she pulled out of his embrace and felt her way over to the table. Fumbling in the inky darkness, she found the matches and struck one, holding it away from herself for a moment while the sulfur burned off. Then with her free hand she lifted the lamp chimney and touched the match to the wick. Replacing the chimney, she shook the match out and then turned back to face the Kid. He had the funniest look on his face.

"You're so beautiful, Lettie," he said softly.

The compliment warmed her in places that had been cold for a long time. She knew it wasn't true, of course, and she'd been in rooms like this with too many different men to be affected by mere flattery. What had touched her about the Kid's remark had been the absolute sincerity of it. Whatever the truth might be, the Kid believed she was beautiful. For the first time in her life, she actually felt like she was. She smiled at him.

"You're not so bad yourself, cowboy," she said quite honestly, slanting him a provocative look.

She had expected him to come to her then, but he held back, and she realized that he had grown suddenly shy. She even thought he might have been blushing. Knowing instinctively that it would never do to let him think she had noticed, she rubbed her hands together briskly to warm them and said, "I think I'll light that fire now. How about

214

a drink?"

He did not reply at first but simply watched her go about the motions of building and lighting a fire in the small stove that served for both cooking and heating in the tiny cabin. When she had finished, she once more turned to look at him, giving him an inquiring glance. "Did you want something to drink?"

"Hot cocoa?" he asked, slanting her a grin.

She almost sighed with relief. He had recovered from his momentary bashfulness. She grinned back at him. "I had something a little stronger in mind."

The Kid shook his head. "I'm feeling strong enough. Come over here." He beckoned with his hand.

Lettie hesitated only an instant before going to him. She would have to be careful. The Kid was young and vulnerable. If things did not go well between them, he might blame himself, might think he wasn't man enough for her or some other such nonsense. She could not risk that. She needed him, needed his protection. She stepped into his arms.

They kissed for a long time while tongues mated and hands groped. As the room warmed, they shed their coats, letting the garments fall unheeded to the floor while the two of them continued to nuzzle. When Lettie sensed that he was losing control, she drew slightly away and took his hand, leading him toward the bed. He followed willingly.

She undressed for him then, letting each piece of clothing slide seductively away until she stood naked before him. He groaned out her name, but before he could move toward her, she reached up and began to unbutton his shirt. By the time she had opened it, his breath was coming in shallow gasps and his whole body was trembling. When she had opened his longjohns as well and run her hands over the smooth plane of his bare chest, he could stand it no more, and he hauled her into a bone-crushing embrace.

"You're freezing," he whispered into her hair, running his

215

hands over her back and buttocks.

"I thought you'd warm me up," she replied.

She was a little startled when he pushed her away.

"Get under the covers," he commanded, pulling back the bedclothes. "Right now, before you freeze off something important."

"Yes, sir," she said around a smile, sliding between the icy sheets. She shivered deliciously and then pouted. "It's cold in here, too."

"I'll only be a minute," he promised, sitting down beside her to pull off his boots. He actually took far less than a minute to finish undressing, and when he straightened from stepping out of his longjohns, Lettie gave a delighted gasp.

"Kid! You should have warned me!" she told him with mock horror, making him grin. The truth was that she was grateful. She wasn't likely to have any trouble keeping the Kid's interest, at least not tonight. For a minute there, earlier on, she had been afraid that he had held her in so much awe that it would affect his performance. Her fears had been groundless, though. Everything was going to be just fine.

It was, too. What the Kid lacked in expertise, he made up for in enthusiasm, and although Lettie was a little worried that she might have some bruises tomorrow, she was pleasantly surprised to discover that she had almost enjoyed the encounter.

Afterward he held her tenderly, stroking her hair and planting tiny kisses on her face. Lettie savored the moment. She could never remember being held like this.

"Was it . . . I mean, did you like it?" he asked just as she was about to drift off to sleep.

She came alert instantly, sensing his insecurity. It wouldn't be enough for him to pleasure himself. He needed to know that he had pleased her, too. One part of her brain registered the fact that this was of paramount importance to her because it proved he cared about her and virtually assured her future protection. Another part of her simply delighted in the heady sensation of being loved.

"Mmmmm," she purred, moving against him. "You're quite a man, Kid Collins. I wonder how I ever got so lucky."

She heard his sigh of relief and felt him quicken against her as she had guessed he would.

"Lettie?" he asked, renewed need thick in his voice.

"Come here," she ordered. "I'm still cold. I don't think I got enough of you before."

"That's funny, I'm still cold, too," he said, moving over her again.

While the Kid was getting warmed up, Cole was trying to cool down. He'd worked himself nearly to death today in an effort to attain complete exhaustion. He'd thought surely if he were tired enough, he would be able to fall right to sleep. He'd been wrong, though. He wasn't falling right to sleep, and he had to suffer the added torture of knowing just exactly what . . . and who . . . would put him right to sleep. And knowing she was in the next room.

The whole evening had been an ordeal. He'd decided to act like nothing had happened, and a good thing he had because that's exactly how Rachel had acted. Oh, she'd given him a little smile when he'd first come in and said hello and everything. He guessed it was easy enough for her to smile, though, knowing she had him right where she wanted him. Then she'd watched him all evening, almost like she was waiting for something. What it could have been, he couldn't imagine, but finally she'd gone on to bed.

He had used up all his willpower to let her go alone, too. It was almost funny. For some reason he'd imagined he would be able to let a whole week go by before making love to her again. A week had seemed like the proper length of time. Short enough that he wouldn't go stark raving mad and long enough that she wouldn't get the idea he couldn't stay away.

Yes, it should have been exactly the right amount of time.

He'd only gone to see Lettie once a week and sometimes even less often. Of course, he hadn't had to see Lettie every day, or eat with her or watch her move around the house or smell her perfume in every room. Hell, he could even smell it in his own room. For one wild second he wondered if maybe that witch Lupe had sprinkled some in his bed to drive him crazy. Then he decided it was more than likely just his own imagination. He was probably perfectly capable of driving himself insane without any help from the old woman.

Sighing, he stared up into the darkness. Only six more days and then the week would be up, he told himself grimly.

Rachel lay in her own bed staring at her own darkness. She had vowed to be a good wife to Cole Elliot, but she had never imagined the job would be so undemanding. Oh, last night had been wonderful. The mere fact that he had come to her had been more than enough, but she also knew he had come because he had needed her. She wasn't exactly certain how the physical act of making love met the needs and soothed the pain she had sensed in him, but she knew it had, and that was all that mattered.

When she had awakened to an empty bed, she had known he had purposely slipped out without waking her. Whether he had been too shy to face her or hesitant about revealing his feelings or afraid of another argument like the one they'd had after their first night or whether he had just been trying to be considerate, she had no idea. Somehow she hadn't been surprised, though. She had suspected he would be gone.

She had also suspected he would be wary when he came home again. She had tried to act normally, although exactly what was "normal" for their marriage was a little difficult to ascertain, but her smiling welcome had bounced right off him. He still wasn't ready to open up to her, to let her see past the tough exterior. What he didn't know, what he didn't even suspect, was that it was far too late to hide from her. She knew him now, understanding for the first time why the Bible used the word "know" to indicate sexual relationships.

Yes, she knew him intimately, in the darkness with all barriers cast aside.

He could pretend if he wanted to. He could convince even himself that he was hiding his true feelings from her. She'd seen the longing in his eyes tonight when he'd looked at her, though. She knew how much he wanted to be in her bed right now. Smiling a little at the foolishness of his stubborn pride, she acknowledged that it was also something she could not fight. He'd just have to learn for himself that whatever he imagined he would be giving up by falling in love with her wasn't worth holding on to. She only hoped he figured it out soon.

Chapter VII

"Hot Iron!"

Cole could hear the call from where he sat his horse, even though the men doing the branding were nothing more than tiny specks in the distance. He studied the scene below, the milling herd, the choking dust, the men going through the motions with practiced ease. The man on horseback cut out an unbranded calf from the herd, separating it from its mother, and then roped it. Dragging the calf to the fire, he turned it over to a man on foot who threw it to the ground and called for the branding iron. Yet another man applied the brand while the second cowboy used his knife to mark the calf's ear and then, if the calf were a male, moved to castrate it with one swift swipe. After dabbing some creosote dip on the cuts to keep the flies away, he released the calf which ran, bawling, to find its mother.

Repeated with endless monotony, the process took on the structure and grace of a dance. The mooing, bawling herd provided a discordant accompaniment.

Cole watched intermittently, often swinging his gaze to study the surrounding landscape for intruders, and then looking back to check the positions of the other sentries. He'd had to work roundups with guards before, in other places at other times, but never had his vigilance seemed so vital. He supposed that was because this time he had a vested interest in seeing that this cattle made it safely to market under their original ownership.

Smiling grimly, he considered his new sense of responsibility. It was ironic how often in years past he'd been grateful not to have such responsibility, how often he had been only too glad to take his pay and ride away when the fighting was over. He had loved the freedom and thrived on the excitement of constant danger. As soon as the threat of that danger passed, he had become bored. This time, however, he could hardly wait for the danger to pass. This time, the outcome mattered far more than just being certain of getting paid off in the end. This time the outcome would affect Rachel.

Cole sighed at the thought of her. In spite of his resolution, he simply had not been able to stay away from her. Once a week, ha! He'd been a fool to ever set such an impossible goal for himself. He was doing good to keep it down to twice a week, even with her still sleeping in the other room.

Reaching into his vest pocket, Cole pulled out his Bull Durham sack and began to roll himself a smoke. Whenever he thought about their sleeping arrangements, he needed some distraction. How on earth they'd ever gotten into separate bedrooms and why he'd felt like he should go along with the idea, he would never know. Oh, he could have just told her to move her stuff because she was bunking in with him from now on, but for some reason that never seemed like the right thing to do. She already had a pretty good notion of how much he wanted her. If he turned to her every night, the way he wanted to and the way he would if she slept in his bed, she would know for certain. He simply could not give her that power over him.

Things would be different if she wanted him, too, of course, and sometimes in the dark of night when she was warm and soft in his arms, he could almost convince himself that she did. Then dawn would come and with it the

222

reminder that she was only doing her duty to keep him home. Not that he'd ever be going out for it again. No, she'd ruined him there. In his younger days, he'd thought that sex was the same no matter who the woman was, but now he knew different. Making love with Rachel was like nothing he'd ever experienced. Separate bedrooms or not, he guessed he was a lucky man.

Or he would be if Rachel felt the same way about him. Cole took a deep drag on the cigarette he had just lit and pondered the potential for such a situation. He couldn't expect her to fall in love with him, of course, not with a man who'd never had a home, who made his living selling his gun, who could barely read and write. That would be asking a little much. But maybe he could win her respect.

Cole straightened in his saddle. Of course. Why hadn't he thought of it before? In fact, she probably already respected him. Why else would she have chosen him to be her husband? She knew he was the best man to lead a fight. All he had to do now was prove her right.

All he had to do now was beat Statler.

Squinting into the distance, Cole tried to decide if he'd seen movement. With a curious sense of disappointment, he realized that he hadn't. Suddenly, he was itching for a confrontation with Statler and his men. Until now, he had been glad that Statler's harassment had been fairly minor, limited to an occasional potshot taken when they'd ridden into an arroyo to collect some steers or when somebody'd gotten separated from the rest of the men. Cole knew a surge of excitement at the thought that from this time on, they could expect an attack at any time. The branding would be over in a day or two and then they would begin the full gather of the cattle.

When Statler came, Cole would be ready for him. This was a fight Cole intended to win. He owed it to Mr. McKinsey for taking him in and giving him a home and then making him a friend. He owed it to the Circle M and the men because they had been entrusted into his care. But most of all, he would fight for Rachel. Winning would mean winning her, winning his rightful place in her life. And he would win. He had to.

Rachel looked up from the book she had been trying to read for the past two hours, and for the tenth time in as many minutes tried to stare a hole in the office door. She had been sitting in the parlor all evening waiting for Cole to finish his meeting with Miles, and she was just about ready to march in there and demand to know what they were discussing. She had already guessed that it was important.

From what Cole had told her, she knew they had finished with the branding. The next step, of course, was to organize a trail drive, but Rachel had a sneaking suspicion Statler wasn't going to let them simply drive her cattle peacefully away for sale. He had already harassed the men on several occasions during the branding. No one had been hurt, but shots had been fired, and the men all had an edge of wariness about them. They knew the trouble had just begun. Cole and Miles would be planning for the attack they expected.

At long last she heard the outside door open and close and she knew Miles had left. A few more minutes passed, and Cole came out. Rachel closed her book and waited expectantly.

Cole seemed a little surprised to see her still sitting there. It was very late, after all, but didn't he know she would wait up for his report? "What are your plans?" she asked.

Now he really was surprised, and Rachel knew that once again he had underestimated her. He was obviously having a hard time believing that she had guessed what his confab with Miles was about. "Plans?" he hedged, sitting down in a chair opposite her with an air of caution. Rachel tried not to notice how his worn jeans hugged his thighs or the way his shoulders moved under his shirt when he reached up and pushed the shock of hair off his forehead.

"Yes, plans," she echoed impatiently. "What are you going to do to stop Statler?" That is what you and Miles were talking about in there, isn't it?"

She saw a tiny glint of admiration sparkle in those blue eyes. Irritation tweaked at her because she knew he had been amazed at her perception. "We're going to round up a herd, just like we were really going to run a drive north," he explained. "Then we're going to wait for Statler to try to rustle it."

It sounded so simple. Rachel lowered her eyes and ran a fingernail over the spine of the book that still rested in her lap. Too simple. Sitting around waiting to be attacked by a gang of murdering rustlers was not a healthy thing to do. It was, instead, a rather dangerous thing to do. They would have no way of knowing exactly when they would be hit or where or even how many attackers to expect. Hampered by a large herd of nervous cattle, her men would be sitting ducks. Her man would be a sitting duck. The thought settled in her stomach like a lead weight.

Rachel slowly raised her head. The blue eyes she loved so well were watching her carefully, waiting to see what her reaction was. She tried not to show him how frightened she was. "When are you going to start the roundup?"

"Tomorrow," he said. The word hung in the air like an ugly cloud. "I figure it'll take a couple-three weeks to finish the gather," he added. "We'll have to sleep out, to guard the herd."

Sleep out. Now Rachel understood the hungry way he was watching her. He was telling her that this was the last time he would be sleeping at home for a while. In spite of the skirmish that fear was holding with her nerves, she almost smiled. The man was an absolute caution. Here he was, planning to go out tomorrow to risk his life for her, but the thought uppermost in his mind was that he wanted to make love with her one last time before he left. And he wasn't even

225

going to come right out and say so.

As if she'd mind. Had she ever done anything to make him think she would? She knew that she hadn't. In fact, she had done everything she could think of—within the bounds of common decency—to let him know that she didn't mind one bit. Still he persisted in acting as if her bed were some sacred shrine that he could only visit on occasion. And after the second time when she had told him he should have knocked, he even did that. Sometimes Rachel thought she might cheerfully strangle him.

At other times she toyed with the idea of simply moving into his room, but something within her rebelled at the thought. She knew that he didn't quite trust her and might very well suspect her motives, and to tell the truth, she didn't quite trust him either. He had never, not even in the heat of passion, said anything to indicate that he returned her love. Although she felt sure that he cared for her, she couldn't do anything so brazen as forcing herself on him until she had some proof. She had used up just about all the brazenness she possessed in getting her marriage consummated in the first place. In fact, she decided with perversity, if he wanted to bed her tonight, he was going to have to say so.

Cole watched her closely, wishing he could hear what was going on inside that pretty little head and trying to decide whether she had gotten his hint or not. Maybe he should have made the plan sound more dangerous, maybe tried to scare her. The thought of a tearful Rachel clinging to him was a little repugnant, though. And he didn't want her coming to him out of gratitude, that was for damn sure.

He knew he was a fool to care what her reasons might be, but he did. Even as he let his wayward gaze stray to the bodice of her dress and allowed his wayward imagination to recall just how those luscious mounds felt under his hands and mouth, he knew that it mattered very much why she came.

Rachel watched him closely, wondering what was going

on inside his head. He was probably calculating how much longer until she would go off to bed and how much longer after that until he could follow her. Oh, no, Cole Elliot, that's not the way it's going to be tonight, she thought to herself. Not only would she not make it easy for him, she would make it very difficult.

"I guess you're going to have a busy day tomorrow," she ventured innocently. He did not reply, and Rachel pretended not to notice the suspicious way his blue eyes narrowed. "You'll need to get a good night's sleep, so don't feel that you have to wait up for me. I'll just sit here and read for a while. Good night," she told him sweetly. Then she ostentatiously opened the book she still held and began to read.

Cole sat there a full minute in stunned silence as he fumed over the fact that he had been dismissed. Just what in the hell was she trying to pull? For a second there he had thought that maybe she hadn't understood what he wanted, but he quickly dismissed that thought. She wasn't stupid, and she wasn't innocent either. No, she was doing this on purpose, the scheming little . . . and then he noticed something. Something very peculiar. "Rachel," he murmured menacingly.

Delicious little shivers danced over her body, but she schooled her expression to blandness. Steeling herself to meet those glittering blue eyes, she peered cautiously over the top of her book. "Yes?" she inquired, pleased that her voice was not quivering as the rest of her was.

Cole rose slowly from his chair and crossed the space between them with two very deliberate steps. He stopped just inches from her knees.

Rachel slowly raised her dark brown gaze to meet his piercing blue one, and by the time she could see his face, her heart was pounding wildly, so wildly she thought he must hear it, too. She knew she should speak but her throat felt paralyzed, so she just stared.

Cole glared down at her for a long moment. Then he

reached out and grasped her book. With painstaking care he turned it over and returned it to her hands, right side up.

Heat flooded to her face, but not from embarrassment. "Oh, my," she said without the slightest trace of sincerity, and gave him a wicked and very unrepentant smile.

He made a noise that was part growl, part groan. With one hand he pulled the book from her hand once more and tossed it aside. With the other, he simultaneously grasped her wrist and jerked her to her feet, straight into his arms.

Rachel made a startled sound but it was muffled by his mouth, which ground down on hers with punishing force. She returned his kiss with equal force, sliding her arms around his neck and clinging as if she would never let go. He was clinging, too, even more fiercely, until she had to rise up on her toes to meet him. His hands clasped her buttocks, feeling for her softness beneath the layers of petticoats and cradling her against the heat of his desire.

She heard his moan and echoed it, sharing his frustration at the barriers that thwarted their efforts to get closer. Her arms were around his neck now, and she moved against him with an urgency that he matched.

Cole groaned again, knowing that he had to have her and soon. There was no time for niceties or rituals. Without any conscious decision to do so, he scooped her up into his arms and headed for the bedroom. She pulled her mouth away from his, and he thought she smiled before she snuggled down against his shoulder. He almost missed a step when she started nibbling on his neck, and when her tiny teeth closed over his earlobe, he actually stumbled.

"Careful," she murmured into his ear, her warm breath sending shivers down the entire length of his body. He whispered a silent prayer that his legs would continue to function until he got her to the bed, knowing that it would take a small miracle.

Without hesitation, he entered his own room and kicked the door shut behind him. Tonight he wanted her in his bed, the way it had been the very first time. Tonight he didn't want to feel like an intruder or a supplicant. Tonight was his night.

In the total darkness, he moved instinctively to the bed and they tumbled down together in a tangle of arms and legs and petticoats. For a while they simply cuddled and kissed, fully clothed. Cole explored every inch of her mouth, swirling his tongue in the moist, sweet cavern, drinking of her essence as if that were enough to satisfy the craving that he felt.

Rachel let him drink, even though it wasn't enough, not nearly enough, and she teased him, her own tongue tasting and tangling. Meanwhile, his hands were questing, roaming over the breasts that were still so tightly bound, and rummaging among her skirts to find the secret, sensitive places. Then he started on her buttons, but either he was out of practice or else just a little bit clumsy in his haste. After a moment of struggle, his head lifted and she could imagine him squinting, trying to see in the darkness to do the job that was so vital. His muffled curse told her that he was having no success.

"Need some help?" she asked, brushing his hands aside and making short work of the tiresome buttons that ran the length of her bodice.

He didn't move. He was very close, one leg thrown over hers, and she could hear every rasping breath he took, could almost imagine that she heard the beating of his heart. But perhaps it was only her own she heard. He couldn't see what she was doing, could only hear the rustle of the cloth, so she swiftly opened her camisole as well, baring the breasts that ached for his touch.

Still he waited, poised over her so that the heat of his body enveloped her like an invisible cocoon. She longed to take his hand, to draw it to her, but she lacked the courage to be so bold. Instead she reached out for his own buttons and opened his shirt. The instant her fingers touched the material and he realized her intent, his breath caught with a rasp. He held it for the small eternity while she worked her way down the placket, and then released it with a groan when her silken hands reached inside the opening to draw him close.

First hands to chest and then breast to chest and mouth to mouth. They came together as if the flesh of their bodies were irresistibly compelled to join. For delicious minutes they brushed skin to skin, smooth satin against furred velvet, until that, too, became too much and not enough.

There was no help for it. They had to separate long enough to free themselves from all constrictions. Struggling, grappling with boots that would not give and bows that knotted and sleeves that stuck, they tussled side by side, bumping knees and elbows, testing each other's progress with hands that brushed not quite by chance.

At last they both lay still, each telling the other by their complete silence that they were ready. For several heart-beats, neither of them moved. Each listened to the other's breathing; each imagined, drawing out this delicious moment of anticipation on gossamer threads of willpower until nerve endings fairly crackled from the strain.

Rachel wanted him, ached from wanting him, but she dared not move. This was a contest, one in which the loser would win, and she very much wanted him to win. Silently, she called his name, called him to her. Her heart wept within her, tears of joy and wonder that gathered in those secret places, waiting for him.

"Rachel." Her name on his lips was both entreaty and command, triumph and surrender, and he did not wait for her response. Even as the word escaped, his arms enfolded her, drawing her to him.

In the thundering silence where mere words cannot be heard, they came together in a communion far more intimate. Hands and lips stroked and caressed; bodies molded together, seeking, seeking. He probed and prodded, searching for a refuge. She opened, offering him sweet

230

sanctuary. She gave him that mysterious refuge, and he returned an offering that was life itself. Together they climbed the heavens and touched the fleeting glory that unites. Even more together, they sank back to earth, bound to each other in the fusion of shared ecstasy.

Much later, sated and snuggled under the covers in the haven of his arms, where she would have believed herself safe from such assaults, Rachel tasted fear again. For a short, blissful time, she had been able to forget the danger that lay ahead. Now, once again, she remembered.

"Cole?"

"Hmmm?" His muttered response was more reflex than comprehension.

"Please be careful," she whispered into the warmth of his shoulder. Tears stung her eyes and laced her voice. "I love you so."

His arms tightened around her for a moment and then relaxed, but he did not respond.

In the morning, he was gone.

Seventeen days of ornery steers and flies and saddle sores and rocky beds. Seventeen days of waiting and still no sign of Statler. And seventeen days without Rachel. Cole was feeling about as sociable as an old sow grizzly stuck in a rusty bear trap when the Kid rode up to him in camp that afternoon.

As usual, the Kid was grinning ear to ear. His golden hair wasn't quite as pretty as he liked to keep it, owing to the long hours he'd been working lately, and his clothes were dusty and sweat-stained, but he still managed to look dapper enough to set Cole's teeth on edge. What in the hell did the young pup have to look so happy about?

The Kid swung one leg over his saddle horn and pulled out his Bull Durham sack. "A fellow could get mighty tired of looking at the back end of a steer," he commented cheerfully as he rolled himself a smoke.

"Kicking won't get you anywhere unless you're a mule," Cole informed him sourly, squinting out at where the herd grazed peacefully.

"You think this is a good place to make a stand?" the Kid asked, ignoring Cole's grouch.

"Good as any," Cole grunted, giving a cursory look around. He'd chosen the camp specifically because it was on high ground and had lots of cover.

"Hope you're right," the Kid remarked with elaborate casualness.

Something in his voice brought Cole's head around.

The Kid's grin broadened. "Francesco's been signaling for five minutes," he said, nodding in the direction of one of their sentries.

Sure enough, a series of mirror flashes told him that about fifteen men were approaching rapidly. "Why the hell didn't you say something?" Cole shouted, running for his horse.

"I thought I just did," the Kid remarked to no one in particular, since Cole was already gone.

Cole began shouting instructions that were largely unnecessary. The other men had also seen the signal and were moving into the positions Cole had previously assigned them. The cook began unloading spare rifles and ammunition from the chuck wagon and stacking them where they could be easily reached. Watching all the preparations with satisfaction, Cole checked the loads in his own rifle.

This was what he'd been waiting for, and he felt his blood surge with the familiar excitement. This was his chance to prove himself to Rachel once and for all, to show her that she had made a good choice. He pulled up at his own appointed station and swung down from his horse. Tying the animal securely to a scruffy bush, he crouched down in the rocks to wait, his eyes scanning the horizon.

The shots came from his left, much sooner than he had expected and from the wrong direction. Swinging around, he took in the whole scene. It had been a trick, a lousy trick, but it was too late now. Even as he grudgingly acknowledged the brilliance of Statler's plan, he cursed and dove for cover.

One lone rider had sneaked past their sentries. Waving what appeared to be an animal skin—Cole guessed it to be a freshly killed wild cat of some kind—that rider was sending the herd into a panicked run, *right toward the camp!*

One of his men had spotted the rider and fired, but it was like trying to stop an avalanche. The ground shook as the thundering hooves churned the ground, and faintly, as if from a great distance, Cole heard the pop of more gunshots. Statler and his men had arrived. They would finish off whoever was left after the stampede. Yes, it was a brilliant plan.

Seventeen days, Rachel thought with disgust as she pulled the brush through her thick, dark hair. At least the day was over, though, and she could go to bed now. Once she fell asleep, a process that was becoming increasingly difficult with each passing day, the hours would fly by and then she would begin the horrible waiting all over again.

The odd numbered days were the hardest. Every other day, Cole sent two men from camp to spell the two men he had left guarding the ranch. This system served the dual purpose of providing her with news on the progress of the roundup and of giving each of the men a periodic rest. Unfortunately, Cole himself was never one of the two men who came.

She should have known it would be like that. Cole would be thinking about the welfare of his men, but would never consider taking a day off for himself. No, he had to be there in case Statler's men attacked. Even Miles was allowed a turn at leisure, but not Cole.

Sighing, Rachel laid her brush down and rose from her dressing table. It was very late. Maybe tonight she'd be able to fall asleep quickly. She was just untying the sash of her robe when she heard the horses.

At first she thought she was imagining it. Running to the window, she peered out into the darkness but could see nothing. Waiting, her heart pounding a tattoo against her ribs, she watched. Finally, they were there, men and horses, filling the ranch yard. She could hear them more then see them. Their shapes made darker patterns in the already dark night, and they kept their voices low. Someone lit a lantern, but she could not identify anyone in the grotesque shadows that it cast.

Was the front door locked? Not that it would make any difference, of course. If they wanted in, they would break the door down, but still she raced to the front room to see. She was too late. She could hear the tramp of boots across the porch, an unfamiliar step, and knew that he would reach the door before she would.

"Who is?"

Lupe's voice came to her from the shadows at the far side of the room.

"I don't know," she replied, her voice trembling slightly. If she only had a gun . . . A gun! She did have a gun! The derringer was lying on the table beside her bed. For one agonizing second she cursed herself for forgetting it, but even before she could think to go after it, the door opened and he was there.

"Cole!"

Flinging herself into his arms, she felt him stagger slightly from the impact, but he recovered instantly and his arms closed around her. He smelled of horses and sweat, but she didn't care. He felt good, so solid and so strong. "Thank God you're all right!" she whispered fervently against his chest.

Cole himself was thanking God as he stood holding her, running his hands over the silken length of her hair and inhaling the fresh scent of roses. This is the way he had dreamed it would be, Rachel in his arms and glad to be there.

He'd come home. Closing his eyes, he savored the sensation.

After a long time, he thought to tell her why he was here, although he knew from her reaction that she must have guessed. He pushed her slightly away so that she looked up at him. Framing her face in his hands, he gave her the news he knew she had been waiting for: "It's all over."

She had guessed as much, but hearing the words spoken aloud gave her a wondrous joy, and she smiled up at him. The smile lasted only a second. In the faint light that shone from her bedroom doorway, she now saw the lines of fatigue that etched his face and noticed for the first time the way his shoulders sagged and remembered once again the lateness of the hour. She remembered, too, the unfamiliar footsteps she had heard, Cole's pace slowed by fatigue.

"You must be exhausted," she decided, sliding reluctantly from his arms. "Sit down, I'll fetch a light," she told him, scurrying off to retrieve the lamp from her room.

When she returned, she saw that he had removed his hat and the heavy leather vest he had been wearing and had slumped down in the wing chair by the fireplace. Setting the lamp on a table nearby, she went to him. "Can I get you anything? Are you hungry?"

The clank of a tray hitting a tabletop made them both jump. Lupe eyed their reaction with disdain. The tray contained a steaming cup of coffee and a plate with three thick sandwiches on it. "Food," she explained unnecessarily.

Rachel gave her a grateful smile. In the excitement, she had forgotten all about Lupe, but as usual Lupe had not forgotten about them. Once she had seen that it was Cole who had come, she had gone about her business.

Cole gratefully picked up the coffee and took a long swallow. Then his startled gaze found the old woman grinning that toothless, knowing grin. The witch had put a shot of whiskey in the coffee, bless her shriveled little heart, and he found himself grinning back. "Thanks," he mumbled, picking up one of the sandwiches and thinking maybe, just maybe, Lupe wasn't so bad after all. Lupe muttered something incomprehensible and disappeared again.

Rachel waited patiently while Cole disposed of the sandwich in a few giant bites, and then she could stand it no more. "What happened?" she demanded, pulling over the three-legged footstool and perching on it.

Cole chewed the last bite slowly and then washed it down with some coffee, enjoying the sight of her. She looked almost like a little girl, squatting on the stool like that, with her hair loose and her knees drawn up and her eyes all big and expectant. Almost, but not quite. He would have preferred to have her sitting in his lap, but he was much too dirty for that. For now, he'd have to be satisfied with just looking at her. With a small sigh of regret, he began his story.

"Statler tricked us. We had sentries out, and one of them spotted Statler and his men heading for us from the north. We were all ready for them, except, like I said, he tricked us. They'd sent one man around behind the herd. He had a freshly killed cougar skin—we found it later—and he waved it at the herd."

Rachel's gasp told him he did not have to explain. She knew what the scent of a wild cat would do to a herd of cattle.

"They ran right over our camp, and then Statler and his men rode in right behind them," he continued, the evenness of his voice conveying the horror of it more vividly than melodramatics could have done. "I reckon Statler figured they'd just throw some dust over what was left of us and ride off with the herd." Rachel nodded her understanding, wondering how such a perfect plan had gone awry.

"Luckily, all the men had their horses nearby, and some of them managed to climb on and ride out the stampede. The rest of us just hunkered down and covered our heads."

"You were in the middle of it?" Rachel asked, fear clawing at her heart even though she knew that he could not have been hurt since he was sitting right here in front of her.

He nodded, his mouth stretching into a mirthless grin. "I

was in some rocks, so I was pretty safe. They went all around me, though. One even went right over top." He made an arching motion with his hand to illustrate the flight of the steer and watched in fascination as her dark eyes grew round. He'd never told a story like this to such an appreciative audience, and he began to warm to the task.

"Somehow, I reckon because we were all dug in for the fight, not one of our men got trampled. Statler wasn't figuring on that, though, so he and his men just came riding into our camp as bold as you please."

Rachel leaned forward on her stool and placed one hand on his knee. Her eyes never left his face, so he was pretty sure she didn't even know she'd done it. He did, though. Her tiny hand was burning a hole right through the denim and up his thigh. He had just realized that under that robe she was only wearing her nightdress and under that he knew she'd be wearing only Rachel. Swallowing past a sudden tightness in his throat, he tried to sound normal as he continued his story.

"None of our men even knew if anybody else was still alive, but almost like we'd planned it, everybody just reared up and started shooting. We got them in a crossfire, so even though there were only four of us left, it was like shooting fish in a barrel. They panicked and took off in all directions, the ones who still could, but our men—the ones who'd ridden away from the stampede—swung back and picked them up. A few of them got away, but the ones that didn't won't be rustling anybody's cattle again."

There, that told her that they were all dead. He wouldn't bother to explain that not all of them had died from gunshot wounds, that he and the men had hanged the survivors. She already looked shocked enough.

He did have some important news for her, though. "We found out who killed your father." He watched the pain cloud her eyes for a moment before she overcame it, waiting bravely for the information. "It was that fellow Kirk. You

237

remember, the one who ambushed me and Miles? The one who got killed?"

Rachel nodded. "How did you find out?"

Cole shifted uncomfortably, not wanting to explain exactly how they had managed to obtain the information. "We talked to some of the men who didn't . . . who were still alive. Kirk had some help, a couple others, but they're all in hell now, too," he concluded grimly.

Rachel nodded again, tears fogging her eyes. It was small comfort to know that her father's murderers had gotten their punishment. She supposed that was because no punishment could ever bring Sean McKinsey back to life. For one awful moment, grief at her terrible loss almost overwhelmed her, but she remembered just in time that she need no longer bear it alone. Instinctively, she moved toward Cole, up and into his lap, where she knew she would find solace.

Cole muttered something about being awfully dirty, but she ignored him, wrapping her arms around him and burying her face in his shoulder. His arms embraced her, as if to shelter her from the hurt, and they did. She sat like that for several minutes until he had absorbed all her pain, and the threat of tears had passed. Her father was gone, but she still had Cole, and thank God, he was safe and sound and out of danger.

Then she remembered one other important item of business, something Cole had not mentioned yet. "Statler's dead, too, then?" she asked, lifting her head to see Cole's face. She thought she knew the answer, but Cole's suddenly grim expression disabused her of that notion.

"He was hit," he said slowly, absently stroking her hair in a gesture of comfort. Cole knew the old bastard was hit because he was the one who had shot him. Got him right in the brisket, too. He'd never been so sure of anything in his life, but they just hadn't been able to find a body. "He was hit," he repeated, "but he got away. We never did find him."

Rachel straightened in his arms. "Didn't you go to his

ranch? Surely, that's where he'd go if he was hurt."

He had thought of that, of course. "Yeah, after we finished up at the camp, we rode into town and picked up the marshal. We wanted everything legal, with witnesses and everything. But when we got to Statler's place, everybody'd gone. I guess somebody who'd got away had warned the rest of his men, and they'd run for it."

"But what about Statler?" she asked, worry lines creasing her forehead.

Cole reached out one long finger to smooth them away. She didn't need to worry anymore. She had him to take care of her now. "Statler might have got away, but he won't last long. He was hurt bad, and he's got no place to go, nobody to take care of him. You won't be seeing him again, honey."

Honey. The endearment washed over her in sweet waves, and for just a heartbeat she sat perfectly still and savored the sensation. Then she lifted her mouth to his. He was tender at first, almost tentative, but not for long. Her lips parted at his encouragement, his arms crushed her to him, as if he would never let her go. The kiss went on and on, tongues mating, hands clinging, breaths mingling. Neither of them noticed Lupe until she cleared her throat.

They both jumped guiltily, coming up from the kiss with a jolt. Lupe observed them without batting an eye. "You bath, he is ready," she informed Cole.

Cole briefly considered telling the old bat what she could do with her bath, but then he recalled that he was probably pretty rank, having ridden more miles that day than he cared to remember. He didn't want anything to spoil what he had planned for the rest of the evening, so he supposed he'd better get cleaned up. "Yeah, thanks," he replied with some graciousness.

Rachel watched the exchange with resignation, but waited until Lupe had gone before sliding reluctantly from Cole's lap. He stood a little stiffly, and she pretended not to notice the bulge in his pants.

"Yeah, well," he began, knowing he needed to go but also hating to leave Rachel. "I won't be long," he promised finally.

"Good," she replied. She almost asked if he wanted her to wash his back, but thought better of it. The things she had planned for the rest of the night were going to be shocking enough, so she simply folded her hands in front of her and gave him a smile full of promises.

He blinked. "Not long at all," he repeated, and hustled himself off to his bedroom.

Half an hour later Lupe returned for the tray and found Rachel huddled in the big chair, still waiting. The old woman clicked her tongue in disapproval and chewed Rachel out in rapid-fire Spanish.

"I can't just walk in on him," Rachel defended herself.

Lupe did not even dignify such an inane remark with a reply. Sniffing indignantly, she moved swiftly over to a sideboard cabinet. Throwing open the door, she reached in and came up with a bottle of whiskey and a glass. "Take him this," she ordered, thrusting the items at Rachel.

Rachel took them obediently, but still she hesitated. He had promised to hurry but maybe he'd changed his mind. After all, he was exhausted.

Lupe made an exasperated sound and muttered something like "Stupid gringos." Rachel stiffened her spine and turned resolutely on her heel. They were married, after all, she decided. There was no reason on God's earth why she shouldn't see him taking a bath!

Still, her ingrained breeding forced her to tap very lightly on his bedroom door before going in. She waited a moment, and when she did not receive a reply, she grew suddenly alarmed. Throwing open the door, she stepped inside.

She might have laughed at the sight that met her eyes if she hadn't been so relieved. Cole was still in the tub, his long legs drawn up to accommodate himself to the hip bath, big knees splayed wide, and he was sound asleep.

Smiling and feeling very much like a voyeur, Rachel closed the door softly behind her and tiptoed across the floor until she stood beside the tub. He had washed his hair and the wet locks were slicked straight back from his face, looking almost black in the flickering lamplight. Beads of water glistened on his face and chest, clinging to his eyelashes and curling the mat of hair that furred his chest. She indulged herself, studying the way the brown of his face and neck ended abruptly where his shirt had shielded his skin from the relentless sun. Then she examined his arms, the corded muscles that looked powerful even in repose, the bronzed hands that had fought for her today but which could love her gently, too.

Delicious shivers teased the backs of her legs, and she shifted from one foot to the other, taking care not to drop the bottle that trembled in her suddenly nerveless fingers. Then there were his legs, that part of him that she had never seen. Dark hairs curled over the knees that stuck awkwardly out of the water, and a rider's muscles slabbed the thighs that were only partly visible. She knew a wicked urge to run her fingers down those thighs and under the water, but she resisted, deciding that was probably not the best way to wake him up.

"Cole," she whispered. He did not move. "Cole," she repeated, more loudly.

He awoke with a startled grunt, blinking at her a few times to get his bearings. She knew the instant that he realized where he was because he closed his knees with a slap that sent water sloshing everywhere. She knew a moment's guilt for embarrassing him. Only a moment's, though. His modesty was wasted since the water had been much too murky for her to see anything important. Unfortunately.

"Lupe thought you might like this," she explained, holding up the glass and bottle.

"I guess I fell asleep," he explained unnecessarily, passing a wet hand over his face. He'd only intended to close his eyes for a minute. The water had felt so good, and he was so warm, that he guessed the day had caught up with him.

Neither of them moved for a few seconds, and then Rachel realized that he couldn't very well move from where he was. Glancing around, she noticed a stack of towels that Lupe must have laid out for him. She set the bottle and glass on the washstand and handed him a towel.

He murmured his thanks and ran it over his face and head, drying and mussing his hair at the same time. Then he made a few swipes at his chest before looking up to find her staring at him.

With a slight sense of disappointment that he wasn't about to stand up with her watching, she handed him another towel and discreetly turned her back, wandering over to the bed where she made a great show of turning back the covers.

The splash told her when he had risen, and she caught her breath, closing her eyes against the vision of long, lean flanks. She knew them by touch, knew just what they looked like although she had never actually seen. He really was a beautiful man, she knew he was. Still a little on the thin side, but beautiful nevertheless. Now that she would have him home, all to herself, she would set about fattening him up. Then she wondered, with a small wicked smile, if making love to her at night would keep him thin in spite of her efforts.

Cole toweled off as quickly as he could. It was a job, since his steeped muscles were refusing to respond. He glanced around, but the only clothes within reach were the filthy ones he had discarded, and he couldn't very well put them back on. The rest of his things were tucked away in the bureau right behind where Rachel was standing. He didn't own such a thing as a nightshirt or even a robe, so for lack of anything better, he knotted a towel around his waist.

"Did you find anything at Statler's house?" Rachel asked out of the blue. "Any evidence that he was behind the rustling, I mean?"

She didn't turn around when she spoke, but continued to fuss with the bedclothes and fluff the pillows. Her hair was loose. He'd never actually seen it loose like that, brushed smooth. It reached all the way to her waist and it was shining in the lamplight. "We didn't find anything but an empty cash box. Somebody'd burned all his papers in the fireplace. The ashes were there but nothing that we could make anything of," his mouth said. His mind was elsewhere; under Rachel's nightdress, to be exact. He took a step toward her.

Hearing that step, Rachel turned around. "That's too bad," her lips said. Her mind was elsewhere, though. Damn that towel, she thought. His legs were so long and straight. Her mouth went dry and all the moisture in her body seemed to collect in one central place.

Rachel gave a small, nervous laugh to cover skittering emotions. "You'd better get in bed. You'll catch your death," she chided, hoping she sounded wifely and concerned instead of eager and wanton. He might have called her "honey," but he hadn't yet said he loved her. Until then, she couldn't let him know how much she loved him back.

"Yeah," he agreed, only too glad to move toward her. But she stepped back from the bed, out of his way as he approached. He could tell from the way her hands were fiddling with the front of her robe that she was nervous, and he wondered why. It wasn't like they'd never done this before.

Then he realized what it must be. She was nervous because the light was still lit. She'd never seen him in the altogether like this, and she must be pretty overwhelmed. To make matters worse, he was beginning to feel a very familiar sensation that told him not all the muscles in his body had been totally relaxed by that bath. If he didn't get under the covers pretty quick, he might just scare her to death.

With as much haste as was seemly, he turned his back to Rachel and climbed into bed, pulling up the covers with a sigh of relief.

Rachel watched in confusion. She'd been so certain that he would take her in his arms, that he'd lift her onto the bed, that he'd kiss her passionately and pick right up where he'd left off when Lupe had interrupted them with the bath. For a minute, she didn't know quite what to make of it. Was he too tired to make love to her? Had he realized that now, and was he trying to get out of it gracefully. Well, she wouldn't throw herself at him, much as she wanted to. She would give him a few more minutes, though, just in case.

"I'll hang that towel up for you," she offered, holding out her hand.

He needed a minute to recall just which towel she was referring to, and another minute to unwrap it from his hips and free it from the tangle of sheets.

Rachel accepted it gingerly, knowing it was warm from his body and resisting the urge to hold it close. She went over to the washstand and hung it up, and there she noticed the whiskey bottle which had been her excuse for coming in the first place.

"I forgot all about your drink," she exclaimed, thrilled to have an excuse not only to stay a little longer but to go back over to the bed. She snatched up the bottle and glass and took them to him.

She had the cork halfway out of the bottle when he said, "I don't need a drink, Rachel."

Her head came up, disappointment clearly written across her face. "Oh," she said, pushing the cork back in. She set the bottle down, not knowing what else to do.

Why didn't she come to bed? What was she stalling around for? Cole shifted under the covers, lifting one knee to make a tent over his loins that would hide the evidence of his impatience.

Rachel watched him. He had the funniest expression on his face. He looked awfully uncomfortable. Maybe he couldn't wait for her to leave. "Are you very tired?" she asked in one last attempt.

He stared at her a long moment as he finally realized why she had not yet come to bed. Now he remembered what it was that irritated him about her. It was her damn manners. He grinned slowly, a grin that was part self-mockery and part teasing. "I'm getting damn tired of waiting for you to come to bed," he growled, reaching out to snare one delicate hand and reel her in.

"Oh!" she said, a small startled sound as she stumbled forward. "Well, why didn't you just say so?" she asked indignantly as he drew her inexorably across his lap.

Cole almost replied that he just had said so, but then he recalled another, similar conversation he had had earlier in the day along the same lines. With that memory had come another, of what had happened afterward, and for one awful moment, the faces appeared, the faces of dead men, old ones and new ones and Statler's most of all. But then Rachel was there and her nightdress was gone and so were the faces.

Will Statler came back. Cole's bullet had glanced off a rib so that the wound that had looked so serious hadn't been serious at all. He had more men with him this time, lots more men. Some were new and some were old and some were the dead ones that Cole had buried.

They came to the ranch and Cole was there alone with Rachel. They shot him, again and again. He didn't feel any pain, but he could see the wounds and the blood, his blood, pouring out. Statler was laughing and saying that now he would have everything, the ranch and the cattle and most of all Rachel. Statler was holding her and then he laughed again and tried to kiss her. She fought him. She was crying and calling to Cole, calling his name, but he couldn't move, couldn't help her because he was dead. He was dead, and he couldn't move, but he could see it all, Statler with his hands on Rachel and Rachel crying and calling him.

"Cole! Cole!"

Rachel's hands were shaking him and her voice cut through the fog. Gradually, the dream faded, leaving behind only the horror of it. He could just barely make out her face in the pale moonlight that bathed the room. "Rachel?" he asked, reaching for her.

"Yes, I'm here. What is it? What were you dreaming?" Concern threaded her voice, anxious hands stroked his face as she came into his arms. She had been afraid at first, having awakened to his thrashing and his muttered words of alarm. Then she had realized that he was having a nightmare, was perhaps reliving the horror of the day. She had wondered earlier at his ability to tell her the story so calmly, to pass off the danger and death he had faced as if it had been nothing. Now she knew he felt the same revulsion she did over the killing, but he had been hiding that emotion from her.

Or attempting to. Now, of course, she held his sweat-dampened body against hers and she knew the truth. "It was just a dream," she soothed as he pulled her down to him.

He knew that, of course. It wasn't the first time such dreams had haunted him when men had died at his hand. It was, however, the first time he had had Rachel there to comfort him. He found her lips with his, lifting her so that her small, slim body rested on top of his, her hair falling down in an ebony curtain around them, blacker than the darkness and redolent of roses.

One of his hands tangled in the silken skein, the other slid down the length of her to cup her buttocks. She felt so good under his hands that for a moment just touching her was enough. The moment was short-lived, however, and soon touching was not nearly enough. She moved against his swelling desire, and he responded instinctively, reaching both hands down to lift her to him. He swallowed her gasp of surprise and gave back a sigh of contentment as she settled around him.

At first Rachel lay still, adjusting to a thousand new sensations, but then his hands urged her, encouraged her, and she realized that this wasn't so very different from the other way. She began to move in the now-familiar rhythm, timidly at first, but with increasing confidence, enjoying the freedom of her new position. Rewarded by his moans of pleasure, Rachel tested her power, setting a slower pace than he ever had. Their earlier coupling had been quick, even quicker than usual. After their long separation, neither had had the patience or the ability to prolong it. As pleasant as that encounter had been, it had not come close to satisfying two weeks' worth of need.

This time things would be different. The edge of their desire had been blunted, their bodies rested by a few hours of sleep. And Rachel was in charge.

She moved on him with agonizing slowness, allowing the length of her body to slide along his with each tantalizing stroke. Iron hands gripped her hips, trying to force her to move faster, but she resisted, coaxing those hands to her breasts instead. Teasing, tormenting, again and again she brought him to the brink, but each time she sensed he was about to fall, she stopped, holding him there until she felt him relax. Then she would start again.

Once she heard him murmur, "Witch," but she knew there was no malice in the epithet. He was much stronger than she. He could take control whenever he wanted. His submission was completely voluntary, but that knowledge only made her dominance more exciting. Knowing that at any moment he might wrest back his supremacy was intoxicating.

Drunk now with her own power, she grew relentless, turning teasing into torture. How long he might have borne such torture, she never learned, however. In her megalomania, she had forgotten to account her own weakness. As she tormented him, she also tormented herself.

The warmth that came from giving kindled the fires of desire. As his passion mounted, so did her own. It grew within her, burning brighter, blazing hotter, raging out of control until it consumed her. The spasms caught her unaware, rippling upward and outward, molten and delicious, and they triggered his own. She collapsed as he shuddered under her, letting those shudders ripple through her, doubling her pleasure.

They lay together like that for a long time, lazy hands stroking here and there, breaths mingling, bodies cooling and calming. At last Rachel smiled against his skin, recalling what had started all of this in the first place.

"What were you dreaming about?" she asked sleepily.

Cole drew in a breath and let it out slowly. He had felt her smile and smiled back, although he knew she could not see it. "I was dreaming about what we just did," he lied, loath to tell her the truth and shatter the mood.

Her languid body became alert at his "confession," and she raised her head in a vain attempt to make out his expression. "You were having a nightmare about that?" she asked skeptically.

"Sure," he insisted. "I was dreaming that I wanted to and you didn't. That for damn sure qualifies as a nightmare."

Laughter bubbled from her throat, gurgling and splashing all around him, drowning all lingering specters from the past and washing him clean. God, he felt wonderful, lying there, holding her, with her hair making a sweet, silken web all around them. He belonged here, now. He'd earned the right to possess her, and he'd even made her care about him, a little bit, anyway. Life was good.

His laughter joined hers, startling her into a moment of silence. But only a moment. Her joy soon gurgled out again at the sound of his happiness. She had never heard him laugh so unrestrainedly before, and soon they were both convulsed, clinging together under the tangle of bedclothes until sheer exhaustion quieted them into a huddled quivering mass of pure delight.

Long after Rachel slept, Cole lay awake. He could not bear to close his eyes just yet, not when all his dreams were coming true right before them. Dreams were funny things, he mused. On that last night, just before he'd left to start the roundup, he'd dreamed that Rachel had told him she loved him. At least, he'd thought it was a dream. Now he wasn't so sure. She hadn't exactly said that she loved him tonight, but she'd certainly made him think it. Why else would she have done what she had done?

She might have done it because she was grateful, of course. She knew he'd risked his life for her today, and she might simply have been rewarding him by giving him what she knew he liked. And giving him what she thought he had earned. But giving had made her happy, too. He knew from the way she had laughed at what he now realized was his off-color joke. He never should have teased her about a thing like that, but in the dark he had a tendency to forget that Rachel was a lady. In fact, Rachel seemed to have the same tendency. He planned to encourage that inclination.

Cole smiled in the dark, knowing full well that a man who'd lived the life Cole Elliot had lived had no business lying here in bed with Rachel McKinsey. It was a very large miracle that she'd ever been desperate enough to think she needed him. He'd proven that he could take care of her, though. He'd gotten rid of Statler and that threat, and now she was safe. In doing so, he had made her care for him as a man, too. He could still see the look on her face when she had realized he was safe, could still feel the way she had held him those first few moments in the parlor.

But now, in the peaceful afterglow of their lovemaking, Cole had the leisure to remember that the job of saving the Circle M was not yet over. In fact, another, very real danger threatened, a danger of which only Cole was aware. Unless they managed to sell off the cattle that had stampeded today, there simply would not be a Circle M in a few short months. Back when he had been trying to avoid Rachel, Cole had spent several of his evenings examining the ledger books. A conference with Mr. McKinsey's banker had confirmed Cole's worst suspicions: paying a crew of professional gunmen had drained most of McKinsey's reserves. They needed some cash money and quick.

That meant a cattle drive. The herd of steers they had rounded up would have to be rounded up again and driven to Kansas and sold. With the price of beef being what it was, they'd clear a small fortune, even after paying off the men with a bonus thrown in. Without Statler to worry about, getting those cattle to market would be a downhill slide. Once again, Cole would pull Rachel's iron out of the fire.

Except . . . Cole frowned in the darkness. Who could he entrust with such an important job? Many things could happen to a herd of cattle between here and Kansas, and even more things could happen to the money they would bring when sold, the money that was so vital to Rachel's future. Not that Cole was afraid to trust the men with that amount of money. They had all more than proven their loyalty to the brand, and he knew they would get the herd through and the money back here or die trying. That was just the trouble. Sometimes things happened that simply weren't a man's fault. What if one of his friends lost the money somehow? How could he ask someone else to take a responsibility like that?

Rachel stirred, murmuring something in her sleep. He drew her closer to his side and she quieted, cuddling contentedly against him. For a while, he just held her like that, not even letting himself consider his alternatives. He knew, deep in his soul, that taking care of Rachel was the most important job he had ever done, and that getting rid of Statler was only the beginning. If he wanted to be sure that the ranch kept operating, insuring Rachel's future, someone had to take that cattle north. As much as he hated to even consider it, that someone would have to be Cole Elliot. He simply could not ask anyone else to accept such a burden.

The trip would be a long one, two or three months at least, and Cole wanted to groan just thinking about leaving Rachel for that long. His only consolation was in knowing that he was doing exactly what needed to be done, exactly what Mr. McKinsey would expect him to do. When he got back, they'd be all set, and he would never have to leave her again. And he would have proven to Rachel once again that she'd gotten a good deal when she'd tied up with him. He'd show her that he had even more to offer than his gun. The thought provided him with a small measure of comfort against the lonely months that stretched ahead.

Chapter VIII

"I still don't see why you have to go!" Rachel insisted with exasperation, glaring across the breakfast table at Cole. She had awakened early this morning but not quite early enough to beat Cole. He had been gone from the bed, but she had found him at the table, finishing up his breakfast.

He sat with her until she, too, had finished eating, and for a few minutes Rachel had enjoyed the cozy intimate feeling of sharing this time together, of exchanging secret smiles when Lupe wasn't looking, of acting very married. Then he told her about his plan.

"I told you," he explained patiently, knowing that he was right. "It's a long, dangerous trip. Taking the herd north isn't something I can ask somebody else to do."

"Why not?" Rachel demanded. "Other people do it all the time!" It was true. Very few ranchers traveled with their herds, perferring to stay home or at the very most take a train north and meet their herd when it reached its destination.

Cole didn't answer, but she could tell by the way his lips had thinned down that he was angry. "And besides," she added, "what makes you so all-fired qualified? How many times have you taken a herd north?"

"Twice," he said quietly, shattering her argument.

Twice. Rachel could hardly believe it. Many men had

gone on such a trip once, just for the excitement, just to say they had done it. Few men ever did it more than once, though. The work was just too difficult, too dangerous and too boring. Trust Cole Elliot to be the one man in a million to whom such things did not matter. Not only had he done it twice, but here he was, insisting on doing it again.

"Do you know how long you'll be gone?" she asked sarcastically, not because she needed to know but because she wanted to make a point.

"I figure two and a half, three months," he admitted reluctantly. This was a subject he was very unhappy about and did not want to discuss.

"Or maybe four or five months," Rachel pointed out, revising his estimate upward. Any number of things could slow a herd down and drag the trip out to almost twice the usual length. She'd just gotten over missing him for seventeen days, and the thought of missing him for three months or more was something she didn't even want to consider. It wasn't bothering him a bit, though. He couldn't be thinking about leaving her again so soon if he'd been even half as miserable as she had. Last night she had been certain that he had suffered, but apparently, she was mistaken. "You're going to leave me here, all alone, for all those months?" she asked in an injured tone, testing her theory.

Cole could have groaned aloud. Instead, he stood up quickly, his chair making a sickening scraping noise against the plank floor. He needed to cut this coversation short. Arguing wasn't going to change the facts, and the facts were that he must make this trip if he wanted to be sure that Rachel would never want for anything again. "You won't be alone. I'll leave some of the men here and Lupe is here . . ." That wasn't what she'd meant, and he knew it, but it would have to do. He was going, and that was that. The sooner she accepted it, the better. He only hoped he could come to accept it himself.

"It's crazy!" she insisted. "There's no reason for you

to go!"

"I'm going," he told her, his voice hard.

Rachel blinked. He had never spoken to her in that tone. It was the way he'd spoken to Statler that day in the restaurant, cold and mean. She'd never expected him to be that way with her, but apparently she had been wrong about that, too. Biting back her hurt and her anger, she simply straightened in her chair and glared at him. Arguing wasn't going to change his mind, anyway. She knew that from the stubborn set of his chin. No, she wasn't going to argue anymore. She had other ways to convince him. She'd give him a little taste of her displeasure, and then she'd give him a very stimulating reminder of what he would be missing if he went on this trip. If that wasn't enough to keep him here, then nothing would be.

Cole scowled down at her. She hadn't agreed, hadn't even pretended that she was going to, but at least she didn't look as if she was going to fight about it anymore. That was something. He gave her a small nod of approval. "I'm going down to the bunkhouse to see how the men are doing," he said, deciding that a strategic retreat was his best move at the moment.

For the first time, Rachel had a very disturbing thought. "Was anyone hurt yesterday?" Once she had learned that Cole was all right, she hadn't given a thought to any of the rest of the men, she suddenly realized with a burning shame.

Cole gave a one-shoulder shrug. "A couple scratches, that's all," he said, passing it off.

"You should have said something. Lupe has a salve . . . I'll tell her to go down and check on them," she offered, rising from her chair. Guilt over her thoughtlessness moved her quickly, and she was gone before he could refuse her offer.

Cole didn't really want that old witch fussing around his men, but then he remembered that the other men didn't seem to have the same aversion for her that he did. In fact, now

255

that he thought about it, they were always going to her for something or other, warts or boils or cankers. They swore by her remedies, too. Funny, but Cole had always thought that witches could give those sorts of things, not cure them.

Cole spent some time down at the bunkhouse, rehashing the previous day's events with the men and assuring himself that Lupe wasn't going to poison anyone. Along about noontime, the sheriff arrived.

Cole met him in the yard in front of the house.

"Howdy, Mr. Elliot," he greeted. "Heard you had some trouble yesterday."

Cole almost grinned. In the first place, the sheriff had not called him "Mr." the last time he had come to discuss the trouble with Statler. That was a measure of how far up in the world Cole had come. In the second place, Cole liked the way the sheriff referred to the massacre of Statler's men as "some trouble." Cole had gotten the feeling that the town marshal was somehow in cahoots with Statler, judging from how upset he had been yesterday. The sheriff gave no such indications.

"A little trouble," Cole affirmed, shaking the lawman's beefy hand. "Come on in and set, and I'll tell you all about it."

Sheriff Davis followed Cole up the steps and into the ranch office. The two men seated themselves in the same chairs that Cole and Rachel had occupied to discuss their marriage a few short months before. But Cole didn't think about that. Instead, he studied the sheriff.

The man was big, as tall as Cole and twice as broad. He was also a decade older, and he'd seen too much trouble to be very concerned about something that was already over and done with. "I got Aldrich's wire late last night," the sheriff began, referring to the message the town marshal had sent him. "He said that Statler's men were trying to steal your cattle. That right?"

Cole nodded. "They've done a lot more than that, too." Cole reminded the sheriff about the incident with the two

256

men who had ambushed him and Miles, and then told him about the incidents that had followed. "We knew who was doing it all the time, but there was nothing we could do until we caught them in the act, so we set a trap. They fell into it." He gave the sheriff a brief account of what had happened the day before, and about how they had failed to find Statler but believed him to be dead and about how his men had scattered.

"It looks like you were in the right of it, Mr. Elliot," the sheriff conceded. "You say you didn't catch any of his men alive?"

Cole hadn't said that, exactly. He'd only said that all of Statler's men were either dead or gone. "All the ones we caught are dead. Of course, if you don't believe me, you can dig them up, just to make sure."

The sheriff responded to Cole's grisly suggestion with a mirthless grin. "I'll take your word," he said. "I should probably thank you, too. You saved the law the trouble of hanging them."

Cole nodded, and the two men studied each other in silence. Plainly, the sheriff knew Cole had taken the law into his own hands, but believed he was justified in doing so. The sheriff would give Cole and his men no trouble for meeting out their own vengeance.

The sheriff's expression grew pensive. "You buried them, eh? A lot of men would have left them for the coyotes."

Cole had considered doing just that, but since some of the men had been hanged, he'd decided it was better to plant them. "I didn't want to have to explain to my wife what the coyotes were howling about," he said by way of explanation.

As if on cue, Rachel tapped on the door. She had been listening, of course, and had decided that the sheriff had pumped Cole long enough. She stepped into the room wearing her best finishing school smile. "Well, hello, Sheriff. I hope I'm not interrupting anything important," she said, giving the large man her hand.

Both Cole and the sheriff rose when she came in, and the sheriff very graciously assured her that she hadn't interrupted a thing.

"You'll be staying for dinner, then, won't you?" she inquired, her smile never wavering. Quite consciously, she stepped back until her shoulder brushed Cole's arm, silently telling the lawman that she stood with her husband in everything.

"Thank you, ma'am, I'd be proud to," he replied, returning her smile with one that was slightly envious at Cole's good fortune. "If you don't mind, I'll mosey on down to the bunkhouse and ask the men a few questions first, though. If you'll excuse me?"

Rachel nodded her consent, and she and Cole stood silently watching him until he was well out of earshot. "He seemed to accept your story," she commented.

Cole couldn't hide his surprise, and she gave him a defiant look, daring him to chastise her for eavesdropping. "Do you think there'll be any trouble?" she asked.

He shook his head, as much in wonder as in answer to her question. He simply could not picture proper Miss Rachel listening at the keyhole. "Not from him. Aldrich wasn't too happy, but I think that's because Statler was paying him off to look the other way. He was a little too eager to think well of that son of a . . ." He let his voice trail off, suddenly remembering to whom he was speaking.

Rachel nodded absently, turning to watch the sheriff enter the bunkhouse. "I hope you told the men what to say," she remarked.

Cole frowned and took her arm, turning her back to face him. "We didn't do anything wrong, Rachel," he assured her. "Davis is a reasonable man, and he understands that. We don't have to hide anything."

Rachel almost surrendered to the impulse to throw her arms around him and tell him she knew that was true and that she had never doubted him for a minute, but she

258

remembered just in time why she shouldn't. She was still mad at him for wanting to go on that horrible trail drive. As a compromise, she said, "I know you don't have anything to hide. I just wasn't sure the sheriff would agree," and then, "I'll go tell Lupe that we have company for dinner." Reluctantly, she slipped free of his grasp, ignoring the way he was still frowning at her.

Dinner was an uncomfortable affair. Cole couldn't seem to think of anything to say, probably because he was too busy watching Rachel. His attention kept wandering to their last conversation and the haunting suspicion that she believed him guilty of some sort of wrongdoing. If she did, then all the more reason for him to make this trip and prove to her once and for all what kind of a man he really was.

Rachel tried to cover Cole's silence by being charming and witty, straining her ingrained manners to the limit. The sheriff seemed not to notice the strain, or maybe he really didn't notice. At any rate, the meal was an ordeal that Rachel was glad to see end.

When the sheriff had gone, Cole went down to the bunkhouse to talk to Miles. He told him his plan to take the herd to Kansas.

"There's no reason for you to go, you know," Miles pointed out.

Cole bit back his irritation. After all, Miles couldn't know that he had repeated Rachel's objection almost word for word. "I've got to make sure that the herd gets through and that the money gets back," he pointed out.

"You've got men you can trust to do that," Miles said. He was watching Cole's reaction to his arguments through narrowed eyes. Something wasn't quite right here. The last thing Cole should want to do right now was leave home for the whole summer. This was his chance to spend some time with his new bride, something he hadn't had much opportunity to do lately.

Cole got up from the chair he had been straddling and

began to pace the room. It was his old room, the one he had occupied as foreman and the one Miles used now that he had assumed Cole's duties. "Don't you see? This is something I have to do myself," Cole insisted, gesturing with his hand, as if by doing so he could more easily convince Miles.

Miles observed his friend's restlessness from where he reclined on the bed. He pursed his lips thoughtfully. "What does your wife think about it?" he asked.

"That doesn't matter," Cole snapped, telling Miles by his manner that it mattered very much, indeed, but that he wasn't going to let that change his mind. Cole stopped his pacing, placed his hands on his hips and cast Miles a beseeching look. "This is her cattle, her money. If anything happens to it . . ." He paused, waiting to see if Miles understood.

He did, but he understood more than that. "Maybe she wouldn't be too happy if something happened to you, either. Did you ever think of that?"

"Nothing's going to happen to me," Cole said, dismissing such a possibility with a wave of his hand and beginning to pace again. "And it's my job to take care of her and to take care of the ranch, isn't it?"

Miles frowned. "I wouldn't exactly call being married a 'job.'"

"You know what I mean," Cole insisted.

Miles's frown deepened. He had been so sure that things were finally working out between Cole and Miss Rachel. The tension he had sensed between them in the early days was gone now, and he knew that Cole worshiped the ground she walked on. She liked him, too. Just how much, Miles had no way of judging, but he'd seen her look at Cole with affection from time to time. Cole was a likable person, once you got past that tough front that he always put up, and Miles guessed that Miss Rachel had finally gotten past it. Cole had certainly won her loyalty, or should have, by whipping Statler, too. But for some reason Cole still felt like he had to prove himself to her. Miles wondered whether he really did.

"It's part of your job to protect her, too," Miles pointed out. "Some of Statler's men might still be around, just waiting for a chance to get a little revenge. Leaving her here alone would give them a perfect opportunity."

"Not if I leave you here, too," Cole said. Seeing Miles's slight surprise, he added, "Nobody will bother her with you here. Hell, she'll be safer with you than with me, and you know it."

A shadow clouded Miles's eyes, blanking them of all expression for a moment, and Cole was instantly repentant. By unspoken agreement, Cole had never mentioned Miles's reputation, knowing the pain it caused him. "Hey, *amigo,*" he said. "I didn't mean to . . ."

"Forget it," Miles said. He even smiled reassuringly, but the smile did not quite reach the sadness in his eyes. "You're right, as usual, but somehow I don't think Miss Rachel will see things the same way. Given a choice between her husband—her handsome, young husband," he added in a friendly attempt to goad Cole, "and a dried-up old man to be a nursemaid, I don't think she'd pick me."

"She won't have a choice," Cole declared.

Miles wasn't so sure.

Cole glanced up from where he sat, but when he saw that Rachel still had her nose stuck in that book, he went back to work again. All evening he'd been busily plaiting a handle for a new quirt, a job that required a lot of attention and one he had chosen when he saw the mood that Rachel was in at supper. That way he could pretend he was too busy to notice that she was ignoring him.

She was still mad about him going to Kansas. He'd figured that out from the few remarks she had made during the meal. He was flattered that she didn't want him to go, but he kept reminding himself of how important this trip was to the future of the ranch. She might not like the idea, but that was just because she didn't understand. He was the man, and he had to do what he knew was in her best interest whether she liked it or not.

Still, he didn't like sitting here like this. All evening she'd been as quiet as a gopher with its throat cut. Of course, he didn't like arguing with her either, but this was somehow worse. At least if they were fighting, there was a chance that they'd end up in each other's arms. This way, he might as well still be out on the range.

The slap of her book closing brought his head up. Without looking at him, she set the book aside and rose to her feet, straightening her dress as she did so. He couldn't help but notice the way it clung to her breasts.

Rachel tried not to notice the look in his eyes. When he looked at her like that, the hairs on the back of her neck prickled and gooseflesh formed on the backs of her legs and she wanted to throw herself into his arms. That would never do, however. She had her plan, and her plan was to make him sleep alone tonight. He had to learn the price of earning her displeasure. Tomorrow would be the second part of her plan. Tomorrow, when she had made her point, she would sleep with him and show him what he'd be missing if he went to Kansas.

"I guess I'll go to bed now," she said in a carefully neutral voice.

Instantly, Cole laid the quirt aside and stood up, ready to follow her. This was what he'd been waiting for. She might not be talking to him, but she didn't need to say a word for what he had in mind.

Seeing him rise, Rachel threw him a haughty look that stopped him in his tracks. While he hesitated, she turned on her heel and flounced to her bedroom door, almost daring him to try to follow.

Cole's eyes narrowed down. What in the hell was she up to? "Rachel?" he said sharply.

She turned back, her hand on the knob, a look of polite inquiry on her face. She waited, hoping he could not guess how fragile was her facade. Behind her calm, detached expression, her heart was pounding. Did she really have the strength to refuse him? Her confidence evaporated as he closed the distance between them with purposeful strides.

"I'm really very tired," she said, lifting her chin to give the impression that she was looking down her nose at him. No mean feat, considering he was almost a foot taller than she.

Cole knew good and well she wasn't tired. She was just mad. He could see the anger simmering in the depths of her brown eyes. With the proper encouragement, she would be hissing and spitting at him, and that was exactly what he wanted. While he didn't know what to do with this cold, aloof Rachel, he knew exactly how to handle the hellcat. "Are you too tired for this?" he asked, hauling her into his arms.

Rachel's reaction was immediate. The instant his lips covered hers in a devouring kiss, every nerve in her body leaped to attention. She curled her hands into fists in a desperate attempt to keep them from reaching for him. Using every ounce of willpower she possessed, she forced her body to remain limp, forced her lips not to kiss him back, forced every one of her senses not to be overwhelmed by the feel and smell of him, forced her brain to remember her plan. If she gave in now, he would never take her seriously again.

After what seemed an eternity, he finally lifted his mouth from hers. His breath was ragged and she could feel the heat of his desire pressed tightly against her hips. His blue eyes searched her face for reaction.

Praying that he would not notice how her nipples had tautened, that he would not read the longing in her eyes, that he would not sense her trembling need, she drew a steadying breath. "Good night," she said with as much finality as she could muster.

Cole swore in frustration. What in the hell was wrong with

her? His hands tightened on her arms as he fought off the impulse to shake that impassive expression off her face. "Rachel," he muttered in warning even as he pulled her close for another assault.

But Rachel knew her limit. If she allowed him to kiss her again, no matter how furiously, she would be lost. She turned her face so that his lips came down on her clenched jaw. "I said I was tired," Rachel reminded him hoarsely. "Are you going to take me against my will?"

That did it. Cole recoiled as if she'd struck him. Using the one moment of his stunned surprise, Rachel broke free and escaped into her room, slamming the door behind her. For long minutes, she sagged against it, expecting to hear the sound of splintering wood or muttered curses or shouted fury. Instead, she heard nothing except the gasp of her own breath and the thundering of her own heart. At long last, even those sounds settled down to normal, and Rachel felt the tension drain from her. She had won. She would not acknowledge that the victory felt a little hollow. Tomorrow, she would make it all up to him, anyway, and then he would understand the price he would be paying if he left her. She would have him just where she wanted him. And how she wanted him! Trembling in the aftermath of her own desire, Rachel stumbled over to her bed. She only wished she could sleep until it was time to go to bed again—with Cole. How would she live through tomorrow?

Cole stared at the closed door for a long time, his whole body shaking with rage. Take her against her will? Where had she ever come up with an idea like that? How many nights had he lain alone in his own room, suffering the torments of hell because he couldn't do that very thing? He had half a mind to break down the door and tell her that, too, except that he realized how idiotic he would sound if he did so.

Damn her. What a fool he'd been to think that she was any different from all the others. Why, he'd even deluded himself into believing that she cared for him, that she shared his bed because she enjoyed it. No, it was just like he'd suspected in the very beginning. She gave him what she knew he wanted to keep him around, but she'd cut him off the minute he did something to displease her. Or maybe she'd just decided she didn't like sleeping with a gunfighter, he thought bitterly.

Turning on his heel, Cole strode across the room to the cabinet where the whiskey was stored. He muttered a curse when he threw open the door and found the bottle was gone. Then he remembered. It was in his room. Rachel had brought it to him last night, last night when she'd been all sweetness and light.

And gratitude. Yes, she sure knew how to show gratitude, he recalled bitterly as he closed the cabinet with a snap. Cole muttered another, very satisfying obscenity, and strode into his own room. Resisting the urge to slam his own door, not wanting to give her the satisfaction of knowing how furious he was, he looked around for the bottle Rachel had brought him last night, the bottle he hadn't wanted then. Tonight was different.

Rachel had no trouble sleeping late the next morning. She hadn't even closed her eyes until the wee hours and then had slept fitfully, tormented by dreams that Cole had forced his way into her room and demanded his rights. She had been terribly disappointed to discover they were only dreams.

Rachel was already having second thoughts, wondering if her plan had been wise, when she wandered out to breakfast. Lupe brought her a heaping plate of flapjacks.

"He is gone," Lupe informed her.

Rachel dug into the flapjacks without even looking up. "I figured he would be. Just wait until he gets back tonight, though," she advised the old woman, silently wishing away the hours in between.

"He not be back."

Lupe started to shuffle away, but Rachel's startled

"What?" drew her back.

"He say he be gone a while. He roundup again. The other men go with him," Lupe explained.

"He can't do that!" Rachel cried, jumping to her feet and knocking over her chair in the process.

Lupe watched her with barely disguised amusement. "He do it."

"Oh, Lupe, that man is impossible!" Rachel declared, righting her chair with furious motions. And then the pain set in. He hadn't even waited to say good-bye. Suddenly, Rachel began to have serious regrets about her plan.

"*Sí*, impossible," Lupe agreed sagely.

"Do you know what he's going to do?" Rachel asked, numbly seating herself in her chair again and not even noticing that Lupe nodded. "He's going to round up that herd again and take it all the way to Kansas. He's going to take it himself, when he's got a bunkhouse full of able-bodied men who could do it for him. Did you ever hear of anything so ridiculous?" she demanded in despair.

"Do you tell him to stay?"

"Of course I did," Rachel insisted, "But he's the most stubborn man alive. He's made up his mind, and he won't listen to reason."

"You can make him stay," Lupe suggested mildly. "Tell him."

Tell him. The words seemed to echo through Rachel's mind. Yes, she could tell him her secret. That would do it, that would keep him here for sure. Or would it? She wasn't even really certain about that when she remembered the way he had left her this morning without a word. She laid a protective hand over her abdomen. "No, I can't."

Lupe mumbled something disapproving.

Rachel's head came up defiantly. "What if I told him and he still didn't stay? Besides, if he won't stay because of me, then I don't want him to stay for any other reason."

Lupe clicked her tongue. "Stubborn man, stubborn

woman." Rachel glared at her, but she ignored it. "Eat," the old woman commanded, pointing a bony finger at the plate.

Rachel was no longer hungry, but she dutifully began to put food into her mouth and chew and swallow it. "Did he say how long he'd be gone?" she asked, vaguely regretting how important the answer would be to her.

"Two week. Maybe three. He not sure," Lupe said.

Rachel gagged down another mouthful, even though the flapjacks now tasted like sawdust to her. Two weeks. Knowing Cole, he wouldn't come home until the roundup was finished, either, and then he'd be gone for three months. That meant she'd probably only see him one more time before he left. She blinked against the sting of tears.

Where had she gone wrong? Lupe had promised her that he would love her once they had made love, but Lupe had been wrong. Oh, he liked making love, but that was obviously not enough. She had been a fool to give her heart to a man who didn't love her back. The only problem was that realizing it too late didn't help a bit. And it was too late, far too late to do anything about it.

Cole rode slowly into the ranch yard, forcing himself not to hurry, not to let on how anxious he was to get home. They had made the gather in record time, one day short of two weeks, but still they would be getting a late start. It was already May and that meant that if they lost any time at all on the trail, they might be among the last herds to arrive in Dodge City. The men were holding the herd nearby, and in the morning they would head north. Tonight, though, he would be with Rachel.

Just thinking about it made his mouth go dry. During the long days and nights of the roundup, he had spent a lot of time thinking about her, trying to figure her out. Although he had not been able to do so, he had somehow managed to forget how furious he was with her and remember only how

267

wonderful she was. But furious or not, he couldn't recall ever feeling like this before about another woman. He'd known several, through the years, who had held his interest for a period of time, several whom he had always looked forward to seeing, but he had never felt exactly this way before. It had something to do with Rachel being Rachel, he knew. Sometimes he wondered if the old witch hadn't put a spell on him or something. All he was really certain of was that he was going to have a hell of a time riding away from here in the morning, no matter what kind of a greeting Rachel gave him tonight.

Looking around the neat ranch yard, Cole observed that he also had a feeling for the place that had nothing to do with Rachel at all, a feeling of peace that a man gets only when he knows he has come home. He had experienced that peace the first time he had ever laid eyes on the ranch, even before he'd accepted a job from Mr. McKinsey. It was almost like he'd known that this, of all the places he had ever been, was the one where he would finally settle. Cole sighed, reflecting that he wasn't ever likely to be more settled than he was now.

Rachel was in the kitchen, up to her elbows in bread dough, when she heard him calling her. "In the kitchen," she called back without thinking, her heart racing. Then she moaned in despair, remembering that she was wearing a ragged old housedress and her hair was a mess, and because her hands were covered with dough, there wasn't even anything she could do about it.

He appeared in the doorway, pausing there first to test his welcome. "Hello," he said quietly when he had taken a minute just to look at her.

"Hello yourself," she replied, a smile trembling on her lips. Her heart had skidded to a complete stop at the sight of him, but it was going again now, although it was tripping along a little too quickly.

She watched him watching her while her hands frantically worked at scrubbing off the remnants of the dough. She tried

268

to remind herself that she was still mad at him, that he was the most infuriating man alive and that he was planning to leave her for the entire summer without so much as a thought to her feelings in the matter. At that particular moment, none of that seemed very important, however. What was important was that he was coming toward her, and she wanted very much to be in his arms.

Cole knew he was taking a chance. She might still be mad at him, and she sure hadn't said anything to make him think any different. She might turn away from his kiss, and if she did, he wouldn't be responsible for what might happen next. Still, he knew that if he didn't get his hands on her soon, he was going to go right out of his mind.

Rachel forgot all about the dough as his arms came around her, and she embraced him back, lifting her face for the kiss she had craved for two long weeks. He tasted of tobacco and Cole, a combination she found irresistible, and she willingly parted her lips for his sweet invasion.

His arms tightened, pulling her against his solid strength, and she gloried in the feel of him, in the way her soft curves molded to him. Her hands traced the sinewy muscles of his back and shoulders, relearning his body and memorizing it for the lonely time to come.

When at last he lifted his mouth from hers, they were both breathless, both weak from wanting. Rachel resisted the urge to pull him back to her, knowing that the kitchen was hardly the place for such wantonness. Instead, she concentrated on breathing, something that had become a conscious effort, and watched the reluctance in his every move as he forced his hands to release her.

Cole drew a ragged breath and stepped away from her, knowing that if he did not do so, he would take her right there on the table beside the bread dough. Imagining what her reaction would be to such a thing brought a wry smile to his lips.

"Is the roundup over?" she asked a little unsteadily as her

269

eyes devoured him. He was taller than she remembered, and maybe a little more bronzed. Everything else was still the same, though. The same broad shoulders, the same narrow waist, the same long legs. His eyes were still the bluest blue she had ever seen, too, and they couldn't seem to get enough of looking at her.

"Yeah," he replied, his voice a little husky. Cole thought she was the most beautiful thing he had ever seen. The old dress she was wearing was soft and faded from many washings and clung faithfully to the generous curve of her breasts. She had unbuttoned the top three buttons and he could see the milk-white skin beneath, glistening from the heat of the kitchen. The opening stopped just short of the shadow between her breasts, but he could imagine it, imagine placing a kiss right there, imagine tasting the salty tang of her skin with the tip of his tongue.

"It hasn't even been two weeks yet," she said, flushing slightly at the direction of his gaze and wishing once again that he had not caught her looking so shabby. She had forced herself not to even begin watching for him until after tomorrow. That was why he had caught her off guard. She watched in fascination as he wiped his palms along the thighs of his jeans, remembering how those hands felt rubbing along her naked flesh. She shivered slightly.

"I pushed the men hard. I was in a hurry to get back," he said. He couldn't remember ever seeing her like this outside of bed. Her hair was coming loose from where she had it pinned up, and he liked the way some strands were falling down around her face. And her face. He would have sworn that she got prettier every time he saw her. She looked different, somehow, fresher or brighter or happier or something. He wasn't exactly sure what it was. He only knew that it was true.

"I'm glad you're back," she said, pleased by his hint that he had missed her. The flush that had warmed her cheeks spread to heat more distant parts of her body.

270

"Well . . ." he said, not quite certain what to say or do next, only sure that he couldn't do the thing he most desired, "looks like I've got time to take a bath before supper's ready."

Rachel wrinkled her nose in a comic grimace. "You look like you could use one," she remarked, only now noticing that he was still wearing his range clothes and that he'd carried a goodly portion of the range in with him.

Cole grinned, showing his dimple, and slapped a small cloud of dust from his shirt. "Yeah, the truth is, I'm so rank I'm starting to wind myself."

At the sight of that beloved smile, something inside Rachel melted, very slowly and very sweetly. She loved him so much. "There's hot water in the boiler," she said, wondering even as she did so how her voice could sound so normal when every nerve in her body seemed to be tingling.

He nodded, and she watched in fascination as he walked over to the boiler and drew off two buckets of hot water. She loved the loose-jointed, graceful way he moved, the way his shirt pulled tight across his shoulders when he stretched. She inhaled deeply and let out her breath in a shaky sigh.

"Well, I'll see you later," he said, forcing himself to lift the buckets and head for the door. She was still smiling. That was a good sign. And she'd kissed him. Boy, howdy, had she kissed him, so she wasn't mad anymore. He only had one night, and he didn't want to waste it fighting.

When he was gone, Rachel sighed again. She only had one night to convince him to stay and what a night it was going to be. A secret smile curved her lips and she hugged herself in anticipation. That was when she noticed that her hands were still quite doughy and she remembered what she had been doing when he came in. Quickly, she returned to the table and began to work the dough furiously, throwing in more flour until it reached the proper consistency so that she could knead it and shape it into loaves. She didn't have much time, not if she wanted to be bathed and dressed herself by suppertime.

Rachel sat primly erect at the table, her tight corset giving her no other choice, and she smiled her secret smile again. It was a wicked thing to have done, but she was feeling very wicked indeed tonight. She'd read about it in a book, a book that one of the girls at school had sneaked in, and she had promised herself that if she ever had the opportunity, she would try it. But that would come later, she reminded herself, and glanced up to see that Cole had finished his meal and was waiting for her.

He looked very much as he had the day they had gotten married. He was wearing the same clothes and his hair was all slicked back. There was something very different about him tonight, though. Rachel thought it was his eyes. Whenever he looked at her, she had the alarming sensation of intense heat, almost as if those azure eyes had the power to burn through her clothing and scorch the bare skin underneath. It was a delicious sensation.

Rachel laid down her fork and rose gracefully from her chair. "Shall we go into the parlor?" she asked coolly, in marked contrast to the way she was feeling.

Cole rose and followed her into the other room. God, she looked wonderful, he decided, watching the sway of her hips under the bustled drape of her skirt. As inviting as she had looked this afternoon in the kitchen, this was the Rachel that most excited him, the one who was so neat and ladylike on the outside, but who, underneath all those fancy clothes, was a fiery little vixen. Cole drew a ragged breath and wondered how long he would have to wait before he could decently suggest they go to bed. He didn't want her to think he'd only come home for *that*, but he didn't think he could wait much longer, either.

Rachel sat down in one of the wing chairs and smoothed the skirt of her violet gown. She had chosen it especially because of the way it fit her so perfectly, accentuating the curves her corset had pushed into prominence. One glance at

Cole's expression told her she had made the right choice. With elaborate casualness, she took up her embroidery. From the corner of her eye, she observed Cole as he strolled over to the fireplace, where he carefully rolled and lighted himself a cigarette. Draping his arm across the mantel, he stood there and smoked it. She knew he was watching her, but she didn't look up. Instead she continued to sew, pushing the needle in and out, in and out, basking in the golden glow of his attention.

"Did you have any problems getting the cattle rounded up?" she asked after a while.

Cole inhaled deeply and let the smoke out on a long breath. "No, nothing big. The herd's a little nervous, though. I reckon being stampeded like that made them kind of skittish. They'll probably settle down once we get moving." It seemed like a pretty silly thing to be discussing, when he really had a million other, important things to say to her. He wanted to know what she was going to do while he was gone. How would she occupy her time? Would she miss him? Had she missed him the other times he had been gone? Would she worry about him? Did she really understand why he had to go? Did she know how much he hated to leave her and that only his compelling need to prove how well he could care for her could make him go?

But he didn't say any of those things. Instead, he crushed out his cigarette on the hearth and rolled another and glanced impatiently at the clock. Had the damn thing stopped? Only two minutes had passed since he last looked at it, but he could have sworn it had been at least a half an hour. He was beginning to think that he would lose his mind long before it was late enough to suggest going to bed. He began to pace the floor.

Rachel bit down hard on her lip to keep from smiling. Now he was pacing. She didn't need much imagination to know what was bothering him. Why he didn't just scoop her up and carry her into bed, she couldn't imagine. She guessed it had something to do with some overblown sense of propreity. How shocked he would be to know that she was seriously considering scooping him up and carrying him to bed. She was fairly certain that she didn't have to be quite so bold to accomplish her purpose, however.

Very ostentatiously, she bit off the thread of the flower she had just finished and held up her work to admire it. Then with a satisfied sigh, she stuck the needle safely into the material and tucked the whole thing back into her sewing bag.

Knowing she had his complete attention, she stood up and said, "Well, I think I'll go to bed now."

Cole glanced briefly at the clock and confirmed his impression that it was entirely too early to even think about going to bed. His eyes narrowed suspiciously. What was she up to this time? If she thought she was going to pull that same trick again, she had another think coming. "Oh, no, you're not," he said, tossing his cigarette into the fire and planting his hands belligerently on his hips.

Rachel stared up at him in complete surprise. "I'm not?"

"No, you're not," he confirmed, advancing on her menacingly, "and don't try to pretend that you're tired, either."

"I'm not tired," she said faintly, baffled at his sudden hostility, and then, suddenly the word "tired" triggered a memory. That was the excuse she had used the last time. "I'm not a bit tired," she hastily assured him. "I just thought that since this is your last night, you'd want to get . . . started . . ." Her voice trailed off uncertainly as she realized how brazen she sounded. What would he think of her?

Now it was Cole's turn to stare. Good God, did she really mean . . . ? "Rachel." Her name was a growl, deep in his chest, and before she could even lift her head in acknowledgment, she was in his arms.

She made a muffled protest against his lips as her feet left the floor, but they were already at the bedroom door before

274

she managed to break free of his kiss to gasp, "Get the lamp!"

Cole stumbled to a halt, his amazed expression almost comical. "The lamp?" he repeated incredulously.

"Yes, the lamp," she said as primly as she could, considering she was being held high against his chest. "I need some light to get out of this outfit," she informed him as seriously as she could under the circumstances. What she did not add was that she needed the light so that he could see her getting out of it.

"The lamp," he repeated, obviously thoroughly puzzled, but he turned and retraced his steps, still holding her, until they reached the table where the lamp rested. "Help yourself," he said, lowering her so she could reach it.

Struggling to control her growing excitement, Rachel captured her prize and held it carefully away from his face as he once again headed for the bedroom. This time he did not stop when he got to the doorway but went inside, kicking the door shut behind him. Still without stopping he went directly to the bed where he set her down with exaggerated care. With even more exaggerated care, he took the lamp from her hands and placed it gingerly on the bedside table.

Rachel was busily reviewing the next step in her plan for the evening until he turned back to her and she saw the expression in his eyes. He was not going to wait for the next step. "Cole, wait!" she cried, but she was too late.

He lunged, his weight carrying them both down onto the bed. This wasn't the way she had planned it, she thought in some distant part of her brain, but somehow that no longer mattered. His hungry mouth blocked any protest and after a few seconds, she forgot about making one.

His hands framed her face, holding her still for his kiss, and his fingers slid back into the velvet of her hair. In another moment he was rooting out the pins that held it so tightly against her head until at last she felt it tumble free. His fingers combed through the silken length of it and he rolled over, carrying her with him so that she lay on top of

275

him, her hair falling around them in an ebony cascade. "Oh, Rachel," he moaned, nuzzling her neck beneath the rose-scented tresses.

Rachel thought for a moment that she might die from the sheer joy of it until she realized that her real death might very well be imminent. "I have . . . to get . . . out of this . . . dress . . ." she gasped, finally equating her breathlessness with the tightness of her corset and not with Cole's passionate assualt. She had to struggle a moment until he reluctantly released her and allowed her to slide down off his body until her feet touched the floor.

Awkwardly, she staggered upright, almost losing her resolve when she saw the bluest eyes in the world devouring her every move. But she had to get rid of the dress, no matter what else happened, she told herself sternly. And besides, she had her wicked little surprise. Newly resolved, Rachel straightened beside the bed and backed up a few steps.

As if he were attached to her by some invisible cord, Cole rose as she retreated until he sat upright. That azure gaze never left her as he reached down and pulled off first one of his boots and then the other.

Her chocolate-colored gaze never left him as she swiftly undid the myriad buttons of her dress. Mesmerized, she watched his hands move to loosen his own buttons and pull the tail of his shirt loose from his pants and then strip the garment from his broad shoulders, baring that broad furred chest. As if in answer, she peeled the violet dress from her own shoulders and let it slide slowly to the floor.

Cole admired the ivory expanse of her bosom lifted proudly above the constriction of her corset, and anticipated how the satiny flesh would feel beneath his hands and mouth. He had just gathered himself to reach for her when something very startling registered on his consciousness.

"What the hell . . . ?" He stared. And then he gaped. He'd never seen anything like it.

Rachel felt the heat from his eyes as a tangible force that

seemed to scorch her naked skin. She knew she must be blushing down to her very toes, but things had gone too far to back out now. With fingers that trembled slightly, she untied her petticoats and let them fall in a taffeta pool around her feet.

Cole continued to gape. Standing there in her corset and her drawers with her hair all wild and tangled, she looked like a vision from his wildest fantasies. As if that wasn't enough, though, the corset was red! Bright red, with black lace on it. No, he really had never, ever seen anything like it.

She had shocked him, she realized, really shocked him. The knowledge pleased her. She had wanted to make this night the most memorable one they had ever shared, and from the way he was looking at her, she had a feeling he would never forget a moment of it. Daintily, she stepped clear of the pile of petticoats. "You'll have to help me with my corset," she informed him.

Those blue eyes narrowed suspiciously once more. "Help you how?" he asked somewhat hoarsely.

"You'll have to unlace me," she said, placing her hands on her hips expectantly.

Cole watched those hands, noticing the way the corset cinched her in and lifted her breasts invitingly. "I don't know how," he said, even as he rose from the bed and moved toward her. Was the thing made out of satin? It was shining in the lamplight and he wondered if it felt as soft as it looked. It looked, except for the color, almost like human skin. Like Rachel's skin.

"There's nothing to it," she promised, presenting him with her back and whipping the length of her hair off her neck and over her shoulder to rest on her breast. "Just unlace it like you would a shoe."

Cole stared in horror. Oh, it was just like a shoe, all right. Like a shoe with a hundred eyes. He reached out and very gently pulled loose the bow that rested on her lower back. The first few holes were relatively easy, but with each hole the laces grew longer and it took longer to pull them free. He let his knuckles brush against the surrounding material. It *was* satin and it did feel just like Rachel's skin. It was even warm from her body.

The laces slid free of another pair of holes, and Cole drew an unsteady breath, inhaling the scent of roses and Rachel. He tried to concentrate on what he was doing, but he kept thinking how he had never noticed that the back of her neck was so beautiful or that the lamplight turned the skin of her shoulders to the color of fresh cream. His gaze kept straying over her shoulder to where that creamy skin swelled gently and disappeared beneath the silk of her chemise. He worked mechanically now, pulling the ever-lengthening laces by touch, not even watching anymore how the red satin slowly separated.

Rachel closed her eyes, sensing the heat of his body so close to hers. She could smell his musky scent and knew from the scent that when she turned, his body would be moist to the touch, the way it was when he was inside her. She shivered slightly as invisible fingers raised gooseflesh up the inside of her thighs and his warm breath flowed over her naked shoulders in increasingly ragged gasps. Every tiny hair on her body stood to attention and the blood sang through her veins, trilling a siren song that grew louder and louder until it was a roaring in her ears.

As if from far away, she felt the laces whisper free of the last holes, felt the bulky satin slide away and fall to the floor. And then Cole's arms came around her, encasing her in a corset of flesh and bone that drew her close and stopped her breath. His mouth came down on the bare skin of her shoulder, tasting and devouring, until she could stand it no more and turned in his arms, lifting her face for his kiss.

Lips and tongues explored while hands sought out familiar territory, tracing hills and valleys through flimsy silken barriers and molding vibrant flesh to vibrant flesh. His hands cupped her buttocks, lifting her to him, and she

278

wrapped her legs around him, clinging to his strength as he carried her to the bed.

Cole sank down into the feather tick and fell backward, intending to carry Rachel with him, but she resisted, breaking the sweet seal of their mouths and raising up slightly. With an impudent grin, she wiggled to a sitting position, straddling his hips with their bodies in intimate contact through the barrier of their clothes and her legs spread wide on either side of his body. She gracefully removed one garter and began to peel down her stocking. Cole watched in fascination, propping his arms beneath his head to better observe the operation.

"Thank you for helping me with my corset," she said, not bothering to hide her smile. She could not keep her eyes from the bare expanse of his chest.

Cole waited until the black silk had slid clear of her leg, revealing the gentle curve of one calf and the delicately arched foot. "How in the he— world do you get out of it when you're alone?" he inquired lazily while she removed the other garter.

Rachel rolled the second stocking down and down and off and tossed it over her shoulder. "I unhook it down the front," she informed him casually.

"What?"

Cole reared up but Rachel had scrambled free. Now on her feet, she swiftly untied the drawstring of her drawers and let them fall. Clad only in her chemise, which barely reached to the tops of her thighs, she managed to look contrite. "I'm sorry I tricked you," she lied.

"You're going to be," he promised just before he lunged for her.

In the wrestling match that followed, Rachel's chemise disappeared and so did the rest of Cole's clothes, the lamp somehow went out and they managed to wriggle underneath the covers where they quickly warmed the cool sheets with their passion. They came together almost frantically, desperate in their needs and wants. Rachel clasped him to her, wanting it never to end but compelled to satisfy the merciless craving that threatened to destroy.

They lay for a long time afterward, weak and panting, in a tangle of arms and legs. Rachel smiled in the darkness, remembering how she had planned the scene with the corset even before she had ever met Cole Elliot, knowing how exciting it would be to tease her man. "Do you forgive me for the corset?" she asked. They were lying nose to nose and even in the dark she felt his answering smile.

"Does that thing really open down the front?" he asked, his voice rumbling lazily from deep in his chest.

Rachel nodded, rubbing her nose against his in delicious intimacy. "Uh-huh."

"That was a rotten trick," he said, but she could hear the laughter in his voice. "And you should get what you deserve." Before she could ask just what that might be, one large hand swooped underneath the covers and placed a very awkward slap on her bottom.

It didn't hurt. It was, in fact, more of a pat than a slap, but Rachel entered into the spirit of the game once more, squealing in outrage and thrashing around beneath the bedclothes in an attempt to land a blow in vengeance. Quite by accident, she found herself grabbing something else entirely.

At first she couldn't imagine what it was, but realization came the moment she heard Cole's gasp. She released it instantly. "Oh! I'm . . . I'm sorry," she stammered, mortified. "Did I hurt you?"

"N—no," he assured her a little breathlessly. "It didn't hurt at all."

His voice sounded so funny that she thought he might be lying. Then she considered. His breath was coming fast, the way it did when . . . A new possibility occurred to her.

"Are you sure?" she asked provocatively, running her hand over his chest, tangling her fingers into the hairs that curled there.

"Yeah," he said on a deep breath that came out a little shakily.

"Good. I wouldn't want to hurt you," she purred, letting her hand stray lower and then lower still. The hair thinned out and then reappeared. She was slightly surprised to discover that he had hair down there just as she did. Then she found what she was seeking. It was smooth and soft and warm, nestled at the apex of his legs. Her fingers closed around it tentatively.

"Rachel," he said warningly, but she knew he didn't mean it. She thought how odd that she had always imagined it being bigger and harder, and then, suddenly, it was. "What's happening?" she squeaked in alarm.

Cole moaned as he rolled them both over. "You're asking for trouble, that's what's happening," he muttered, pinning her down into the deep feather mattress. His kiss silenced any questions she might have had.

She didn't have any, though. When he moved over her, she had all the answers she needed.

This time he was slow, as slow as she had been on the last night they had made love. This time he was the tormentor and Rachel the victim. She submitted willingly, though, allowing him to have his way with her. The warm glow that welcomed him soon grew hotter, fanned steadily by his delicate ministrations, and Rachel melted into it, swirling and dissolving until she was a mass of molten colors that flickered and glittered and shimmered and gleamed. Still he kept on, until each breath was a sob and Rachel could not tell if it were he or herself who was sobbing. The end came just when she knew she would not live a moment longer, and it came with a flash of brilliance that blinded her, closing out all else and sealing the two of them into their own private place, forever.

Forever, she muttered as she felt asleep in his arms. He would never leave her now. She was certain of it.

In the morning, when dawn teased its way into the room to disturb her, she reached out for him once more but the bed was empty.

"Cole!"

Rachel sat bolt upright in the bed, frantically scanning the room for him. Mercifully, she found him, and her whole body sagged in relief.

He was standing at the washstand, shaving in the morning light. With his startled face still marked with stray streaks of lather, he looked awfully dear, and she took a few seconds just to stare at him. "I was afraid you'd gone," she said softly, a small smile curving her lips. She should have known he wouldn't have left her.

"No, I . . ." His voice was husky and he had to clear his throat and try again. "I wouldn't do a thing like that."

He was staring at her quite intently, and she suddenly felt self-conscious, knowing that her unbound hair would be a mess. Reaching up a hand to brush it back from her face, she became aware of something else that was unbound—and completely exposed! With an embarrassed cry, she yanked up the covers that had fallen to her waist and held them modestly to her naked breasts. Her face was hot with embarrassment, but when she again met his eyes and saw the frank admiration there, her discomfort faded and the heat in her cheeks settled down to warm the rest of her.

Cole picked up a towel and wiped his face. "No, I wouldn't leave without saying good-bye. I was just letting you sleep until I was ready to go."

Rachel gaped at him. *Go?* How could he still be talking about going? "You aren't really going to leave me?" she asked incredulously. Not after last night, her mind screamed.

Cole turned back to her and took a deep breath. He was wearing only his jeans, and Rachel watched his bare chest rise and fall. Irrelevantly, she noticed that he was still too thin. "Rachel, this cattle will bring a lot of money, maybe as much as ten thousand dollars. Do you know how important that money is to the Circle M?"

She shook her head dumbly. Didn't he know there were other things that were important, too?

"Well, I'll tell you," he said, forcing the words out. He hadn't wanted to scare her, but he was going to have to tell her the truth or she'd think he was leaving her because he didn't care about her feelings. "I've looked at the books and as near as I can figure, without that money, the Circle M won't last another six months." He took a few steps closer to the bed. "Do you understand? In six months you'll be broke."

"Somebody else could take the cattle," she said stubbornly.

"And what if something happened?" he demanded, angry now, although he wasn't certain at whom his anger was directed. "What it they didn't get through? What if they got cheated? What if they got robbed? What if they never made it back here?"

Those sky-blue eyes were like chips of ice, and she could see from the set of his jaw that he would not be swayed, but she felt compelled to try. "The same things could happen to you," she pointed out.

She could almost see some of the anger drain out of him. "Then it would be on my head." He made a beseeching gesture with his hand. "Don't you see? I can't let anybody else take this chance. It's too important." He paused, letting his hand drop. "It's too important to you."

That was it, then. At last she did understand. He was doing this for her. As much as she wanted him to stay, she also knew a sense of gratitude for what he was doing. It was natural, she supposed, to feel cherished by his gesture. She only wished she could feel happier about it.

Forcing a small smile, she made a feeble attempt to let him know she accepted his decision even though she could not like it. "Why don't you come over here and kiss me good-bye then?" she asked.

There was certainly nothing he wanted to do more, but he hesitated. He remembered only too well that underneath those blankets, Rachel was stark naked. He could still see the way her breasts had looked, so round and smooth with tiny pink nipples that pointed up with sassy impudence. If he went over there and kissed her, one thing would lead to another, but the sun was already well up and the men would be waiting and . . .

Sensing his hesitation, Rachel loosened her grip on the blankets and let them fall again. This was one argument she was determined to win.

Cole watched the blanket fall. The men could wait.

It was the first time they had made love in the light, the first time eyes had seen what fingers and hands had learned so well. Each could only marvel at the beauty of the other, and they spent a long time silently appreciating each other in the dapple morning sunlight.

When they finally came together for what each knew would be the last time for a very long time, they did so tenderly, drawing out the moment of possession. Murmured love words passed from lip to lip, mingling with warm breaths and kisses. Hands stroked reverently, memorizing what would soon be gone. Hips churned gently in familiar rhythms, giving and receiving until the giving became receiving and each blended into the other. At the ending such distinctions mattered not at all.

After a long time, Cole stirred. "It's getting late," he murmured. With infinite reluctance, he began to untangle himself from her embrace.

Grudgingly, she released him, allowing him to rise but holding him in the bondage of her gaze. She adored him with her eyes, only half aware that he was doing the same to her. After long moments, he reached down and drew the blanket back over her. "There," he said with a self-mocking grin. "If I have to keep looking at you, I'll never get out of here."

"I wouldn't mind," she said. She saw his lips tighten momentarily but then the grin was back and he was going for his clothes. She watched him dress, studying every movement, memorizing every line, every muscle, every inch of him. Three months was a long time.

When he was finished, he turned back to her briefly. "I'll grab a bite to eat while you get dressed," he said, and he was gone before she could reply.

As usual, Lupe had his breakfast ready. She didn't even remark on how late it was or that his food had grown cold. She only watched him in stoic silence until Cole started to wonder if his petticoat were showing or something.

But he had more important things to think about, he decided grimly. Like Rachel. If he lived to be a hundred, he knew he'd never understand her. One minute she was the perfect lady and the next she was wearing a red corset, of all things. And making him unlace it, too, knowing—as she must have known—that it would drive him out of his mind. And then there was this morning.

Thinking back, he realized that Rachel had actually seduced him. He'd never been seduced before. It was a funny feeling, and he wasn't quite sure if he liked it or not. Oh, of course he liked *it,* all right. What he didn't like was not being in control, not when he still couldn't quite trust her. He just wasn't certain whether her passion came from genuine affection or a desire to control him. And she was definitely trying to control him. She didn't want him to go on this trip and she had let him know. He was still going, but she'd thrown her half hitch on him all the same. The ropes were pinching and he knew he was getting out only by the skin of his teeth. Next time . . . Next time, he had the unsettling feeling that no matter what he decided, he would do whatever Rachel wanted. The knowledge rankled.

She still hadn't come out of the bedroom when he had finished eating. Cole knew he didn't dare go back in there with her or he wouldn't get to leave today at all, so he went down to the corral to saddle his horse. He was glad no one was around, because all of a sudden he was feeling mighty unsociable. The closer he got to time to leave, the less he wanted to go and the more he knew he had to, if only to prove to Rachel and himself that he would do what he knew was right no matter how hard she tried to convince him otherwise.

Memories of last night and this morning teased at him as he roped the gelding he had ridden in the day before and tied it to the fence. If only he had some clue about what went on inside her head. She must care for him a little. She couldn't have been pretending. Nobody, and certainly not a lady like Rachel, could act like that just out of a desire to control somebody, he reasoned as he went inside the barn to get his saddle.

"'Morning," Miles said cheerfully. He had wandered over from the bunkhouse and stood leaning against the barn when Cole came out.

Cole grunted a greeting and went to saddle his horse. Miles frowned at his back. When the gelding shied from Cole's brisk movements, Miles called out in warning, "Watch what you're doing there."

Cole ignored him and threw the saddle blanket over the reluctant animal's back.

Miles stared at him, completely puzzled. Of course, Miles had expected him to be kind of down, what with him having to leave Rachel and all, but Cole looked downright mad. What could have caused that? Miles considered a moment, and then a knowing look lighted his eye. "Hey, now," he soothed, certain he had discovered the reason. "Don't be like that. She can't help it."

Cole whirled on him, wondering how Miles could have guessed about his problems with Rachel. "What do you mean?" he asked warily.

Miles gave him an understanding smile. "You come in here randy as an old range bull and find out it's the wrong time of the month. It's not her fault . . ."

"It's not the wrong time of the month," Cole snapped and bent to pick up his saddle.

Miles considered. What else could have put Cole in such a foul mood? "You mean she just turned you down?" he wondered aloud.

Cole whirled on him again. "She didn't turn me down! Now mind your own damn business."

But Miles wasn't about to be deterred. "This *is* my business. I've got to stay here with her all summer and if you two had a fight . . ."

Cole gritted his teeth in an attempt to hold in his temper. "We did not have a fight," he explained with elaborate patience, "and she did not turn me down." He turned with an air of finality to pick up the saddle again.

Miles watched him throw it over the horse and cinch it tight. Cole was heading back to the barn for the bridle when Miles figured it out.

"Look, *amigo,*" he said, following Cole into the barn, "you can't expect a nice girl like Miss Rachel to like sex as much as you do . . ."

Roaring a curse, Cole whirled on Miles a third time. "She likes it too damn much," he blurted before he could stop himself. For a long moment the two men stood staring at each other, neither quite believing that Cole had really said what he had.

Embarrassed that he had confided a thing like that about his wife, Cole tried to go after the headpiece, but Miles caught him by the arm.

"What are you saying?" Miles asked, accusation in his voice.

Cole shook free of Miles's grip, glaring at his friend in irritation. What *was* he saying? Since he really wasn't certain himself, he had to grope for the words to explain. "It's just . . . it's hard to believe that a lady like Rachel would . . ." He gestured vaguely.

"Are you saying Miss Rachel isn't a lady?" Miles demanded.

"Of course not!" Cole snapped, unsure whether he was more angry with Miles or himself. He was behaving like a damn fool, all because he couldn't quite reconcile the way Rachel acted in bed with the way she acted other times. And because he was unable to understand the why of it.

Miles's spectral eyes glared at him, reading his confusion. "You jackass," Miles said, knowing he was the only one in the world who could get away with doing so. "If you've got a woman who likes it, you ought to get down on your knees and give thanks. Don't you know that a lady like Miss Rachel would only be that way because she loves you?"

Cole's mouth dropped open. Love? Could Rachel really love him? Before he could even consider the answer to that question, however, he heard her calling his name.

"There she is," Miles hissed. "Now you march over there and you kiss her good-bye like it's killing you to leave her and no more of this crazy talk. I've got to be here with her all summer and I want her happy. I don't want her mooning around here with her heart breaking because she thinks you think poorly of her."

Cole opened his mouth to protest that he most certainly did not think poorly of her, but Miles said, "Go!" and gave him a gentle shove to send him on his way.

Muttering an imprecation about meddling old fools, Cole did as he was told. It wasn't very difficult. It really was killing him to leave her. She was standing on the porch and she was dressed the way he always pictured her. Wearing a pretty blue dress with flowers all over it, she looked as prim and pure as if no man had ever laid a hand on her. Her hair was pulled neatly back and tucked into a tight bun with not a strand out of place. A far cry from the naked, tousled, glowing creature who had lured him back into bed this morning.

She came down the stairs toward him and stepped right

into his arms. That was when he knew that no matter what she looked like on the outside, she was still that creature, and Miles was right, he ought to get down on his knees and give thanks. Later, though. Right now, he'd just kiss her.

Rachel clung to him as if her life depended on never letting him go, and at that moment, she thought it might. How could he leave her like this? He couldn't possibly care for her if he were able to leave, and if he didn't love her, what would bring him back again? The pain from these torturous thoughts tore through her even as the fervency of his kiss belied them. He had to care for her, reason insisted. He couldn't make love to her the way he did if he didn't love her just a little. He would come back for that. He would. He simply had to.

At long last, Cole reluctantly lifted his head, wondering if he were out of his mind to be saying good-bye to a woman like this. Her own breath was as ragged as his, and he saw to his surprise that she was crying. Not crying hard or anything, but her eyes were wet and she looked awfully sad. This was killing her, too, he realized with startling clarity. Maybe she did love him, a little bit, anyway.

A wave of regret washed over him, almost overwhelming his resolution. "I have to go," he whispered, as much to convince himself as to convince her. "I have to make sure you're taken care of," he said, and this time he believed it once again.

Rachel nodded her reluctant understanding. Then she reached up and laid her hand along his smoothly shaven cheek and remembered that once she had not thought him handsome. Now she knew that he was the best-looking man she had ever seen, and she loved him so much she thought her heart might burst from it. "You'll be careful, won't you?" she asked. Trailing cattle was dangerous. Men sometimes got hurt or killed doing it. There were lightning storms and stampedes and raging rivers and a host of other mishaps.

"I'm always careful," he lied, silently promising himself

that he would be this time, just for her.

"And you'll write to me, to let me know how things are?" she asked.

He hedged at this. "There won't be much to write about . . ."

"I don't care. I just want to know that you're all right," she insisted.

He nodded, not really promising. "It's late. The men'll be waiting," he reminded her with regret.

Slowly, she released him, but he couldn't leave her quite yet. "Walk me to my horse," he commanded, taking her hand.

By the time they reached the barn, they had their arms around each other, and Cole noticed with mild annoyance that Miles was grinning at them like a cat with his head in the cream pitcher.

"Have a good trip *amigo,*" Miles said, stretching out his hand.

Cole took it without letting go of Rachel. "And you take good care of my girl," he replied, giving her a loving look.

Rachel memorized that look, perserving it in her heart for the lonely weeks and months to come. He did care and he would come back to her. She knew he would. For one wild moment she considered telling him her secret, just to be certain, but she quickly stifled that urge. No, as desperately as she needed to know he would return, she also needed for him to return to her and only to her. When he did so, he would have earned the right to know. As he dropped Miles's hand, she slid both her arms around Cole and held him close.

Cole returned her embrace for one agonizing moment before she gave a very suspicious-sounding sniff and then lifted her face for his final kiss. The kiss was long and sweet. Bittersweet.

Rachel pulled away first, knowing that soon she would cry, really cry, and wanting him to be gone when she did so. She looked ugly when she cried, and she didn't want him to remember her that way. Pinning a tiny smile on her trembling lips, she stepped back as he slowly let his hands fall away from her.

For a long moment, they just looked at each other, and then Miles cleared his throat. "The men are waiting," he reminded. Cole nodded absently, and turned to mount his horse, hardly taking his eyes off Rachel during the entire process. Only then did he notice that Miles had put the headpiece on the animal.

Not trusting his voice, Cole raised his hand in a farewell salute and kicked the horse into motion. Rachel lifted her hand also and waved. She waved again when he stopped to look back just before topping the rise that would take him out of sight. Whether he waved back or not, she could not see, because her tears had blinded her.

Miles placed a comforting hand on her shoulder. "He'll come back," he assured her.

Rachel dashed away a tear and lifted her chin resolutely. "He'd better," she replied.

Chapter IX

Rachel glanced around the bustling town of Canaan while she waited for Miles to come around and help her down from the wagon. She had holed up out at the ranch for the entire three weeks that Cole had been gone so far, but this morning Miles and Lupe had conspired to bully her into going into town for supplies. Not that Miles wasn't perfectly capable of going alone, but Lupe had muttered something about how Rachel needed to get out to get the stink blown off, and Rachel had decided that she probably was becoming a little sour-tempered sitting around the house all the time.

Anyway, here she was in Canaan. She would do some shopping and stop by to see some of her old friends whom she had neglected in the busy days since her marriage. The outing would do her good. She would also see if she had any mail. Enough time had passed that she might very well have a letter. Or even two.

Miles lifted her effortlessly to the ground, but made no move to step out of her way to let her pass. When she looked up inquiringly, he asked, very softly, "Do you want me to go inside with you?" He cut his eyes very discreetly in the direction of Hank Oliver's Mercantile.

Rachel started to assure him that she didn't need a chaperon, but then she remembered the last time she had seen Hank Oliver, and she changed her mind. Still, pride dictated that she not let anyone, especially her guardian, see her hesitation. "I'm sure you have some shopping to do, too," she replied noncommittally.

Miles nodded and stepped back to let her pass, a small smile of admiration on his thin lips.

Hank Oliver had seen them drive up, but this time he waited behind the counter for them to come inside instead of meeting her at the door with outstretched hands the way he always had in times past. Rachel got the distinct impression that he was pouting.

"Good morning, Hank," Rachel said pleasantly, trying to set a normal tone for their meeting.

"Good morning, Mrs. Elliot," Hank responded, giving Miles a disapproving glance.

Rachel pretended not to notice the slight sarcasm in his voice when he used her new name. She reached into her reticule and produced a list. "Here are the supplies we'll be needing. It's a smaller order than usual, since most of our men have gone on the trail drive."

Hank took the list from her gingerly, being careful not to even brush her fingers with his own, and then glanced defiantly at Miles, as if daring the cowboy to comment on his caution.

Rachel watched the byplay and sighed. So Hank was going to be difficult, was he? Well, she was not going to play along. Deciding that ignoring him was the best ploy, Rachel smiled cheerfully. "I'll look around a little. There are some other things I might want. Oh, by the way, is there any mail for me?" she added with creditable nonchalance.

Grudgingly, Hank moved over to the post office window in a far corner of the store and fetched her a slim packet of mail.

Rachel accepted it eagerly and hastily flipped through it. Not finding what she was after, she went through it again, more slowly. No letter from Cole.

Seeing her disappointment, Miles said, "I'll put that in the wagon for you, Mrs. Elliot." Without waiting for her agreement, he took the mail from her unresisting fingers, tucked the packet under his arm and leaned back against the wall to wait for her.

Reminding herself that only three weeks had passed and that the mails could sometimes be slow and could often be erratic, she exchanged an understanding look with Miles, shrugged resolutely and made her way to the rear of the store. Leisurely examining the contents of each shelf as she passed, she picked up a few items here and there and then stopped beside the bolts of material and began to finger some of the fabric. She could use the next few months to get started on the warm things she would need for winter, she reasoned, and tried to decide on a color.

If Rachel thought Hank was pouting, she was right. He watched her move down the aisle, thinking for the thousandth time how she should have been his wife and not the wife of that dirty gunslinger. His lips thinned in anger as he remembered yet again how she had betrayed him, how she had ruined all his plans.

And Hank had many plans. Henry Oliver had been nothing but a clerk back in Richmond, without much prospect of ever becoming anything else when fate had taken a hand. He'd gotten a letter from a lawyer he did not know informing him that his uncle, whom he had never heard of, had passed away, naming Henry's father as his heir. Since Henry's father had predeceased his brother, that made Henry the recipient of his uncle's entire estate. The "estate" had turned out to be this store.

Henry's experience as a clerk had held him in good stead, and he had recognized immediately the possibilities open to the owner of the one and only source of supply in this small Texas outpost. Oh, he hadn't liked Texas very much. He hated the tiny town, the heat, the dust, and the crudeness of the people with whom he was forced to deal. His innate

295

charm had served him well, though, enabling him to hide his prejudices and helping him to make a place for himself in the community.

He turned what had been a satisfactory business into a thriving one by updating the merchandise and trading on his good looks and Eastern manners to entice the ranchers' wives into buying things they would otherwise have thought unnecessary. The men also liked him because of his pleasant bearing. They had begun to call him "Hank," and although Henry hated the tough-sounding nickname, he had recognized it as a sign that he was accepted and bore it as best he could.

Yes, everything had been going well, Hank reflected as he watched Rachel browsing along one of the aisles. So well that he had raised his sights a bit. After all, a successful businessman in town bore certain responsibilities. The town, so loosely run at the moment, would eventually need a mayor. A mayor might set his sights even higher—the state government someday, perhaps even senator or governor.

His vague dreams had begun to crystallize the moment he met Rachel McKinsey. Not only was she lovely to look at— the most beautiful girl he had seen since coming to this god-forsaken place—but she was educated and well-mannered and cultured, all the things a governor's wife should be. His easy conquests of all the other local girls and women had boosted his opinion of his own attraction, and so he had not been the least surprised when Rachel welcomed his attentions.

He had been "sitting" her, as the cowboys said (although Henry hated the expression, feeling that it sounded too much like what a hen did with her eggs), for months and months. He had decided to take it slow, certain that a girl of Rachel's delicate nature should not be rushed. He also had a vague feeling that Mr. McKinsey did not entirely approve of him, and Hank needed time to convince the old man that he was the perfect husband for his precious daughter.

Hank had begun to think that he had succeeded, too, and that McKinsey had finally come around. If he didn't exactly seem overjoyed to see Hank each time he came to call, at least he seemed resigned. Knowing how McKinsey doted on the girl, Henry also knew that the old man would give her whatever she wanted, even if what she wanted was Hank Oliver.

Everything had fallen into place quite nicely, and then McKinsey had turned up dead. Hank knew immediately what that event would mean to him. He only needed a few moments to decide that he should rush right out to the ranch and offer his strong shoulder for Rachel to weep on. He would help her with all the unpleasant details of running the ranch and make himself indispensable. The fact that he knew nothing of running a ranch did not bother him in the least. Surely, an innocent girl like Rachel would know nothing about such things either, and he could easily bluff his way through. Then, after a decent interval, he would propose to her.

Hank frowned as Rachel reached the end of the aisle and wandered out of his range of vision. Marriage to Rachel would have made him not only a successful merchant with a lovely wife but a wealthy rancher into the bargain, something he had not even bothered to consider before since the old man had been in excellent health and could have been expected to live another forty years at least. Yes, everything would have been perfect for Henry Oliver if he had only heard about McKinsey's death a few days earlier. Hank's frown became a scowl.

Unfortunately, the news had not reached him until the very morning that she had come waltzing in and announced her marriage to Cole Elliot. Fate was a fickle thing. First it had dropped a potential fortune in his lap by giving him the store and then it had tantalized him with another potential fortune before snatching it ruthlessly away.

A few days, if only he had learned about McKinsey's death

a few days earlier, how differently things might have turned out, Hank thought bitterly, turning toward the storeroom. That snake Elliot would not have had time to play on Rachel's fears and pressure her into such an unsuitable marriage. Most of all, he wouldn't have had time to snatch her right out from under Henry Oliver's nose. Every time he thought of it—and he thought of it often—he was filled with a cold fury. Someday, he had vowed impotently, he would get even with Elliot. And someday, if fickle Fate allowed, he would rescue his poor Rachel from that blackguard.

Later, when Hank had finished loading her supplies onto her wagon, Rachel asked him to cut her several yards of outing flannel. He gave her a funny look. With summer coming on, outing flannel was not the fabric of choice for most people, but the coolly defiant look she gave him back made him shrug and begin to measure.

She was so different, so changed from the Rachel he had known before, he noted sadly. He should have expected it, he guessed, what with her living with that brute and having to submit to his lusts. The very thought made Henry shudder slightly, but he reminded himself that she had consented to her own downfall. Bitterly, he lashed out at her.

"I hear Elliot took your cattle north to sell," he said.

Rachel heard the thread of anger in his voice. "That's right," she confirmed warily.

"I also hear cattle is going for twenty dollars or more a head now. That's a lot of money you've trusted him with," Hank pointed out.

Rachel stiffened in anger. Just what was he implying? "Cole is my husband," she reminded him.

"But what do you really know about him?" Hank insisted. "He was nothing but a common gunman when he came here. That's why your father hired him, if you remember, because he was a man who didn't mind bending the law or even breaking it, if it came to that."

"Oliver," Miles's voice cut in warningly, threateningly, but

298

Rachel raised her hand to him to stop his interference. This was something she needed to handle herself.

Her face was burning with the force of her rage, but she tamped it down and held it in check, knowing that hysteria would only convince Hank that she, too, mistrusted Cole. "Cole is my husband," she repeated through clenched teeth. "I would trust him with my very life. Certainly, I can trust him with a small part of all I own."

Hank's anger left a sour taste in his mouth, and he almost felt like weeping as he watched Rachel's eyes grow cold and haughty. Poor Rachel. Poor, dear, innocent Rachel. Her pride would never allow her to admit she had made a mistake, he knew. He could only guess at the indignities she had suffered at the hands of that fiend, and yet she could still defend him. It was so tragic. Once more Henry vowed silently to save her if it ever came within his power to do so.

Seeing that she had successfully silenced Hank's insinuations, Rachel waited stoically while he measured out her material and wrapped it. She snatched the bundle from him when he offered it to her, not even noticing the pitying look he was giving her. "Put it on my account," she snapped, and hurried out of the store.

Fortunately for Rachel, not all her friends were as suspicious of her husband as Hank Oliver had been. The rest of them were much more interested in hearing all the details of the fight with Statler and his men, and with discussing Rachel's opinions of married life. The young women Rachel's age thought Cole Elliot made a strikingly romantic figure after the way he had fought so gallantly for her, and their admiration raised Rachel's spirits somewhat. While she chatted with her friends, she even managed to successfully push Hank Oliver's vicious remarks to the back of her mind.

When the visits had ended, however, and Miles was helping her into the wagon for the trip home, the memory of those remarks came sneaking out again to tease and torment her. She was certain Hank was wrong about Cole's character, but Hank had been right about one thing, at least: she really didn't know much about Cole Elliot. How could she be so certain that he was not the kind of man who could steal from her?

"Folks have called Cole Elliot a lot of things, but nobody's ever called him a thief," Miles remarked as if sensing her thoughts. In fact, he had known exactly what she was thinking about. He himself had thought of little else all day, and from the way Rachel was twisting her wedding ring, she obviously had Cole on her mind.

Rachel looked up gratefully. For a moment she studied the face of the man beside her. He was such a strange man, mysterious almost. The lines on his face betrayed the fact that he seldom smiled, and Rachel had a suspicion that there had been little in his life about which he could smile. How she knew such a thing was beyond her, but she was certain that he had experienced tragedy, great tragedy. Suffering was stamped too clearly on his features for her to doubt it.

She also knew that he could be cruel and that he had killed. He would not have been working for her father if it were otherwise. Still, she could see a softer streak in him, the tender side that had prompted him to defend Cole to her just now and the sensitivity that had told him how much she needed to hear that defense.

Needing reassurance, though, she challenged him. "Cole said the cattle might bring as much as ten thousand dollars. That is a large amount of money."

"Cole considers it your money, Mrs. Elliot," Miles assured her. "He'll bring it back or die trying. He thinks the world and all of you, you know."

Rachel still wasn't entirely convinced of that. "I can't help thinking that if he did 'think the world and all of me,' he wouldn't have left me in the first place," she said, her lips twisting in wry self-mockery.

Miles shook his head, silently cursing Cole Elliot. How could the man have lived with her all this time and not have let her know how he felt? "He figured it was mighty important to get that cattle to market safe and sound. He didn't think he could trust anybody else to do it."

But Rachel had heard all this before. "What about me? Don't I need to be safe and sound, too?" she asked, her frustration flooding back again. She didn't really think she was in danger, but it was certainly a valid argument. "What if some of Statler's old men come back? That's a possibility, isn't it? Shouldn't Cole be here to keep me safe?"

Miles shifted uncomfortably on the wagon seat. "He thought of that."

Rachel perked up at this information. "And what did he decide, that I'm less important than those cows?" she challenged.

"No," he hastened to assure her. "He . . . he decided that you'd be safe with me here to protect you."

"Safer than I would be with him?" she demanded, unconvinced.

Miles's lips thinned down until they whitened from the strain. "Yes."

Rachel stared at him for a long moment. She had only been arguing for the sake of argument, wanting Miles to confirm her faith in Cole, but somehow the conversation had strayed into uncomfortable territory. Studying the stiff set of Miles's shoulders and the grim expression on his face, she knew they had touched on a subject that Miles found distasteful, the subject of his ability to protect her, which meant, boiled down to its essence, the subject of his reputation with a gun.

"Miles, who are you?" she asked softly. It was something she had never considered before. He had just been one of her father's men, one of his hired guns, just like all the rest. Clearly, though, he was far more than that if Cole felt he could trust her very life to the man, that she would, in fact, be safer with Miles than with Cole himself.

Miles took a deep breath and let it out with a weary sigh.

"They call me Parson Black."

Rachel gasped. In a land where law was a sometime thing, where often a man's only assurance of living to see another day rested squarely on his hip, this was a name to conjure with. She had heard things, awful things, but somehow she could not believe them. "I can't believe you did the things I've heard," she whispered.

Miles smiled a mirthless smile. "Sometimes I can't either," he replied.

It was true, then, all of it, or at least some of it. "Why?" Rachel demanded, knowing it was none of her business, knowing that if she were a man, she might very well be looking down the business end of his Colt as a reward for her boldness.

Why? Miles had often asked himself the same question, although no one else ever had. Perhaps if he explained it to her, told her the whole story as he had never told another living soul, then perhaps he would begin to understand it himself.

"During the war," he began, haltingly at first, "I saw too much killing. Like a lot of men, I promised God that if He got me out alive, I'd pay Him back." Miles laughed bitterly. "I even tried to. I became a preacher."

Rachel could only stare in open-mouthed wonder. When she had asked her question, it had only been a reflex. She had expected an angry rebuke or, at best, a gentle admonition to mind her own business. Never had she expected him to answer.

Miles was oblivious to her reaction, though. He was hardly even paying attention to his driving, letting the horses find their own way. He was speaking almost to himself, telling the details thoughtfully, weighing each one, testing them to find any secret meaning that he might previously have overlooked.

"I got married, too, after a while. Annie was her name. She was a gentle thing, so trusting. She worked alongside me, helped me in everything I did. She didn't even mind being poor, as long as we were together." He drew a ragged breath as the memories assailed him, but he pushed them back before they could overwhelm. "One day they came for me. A man in my congregation was sick. They wanted me to pray for him, so of course I went. Annie stayed behind. I didn't know I'd be gone so long, and there was the cow to milk and all . . ." He let his voice trail off, lost in a momentary reflection while he examined those old excuses to see if they were valid. They weren't, but he went on.

"The man died, but he was in a bad way for a couple of days, and I stayed with him. Then there was another day for the funeral. When I got home . . ."

Sensing the horror, Rachel did not want to know what he had found when he had returned home, but she could not force the words to stop him past her constricted throat.

"The men were renegades. They'd been raiders during the war, using the war as an excuse to commit crimes. When the war ended, they'd just kept on." His voice was strained now, as if it came from a great distance, someplace deep inside him. "They were gone by the time I got home, but from the way things were at the house, it looked like they'd been there a couple of days. I never knew if they'd really meant to kill her, but there were three of them, and she was a tiny little thing . . ."

Rachel's sob startled him. He had even forgotten that she was listening. Tears were rolling down her cheeks, and she had a hand pressed over her lips, but she had not been able to keep the sob from escaping. She could feel his pain, the pain that went so deep that it hardly even showed on the outside, except in his eyes.

"I'm glad that you can cry for her," he told her with an eerie lack of expression. "I never could. It hurt too much for tears."

After that, he was silent for a long time, and Rachel thought perhaps he was finished or just unable to go on, to explain the rest of it. She never would have asked to hear the end of the story, but at last he spoke again, still in that same flat, expressionless voice that chilled her to the bone.

"I guess I went a little crazy. It's hard to know. I felt like I was in my right mind, and everything I did, I planned out very carefully. I was very calm and cold-blooded about it all, never wild or out of control. Still, it's hard to know.

"I tracked them down. It took a while, and once they knew I was on their trail, they split up, and that made it harder. It was more than six months before I caught the first one. I killed him and then I . . . I killed him," he repeated softly. He wouldn't tell her the other things he had done, the unspeakable things. If she had already heard about it, there was no use, and if she hadn't, she didn't need to know.

"Then I found the other two. Like I said, it took a long time. More than two years, all told." He gave a weary sigh, as if he had just relived those long, lonely years. "When it was over, I was a 'known' man. It was easy to get jobs, especially jobs requiring the use of a gun."

Rachel wiped the moisture from her cheeks. After a long silence, she placed a comforting hand on his arm and said, "I'm sorry I put you through all that, Miles. I didn't know . . ."

Miles looked down at her hand in surprise. When he lifted his eyes to hers, they were full of gratitude. "Don't be sorry, Mrs. Elliot. I think I needed to tell someone that story, someone who'd care. Besides," he added with a sad smile, "you needed to know why Cole thought you'd be safer with me than with him. You see now, don't you? No man would ever bother a woman if they knew they'd have to deal with me."

Rachel nodded and gave his arm a reassuring squeeze before withdrawing her hand and letting it drop back into her lap. "I think, maybe . . . I mean, after all that, you could call me 'Rachel,' don't you think?" She smiled tentatively.

Miles returned her smile with a grin that actually erased the ever-present sadness in his eyes. "I'd be honored . . . Rachel," he said.

After they had ridden along in companionable silence for a while, Miles said reassuringly, "Don't pay any attention to Hank Oliver. Cole will be back, you'll see. Before you know it, too."

Rachel sighed. "I hope so, especially since . . ." Her voice trailed off uncertainly.

"Since what?" he demanded suspiciously.

She didn't really know if she should tell him or not, but even if she didn't, he'd find out pretty soon anyway. "Since I'm going to have a baby."

Miles swore and then apologized profusely. When Rachel had assured him she was not offended, he raged, "I can't believe Cole would leave you in that condition."

"Oh, he didn't," Rachel defended him. "I mean, he didn't know. I didn't want to tell him."

Miles glared at her in exasperation. "Why the hell not?" This time he didn't bother to apologize, and Rachel thought it was probably because in his opinion she deserved to be sworn at.

Rachel considered telling him huffily it was none of his business, but in view of the confidences they had just shared, she knew that would have been petty. Still, she found it difficult to put her reasons into words that she thought Miles would understand. "At first, I kept thinking I could talk him out of going, and then, when I realized he was going no matter what I said, I was afraid to. I mean, what if it hadn't made any difference?"

"It would have," Miles declared.

Rachel hoped he was right. "Anyway, I also thought that I only wanted him to come back because of me, not because of anything else," she concluded lamely.

Miles had picked up on her uncertainty, though. "You

thought? Have you changed your mind?"

Rachel nodded miserably. "Now I just want him to come back. I don't care about 'why' anymore."

This time it was Miles's hand that reached out to comfort. He patted her shoulder awkwardly, much as he had the morning that Cole had left. "He'll be back," Miles promised her again.

Rachel prayed that he was right.

"I'd better be going," the Kid said reluctantly.

Lettie nodded and then lay there watching him rise from her bed and begin to dress. It was late, but he still felt he had to get back to the ranch. He never stayed the night with her anymore, not since Cole had left.

Lettie sighed and rolled over on her side. Not since Cole had left him in charge of watching over that wife of his, she thought bitterly. Rachel McKinsey Elliot had an annoying habit of worming her way into all of Lettie's relationships. First there was Cole and now the Kid. Even Hank Oliver was still head over heels.

After Lettie had started seeing the Kid, she had expected Hank to get mad and drop her. He hadn't, though. In fact, Oliver hadn't acted like he even cared. He still continued to see her one or two nights a week, weeknights when he knew the Kid would not be in town. It wasn't that he didn't know about the Kid, either. Once he even saw a silver concho that had fallen off the Kid's vest at her place. She had laid it on the washstand where the Kid would be sure to see it the next time he came.

Oliver had picked up the silver disk and looked at it. "This belongs to Kid Collins, doesn't it?" he had asked with mild curiosity. When she had told him that yes, it did, he had simply put it back down and gone on about his business. That was when Lettie had known exactly what he thought of her, and that he really didn't care a fig for her. She should have told him then to get his jollies someplace else from now on, but somehow she hadn't been able to do it. She knew her decision had something to do with Rachel McKinsey Elliot, but she wasn't sure exactly what. It wasn't like she'd stolen Oliver from the woman or anything, nothing she could feel was revenge for having lost Cole. It was something, though, and she continued to see him, in spite of her misgivings.

She probably should have been afraid of the Kid's finding out. At least she was sure that he wouldn't take the news that he was sharing her favors as lightly as Oliver had. The Kid wasn't very likely to find out, though. No one in his right mind was going to want to be the one to tell Kid Collins that Hank Oliver was playing dip the wick with his girl.

The Kid was dressed now, and he leaned over to give her a kiss good-bye. As he did so, he pressed a gold coin into her hand. "Buy yourself something nice," he whispered.

Lettie's fingers closed around the coin. The Kid was sweet. He always gave her money, but he made it seem like a gift. Hank Oliver simply paid her.

Suddenly, she remembered something she had heard that the Kid would want to know about. "Kid, wait," she said, stopping him on his way to the door. She propped herself up on one elbow. "There's a rumor going around. I heard it from a couple different fellows who came in the saloon this week. They said they'd heard that Will Statler was still alive."

The Kid frowned. "You're sure they'd just heard about it? Had either of them actually seen him?"

Lettie shook her head. "They'd just heard. He had a gang operating in the hills. Some of the men that got away from you all joined them. These fellows had heard that Statler was with them, too, that he's turned outlaw now."

The Kid's characteristic smile returned. "It's probably just a rumor, honey. Don't worry about it." He smoothed his golden curls and put on his hat.

Lettie watched him with a small trace of jealousy. It was tough being with a man who was prettier than she was, and the Kid was a lot prettier than she was. Of course, the Kid was a lot prettier than most everybody, but that was small consolation. At least she knew that he cared about her. He'd even said that he loved her. That was more than any other man had done. More than Cole Elliot had done. Lettie wondered acidly if Cole Elliot told his wife that he loved her.

"Take it easy," the Kid called to her as he opened the door. "Keep it warm for me," he added with a wink.

"Be careful," she replied, a little surprised to discover that she was really worried about his returning to the ranch after dark. He'd done it plenty of times before, after all. Maybe she was going soft on the Kid, she reflected as the door closed behind him. Shrugging, she lay back down in the bed that still smelled of their passion. She supposed that worse things could happen.

May blended into June and then July. The intense heat of summer kept Rachel away from town most weeks, giving her an excuse to avoid Hank and his sly remarks. He'd never come right out and said anything bad about Cole again, but he often inquired about whether she'd heard from him lately, knowing full well that she hadn't because he was also the postmaster. Then he would be excruciatingly sympathetic toward her until her teeth ached from clenching them.

An unseasonable break in the summer weather tempted her from the house one day in July, however. Knowing this might well be her last chance to travel in comfort before she would be too big with child, she told Miles to hitch up the wagon and take her to town. Hank Oliver be damned, she decided, smoothing the front of her dress over her gently rounded belly.

This was the first time she would be appearing in public in her maternity clothes. She knew that Cole would be home soon, and she wanted to be accustomed to wearing the bulky dresses long before he arrived. She also wanted everyone to be aware of her pregnancy so that any talk that might go around would have died down by the time he got back.

Rachel put off her trip to the Mercantile until the very end of the day. She had hoped that perhaps the rumor of her pregnancy would have reached Hank by then and would not come as such a complete surprise. Unfortunately, it hadn't.

"Good afternoon, Hank," she called with false cheerfulness as she breezed into the store.

Hank's head came up from where he was counting out change for Mrs. Siddons. The stilted words of greeting that he had planned to speak lodged somewhere in his throat, causing a slightly strangled sound to emerge. His face turned first chalk white and then beet red. He couldn't seem to move or to continue counting the change, but his customer was far too interested in Rachel's condition to even notice.

"Why, Rachel, I had no idea," Mrs. Siddons was saying. "Congratulations!" She bustled over, eyeing Rachel carefully from head to foot. "It's a boy, you know," she declared confidently. "I can always tell. You're carrying high and that's a sure sign."

Rachel nodded pleasantly. So far that day she had heard predictions of a girl from no less than three other people who had cited the same reason. How any of them could possibly tell whether the tiny mound of her stomach were high or low, she couldn't imagine.

"When are you due?" Mrs. Siddons inquired in a stage whisper.

Rachel balked at answering, knowing how the old biddy would be counting on her fingers. "Before Christmas," she hedged.

"How nice," Mrs. Siddons replied, but Rachel could tell

from her distant expression that she was already planning whom she would tell next. The fact that her sister, the Widow Johnson, was not with her gave her a decided edge, since this juicy piece of gossip would be hers alone, unlike the news of Rachel's wedding which she had had to share. Rachel did not have the heart to tell her that after all the visits she had paid today, the news would already be common knowledge.

With a hasty farewell and without even waiting for her change, Mrs. Siddons bustled out of the store. Rachel watched her go with a small sigh of relief and then turned to face Hank Oliver.

Hank had recovered somewhat, although his ears were still slightly pink. Rachel greeted him again. "Hello, Hank. Nice weather we're having, isn't it? A pleasant relief. I wonder how long it will last."

He seemed about to reply. His lips even moved, but no sound came out. At last he managed to croak a "Yes."

Rachel stared at him, suddenly at a loss. She had expected him to be angry, perhaps even bitingly sarcastic, but she had never expected this speechless horror. She was married, after all. It was only natural and certainly nothing to be ashamed of. In point of fact, she was very proud of her condition, and happy, too, and she wasn't about to let Hank Oliver spoil things for her.

Without another word, she strode purposefully to the back of the store where she picked up a bolt of pink outing flannel and then carried it to the front of the store.

"Could I have three yards of this?" she inquired, pretending not to notice the peculiar way Hank was still staring at her.

When he made no move, she thrust the bolt at him, forcing him to take it. The abrupt movement seemed to break his trance.

"Y—yes, three yards, did you say?" he stammered.

310

He measured the cloth with infinite care, and as he did so, he regained his composure. So she was pregnant, was she? Well, it served her right for what she'd done to him. And due before Christmas. The satyr hadn't wasted any time, had he? Hank's lip curled in distaste. Well, Hank wouldn't give her the satisfaction of knowing how deeply she had hurt him.

He cut the flannel and folded it carefully. Then he gave her a questioning look. "Pink?" he inquired. "I thought Mrs. Siddons predicted a boy?"

Rachel gave an inward sigh of relief. At least he wasn't going to be difficult. He didn't even sound sarcastic. "I don't trust Mrs. Siddons's opinions. Besides, I already have plenty of blue things," she informed him with a friendly smile.

Hank nodded, remembering bitterly the blue flannel he had sold her several months ago. She had known her guilty secret even then. "Will there be anything else?" he inquired.

When she had assured him that she needed nothing else, he wrapped the fabric carefully and handed it to her. "Oh, you'll be wanting your mail, won't you?" he asked.

He said it a little too casually, alerting Rachel's instincts for self-protection. She waited with apparent patience while he collected her letters, and then accepted them graciously, hardly even sparing them a glance. "Thank you, Hank," she said cheerfully, wished him good day, and left.

As soon as she was out of sight of the store, she paused, tucking her parcel awkwardly under her arm, and flipped through the letters.

Nothing.

Heaving a furious sigh, she jumped as someone snatched the letters out of her hand. Her startled gaze met Miles's rebuking one. Without a word, he tucked the letters out of sight into a vest pocket.

"Let's go home," he suggested.

"He didn't write!" Rachel informed him. "It's been almost three months, and he still didn't write! He *promised!* Of all

311

the rude, inconsiderate . . ." she ranted.

"Calm down," Miles soothed with infuriating calmness. "Be careful or you'll mark the baby."

". . . thoughtless, mean, ungentlemanly . . . *mark the baby?*" Rachel exclaimed, having finally registered Miles's amazing remark.

"Sure," he replied with a grin, taking her by the elbow and directing her toward their wagon. "If the mother gets mad all the time, doesn't that make a red mark on the baby?"

Rachel glared up at him. "That's a strawberry mark, and it's caused from eating too many strawberries, something I don't have to worry about, because I haven't even seen a strawberry, much less . . . And stop trying to distract me," she said in annoyance, shaking her arm free of his grip and stopping dead in the middle of the sidewalk. "Finding out its father has been hurt or killed or some terrible thing is far more likely to mark the baby, anyway."

"He hasn't been hurt or killed," Miles assured her.

"Then why doesn't he write?" she demanded.

"People are starting to stare, Rachel," he warned.

Rachel glanced around. Sure enough, her behavior was drawing some very unwanted attention from passersby. Consciously twisting her scowl into an artificial smile, she allowed Miles to escort her over to their wagon. "Then why doesn't he write?" she asked again, this time around her fixed smile.

Miles looked down into her flushed face and noted the tears of disappointment sparkling in her eyes. "I reckon he's ashamed to," he said.

Rachel's mouth dropped open. "Ashamed? Why on earth should he be ashamed?"

Miles sighed wearily. "Think about it for a minute. You've been to school. You're smart and educated. Cole, well . . ." Miles shrugged. "Oh, I reckon he can read and write and cipher, enough to get by, anyway. But just barely enough. If he was to write you a letter, it would be like advertising that he's nothing but an ignorant cowboy. He doesn't want you to see him like that."

Rachel could have moaned in frustration. "Doesn't he know that wouldn't matter? I don't care if he's completely illiterate! He could just put his mark on a piece of paper and send it to me. Anything, I don't care, as long as I know he's still alive!"

Miles gave her an understanding smile. "Don't you think that if anything had happened to him, one of the other men would have let us know?" He let her mull this over. "Look, Rachel, no news is good news. If something really awful had happened, we would have heard. Since we haven't heard anything, we have to assume that everything is fine."

Rachel considered. She knew Miles was right, but that didn't make it any easier to swallow. She wanted a letter, a love letter. Of course, she should have known better than to expect something like that from Cole Elliot, but that hadn't stopped her from wanting it.

Miles saw the acceptance come slowly. "He'll be home soon," Miles pointed out. "Then you can rant and rave all you want to at him in person."

Rachel's lips trembled into a small smile. "I will, too," she promised, and allowed him to help her up onto the wagon seat, unaware that two very jealous hazel eyes watched her from across the street.

"She's knocked up," Lettie remarked from her post in the saloon doorway.

The bartender glanced up from where he was polishing the bar. "Who is?" Sam asked cautiously, knowing full well who "she" must be.

"Mrs. Cole Elliot, that's who," Lettie snapped, turning abruptly from where she had been standing in the doorway and stalking over to the bar. "Give me a drink."

Sam shook his head in disapproval. "You've been drinking an awful lot lately, Lettie. The Kid wouldn't like it."

"The Kid won't know," Lettie pointed out. "Now do I get that drink or do I have to go back there and pour it myself?"

Reluctantly, Sam reached beneath the bar for a bottle and a glass and poured her a shot. She downed it in one gulp.

When she set the glass down, her eyes were wet. It could have been from the burn of the whiskey, except that she said, "That should have been mine, Sam. That should have been *my* baby."

"Oh, Lettie, honey, don't," Sam pleaded. He had been watching the jealousy eating her alive for months now. For a while he had hoped that the Kid would make her forget, but obviously she wasn't really serious about the Kid. If she had been, she wouldn't still be seeing Hank Oliver on the side. There had been others, too, occasional strangers who were just passing through town. Lettie was turning herself into a whore right before Sam's eyes, and there wasn't a damn thing he could do about it. "Cole Elliot isn't worth it," he argued.

Lettie smiled sardonically. "No, he isn't, is he?" she said, and poured herself another drink.

Although no word came, Rachel began to anticipate Cole's imminent return. Each morning she dressed with care and fixed her hair just so and waited. Each night she undressed and brushed out her hair and told herself that tomorrow would be the day. Except that it wasn't, and she would repeat the whole process yet again. And again. And again.

July sizzled into August. Each blazing day burned into another with agonizing slowness. Miles began to send the Kid into town every two or three days in hopes that he might hear some news or find that long-awaited letter.

He didn't.

Rachel would wait at the window, watching for the Kid's return, and one day, after the Kid had handed over the mail to Miles, they stood for a long time in deep discussion. Later, when Miles brought her the letters, she challenged him. "What was the Kid telling you out there?" she asked.

Miles feigned surprise. "Nothing, not a thing. Why do you ask?"

Rachel wondered that he could have lived this long and still have been such a rotten liar. Fear sent its icy fingers up her spine. "It was about Cole, wasn't it?" she guessed. "You heard something and you're afraid to tell me."

"No, no, of course not," he assured her, but he could see that his assurance meant nothing to her. Much as he hated to, he would have to tell her the truth. As bad as the truth was, it was far better than what she was imagining.

"The Kid heard something about Statler," he said.

Rachel's shoulders sagged with relief. "What about him?" she asked, not really caring as long as it wasn't bad news about Cole.

Miles frowned. "All summer we've been hearing rumors that Statler is still alive, off in the hills somewhere, still running his gang of rustlers or what's left of them."

"But I thought he was dead. Cole said . . ." Rachel began and then she remembered. "You never found his body, though, did you?"

Miles shook his head. "Up until now we figured it was just a rumor, somebody trying to scare us. Today, though, the Kid ran into a fellow who claims he actually saw Statler, alive and well."

The icy fingers went to work on her spine again. "Do you think he'll come back here?"

Miles shrugged. "I reckon there's nothing he'd rather do, if he thought he could get even with us. That's the rub, though. I figure he's not strong enough yet. He'll need more men than we left him with. It'll take him a while to build his operation

315

back up. He's operating pretty far away, too. I don't think we have anything to be worried about just yet."

"But you think we will have something to worry about someday, don't you?" she asked.

"It's still just rumors. That fellow could have been mistaken. He didn't really know Statler. The man he met just claimed to be him. That don't mean he really was. No use borrowing trouble until we know for sure."

Miles's argument made sense, but gave Rachel little comfort. Now she not only had to worry about whether or not Cole was really coming home, she had to worry about what might happen to him if he did. No, she mentally corrected, *when* he did. She would not give up hope.

Hoping became increasingly more difficult as the days dragged by, however. The heat drained her energy and depression sapped her spirits. Her only comfort was the child that grew larger every day, persistently reminding her of its existence with strong, well-placed kicks that jarred her out of gloomy daydreams and woke her out of frightening nightmares.

As the child grew, Rachel found herself torn between the desire to see Cole and her reluctance to have him see her. Her mirror showed her a bulky body, swollen well past any degree of attractiveness, and a haggard face with shadowed eyes and furrowed brow. Her once-luxuriant hair hung limp and lifeless, resistant even to Lupe's determined care and brushing, and for the first time in her life, Rachel considered chopping the whole mess off short.

When September came, Rachel did not even turn the calendar for three days, as if by refusing to do so, she could deny the passage of time. September. One whole month past the three months that a trail drive usually took. Many things could have held them up, of course. Miles reminded her of that daily. They'd gotten a late start, too, and might have had to take a roundabout route to be assured of adequate graze for the herd. Rains could flood a river, leaving it impassable for days. That could have slowed them up, as could have any number of other things.

After a while, though, even Miles ceased to make excuses and began to stare anxiously at the horizon. Where could Cole be?

And then the telegram arrived.

Chapter X

Cole hadn't exactly been a saint, but he sure didn't know what he'd ever done to deserve such a disaster. Never had he even heard of anything like it. It was funny, when he thought back. He'd even mentioned to Rachel how the herd was a little nervous but how he was sure they'd settle down once they got trail broke. The trouble was, they'd never gotten trail broke, or at least not so's you'd notice.

The first time they'd stempeded, there'd been a thunderstorm. They were only three days from home, and they'd lost another two days gathering the herd up again. After that, things had gone from bad to worse to . . . well, he didn't even know a word to describe it.

Those damn cows had run every chance they'd got. They'd run at every thunderstorm, of course. They'd run whenever a coyote howled. They'd run whenever a prairie dog barked. They'd run whenever somebody sneezed. Once they even ran for no reason at all.

It got so the men didn't even bother to unroll their bedrolls, knowing that they'd probably no sooner get snuggled down inside than the ground would start to shake, and they'd be running for a horse to chase after the thundering herd. Miraculously, no one had been seriously injured in all of the times it had happened. Once they'd been pretty sure that they'd lost one man since somebody had actually seen him go down right in front of the herd, but for some reason, all those brainless animals had run right around where he was curled up on the ground. His horse had been trampled to pulp, but the rider had gotten up only slightly more dirty and none the worse for wear then when he'd gone down.

When they'd first set out, Cole had suspected that they'd be among the last herds to arrive, but he hadn't reckoned on being the very last one. It had worked to his advantage, though, and the buyers had fought over his herd, bidding against each other in a last-ditch effort to finish with the highest sales for the year. Even though he'd arrived twenty-five head short—that's how many had made good their escape during the multitudinous stempedes—he had made up for it by getting top dollar for the ones he did have.

With great satisfaction, he wrote out the telegram to Rachel saying that he'd sold the cattle and telling her on which train he would arrive home. What wasn't so satisfying was the date he'd have to give her. The trip he had told her would take three months had stretched to almost five. He was almost ashamed to show his face back at the Circle M. But that wasn't going to stop him from going home.

She might be mad at him for taking so long, but he knew Rachel would meet him at the train, if for no other reason than to give him a piece of her mind. He'd missed her so much that even the prospect of listening to her yell at him seemed pleasant. And he had a pretty good idea how to get her to stop yelling, too.

He'd given a lot of thought to what Miles had said. He had been really stupid to worry about why Rachel was so passionate in bed. From now on, he was just going to enjoy it. If Miles was right and she did love him, well, that was great, but if she didn't, that was all right, too. He'd take what he could get and give thanks for it.

Other things were also going to change, once he got home.

No more separate bedrooms, for one thing. He still couldn't remember exactly how that had gotten started, but he was going to put a sudden stop to it. They were man and wife, and they were going to act like it. He had a feeling Rachel would not object, but he didn't intend to let her, even if she tried. From now on they would sleep together, in the same bed, every night.

Cole couldn't help grinning every time he thought about it. In fact, he planned on spending about the first five days he was home in bed, and not much of that time sleeping either. He figured he could wear himself down to a nubbin and still not get enough of her, but he was sure as hell going to try.

He thought about it all the way back on the train. It only took a day to go the same distance he and his men had spent almost five months crossing in the opposite direction. Cole reflected more than once how nice it would be someday if the rates ever got to be cheap enough to ship cattle directly from Texas without having to drive them all the way to Kansas. Of course, he himself was never going on another cattle drive, that was for damn sure. He'd decided that long before he'd ever crossed the Red River on his trip north.

Cole jumped off the train in Stillwater before it had even come to a complete stop. Scanning the platform eagerly, he quickly spotted Miles, but his gaze slid past his friend on its way to find Rachel. She was nowhere in sight.

Miles approached, a smile of welcome on his homely face.

"Where is she?" Cole demanded before Miles could say a word.

Miles's eyes grew wide. "Well, hello to you, too," he replied, feigning offense.

The train had stopped now and the other men were getting off, calling greetings to Miles, who returned them.

"Where is she?" Cole repeated, more urgently this time. Surely, they'd gotten his telegram. How else would Miles have known to be here? But if they had, why wasn't she here?

"She's out at the ranch," Miles said, "and she wants you to

321

hustle on out there as fast as you can."

Cole scowled at Miles. His friend was grinning ear to ear, like a cat with his mouth full of feathers. A very bad sign. He'd never seen Miles looking quite so pleased with himself before. Miles was acting like everything was fine, but if everything really was fine, why hadn't Rachel come to meet him? A very disturbing thought occurred to him. "She's not sick, is she?"

Miles really was offended at that. "Do you think *I* would let her get sick?" he inquired loftily.

Cole was starting to wonder how that smirking mouth would feel under his knuckles. "Then why didn't she come to meet me?" he growled.

"Maybe she wanted your first meeting to be a little more private than the Stillwater train depot," Miles suggested.

Cole considered this a moment. It sounded reasonable and Miles didn't look like he was lying. In fact, he still looked almighty pleased with himself. Before Cole could ask any more questions, however, Miles spoke again.

"What are you waiting for? I've got a horse all saddled up for you, right over there." Miles pointed, but Cole was gone before he even got his finger out. Well, now, Miles reflected, that was a good sign. Maybe things were going to work out just fine in the Elliot household after all.

The usually long trip from Stillwater seemed even longer to the man who had been waiting almost five months to make it. Excitement and anticipation had churned into a hot ball in his stomach and tingled out to spark on every nerve. He'd missed her with all of him, but certain parts of him had missed her more than others, he observed wryly as the ranch buildings came into view. It wouldn't be long now, though.

Rachel watched him ride up. She was standing at the front window, hiding behind the curtain. As much as she longed to run out and down the stairs and across the yard, to put a swift end to these long months of waiting, she didn't dare. Running, of course, was out of the question considering her condition. But more than that, she was a little afraid of what his reaction was going to be when he saw her, and so she wanted as much privacy as possible for their first meeting. Nervously, she reached up and checked her faultless hair for the thousandth time that day and then reached down and smoothed the fabric of her dress over her rounded belly. Oh, please, let him be happy, she prayed. When she saw him turn and start toward the house, she stepped quickly away from the window and took her place in front of the hearth. Locking her hands in front of her so they would not tremble, she turned her full attention to the door through which he would come.

Cole had believed Miles when he had said that Rachel was all right, but now he began to doubt again, especially when he rode into the yard and no one came to meet him. The place seemed unnaturally quiet, almost spooky. Had Miles been stringing him along? Swiftly, and with growing alarm, he unsaddled his horse and turned it loose in the corral. By the time he reached the porch steps, he was almost running, and he took the stairs three at a time.

"Rachel!" he called as soon as he cleared the doorstep. Squinting in the dimness, he peered around, searching for her familiar figure.

"Welcome home," she said. She stood stock-still, drinking in the sight of him. He looked blessedly familiar, although he was even thinner than ever and even browner than usual. Longing to rush into his arms, she still did not move. She had to show him her secret, let him see it with his own eyes, before she could hold him. Just another minute, she told herself.

Slowly, his eyes became accustomed to the interior light and she materialized. She was standing across the room, but she hadn't made any move to meet him. Her hands were twisting in front of her and she was fiddling with her dress the way she did when she was nervous. She was smiling, though, and maybe it was just the light, but he thought she was crying a little bit, too. Before he could solve the riddle of why she would be crying and smiling at the same time, she took a step toward him. In the rush to capture her, he forgot all about it.

His arms closed gratefully around her, and he was vaguely aware that she was holding him, too. At first he simply held her, inhaling the sweet scent of roses and Rachel, the scent that had haunted him through countless lonely nights. He laid his cheek against her hair, testing its softness, and then he could wait no longer.

Bending his head, bringing his hand up to cup her jaw, he lifted her face to his. Their lips met in a riot of sensation, tasting, sensing, devouring, bestowing. His arms tightened around her. He wanted her close and closer still. He wanted to feel her breasts flatten against his chest. He wanted her thighs cradled between his. He pulled, but she didn't come closer. He pulled again. Some realization niggled at his consciousness, something he had noticed in that brief moment before she had come to him.

Reluctantly, he pulled his mouth from hers and forced his gaze downward to the bulk that separted them. Bulk? It was Rachel's stomach. He stared. "You're going to have a baby," he said at last.

Rachel blinked back the tears that threatened to blind her. She needed to see his reaction. "Yes," she said with a tenuous smile. What would she do if he wasn't pleased?

At the moment, he was merely stunned. A thousand questions jumbled through his mind. Sorting quickly through them, he came up with an important one. "When?" He wasn't much of a judge, but he could guess that it wouldn't be much longer.

"Two more months, the middle of November." She still could not read his expression.

Cole was doing some fast figuring. Nine months, almost exactly, since their wedding. That meant that it had happened right away, maybe even the very first time. The boys would give him a hard time about that, but that was all right. In fact, he didn't think he would mind a bit. He felt his face moving into a smile, but a new thought stopped that smile. "Did you know about this before I left?"

Rachel hesitated. She had considered lying if he asked her point blank like this. After all, he would have no way of knowing. She found that she couldn't lie to his face, though. "Yes, I did," she said in a small voice.

She saw his surprise. "Why didn't you tell me, then?" he demanded.

Rachel had long since discovered how feeble her reasons sounded when explained to someone else. Still, she had no others to give. "I wanted you to stay because of me, not for any other reason, and when I couldn't talk you into staying, I wanted to know that you were coming back to me and only me."

He found such logic incredible and his expression showed it. "You should have told me," he said, even while he wondered what difference it would have made. Would he still have gone? He would never know for certain now. At the moment, even his original reasons for leaving seemed inadequate, and he was certain that he had been a fool to go on the drive in the first place. Whether anything could have convinced him of that beforehand, however, he did not know.

"I'm sorry I didn't tell you," Rachel said. "Do you forgive me?" For a moment, he had almost looked happy, but only for a moment. She wanted that moment back, and she very much needed him to be happy.

Did he forgive her? As he looked down into her worried face, he knew that he would forgive her anything. His lips twitched into a wry grin. "For the time being, I do," he informed her. "Right now I'm too interested in kissing you to fight about anything."

Rachel thought that sounded like a fine idea and willingly lifted her face to his. His mouth swooped down, plundering hers in a sweet assault to which she willingly surrendered. She clung to him, drawing as close as their child would allow her, and let her hands explore the familiar territory of his back and shoulders, testing the changes that five months of hard work had made in him. He was different, and yet blessedly familiar. The taste and the scent of him enveloped her, stirring sweet memories and even sweeter yearnings. She loved him so very much, she thought her heart might burst.

Cole kissed her for a long time while his hands discovered the changes his child had made in her beloved body. He traced the curve of her back, the fuller curve of her hips and then reached up to her breasts. They were heavier than he remembered, but the nipples still blossomed at his touch, even through the fabric of her dress. Suddenly, the last thread of his restraint snapped. With a groan, he scooped her up into his arms and headed for the bedroom, not even noticing the weight of his extra burden.

Rachel started struggling immediately, but they were halfway to the bedroom door before she managed to break their kiss. "Wait, Cole, we can't!" she gasped.

Cole stumbled to a halt, knowing he couldn't have heard her right. "What did you say?" he asked suspiciously.

Rachel felt her cheeks heating up. "I said, we can't."

"Can't?" he echoed, disbelieving. He stared at her reddening face for a long moment before he finally figured out her objection. "I know it's not bedtime yet, but it's all right . . ."

"No," she interrupted, blushing even more furiously. Did he think her such a prude that she wouldn't make love to him in the daylight? It had been plenty light the last time they had been together. "Because of the baby," she explained.

Now he was really puzzled. "We can't do it in the daytime because of the baby?" he asked.

Rachel closed her eyes in despair. He simply was not going to understand unless she said it right out, was he? Opening her eyes, she did so. "We can't do it *any*time, because of the baby," she told him with profound regret.

"*Any*time?" he repeated incredulously, loosening his grip and letting her feet slide to the floor. This was unbelievable. He'd never heard of such a thing. Of course, he'd never been with a pregnant woman before, either, but he'd still never heard of it. After he thought about it a little, however, he realized that he *had* been with a pregnant woman, quite a few times as a matter of fact. "You were pregnant before I left," he pointed out, remembering that that hadn't prevented such things then, and she had just admitted she had known so she couldn't plead ignorance. He was starting to suspect that this might be a little ploy for revenge because he had left her, but one look at her miserable expression disabused him of that notion.

"It's all right in the beginning, but during the last few months, when the baby's so big, it isn't safe." Rachel twisted her hands together, sensing his frustration but unable to do anything to ease it. The fact was, she was experiencing quite a bit of frustration herself, and apprehension, too. If he didn't really love her, if he had only come back because he liked going to bed with her, what would he do now? How could she possibly hope to hold on to him? And would he turn to that woman in town, whoever she was, for the comfort Rachel could no longer offer?

Totally unaware of Rachel's fears, Cole's attention was completely taken with analyzing the current state of affairs. Suddenly, a new possibility occurred to him. "Did Lupe tell you this?" he inquired suspiciously, certain that he had uncovered the explanation. If it was a plot, then that witch Lupe would be behind it.

Rachel nodded but hastily added, "The doctor told me the same thing, though, so it must be true." She studied his face, easily reading his disappointment, but unable to judge how deeply it ran.

Cole barely stifled a groan. What a welcoming present this was! He'd been pleased about the baby, or at least he thought

327

that he would be once the shock had worn off. The rest of the deal sort of took the edge off of it, though. If only he'd known ahead of time, he never would have . . . "If you'd told me all this before, I never would have gone on that drive," he said in exasperation, forgetting that only moments ago he himself had not been too certain of that fact.

Rachel bristled. How dare he try to put all the blame on her! "If you'd come back when you were supposed to, there still would have been plenty of time," she informed him haughtily.

"Do you think I wanted to be on the trail for five months?" he demanded, his voice growing steadily louder.

"Don't break furniture," Lupe cautioned from across the room, startling them both.

They both glared at her but she didn't seem to notice and came forward on silent feet. Her twinkling eyes studied Rachel and Cole, and her toothless mouth stretched into a grin as she took in their angry expressions. "You are mad because she has baby?" she inquired of Cole.

"No, of course not," he snapped.

She turned her tiny black eyes to Rachel. "You are mad because he come home?"

"No," she gasped, one hand fluttering to her throat.

"Then why you fight?" Lupe asked curiously, her amused gaze going from one to the other.

Rachel's brown eyes met Cole's blue ones. They stared at each other a little sheepishly for a minute. "We weren't fighting," Cole said quietly, still looking at Rachel.

"Then why you yell?" Lupe insisted.

Neither Cole nor Rachel could think of a reply. Several minutes ticked by.

"Don't you have something else to do, Lupe?" Cole inquired without taking his eyes from Rachel's.

Lupe cackled delightedly. "Sí, I get you supper. You will eat. I will call you. But not too soon."

They stood there for a long time after Lupe had gone. "Are

you mad about the baby?" Rachel asked softly. The hand that had rested at her throat slid protectively to her swollen middle.

"No," he quickly assured her. "It's just, I was a little surprised at first, that's all." He grinned wryly, revealing his dimple. "It's sort of like getting punched in the stomach. It takes a minute to start thinking straight again."

How she loved that dimple. She smiled back. "I know the feeling." Only too well, she added mentally, remembering how many times this man's baby had punched her.

"And I was a little disappointed. I had . . . plans . . . for the rest of the day," he explained lamely.

"I know," she said softly. "I'm disappointed, too."

His eyebrows went up. "You are?" She nodded. Cole took a ragged breath as familiar emotions surged within him. "Is there any reason why I can't kiss you? Just kiss you, and hold you?" he asked hoarsely.

Rachel shook her head, unable to speak for the lump that was clogging her throat. He still wanted her, in spite of everything. He must care for her, must want her for more than the physical pleasures they had shared. Tears stung her eyes, making her feel totally ridiculous. The last thing she should be doing was crying because her husband wanted to kiss her.

Luckily, he kissed her then, and she forgot all about crying. His lips touched hers tenderly, almost reverently, allowing their breaths to mingle for a second before sealing the gap between them. He tasted infinitely sweet, familiar yet new, comforting yet exciting. He sampled her mouth, first with just his lips and then with the tip of his tongue, grazing across the soft fullness before teasing for admittance. Once inside, he swirled and probed, finding and tasting every secret of her essence.

As the kiss deepened, so did the embrace, and his arms tightened around her, crushing her, as if he would draw her into himself. Rachel sagged against him, grateful for the strong arms that held her and clinging with a remnant of the desperation she had felt when thinking that she might never see him again. He was so dear, so very precious, and she loved him more than she could ever say. Since she had no breath and no strength left, she did not even try.

At long last, Cole reluctantly pulled his mouth from hers, knowing that if he did not stop soon, he would be unable to, baby or no baby. Panting, gasping, he rested his forehead against hers and simply looked at her. She was so beautiful, with her cheeks flushed and her eyes glowing and her lips rosy from his kisses.

"Now I want to hold you," he told her with a sly grin, "except that I think we'd better sit down. Kissing you seems to do funny things to my knees."

Rachel smiled happily and joined him on the settee, snuggling into the crook of his arm with a contented sigh. The idyllic interlude lasted only a moment longer, though, as she remembered something that still disturbed her.

"Why were you gone so long?" she asked, fingering a button on his shirt.

At the sound of his weary sigh, she glanced up curiously. "You won't believe it," he warned, looking very much the martyr.

"I'll try," she promised, settling back more comfortably.

And so he began his story. Not very much time had passed when Rachel realized that she had never heard him talk for so long a time at one stretch. Delighted, she hung on his every word, marveling that even their usually rambunctious child had stilled, as if the sound of his father's voice had soothed him the way nothing else could.

Cole told her and told her. It felt a little strange at first, but she was such an appreciative audience that he soon warmed to the task. She giggled once at something he hadn't thought the least bit funny at the time, but he found himself smiling now at the recollection. Again she laughed, and then again, and he soon began to embellish his recounting, finding humor where none had been before and even seeing it himself, now that the grind of the trail drive was over. The stampedes had been a continuing nightmare at the time, but in retrospect, they made very entertaining fare. He basked in the glow of her admiration, reflecting on how good he felt to be home. Telling her stories wasn't exactly the way he had intended to spend the afternoon, but it wasn't really too bad. When Lupe interrupted to tell them supper was ready, he was irritated with her all over again, but for a very different reason this time.

By bedtime, they had discovered a rapport that had been lacking in their marriage until now, and it was with great regret that Rachel bid him good night and retired to her own room. As much as she longed to have him hold her through the long, lonely night, she had decided that she would be cruel to torture him by sleeping in his bed when she couldn't provide him with any comfort. Besides, she hated the idea of his seeing her bloated body without concealing clothes.

The next morning, Rachel regretted her decision not to share his bed. When they met at breakfast, the closeness they had developed the day before seemed to have evaporated. Cole treated her well and she tried her best to be warm and loving in return, but something very important was missing from their relationship. Several days passed before Rachel realized what it was. Cole was behaving toward her the way he always had, with the aloof respect and consideration that she sometimes found amusing and other times, annoying. The problem was that they no longer had their nights of passion during which they communed on a more intimate level to make the days bearable. It was almost as if Cole saw her as two different people: Lady Rachel to whom he was unfailingly courteous during the day and the wife to whom he made passionate love at night. Without the lovemaking, he seemed to forget that the passionate Rachel existed.

And Rachel had no idea how to go about reminding him. She couldn't make love with him because of the baby, and even though she regretted her decision to sleep alone every time she crawled into her empty bed, she could not bring herself to change her mind about that either. Her already enormous figure expanded almost daily, and she dared not let him see her in a flimsy nightdress, much less first thing in the morning with her hair a mess and her face puffy from sleep. So she slept alone, night after night, longing for Cole but certain that she would be a fool to ask him to join her.

Cole spent many sleepless nights wishing that she would. As much as he would hate sleeping with her without doing anything, he hated sleeping alone even more. He longed for the comfort of her body next to his, and although he did not like to think of it, he needed to know that she was all right. This need grew progressively stronger as November approached and then, finally, arrived. As her time drew closer, Cole began to remember how dangerous it was to have a baby. With those memories came the very real fear that he might lose her. Some nights it was so bad that he would sneak into her room just to hear her breathe, just to know that she was alive. He watched guiltily as her body grew larger and more uncomfortable, and he winced every time he saw her massage the small of her back or put her swollen ankles up on a stool.

One evening as she sat working on baby clothes, he simply could not seem to keep his eyes off her. It was mid-November, and he was wiser about babies now than he had been. He knew that the time was near, but he also knew that there was no certain way to predict exactly when that time would be. The waiting was driving him loco, magnifying the fears he already felt into absolute terror. To someone who feared nothing and no one, this terror was a debilitating emotion, a force that ate away at his insides because it was not something that he could fight, not something on which he could use his gun. He was powerless against it.

The memories of his mother were what disturbed him most, he knew, but he was unable to stop them. The more he tried not to think about them, the worse they got, and when he closed his eyes, he could actually see his mother thrashing on the bed. And the blood, the blood everywhere. And he could hear her, too, moaning with that awful wail that hadn't even sounded human. The old woman had wrapped the baby up in a rag and carried it out, but not before he'd seen it, all blue and wrinkled. They'd sent him out then, but he'd still been able to hear his mother's cries. He'd hidden in the loft, buried himself with hay, but still he'd heard them. Sometime in the night, the cries had stopped, and he had slept. When they found him the next day, they had told him that his mother was dead.

"Stop staring at me!" Rachel snapped, angrily stuffing the bootie she had been knitting back into her workbag. "I know I'm fat and hideous, but you don't have to stare!" Rachel blinked furiously at the tears that came with alarming frequency nowadays.

Cole came slowly back to the present. He hadn't even been aware that he had been staring, but he reacted instinctively when he saw the tears that Rachel's fury could not conceal. She was getting up, awkwardly heaving herself from the chair, and he knew he had to stop her.

Rachel wanted nothing more than to escape to the privacy of her room where she could hide her ugliness under the blankets and sob out her misery. She loved him more with every day that passed, she reveled in his attention and his consideration, but she agonized over knowing that he could not possibly return her love when she looked like one of those cows he'd driven up to Kansas. Every time he went out the door, she tortured herself with thoughts that he might be going to another woman, and every time he came back *not* smelling of cheap perfume, she hated herself for feeling grateful. In another moment, she knew she would be crying over all of this, and to hide her pain, she had to get away. Her girth slowed her too much, though, and he caught her before she'd gone three steps.

To her horror, she discovered that she was already crying, unable to stop, unable even to explain the reason for her tears. The worst part was that he would see her, and she looked so awful when she cried, as if things weren't bad enough already. She struggled frantically, but she was no match for him. Before she knew what was happening, he was sitting in her chair, cradling her in his lap.

Because she could not stop, she continued to sob, but now he muffled those sobs with the comfort of his shoulder, rocking her as if she had been a small child instead of a giant mother-to-be.

"Don't cry. Please don't cry," he begged her, stroking her hair and massaging her back in the ancient gestures of consolation. Feeling impotent and helpless and clumsy but not knowing what else to do, he continued to talk to her, alternately soothing her with meaningless phrases and urging her to stop crying. It took a long time, but at last she obeyed him. The sobbing slowed to weeping which in turn slowed to an occasional sniffle.

Thoroughly humiliated, Rachel pulled a limp hanky from where she had earlier tucked it in her sleeve and tried to wipe away the worst of the ravages without lifting her head. When she thought she was as close to being presentable as she could get under the circumstances, she sat up straight and daintily blew her nose.

Cole waited patiently, and when she seemed to have composed herself, he asked cautiously, "Are you all right?" She nodded without looking at him. "Why were you crying?"

Rachel drew an unsteady breath. "I don't want to talk about it."

Cole swallowed a sigh of exasperation. This was silly. He already knew the answer anyway. "Were you crying because you're ugly?"

With a gasp that was part humiliation and part outrage, Rachel made a furious lunge for freedom, but his arms closed around her. "Wait a minute, I didn't mean that the way it sounded," he assured her as she struggled and while he cursed his own stupidity. "Let me try again. Were you crying because you *think* you're ugly?" he carefully rephrased his question.

"Let me go," Rachel demanded, still straining to break free of his grasp. Why was he so intent on torturing her?

"Not until you answer me," he threatened.

Rachel surrendered grudgingly. "Yes," she admitted reluctantly. There, he'd gotten his confession. "Now let me go."

She was sitting ramrod stiff on his knees, and he could sense her need for privacy, but he wasn't about to let her go, not like this. "Rachel," he said softly. He got no reaction. "Rachel," he repeated cajolingly, "look at me."

Slowly, stubbornly, she turned her head until they were face to face.

"Rachel, look close," he advised, risking releasing her long enough to point to his own face with one finger. "Now *that's* ugly."

She gasped a protest, but before she could speak, he went on. "The only thing ugly about you right now is your mood."

Totally against her will, the tears were starting again. He was being nice to her, and she simply could not stand it.

Cole shook his head in exasperation. "You are not ugly," he insisted.

"Yes, I am," she blubbered. "I'm fat and awkward and swollen and . . ."

He clasped her to him, smothering her words against his chest. "That doesn't make you ugly," he told her fiercely. "Not to me, never to me."

She really couldn't stand it, but this time when she wept, her tears washed away the misery instead of adding to it. Whether he had meant the words or not, he had said them, and he had almost made her believe them. She would always

335

be grateful for that. She couldn't face him, though, not yet, so she stayed where she was even after the tears had stopped, letting him cradle her, letting him absorb the pain.

This time when she quieted, he could feel the tension easing from her body, and he allowed himself to relax, too. It was bad enough that she had to be so physically uncomfortable because of the child he had given her. She shouldn't have to feel unlovely, too. God, didn't she knew that she was still the most beautiful woman alive, even with her stomach bulging out a mile?

As if she had heard his thoughts and disapproved, Rachel suddenly punched him. Except that Rachel hadn't moved.

"Rachel?" he asked tentatively. Her reply was a watery giggle. "Was that . . . ?"

"Uh-huh," she murmured against his shirtfront. He could hear her smile.

His own lips trembled into a delighted grin. "Does he do that a lot?"

"Constantly," Rachel testified with long suffering, wiggling around to a more upright position at last. "Here, put your hand right there," she advised him, placing it on her stomach.

He waited in breathless wonder for the kick that finally came. "My God," he whispered, and then broke into a full-fledged smile.

Rachel impulsively kissed the dimple that smile produced, but he was no longer paying attention to her. "Make him do it again," he urged, placing his hand more firmly on her abdomen.

She laughed out loud at that. "I can't make him do anything, and if I could, I'd make him *stop* kicking. If you think that's exciting, you should be here when he has the hiccups."

Plainly, Cole did not believe such a thing was possible, but before he could call her a liar, the baby moved again and

336

distracted him. "My God," he said again. "It feels like he's trying to get out."

"The sooner the better," Rachel exclaimed, and they both laughed.

For a long time, Rachel sat there with her head on his shoulder while he waited for the tiny movements of his child. Oddly enough, until this very moment, he had never even thought of the baby as a living being. It had just been a mysterious "something" growing inside of Rachel. But it wasn't, he realized now. It was a real baby, and it would be here soon, please God, alive and well. He had to admit he didn't really care all that much about the baby, though. All he really wanted was for Rachel to be alive and well. Without that, all the babies in the world wouldn't make a bit of difference.

"Time for bed," he told her after a while when he noticed that she was dozing against his shoulder.

Rachel roused reluctantly, groaning when she lumbered to her feet. She had been so comfortable in his arms. "Cole?" she began, a little embarrassed to ask and hoping that he would not refuse. "Would you sleep with me tonight?" She waited, twisting her hands in distress when he did not respond immediately. "I get so lonely . . ."

"Sure," he interrupted, jumping eagerly to his feet. He grinned down into her astonished face. "I get lonely, too," he explained.

Rachel's face puckered and her eyes filled again. He was so dear.

"Only don't start that up again," he begged with comic dismay.

Obediently, she blinked the moisture away and managed a wobbly smile. "I'm sorry. I can't seem to help it. Lupe says it's because I'm pregnant, that all pregnant women cry easily." He nodded understandingly. He was still smiling, and she almost wept again when she noticed the tender

337

expression in his eyes. He really did care for her; he hadn't just been mouthing platitudes. Maybe it wasn't love yet, but whatever it was, it was nice. "I . . . just give me a few minutes to get undressed, please," she requested.

Cole nodded again, watching her go. She hadn't been quite so modest the last time they had slept together, he reflected, recalling the red corset and wondering how long it would be before he got to take it off her again. And the next time he wouldn't bother with those damn laces, he thought wryly.

For the first time in many nights, they both slept well. Rachel could not believe how much more comfortable she was when she braced herself against Cole's strength. Cole was so thankful to have her close, where he could instantly reassure himself of her well-being, that he didn't even mind when tiny hands and feet jarred him awake in the middle of the night.

At dawn the next morning, he left her still sleeping soundly. When he placed a tender kiss on her forehead, she smiled in her sleep, awakening all his protective instincts and stirring all the old fears once again. Breathing a silent prayer that she would be all right, he stole quietly from the room and informed Lupe that he would be working very close to home from now until the baby came. He had a feeling that he wouldn't have long to wait.

When he came in to dinner at noon, he was startled to see how haggard Rachel looked. After her restful night, he had expected her to be blooming.

"My back's been hurting ever since I woke up this morning," she explained when he expressed his concern.

"Did I hurt you last night?" he asked, frowning.

Rachel smiled around her discomfort, touched at the way he was willing to take all the blame. "No, it wasn't anything you did," she assured him. "Lupe says it's just because the baby is getting so big."

"Maybe you should lay down for a while," he suggested, still not completely convinced that he wasn't somehow responsible.

"I will, after dinner," she promised. She had been waiting all morning to see him again, and she wasn't about to go to bed now and miss this opportunity. The thought of lying down was remarkably appealing, though.

Cole noticed that she barely touched her food, but he didn't say anything. He knew she was just sitting there to bear him company. "Why don't you go lay down now?" he asked when he could no longer stand watching the way her face twisted with pain.

"I think I will," she consented with a meekness that surprised even her. The pains in her back were getting more uncomfortable with every passing minute.

She stood wearily, but then suddenly she gasped and gripped the edge of the table. Cole was out of his chair in an instant but a soft popping sound stopped him in his tracks. He followed Rachel's startled gaze to the floor at her feet where a puddle was forming from beneath her skirt.

"It's the baby," she explained with a mixture of relief and excitement. "My water broke. That means the baby is coming." At last. At long last, she added silently.

"Lupe!" Cole hollered, suddenly frantic. "She's having the baby!" He hurried to her side, not certain if it were safe to move her or even touch her but also knowing that she couldn't give birth standing in the dining room. "Lupe!"

But Lupe had already arrived. "Take her to bedroom," Lupe advised. Without hesitation, Cole scooped Rachel up into his arms and hurried off, heedless of her sopping skirt or her protests that she was still perfectly capable of walking.

When they reached the bedroom, he set her on her feet after she refused to let him put her on the bed in her wet clothes. "Calm down, Cole," she told him with a bemused smile. "The baby won't be here for hours yet."

"Oh," he said, feeling suddenly very foolish. He had known that. He had just forgotten for a moment.

Lupe came into the room behind them. "You send for doctor yet?" she inquired casually.

"The doctor!" Cole remembered and tore out of the room.

The men were still at dinner down at the cookhouse, and every one of them knew what was happening as soon as they saw Cole's face. "The baby's coming," he explained breathlessly, but Miles was already on his way to the door. By prior agreement, he had been selected to go and had been trying to keep tabs on the doctor's whereabouts, something that was often difficult to do since the doctor had to travel great distances to treat patients. Miles paused beside Cole on his way out and clapped a hand on his shoulder. "Don't worry. She'll be fine."

"Just hurry," Cole said. Without waiting for a reply, he turned on his heel and did his own hurrying, back up to the house.

He found Rachel clothed in a nightdress and seated at her dressing table. Lupe was in the process of brushing out Rachel's hair and braiding it. Rachel turned to smile at him when he came into the room.

"Lupe says that the back pains were probably labor. I've been in labor all morning," she told him. Her excitement echoed in her voice. Excitement and something else.

Cole didn't know whether her news was good or bad, so he did not comment. "Miles went for the doctor," he reported. "It'll take him a while, though. Do you think you can wait?"

Rachel gave her bemused smile again. "I can, but I don't know if my little friend here can or not," she said, her eyes dancing with delight. She had never seen Cole quite so flustered, and between that and knowing that the baby was coming, she was becoming almost giddy.

Cole couldn't believe the change in her. A few minutes ago she had been in misery. Now her eyes were sparkling and she

340

was smiling. She was very excited and she looked almost happy, too. He silently thanked God that she wasn't as scared as he was.

"Oh! I'm having a pain!" she said, placing both hands on her abdomen. Rachel's eyes closed as her muscles contracted.

The word "pain" alarmed Cole, but mercifully, she did not look as if she were in pain. "Does it hurt much?" he inquired, watching her face pucker in concentration.

After a moment, she looked up. "Not much. Not yet, anyway," she replied. But it would later, she knew. Suddenly, she recognized her excitement for the imposter that it was. Her tingling nerves, her giddiness, all of it was the precursor of fear, fear of the unknown terrors that lay ahead.

Cole knew even less than she, but he knew she would soon be hurting, really hurting, and he didn't want to be anywhere around when it started. He began to back toward the door. "I reckon I'll go outside for a while."

"Don't leave me!" Rachel said in alarm. She knew that men seldom attended a childbirth, but the thought of his leaving put her in a panic. How could she face this alone?

Cole froze, uncertain what to do. A birthing was no place for a man, and it was the very last thing he wanted to witness, especially if he had to see Rachel in pain. On the other hand, he could plainly sense her terror. How could he refuse her?

Lupe bent over and whispered to Rachel, patting her shoulder reassuringly and telling her that she would take care of everything. Then she went toward him.

Cole watched Lupe's approach warily, fighting the urge to shake her off when she latched onto his arm with one of her claws and drew him out the door. "We talk," she ordered, pulling the door shut behind her.

When they were alone, she glared up at him. "Stay with her. She scared."

Cole almost said that he was scared, too, but he caught

341

himself just in time. "You don't want me in there," he said reasonably enough.

"She want you," Lupe declared. "You stay till doctor come."

That could be hours. "But she has you," he argued lamely.

Lupe's withered face crinkled into mock amazement. "I know nothing about babies," she said.

Cole's amazement was not feigned. "And you think I do?" he inquired incredulously.

"You help the cows, no?" she challenged.

An instinctive denial rose to his lips but he swallowed it. No cowboy worth his salt would ever admit to having played midwife to a damn cow, but the truth was that almost everyone had lent a hand at least a time or two. It was just too hard to watch the poor beasties suffer, and Cole guessed that he was even more softhearted than most. But that was different. A lot different. "Rachel's now a cow," he pointed out with perfect logic.

Lupe shrugged philosophically. "Same thing," she decreed. "She want you. You stay till doctor come."

Cole might have argued some more, but Rachel called him then. He could not have refused her anything at that moment, and so, however reluctantly, he went back into the room.

Rachel watched the door, wondering if she dared call him again, and knowing that she would never be able to do this without him. She had just risen in a frantic effort to go after him when the door finally opened and he appeared. He looked, she realized vaguely, as if he were on his way to his own execution, but she knew he was going to stay with her, and that was all that mattered. She gave him a grateful smile.

"What do you want me to do?" he asked with a notable lack of enthusiasm.

Rachel's smile grew as she felt her earlier panic receding. "First of all, hand me my wrapper," she said, pointing to

342

where it hung on a peg on the wall. "And then you can walk with me."

Lupe brought him an old pair of moccasins that she had found under his bed so that he could be comfortable while he walked Rachel around the room. His high-heeled riding boots were simply not designed for strolling and that was all Rachel wanted to do. "It makes the baby come faster," she explained to her skeptical husband. The last thing Cole wanted was for it to come faster, at least not until the doctor arrived.

Rachel clung to his arm, unspeakably glad for the support he was giving her. She was entirely too nervous to lie still in bed and wait for each contraction to come. Walking helped her work off the energy that surged through her, and it made her feel as if she were taking an active part in helping the birthing along. With Cole by her side, she was hardly even afraid anymore.

After a while Lupe handed Cole Mr. McKinsey's old pocket watch without comment. "What's this for?" he asked but Lupe had already turned away.

"It's for you to time the pains with and tell me how close they're getting," Rachel explained as Lupe had weeks ago explained it to her. Rachel paused as another contraction overtook her, and bent slightly forward, breathing deeply until it had passed. She didn't see the way Cole's face twisted in sympathy.

Cole didn't need the watch to know the pains were coming more frequently, and he didn't need anything at all to tell him that they were getting longer and stronger. Rachel hadn't complained, but he knew she was suffering more and more with each one. "Maybe you should lay down now," he suggested for at least the tenth time. He just couldn't believe that all this walking was good for her.

"I think I will," she said, surprising him with her agreement. By that he judged the extent of her fatigue.

Rachel crawled willingly into the bed. Lupe had spread a waterproof oilcloth on it and covered that with blankets and a sheet, so the mattress wouldn't be ruined by the birth fluids. Silently, Lupe fluffed the pillows, enabling Rachel to sit up in comfort. Rachel was feeling tired now, and the contractions were stronger. Each one sapped a little more of her strength until she knew that she could no longer waste her energy on walking.

As her energy faded, her fears grew once again. How would she ever to able to even stay awake, much less do all the work that would be required of her? What if something happened? What if the baby . . . Before she could even finish the thought, she suddenly noticed that Cole was gone. Her whole body tensed and a cry of protest trembled on her lips just as he reappeared in the doorway, dragging a big wing chair into the bedroom and up beside Rachel's bed.

Rachel sagged back against the pillows in relief as he sank wearily into the chair. She gave him a small smile as she realized what the chair meant. He was no longer even considering leaving her. Instinctively, she reached out her hand to him, and he took it in both of his. She squeezed it gently in silent appreciation and then more tightly as another contraction gripped her. As if his touch had somehow transferred his strength to her, Rachel felt renewed. She would be all right now. She would make it. They would make it together.

Lupe scurried out and returned in a few moments with a lighted lamp. Only then did Cole realize that the sun was going down. How could he have been staring at that watch all afternoon and not have known how many hours had passed? Where was that damn doctor? he wondered in irritation.

So distracted was he that he almost did not notice the huge butcher knife that Lupe had also brought into the room. "What are you going to do with *that?*" Cole roared, dropping

Rachel's hand and lunging to his feet.

Lupe grinned her toothless grin, bent down and slid the knife under the bed. "To cut the pain," she explained when she had straightened up again.

Cole stared at her incredulously. Not only was the old bat a witch, but she was crazy into the bargain. It was definitely a good idea for him to stay with Rachel. There was no telling what kind of hocus-pocus she might try to pull.

Rachel watched Cole sink back down into his chair and wished that she were not too tired to smile. Sometimes she wanted Cole to like Lupe a little more, but watching them together was so entertaining that she didn't want it very often.

Another contraction distracted her. This was the hardest one yet. Her stomach muscles knotted painfully, causing her to double over. When it ended, she was panting and moisture had collected on her forehead and upper lip. Lupe bent over and sponged it off with a damp rag. Rachel cast her a grateful look and watched as Lupe twisted some rags into loops and tied them to the headboard of the bed. They were, she knew, for her to slip her hands into and hang onto when the pains got worse. She didn't think she wanted them to get any worse and caught herself wishing that she could change her mind and call the whole thing off. She felt an hysterical urge to laugh out loud at the absurdity of such a wish.

The pains were coming more quickly now, but they were still a good five minutes apart, which meant that her ordeal was far from over. They were getting stronger and had started to hurt, although Lupe had warned her they would be much stronger and more painful before it was over. To conserve her strength, she lay back and rested in between each one, sometimes even dozing. At some point she noticed that Lupe had brought Cole a sandwich and a pot of coffee. He barely touched the sandwich, but he drank the coffee in long, reviving gulps.

Occasionally, Lupe would press a glass to Rachel's lips and she would take a few sips of water. Oddly, she did not feel the least bit hungry, even though she had skipped supper and had not eaten much dinner.

"I'm starting to understand why they call it, 'labor,'" Rachel remarked as Lupe bathed the perspiration from her face once more. Lupe murmured to her comfortingly, and Rachel smiled her thanks. It had been dark for quite a while, but she was afraid to ask the time. She did not want to know how long this had been going on. She could feel her muscles bunching for another contraction, and she drew a deep breath in preparation, reaching automatically for Cole's hand. It was there. He was always there for her when she needed his strength, and she gripped his fingers tightly. The pain came then, sliding around both her sides from the back and meeting in the middle of her stomach where it locked and held and held and held and then slipped slowly away, leaving her panting. She sagged back against the pillows.

"Oh, Lupe," she gasped as the old woman bathed her face again, "I need to push."

"Then push," Lupe advised, crinkling her face into a smile.

Rachel stared at her for a moment until the meaning of that advice sank in. "Is it time?" Lupe nodded sagely and Rachel sighed gratefully and closed her eyes to gather her strength for the next onslaught.

Cole listened to this exchange with alarm. "What's all this about pushing?" he demanded.

Lupe ignored him, bustling around to assemble some towels and sheets and then leaving the room completely to fetch fresh water.

Cursing softly, Cole asked again, this time tempering his voice for Rachel's benefit. "What's this about pushing?"

Rachel lifted her eyelids and gave him a small smile. "It means that it's getting close. I have to push to get the baby out."

Panic surged through him. Luckily Rachel had closed her eyes again so that she couldn't see him blanch. Oh, God, he thought, where is that doctor? Frantically, he hurried over to the window and peered out. It was pitch dark, though, and the only thing he could see was his own worried reflection peering mockingly back. He swore again, running a distracted hand through his hair. What if the baby came and the doctor wasn't here? What if something went wrong? What if the baby died? What if Rachel . . . He couldn't even complete the thought. She stirred, and he was instantly beside her. This time she did not reach for his hand. This time she was struggling to sit up, so he helped her rise from the pillows. "I have to push," she gasped.

Cole watched, but she didn't seem to be doing anything differently than she had all the other times, except that her face was getting red. Somehow he had expected her to use her hands to push the baby out.

This time when she sagged back, she smiled slightly. "That's much better," she murmured.

Better than what, Cole had no idea. She certainly didn't look like it was better. In fact, she looked like it was worse. As Lupe had done, he snatched up the damp cloth and gently wiped her face with it. When he was finished, he stared at her for a long moment. She looked so small, so fragile, lying limp like that in the big bed. Except for the mound of her stomach, she might have been a young child who had fallen asleep after a long tiring day.

Hardly had she gotten settled when another pain started. Rachel's eyes flew open in disbelief. That hadn't been five minutes. She was pretty sure it hadn't even been three minutes. Things were really beginning to happen now. It wouldn't be much longer. She tried to heave herself up, but Cole's arms caught and lifted her, relieving her to work on the contraction. Straining for all she was worth, she bore down against the pain exactly as Lupe had instructed her.

Something was not quite right, though. It wasn't exactly as Lupe had said. Then the pain eased, and Lupe was there, putting Rachel's hands into the cloth loops she had fashioned earlier.

That was it, Rachel thought with a relieved sigh. Now she had something to strain against. Two sets of hands were busily tucking pillows behind her, but she could not be concerned with that. Her attention had narrowed down to focus on one thing and one thing only. She had no time or energy for anything else. With a deep breath, she prepared herself, taking a tighter grip on the straps that held her hands and pulling up her knees. When it came this time, she was ready.

Cole watched in agony as the pains came almost on top of one another. No sooner had she relaxed from one then she was tensing for the next. She couldn't keep this up much longer, he knew. Already her nightdress was clinging to her damp skin and wisps of hair clung moistly to her face and neck. Her skin was pale, clammy to the touch, and she was gasping for breath as if she'd run a mile. She was such a tiny little thing, and so frail. How could she possibly be strong enough to endure such an ordeal?

Wringing his hands helplessly, Cole suffered through yet another of her pains. This time, however, she did not sink back when it was over. Instead she tensed and her eyes flew open.

"Lupe!" Rachel cried, "I think . . . It feels like . . ."

Lupe lifted the hem of Rachel's nightdress, and Cole stared in horror.

"My God, what is it?" he asked.

Rachel drew in her breath for another contraction, and Lupe looked at him as if he weren't quite bright. "Baby's head," she informed him.

Stunned, Cole looked again. It still looked horrible, coming out of Rachel that way, but knowing what it was reassured him somewhat. But only for a moment. If that was the baby's head, then the rest of it couldn't be far behind and that meant . . . Cole cast one last frantic look toward the window, but he knew it was useless. The baby was coming and the doctor wasn't.

"Tell her she can't. Tell her she has to wait until the doctor comes," he commanded Lupe.

The old woman looked up at him in amazement. "You tell her," she replied, glancing meaningfully at Rachel who was too involved in her own private agony to even hear the exchange.

That did it, Cole thought. When this was all over he was going to murder the old woman. He didn't care what they did to him. It would be worth it.

"It's coming!" Rachel gasped. "I can feel it!"

She could, too. She was stretching and it felt like the whole bottom was falling out. There were no breaks at all now between the pains. They simply rolled over one another, easing and swelling, waxing and waning, but never stopping. This was it, she knew, and she bore down for all she was worth.

"Catch it," Lupe commanded, grasping Cole's wrists and forcing his hands into the proper position to cradle the baby's head as it emerged. She was screeching other commands, something about Rachel to push or not push, but he didn't hear exactly. He was too busy trying to get a grip on something very slippery. Before he could, there was more of it, filling his large hands and squirming. Lupe did something to its mouth and when she pulled her fingers clear, it started howling.

Cole stared numbly as the wriggling mass he held pinkened and surged to life and separate parts of it began to move. Soon he recognized those parts as hands and feet and arms and legs. It was a person. A real, human being-type person.

Rachel sobbed in a breath and forced her heavy eyelids to open. It was here; it was born. Straining up, she searched for the baby, but her raised knees were in the way. "What is it? Let me see!" she begged, tears of joy fogging her vision as she heard the wail of her firstborn.

Obediently, Cole lifted his tiny burden, only then noticing the cord that still bound it to its mother. Instinctively careful, he tilted the thing for her to see.

"Oh, it's a girl!" she cried joyously, struggling to free her hands from the bonds so that she could touch and hold and love her child. "She's so beautiful! Is she perfect? Does she have everything? All her fingers and toes?"

Cole stared down at the thing he held. A girl. He hadn't even noticed. If he'd thought about it at all, he would have wanted a boy. But he hadn't thought about it much, so he guessed a girl was all right. From the way it was crying, though, he was pretty sure there was something wrong with it. How could he tell Rachel that? Then he saw the old witch coming after it with a pair of scissors.

"What the hell are you doing?" he demanded, wanting to snatch the baby away out of the old crone's reach but remembering the cord that still bound it.

The trill of Rachel's laughter startled him, and even though he knew he shouldn't take his eyes off Lupe for a second, he had to glance at his wife.

"She has to cut the cord, silly," Rachel explained, smiling with delight. "Hurry, Lupe. I want to hold her."

With swift, sure motions, Lupe tied off the cord and severed it while Cole watched suspiciously. Then she took a towel and wiped the squirming infant, taking it from Cole as she did so. When she had cleaned the baby up a little, she wrapped it in a pink flannel blanket and placed it in Rachel's eager arms.

Rachel didn't know whether to laugh or to cry, so she did both while she peeled away the blanket to examine her prize.

Ten pink fingers and ten pink toes, all curled in outrage. With a mother's instinct, she began to jiggle the screaming bundle in her arms and croon to it the secret words that only mothers know.

At the sound of her voice, the baby instantly quieted, staring up at her with eyes the color of the broad Texas sky, the same eyes she saw when she looked at the man she loved. God was good, she reflected as she placed a kiss on one satin baby cheek. So intent was she that she barely noticed the delivery of the afterbirth or Lupe's attempts to clean her up a bit.

Cole still stood exactly where he had when Lupe had taken the baby from him. Even his hands were still cupped as they had been when he had held it. Slowly, he let them fall to his sides as he watched Rachel snuggle the baby and talk to it. Finally, everything was starting to sink in. It was over. It was all over, and the baby was alive and Rachel was alive. Thank God, she was alive. And happy as a weevil in tall cotton, if the look on her face meant anything.

"Anybody home?"

The question followed a knock on the door that everyone had been too busy to notice. The squat, graying Doc Baines stepped in, knowing he would be welcome, if not needed.

"Where the hell have you been?" Cole inquired angrily, placing both hands threateningly on his hips.

The doctor lifted his eyebrows, but his smile never wavered. "Hello, Cole," he said cheerfully, before stepping past him to look at Rachel. "I see you didn't wait for me, Miss Rachel," he teased. "What have we got here?" He folded back the blanket to get a better look.

"It's a girl," Rachel announced proudly, holding the baby up for him to see. "Isn't she beautiful?"

"Prettiest girl I've seen this week," he replied tactfully as he rummaged in his black bag and pulled out a stethoscope. "Let's see what she sounds like." He put the contraption on

351

and held it to the baby's chest. "Sound as a dollar," he pronounced when he had finished. "Have you fed her yet?"

"No, she just got here," Rachel admitted, a worried frown betraying her concern that she might have done something wrong.

"Go ahead and feed her, then," the doctor advised. "That way we'll know for sure if she's all right, if she can suck and swallow and all that. It's also good for you, little mother. It will keep you from bleeding too much."

Bleeding! Cole looked back at Rachel in renewed alarm. Did that mean that the danger still wasn't over? Before he could ask, however, he saw to his additional horror that Rachel had unbuttoned the front of her gown and exposed one breast—without so much as a blush of modesty and with the doctor standing right there, too!

Cole felt the heat rise in his own cheeks as he watched her coax the baby to take the nipple, which it did with an avid greed that Cole somehow resented.

"Good, good," Dr. Baines pronounced after a few moments. "Did you save the afterbirth for me to see, Lupe?" he asked, walking away in apparent unconcern, as if the sight of Rachel's breast were not the most engrossing thing in the room.

To Cole it was. He couldn't even remember how long it had been since he had seen Rachel's breasts, and he couldn't seem to look away. It didn't even look like her breast, either, or at least, not the way he remembered it. It was larger, fuller somehow, and the nipples were darker, but her skin was just the same as always, smooth and white and luscious. Cole knew exactly how she would feel under his hands. And he knew exactly how sweet she would taste, he reflected jealously as he watched that tiny mouth working.

"Well, now, everything seems to be just fine, but I'll stick around for a while in case you need me," Dr. Baines was saying. "I'll let Lupe fix me some breakfast and maybe catch a few winks before heading back to town."

Feeling a little disgusted with himself for being jealous of a little baby, Cole was only too glad to remember a grievance and lash out at the good doctor. "What took you so long to get here?" he demanded again. "What if we'd needed you?"

"Cole!" Rachel chastened, looking up from her fascination with her infant.

Dr. Baines waved away her concern. "It's all right, Rachel. Your husband is just concerned about your welfare." His smile wavered for the first time and he sighed wearily. "I was with a cowboy up near Stillwater. He'd been gored by a bull." Rachel made a small cry of sympathy but Cole just stood there feeling very much a fool. "There wasn't a lot I could do for him, but I waited with him until it was over." He sighed again and shook his head, and then, as if drawing on some inner reserve, he pulled out his smile again. "Besides, I knew you didn't need me when you had Lupe here. Why, I'll bet she's delivered ten times as many babies as I have. Probably knows ten times as much about it as I do, too, but don't tell anybody, eh?" he added with a wink.

Cole turned on the old woman in outrage. The witch had lied to him, all that business about not knowing anything about babies and how he had to help because he'd pulled a calf or two. Now he really was going to throttle her.

She didn't seem too worried, though. She grinned that hideous grin of hers and just shrugged. "You get out now," she told the two men before Cole could swallow his fury and find his voice. "I clean up Rachel. You go." She made shooing motions with her hands.

"Come on, Cole," Dr. Baines said, clapping Cole on the back. "You probably need a drink anyway, unless you've already had one. Have you been pacing the floor all night?"

The doctor was leading Cole to the door, but Cole managed to cast one black look back over his shoulder at Lupe. "Not hardly," he mumbled, giving her a look that would have raised blisters on a rock. She'd be sorry she ever tricked Cole Elliot.

When the door had closed behind them, Lupe walked over to Rachel. "Change sides," she advised the nursing mother.

Rachel nodded and tried to pull the baby loose. Looking up in bewilderment, she asked, "How do I get her to let go?"

Lupe leaned down and showed her how to break the suction and helped her get the child settled on the other side. Then she went about readying things to give Rachel a bed bath when the baby had finished.

Rachel cooed love words to the baby, enjoying the almost-sensual pleasure of the baby's mouth against her breast. Already the memory of her ordeal was fading, and all she could think of was how beautiful her child was, how sweet and tiny and helpless. The baby was just was Rachel had imagined. The dark fuzz on its head would grow into Rachel's dark hair and the blue eyes belonged to Cole. Now if only she would have Cole's dimple, too.

Her thoughts drifted to her husband then and to all the ways he had helped her during the birth. Remembering how reluctant he had been to stay with her in the beginning, Rachel began to wonder what Lupe might have said to him to convince him to stay. Then she recalled the surprised look on his face when the doctor had mentioned that Lupe was an experienced midwife. "Lupe," Rachel asked accusingly, "did you tell Cole that you didn't know anything about delivering babies?"

Lupe shrugged, much as she had under Cole's outraged look. "He not want to stay. I have to tell him something. I tell him he must help." She grinned wickedly. "He good help. Maybe I teach him to midwife, no?"

The thought of Cole Elliot delivering babies for a living made Rachel laugh so hard that her own baby ceased sucking long enough to register a complaint.

After Lupe had gotten Rachel settled and the men had grabbed a bite to eat, Cole peeked in to check on Rachel. She was sleeping soundly, the baby snuggled in the bed next to her. Only the top of the baby's head was visible from where he stood, and he recalled that that was the first view he had ever had of the child. The thing still didn't look all that appealing.

Not wanting to disturb Rachel, he still could not resist running one kunckle across her smooth cheek. She stirred slightly but did not waken. Cole breathed a silent prayer of thanks that it was all over and that Rachel was safe.

Later he would recall that prayer with bitterness, because it really wasn't over. And Rachel was far from safe.

Chapter XI

Since it was almost dawn when Cole finally crawled into his own bed, he slept most of the next day. When he finally did awaken, he discovered he had missed seeing Rachel, who had been awake part of the day but had just gone back to sleep. As he had that morning, he sneaked in to look at her, to assure himself she was fine.

He watched her sleep for a long time. She was incredibly beautiful. The puffiness of pregnancy had already faded from her face, but the ordeal had left her paler than usual, turning her skin to the color of fine porcelain. Her ebony lashes formed dark fans against her cheeks, as did the raven hair that had been carefully brushed and braided and now lay so sleekly against her head. One delicate hand lay protectively on the back of the baby who was curled beside her, its little legs drawn up under it in what looked like a grotesquely uncomfortable position.

Cole was a bit intimidated by the size of the child and ordinarily would not have dared touch it for fear of doing some irreparable damage to its tiny body. His need for contact with Rachel overcame his hesitation this time, however, and he put his hand over where hers rested on the infant, just to feel her warmth, just to reassure himself Rachel was really there and alive. He could stop worrying now, stop remembering the horrors of his mother's death. Rachel was fine. With a grateful sigh, he tiptoed from the room.

Since it was suppertime, he decided to take his meal with the men. He would make it a celebration of sorts, so he broke out a bottle of whiskey and took it along.

His arrival at the cookhouse was greeted with shouts and catcalls and a lot of good-natured ribbing. It was, he remembered with irony, a far cry from the reception he had received from them when he had announced his marriage nine months earlier.

After they had drunk a few toasts and everyone was feeling mellow, the Kid felt bold enough to ask, "Lupe said you delivered the baby yourself. That true?"

Plainly, he did not think so, and as Cole glanced around, he noted how every man in the room had perked up, eager to hear the answer. He figured they couldn't believe it either. "Yeah, I guess I did," he admitted.

The muttered exclamations of surprise that greeted this admission also contained an element of admiration. Cole marveled at this, reflecting that although Lupe had tricked him, she might also have done him a favor. Not many men could say they'd delivered their own babies. He felt a stirring of pride, and even began to think maybe the old witch wasn't quite so bad as he'd thought. Maybe he might not murder her after all, at least not this week.

It was late when he went back to the ranch house, and Rachel was still sleeping. After checking on her once more, he went to his own room where he lay awake for a long time. Now that the baby was born and Rachel was safe, he could concentrate his full attention on his other problems. Miles had told him the rumors about Statler. In the months since he had returned home, he had even heard a few of them himself, but he wasn't too worried. With winter coming on, he was pretty sure they wouldn't be hearing from Statler for a while, even if he was still alive.

No, they were fine for the time being. With the money from selling the cattle, they wouldn't have any financial problems for a long time, either. In the winter, ranchers usually let some of their crew go since the work load was light. Cole decided he would not do so this year. If Statler was around, Cole would need every man he had come spring, and he wanted to be sure he had men he could trust if the going got rough. They could afford to keep them, so they would. He would tell the men tomorrow, just in case they were worried about getting fired.

With that settled in his mind, he rolled over on his side to go to sleep. He had just about decided life was going to get back to normal when he heard the baby start to cry in the next room. Sitting bolt upright in the bed, he was just about to fling off the covers to find out what was wrong when the sound ceased abruptly. After a moment he figured out what must have happened, surmising that Rachel would have picked the baby up to silence it. He drew a mental picture of the last time he had seen Rachel awake. She had been nursing the baby and he imagined that was what she would be doing now. For a minute or two he entertained the idea of going in there to watch, but rejected it. He didn't want to disturb them, and besides, there would be plenty of opportunities to watch in the future, starting tomorrow. He settled back down, listening to the silence, and eventually fell asleep.

The next morning he went out with the men, business as usual. The only thing he regretted was that Rachel had not yet been awake when he left the house. He would have to wait until evening to see her since they were working far out and would not be coming back to the house for the noon meal.

"Is she awake?" was the first thing he said to Lupe when he came into the kitchen to wash up for supper. Lupe had begun preparing his bath in the kitchen since the weather had turned colder.

"*Sí,* she is mad at you, too, because you do not come to see her," Lupe informed him.

Cole started to argue that he'd been to see her plenty of times but she just hadn't been awake, but he thought better of it. There was no use in arguing with Lupe. She'd just shrug and mutter something nobody could understand, and he'd still have to explain it to Rachel. He'd save his breath.

When he was clean and dressed, he hurried to Rachel's room. His first impulse was to rush right in, but he decided he'd maybe better knock, just in case she was doing anything she didn't want him to see. He tapped lightly. "Rachel, it's me," he said.

"Come in."

Her voice sounded weak, but maybe that was just because it was muffled through the closed door. His suspicions were confirmed, however, when he saw her. The room was dark since it was dusk and the shades had been drawn, but even in the dimness he could see something was wrong.

Rachel smiled up at him, painfully aware how weak her smile was. She was really very happy to see him. She only wished she had the energy to show him. No one had warned her how tired she would become after the baby was born. Somehow she had imagined an instant return to her previous vitality. She wasn't getting any better, either. In fact, yesterday she had felt much better than she did today, and she had been much better even this morning than she was now. "Hello," she said softly, amazed at the effort required to utter one simple word.

Cole scowled, not even remembering to return her greeting. She looked awful. Her face was pinched and drawn, as if she were in pain. "How do you feel?" he asked.

His worried concern touched her. "Tired," she said in a voice that confirmed her statement. With a great effort, she lifted a hand to him.

He took it between both of his. It was warm to the touch. Too warm. Instinctively, he placed one of his hands on her cheek. It, too, was warm. No, he mentally corrected, hot. "Lupe!" he called, and then remembered he had closed the door behind him. Lupe was probably in the kitchen and couldn't hear him anyway. "I'll be right back," he assured Rachel, tucking her hand back down into the bedclothes as if it were a precious object that needed safekeeping.

He hurried to the door, flung it open and called again as he rushed toward the kitchen. "Lupe!" They met in the dining room. "Come quick," he commanded, taking her by the arm.

Lupe had to run to keep up with his long strides. "What is?"

"Rachel," he said, fear lacing his voice. "She's got a fever."

"Dios," she muttered, and Cole's blood ran cold. If Lupe was worried then it wasn't his imagination. Something really was wrong.

"Dios," she said again when they entered the room and she saw Rachel. She scurried over to the bed and placed a gnarled hand on Rachel's cheek, just as Cole had done. Her expression betrayed nothing, but she moved to pull down the bedclothes.

"Don't," Rachel protested feebly. "I'm cold."

Lupe ignored the protest and pulled down the blankets far enough so she could probe Rachel's abdomen.

"Ouch!" Rachel objected, impatient with being mistreated.

Lupe crooned something comforting and pulled the bedclothes back up, tucking them carefully around Rachel and the baby who still slept peacefully beside her.

"Is something wrong?" Rachel asked, noticing Cole's somber expression.

He did not reply, not knowing himself, but Lupe said, "Rest now," and turned away, taking Cole's arm much as he had taken hers moments ago, and leading him from the room.

Rachel watched them go in disappointment. She had wanted to see Cole, to talk to him about the baby, to relive the wondrous experience they had shared. They had to choose a name for the baby, too. She had one all picked out but she wanted to be sure he approved first. This was important and Cole should be here with her so they could discuss it. She opened her mouth to call him back, but suddenly the effort seemed just a little too much and she closed her mouth again. Her eyelids felt awfully heavy, too, so she closed them also. She would do as Lupe had said and rest, just for a minute.

"What is it?" Cole asked in an urgent whisper as soon as the door closed behind them.

Lupe's withered face was twisted into a worried frown. "Childbed fever."

The words hit him with the force of a body blow, robbing him of breath and strength and even sight as the world went black for a moment. Childbed fever. Women died from that.

Seeing his reaction, Lupe grasped him by the arms. "It is not bad yet. Sometimes it does not get bad."

"Is she going to . . . ?" He could not say the word, could not even think it.

"We will take care of her. She will be fine," Lupe insisted, but Cole had the uneasy feeling she was trying to convince herself as much as him.

"Is this something you know about?" he demanded. "Tell me the God's truth this time."

Lupe nodded gravely. "But nobody knows much. You wait and you pray, that is all."

"There must be some medicine," he insisted in desperation.

She shook her head. "Something for the fever, something for the pain, nothing to make her well but time."

That couldn't be all, his seething brain insisted. There must be something else. "I'll send for the doctor again," he said, knowing if there was anything, Dr. Baines would know about it. Without waiting for Lupe's reply, not even caring what her opinion might be, he hurried from the house to find Miles.

It was late when Dr. Baines arrived. Luckily, he had been at his office when Miles had come seeking him. This time he was not smiling. He examined Rachel much the same way Lupe had and then listened to her heart and lungs.

Rachel showed a spark of her usual spirit, complaining she was cold when they uncovered her again and telling the doctor to go away and let her sleep. She was so weak that she sounded like a petulant child instead of the woman Cole knew, and he could actually feel his heart breaking in his chest.

Out in the parlor, the doctor told him much the same thing Lupe had. "She has an infection in her womb," he explained, "but there's not much I can do. I can give her some laudanum for the pain. Sometimes it gets pretty bad. Lupe can brew up something to help bring the fever down and you can give her sponge baths. That helps, too. Keep her warm and give her all she wants to drink." He shook his head wearily. "There's not much else, I'm afraid."

Cole wanted to yell that there had to be something else, but the man's defeated expression convinced him otherwise. It was just like Lupe had said, you wait and you pray.

"I've seen many women recover," Dr. Baines was saying, placing a comforting hand on Cole's shoulder. "She's young and strong and in excellent health. She has every chance." He continued talking, promising to check on her every day, but Cole wasn't listening.

Cole turned numbly and went back into her room. The chair he had brought in during the birth was still there, beside the bed, and he sank down into it. She did not move, but it was a comfort just to watch her breathe.

He must have dozed because the sound of the baby crying woke him. The baby was still in the bed beside Rachel. She had nursed it earlier, while they were waiting for the doctor to arrive, cradling it lethargically to her as she lay on her side, too weak even to sit up. This time she seemed unable even to

363

make that much of an effort.

"Lupe!" he called again, not even knowing where the old woman was or if she could hear him. She must have been nearby, however, because she came instantly.

"Get the baby out of here," he told her, pointing to the squalling infant.

"Can Rachel . . ."

"No, she's too weak. Get it out of here." He watched Lupe pick the baby up. Rachel was thrashing, obviously disturbed by the baby's cries but unable to rouse herself to deal with them.

"The baby . . ." she muttered feverishly.

"Lupe has it," Cole assured her, tucking the covers more securely around her.

"What I feed her?" Lupe mumbled, more to herself than to anyone else.

"I don't give a damn," Cole snapped. "Just get it out of here." At that moment, he really didn't care whether the child starved to death or not. The baby was what had made Rachel sick, and if anything happened to Rachel, he knew he never wanted to lay eyes on it again.

Lupe left with the baby, and Cole heard its howls diminish as she took it farther and farther away. As the sounds died, Rachel's agitation calmed, and she looked around the room with overbright eyes. "I thought I heard the baby cry," she told Cole.

"No, everything's fine," he said, brushing wisps of hair back from her forehead. Everything wasn't fine, though. Her forehead was even hotter now than it had been. "Drink some of this," he urged, offering her a cup of some concoction Lupe had brought. She had told him it would bring the fever down, and he had been pouring it into Rachel every time she stirred.

Rachel drank thirstily. It didn't taste like anything familiar but she was so dry, she would have taken anything. Cole was giving it to her, too, and she trusted him. She had been so sure she'd heard the baby. A lot of time had passed and surely the baby would be waking up soon. Lifting her hand to her breast took a surprising amount of effort, but when she touched the taut skin beneath the linen of her nightdress, she knew she was right. Her breasts were full and aching, her nightdress damp from leaking milk.

Maybe she would ask Cole to give her the baby now, even if she wasn't awake yet. Yes, that's what she would do. In a minute. She would rest first, and then she would ask.

The pain woke her. She had been dreaming she was in labor again, that she had pushed and pushed until every bone in her body ached and still the baby wouldn't come. This wasn't labor pain, though. She knew that as soon as she came awake. Labor pains came and went but this one stayed and stayed. She tried to turn over, hoping another position would ease her discomfort, but the movement caused a storm of agony in all her joints and wrenched loose a moan. No part of her was working correctly.

And then Cole was there, pressing something cool against her lips. She drank and drank. It was water this time, sweet, clear water. He was so good to her. "It hurts," she told him, not really understanding herself the where or why of her pain but knowing instinctively that he would.

He left her then, but before she could even feel the disappointment, he was back and giving her something else to drink. This stuff tasted awful, and she tried to turn away, but she was too weak to resist.

"Drink it, honey," he urged. "It will make you stop hurting."

He had convinced her and she swallowed the vile liquid. He laid her back against the pillows with a tenderness that impressed her even in her groggy state. "The baby . . ." she said, suddenly remembering her responsibilities.

"She's fine," Cole said, or maybe she only dreamed it.

Cole watched her eyes close, and then set the empty glass down on the bedside table. He hated giving her the laudanum, especially after the doctor had warned him it could be addictive. But he couldn't stand seeing her in pain either. After a few moments, her breathing settled into a drugged steadiness that told him she was no longer suffering, and so he allowed himself to sit back down in his chair to wait.

Time became meaningless as the hours stretched into first one day and then another and Cole continued his vigil. Every now and then, Lupe would bring him some food, and sometimes he even ate it. She also seemed to know exactly what he would need to care for Rachel, cool water or hot water, broth or tea or one of her brews, clean sheets, clean towels, a clean nightdress. At first the old woman had tried to convince him to take a few hours and get some rest. Eventually, she had quit saying anything except to instruct him on how to care for Rachel.

He did everything for her. Everything. He changed her gown. He changed her bindings. He took care of her most intimate needs. When she was feverish, he sponged off her beloved body with cool water. When she shook with chills, he crawled into bed beside her and warmed her body with his own. When she cried out in pain, he gave her the drug. When she slept peacefully, he watched, counting every breath she took. And in the dark, haunting hours of this longest of nights, he knelt beside her bed and begged her not to die.

Rachel lifted her eyelids slowly. She was still very tired, but for the first time in what seemed like forever, she was fully awake. The room was shadowed, the dim light from the fading afternoon coming only faintly through the shuttered windows. Still she was able to find Cole. He was dozing in the chair beside her bed. For some reason, she was not surprised to see him there. What did surprise her was the condition he was in. He looked as if he hadn't shaved in several days and his clothes looked like he'd slept in them. Which was exactly what he was doing, she realized with a small smile.

The pain in her breasts had awakened her. She remembered pain before, but that had been another pain. That had been lower, in her stomach, and it had made her dream she was having the baby over and over again. The pain in her stomach was still there, but had faded to a dull ache so now she could notice other discomforts. Lifting her hand, she discovered her breasts felt hard and hot to the touch.

"Cole," she called, her voice rusty from disuse.

He was awake and at her side before she could clear her throat and call him again.

"I have to feed the baby," she told him.

But he wasn't listening. "Rachel, how do you feel? Your fever's down. Do you hurt anyplace?" he asked, laying an experienced hand across first her forehead, and then her cheeks and neck.

"I have to feed the baby. Where's the baby?" she asked, looking around. The baby should be here someplace. Rachel knew she should.

"How does your stomach feel?" he said, pulling down the covers to probe it himself. "Does this hurt?"

"A little," she admitted testily. "Cole, where is the baby?"

"Lupe!" he called in triumph, hurrying to the door and throwing it open. "Lupe, come quick."

She did.

"Her fever broke," he announced as Lupe scurried past him to see for herself.

Rachel was growing more and more irritated as Lupe probed and prodded, too. "Lupe, I have to feed the baby," she tried again.

"*Sí,*" the old woman muttered absently, and then said to Cole, "She is better."

The two continued to discuss her as if she were not present. Rachel seethed silently for a moment before another thought distracted her. She glanced around the room. Even in the dimness she could see that the cradle she had placed in the corner of the room was gone. "Where's the baby?" she demanded, her alarm growing with each passing second. Still they ignored her. Fear gave her the strength she had not had before, and she pushed herself up on her elbows. *"Where's the baby?"*

She finally had their attention.

"She is safe, *chata,*" Lupe soothed, patting her and urging her to lay back down.

"Cole," Rachel pleaded, resisting Lupe's efforts, "I want my baby."

Cole and Lupe exchanged a look as they tried to decide if Rachel were well enough.

Misinterpreting their look, Rachel panicked. "What's wrong? Is something wrong with the baby? Tell me!"

"No, nothing's wrong," Cole hastened to assure her, giving Lupe a defeated shrug. "Go get it," he told the old woman. Well enough or not, Rachel needed to see her baby. "You've been sick, honey. Lupe's been taking care of the baby. That's all. There's nothing to worry about."

Plainly, she did not believe him, and although she lay back down, she did not relax until Lupe came back in carrying a small pink bundle.

A small, pink, squalling bundle. Rachel threw both Cole and Lupe a look of reproach as she took the child from Lupe. "What have they been doing to you, little one?" she asked, tucking the baby in beside her and baring her breast. The tiny mouth had a little difficulty at first with the overfull nipple, but soon was able to latch on successfully. Rachel watched, noting that the baby sucked with even more than her usual greed. "How long has it been since she was fed?" Rachel asked accusingly.

"I feed her all the time you sick," Lupe replied defensively.

Rachel tried to remember. She recalled blurred images and pain and Cole. Most of all Cole. "How long have I been sick?" she demanded.

"Couple days," Cole said, shortening the length of her illness by one day.

Rachel knew he was lying. If she hadn't been able to tell from his expression, she would have known from his beard growth. She was too tired to argue, though. "What did you feed her?" she inquired instead.

Lupe gave one of her eloquent shrugs. "I make her a sugar tit to suck," she explained, referring to something made from wrapping a small lump of sugar in a clean cloth. "I give her milk from a cow."

This was startling news to both Rachel and Cole. Until this moment, Cole had not known or cared what Lupe might be using to keep the baby alive. "Cow's milk?" Cole repeated. "Where on earth did you get it?" Nobody who worked on a cattle ranch would ever be caught dead milking a cow. Cole wasn't even sure he would know how.

Lupe smiled mysteriously. "The men get it for me," she revealed. When both parents still did not believe her, she explained. "I tell them the baby will die without it. They play poker every night. Whoever loses must get milk next day. They be glad Rachel is well again," she added with a wink.

That reminded Cole. "Are you well?" he asked, testing her forehead again.

Rachel smiled up at him. "I'm tired, but I do feel much better. I must have been very sick. What was wrong?"

Plainly, he was loath to say the words. "Childbed fever."

Rachel felt a chill run down her spine. She had been very lucky. Many women did not recover from childbed fever. "I'm fine now. "You'll see," she promised. "I have to get well. I've got responsibilities," she added, running an affectionate hand over the baby's small body.

Cole frowned down at the nursing couple. "Are you sure you should be doing that? You're still awfully weak. Lupe could . . ."

"If I *don't* do this, I'm going to explode," Rachel informed him with a look that said she would brook no argument on the subject. "I need some help. Will you put her on the other side?" Rachel broke the baby's suction and looked up at Cole expectantly.

Cole simply stared right back. She couldn't want him to pick up that tiny little baby. The thing was no bigger than a minute and how on earth was he supposed to get a grip on it? And what if he dropped it? Or squeezed it too hard? Or . . .

When he didn't move, Lupe stepped in and placed the baby on Rachel's other side. Rachel was a little disturbed at Cole's refusal to help, but she was tiring and couldn't expend too much energy on considering it. She sighed with relief as the baby took her milk, and hugged the child more closely to her. "Don't take her away again," she murmured just before dozing off.

Cole leaned over in alarm, but straightened again as soon as he realized she had simply fallen asleep.

"You get some sleep, too," Lupe commanded.

"I'm all right. I'll just sit here with her for a while," Cole demurred absently.

"You get some sleep," Lupe repeated more forcefully. "You look like walking dead man. If she see you in the light, you scare her to death."

Instinctively, Cole put a hand to his face and was startled by the length of the whiskers he found there. "Well, maybe I will get cleaned up a bit," he allowed.

"You sleep, too," Lupe insisted. "I will stay with her. I will call if anything happen. You sleep. She will be sad if you get sick, too."

Cole considered her words. He didn't feel sick, but he might be able to sleep for a few hours. "You'll call me if there's any change?" he asked suspiciously.

Lupe nodded solemnly.

He cast one last glance at Rachel. That damn baby was still sucking away, even with Rachel fast asleep. "You promise you'll call me?"

"Go!" Lupe said in exasperation, pointing toward the door.

He did.

It was more than twelve hours later when Cole woke up starving. Lupe swore to him that Rachel was still asleep, so he took the time for a meal and a shave and a bath. He even went outside looking for Miles to find out what had been going on at the ranch for the last several days, but Miles had not come in for dinner yet. When Cole got back to the house, Lupe informed him Rachel was at last awake and wanted to see him.

This time, because she no longer had any secrets from him, he did not bother to knock. Rachel was sitting up in bed with her knees drawn up. The baby was propped against her thighs and Rachel seemed to be talking to it. She glanced up when he opened the door, and the smile she sent him lit up the entire room. She looked wonderful, incredibly happy and even healthy, with a touch of color in her cheeks.

"Come in," Rachel said. He looked wonderful, tall and lean and rested, and he was grinning at her. "Look, sweetheart," she crooned to the baby. "Papa's come to visit us."

Cole had an impulse to look over his shoulder to see who else might have come in behind him, but then he realized she had meant him. He shifted uncomfortably as the name "Papa" settled awkwardly on him. He'd never been anyone's papa before. This was something he was going to need some time to get used to. "How are you feeling?" he asked perfunctorily.

Rachel rolled her eyes. "If one more person asks me that, I think I'm going to scream. I'm fine," she insisted. "The doctor was here this morning while you were still sleeping, and he pronounced me fit as a fiddle. Now sit down here and talk to me," she ordered, patting the bed.

Gingerly, Cole perched on the edge of the bed. What he really wanted to do was take her in his arms and squeeze her till her ribs cracked, but he didn't think that would be a good idea. She still wasn't completely recovered, regardless of what she said. He would just have to be content to be close to her and to see her smiling once again. God, it was good to see her smile.

"Did you sleep well?" Rachel inquired, still smiling. Looking at him acted as a balm for her eyes and her still-weary body. She marveled at how his physical presence seemed to strengthen her. Then she recalled how he had had the same effect on her when she was in labor, how he had kept her going long after she thought she could not make it. Her heart swelled with love for him.

"I think I slept a little too well," he admitted a little sheepishly. "Lupe must have slipped me some of your laudanum." He'd been a little angry when he realized how long he had slept, but Lupe assured him Rachel was still fine and he hadn't been needed.

Rachel's smile settled down into a more somber expression as she recalled all the other things he had done for her, the things she did not remember, the things she wanted to talk to him about. "Lupe told me what you did, how you took care of me all the time I was sick, how you wouldn't even let her help." She watched Cole shift uncomfortably under her praise. Of course, she had known he would be embarrassed at being reminded of the way he had taken care of her. A man like Cole, who had such difficulty expressing his more tender feelings, would not want to speak of such things, but she had no intention of letting him think she did not know or care. She did know and she cared very much. Her eyes grew moist as she remembered the gentle way he had tended her. "I don't know how to even begin to thank you. You've done so much for me and now this . . ."

"Whoa," Cole cautioned, raising his hands in surrender. "All you have to do is promise never to get sick like that again, and we'll be even. More than even."

Rachel blinked back her tears and wondered if she would ever be able to love him as much as he deserved to be loved. She could remember bits and snatches of her illness and every incident centered on Cole, Cole giving her something to drink, Cole making her comfortable, Cole holding her close and keeping her warm. How much of it had really happened, she would never be entirely certain, but she had a good idea that just about all of it had. She also knew that Cole would modestly downplay his role in her recovery. Her lips trembled into a grateful smile. "I'll try not to get sick again," she promised him.

He returned her smile, but he didn't say anything. Just looking at her was enough. At least until she was better and he could do more than look.

"You haven't said 'hello' to your daughter yet," she chastened good-naturedly, suddenly remembering the baby in her lap.

Cole looked askance at the tiny body huddled against Rachel's legs. Its eyes were closed and it was giving every indication of being asleep. Privately, he thought he was wasting his time, but to humor Rachel he said, "Hello."

Rachel's eyes widened in amazement. What a way to talk to a baby! Didn't he know anything? Then she realized he probably didn't. How could he when he might well have never even been close to a real live baby before now? Testing her theory, she asked, "Would you like to hold her?"

"No," he said a little too quickly, and then amended, "I mean, no, I don't want to wake her up or anything."

Her amazement grew. Was he afraid to hold his own baby? "Have you ever held her?" she asked suspiciously.

Cole considered. "Sure," he replied with restored confidence, suddenly remembering. "I held her when she was born." There, that ought to satisfy her.

"And not since then?" Rachel prodded.

"No," he admitted reluctantly, not liking the determined glint in Rachel's eye.

"Well, then, it's about time you did." She picked up the infant and thrust it into his arms.

"I might drop her," he protested even as his arms automatically accepted the small bundle.

"You aren't going to drop her. Here, put her in the crook

of your arm like this," she advised, showing him how to support the baby, "and put your other hand underneath. Now that's not so hard, is it?"

Cole thought it was extremely hard, but he didn't think Rachel would believe him, so he didn't say so.

Rachel sat back and wryly contemplated her two favorite people. The little one was fast asleep and the big one, for the first time that Rachel could remember, looked totally buffaloed. He hadn't even been this unsure of himself the night this very child was born. Rachel's lips twitched into a wicked grin as she decided to torment him further. "She looks like you," she announced.

Cole glanced down at the baby in surprise. If he had had to choose the person whom this toothless, wrinkled bit of humanity most resembled, he would have picked Lupe, and if he had his druthers about whom he wanted his daughter to look like, he would have picked Rachel. Never in his wildest nightmares would he want a little girl to resemble Cole Elliot. "She does?" he asked skeptically, certain that Rachel would retract her pronouncement.

"Yes," Rachel said. "Her head is shaped just like yours, and she had your hands." Rachel pulled back the pink blanket to reveal the baby's hands. "See how long her fingers are?" she asked, uncurling one tiny fist. "She even has your feet."

Cole glanced down at the baby's minuscule feet in disbelief, but even he had to acknowledge the toes were quite long, as his were. He only hoped the kid's feet never got to be as large as his were. "I just hope her face looks like *yours*," he said, looking doubtfully at the little face. At that moment the baby's eyes opened, and Cole found himself staring into eyes the same color as those that stared back at him from the mirror. "She has my eyes!" he discovered with unexpected delight.

Rachel could have laughed out loud for joy. He'd gotten off to a slow start, but he was falling into the role of proud father at last. "Lupe says all white babies are born with blue eyes but there's a good chance hers will stay blue. Lupe said she's never seen eyes quite that blue in a newborn before."

Cole couldn't seem to stop looking at the baby. He still didn't think she was beautiful the way Rachel did, but maybe she wasn't quite as ugly as he had first thought.

"We need to name her," Rachel said, having decided he was interested in the baby enough now to participate in the decision.

"That would be a good idea," Cole said, thinking if she had a name, they could call her something besides, "the baby" and "it."

"Do you have an preferences?" Rachel asked.

Cole's head came up in surprise. "Me? No, you can name her anything you want," he offered generously.

Rachel breathed a silent sigh of relief. "Then I'd like to call her Colleen."

Colleen. He mulled the name over, and tried to remember if he'd ever heard it before. He didn't think he had. "Was that your mother's name or something?"

"No, I . . . ah," Rachel stammered, a little embarrassed but determined. She took a deep breath and plunged in. "It's Irish for 'girl.' My father used to call me that sometimes and . . ." Her voice trailed off uncertainly and she reached out to lightly stroke the top of the baby's head as she recalled the father she missed so very much. "I wish he could see the baby," Rachel murmured, imagining how proud Sean McKinsey would have been of his first grandchild.

"Maybe he can," Cole said by way of comfort, his blue eyes telling her he shared her grief.

And that reminded Rachel of how very much she loved Cole Elliot and the other reason for the name she had chosen for their child. Brushing away her tears, she told him the rest of it. "And Colleen is sort of the feminine version of Cole."

Cole stared at her. "Why would you want to name her after me?"

Blissfully thankful he had comprehended her convoluted tribute so easily, she was also touched that he could still be so amazed by it. "Because," she told him, reaching out to touch his cheek, "I love you, Cole Elliot." Impulsively, she leaned over and placed a kiss on his startled mouth.

Miles had been right, he thought in the second that followed her declaration, and then she was kissing him, and he was remembering how very sweet she tasted. She had made him just about the happiest man alive, and he was going to tell her so, too, but before he could even get his tongue unhinged, that very same Miles called out, "Anybody home?"

Startled, they broke the kiss, and without thinking, Cole responded, "In here." He could have bitten his tongue off then, but it was already too late. Miles stuck his head in the partially opened door.

"Oh, I'm sorry," he apologized, drawing back. "I didn't realize you were in here, Rachel." He took in the domestic scene with Cole holding the baby. "I don't want to intrude."

Rachel smiled to cover her disappointment. She would have liked about five more minutes alone with Cole, but she knew the mood had been shattered now. Comforting herself with the fact that there would be many other times like this in the future, she said, "You aren't intruding. Come on in. Have you seen the baby yet?"

Miles came in and glanced down at the bundle in Cole's arms. "Not yet," he admitted, giving the infant a cursory inspection. "That's a mighty fine-looking baby you've got there."

"Rachel thinks she looks like me," Cole informed him before Rachel could respond.

Miles bit back a smile at the hint of belligerence in Cole's tone and pretended to study the child. Then he nodded sagely. "Don't worry, though," he comforted, patting Cole on the shoulder. "She'll probably grow out of it."

Cole glared up at Miles, and Rachel's strangled giggle

didn't make him feel any better. He'd have a word or two with Miles in private about insulting his daughter.

"We're all glad you're feeling better, Rachel," Miles was saying.

"I'll bet you are," Rachel replied, her dark eyes dancing with mischief. "Lupe told me about the milk."

Miles rolled his eyes in mock horror.

"Who did the milking?" Cole inquired, not even bothering to hide his smirk and hoping it had been Miles as a small revenge for his earlier remark.

"The Kid mostly. You know what a lousy poker player he is." The mental picture of the dapper Kid with his golden locks and silver-trimmed clothes squatting beside a belligerent cow was more than Cole and Rachel could stand and they both burst out laughing. "Don't say anything to him," Miles cautioned them. "He threatened to nail us to the barn wall if we ever told."

"I'll have to do something nice for him," Rachel said when she had managed to control her hilarity. Then she grew suddenly more somber. "He did save my baby's life."

Cole nodded, acknowledging the truth of her statement and making a mental note that he, too, owed the Kid a debt.

"What did you name her?" Miles asked to lighten the mood once again.

Cole glanced at Rachel but her look plainly said this was his news to tell.

"Rachel named her Colleen." He waited for Miles's reaction. When there was none, he added, "After me."

Miles's eyes grew wide with understanding, and his homely face broke into a pleased grin that plainly said, "I told you so," to Cole.

Cole acknowledged the grin with one of his own, one full of self-mockery. He knew he'd done some stupid things, and not realizing Rachel must love him was probably the stupidest, but that was over now. He owed Miles an apology, too, and probably more than one, now that he thought about it. He had been pretty short with him a couple of times when Rachel had been sick. He'd take care of that right away. But before he could, he suddenly noticed something very peculiar about the baby he was holding.

"Rachel, I think . . ." he began. He pulled out the hand that had been supporting the baby's bottom and examined his large palm. He was right. "She's wet," he reported with dismay.

Rachel thought this was mildly humorous, and although Cole could see nothing funny whatsoever, Miles roared. When Colleen had been transferred back to her mother for a change, Cole stood up, still holding his wet hand away from him as if it had been infected with some vile plague. "You ought to teach her not to do that," he advised Rachel, so seriously that Miles was convulsed and Rachel could no longer restrain herself.

"Well, she should," Cole repeated defensively, unable to ascertain what had caused all the hilarity.

"I will," Rachel promised between giggles, "but it might take a while."

"Come on, Papa," Miles urged, still grinning ear to ear. "I think Colleen and her mother have had enough visitors for now. Let's let them get a little rest."

Reluctantly, Cole followed him out, giving Rachel a small wave before closing the door behind him. She flashed him a happy smile in return.

Rachel made a speedy recovery. Long before her requisite two weeks of rest were over, she was chaffing to be up and around. With winter coming on, she knew she was missing the last of the nice weather, and with it, her chance to take Colleen out to show her off. Now she would just have to wait until spring. Those who wanted to see the baby would have to come to the ranch.

Cole still continued to be a little leery of his child, but Rachel decided the best way to get him over it was to force him. One evening when Colleen was about three weeks old,

Rachel simply announced, "I have to go help Lupe. Will you hold Colleen?" Without waiting for an answer, she handed the child to him and started to leave the room.

"Rachel!" he called in alarm, making the baby jump.

Rachel came back, an inquisitive look on her face. "Yes?" she asked innocently.

"What am I supposed to do with her?" he demanded in consternation.

Rachel gave a good imitation of one of Lupe's eloquent shrugs. "Just hold her. You might want to play with her, too," she suggested helpfully.

"Play with her?" Cole echoed incredulously. How could he play with a person who couldn't even sit up?

Biting down hard on her lip to keep from grinning at his disgruntled expression, Rachel relented. "Well, maybe she's a little too small for playing. You could talk to her, though."

"About what?" Cole glared at his wife.

Rachel smiled mysteriously. "About anything. She won't understand a word you say anyway." Then she turned gracefully and glided from the room, ignoring Cole's demand that she return immediately.

At first Cole felt like a fool, but he had observed Rachel and Colleen in action enough to know that murmuring nonsense to an infant was acceptable behavior. Deciding he had to do something, he began to talk to her, and amazingly enough, she listened with rapt attention to every word.

When Rachel came back a few minutes later and heard his deep voice crooning to the baby, she had to stop and cover her mouth to keep from crying out in sheer joy. He might not have spoken of his love for her, but he had shown her in every way possible how he felt. He had come back to her, he had remained faithful throughout her pregnancy, he had saved her very life, and now he loved their child as well. For just a moment, she thought she might not be able to contain her happiness. Somehow she managed to control her emotions and to pretend nothing earthshaking had just occurred so he would not feel self-conscious.

After that, Rachel handed the baby to him often, and he never seemed to mind. He would talk to her quite naturally, sometimes telling her about his day or sometimes telling her stories about when he was a boy, the happy times before his mother died, or sometimes he would just talk nonsense. She didn't seem to care, either. She listened raptly no matter what the subject, and occasionally responded with comments of her own. Unless she got hungry. In that case nothing he said made any difference, and she just kept nuzzling the front of his shirt like she thought he had something there for her.

Then he would call for Rachel, who did have something for her. Rachel would unbutton her bodice quite naturally and offer Colleen her breast, only too aware Cole was watching her every move. At times she could almost feel the heat from his gaze, and she had no trouble at all guessing his thoughts. She thought about the very same things while she lay alone in her bed at night longing for the day when she could invite Cole to join her there. So much time had passed since they had made love that sometimes Rachel even wondered if she would remember how.

Then again, she would glance up and catch the hungry look in Cole's blue eyes and her body would tingle in familiar ways, and she was certain she would remember *exactly* how.

And Cole would watch the baby sucking eagerly on Rachel's sweet flesh and wonder how much longer he could stand this torment without going right out of his mind. Lupe had warned him he wouldn't be able to do anything for a while after the baby came. She had not told him how long he must abstain, but he knew he had already qualified for sainthood. He certainly didn't want to hurt Rachel, but at times he was in considerable pain himself. Occasionally, he even had to leave the room when Rachel fed the baby for fear he would lose what tenuous control he had left.

Rachel would see him go and sigh with regret. She wanted

him as much as he wanted her, but her body wasn't ready yet. Soon, though, she reminded herself. Soon, and when the time was right, things were going to be better than they'd ever been around here, and Cole Elliot was going to bless the day he'd agreed to marry her.

Meanwhile, Rachel had a few other plans for Cole. One evening shortly after life had begun to settle into a normal routine, Rachel sat reading by the fire. Cole was working on a pair of rawhide hobbles for his horse, and Colleen was lying in her cradle observing the world around her. Rachel took a deep breath and began.

"Hmmmmm," she mused aloud, turning the page of her book with a flourish. "Hmmmmm," she repeated thoughtfully and more loudly.

Cole glanced up curiously.

"Hmmmmm," she said again.

"That must be a good story," Cole remarked.

She had him.

"It's not a story. Not exactly, anyway," she said absently, forcing herself not to look up.

Cole frowned. He was used to her reading in the evenings. It irritated him sometimes, especially when he would say something to her, and she wouldn't hear him the first time he spoke. He couldn't imagine anything being quite so interesting. Perversely, he asked. "If it's not a story then what is it?"

Rachel glanced up blankly. "What? Oh, it's an essay. But it's a story, too. It was written by a man named Thoreau."

"Throw?" he repeated.

"Tho-reau," she pronounced. "Henry David Thoreau. He built himself a house off in the woods and lived there all by himself for a while. Then he wrote all about his experiences."

"Why did he want to live off in the woods by himself?" Cole asked, unaware he had fallen right into her trap.

"He lived in a city and . . ." she began to explain.

"Oh," he said, telling her she did not need to explain

381

further. Cole didn't like cities either.

"Wait," Rachel said as if she had suddenly remembered, "he explains his reasons right here." She thumbed back a few pages. "Here it is. He says, 'I went to the woods because I wished to live deliberately, to front only the essential facts of life, and see if I could not learn what it had to teach, and not, when I came to die, discover that I had not lived. I did not wish to live what was not life, living is so dear; nor did I wish to practice resignation, unless it was quite necessary. I wanted to live deep and suck out all the marrow of life, to live so sturdily and Spartan-like as to put to rout all that was not life, to cut a broad swath and shave close, to drive life into a corner, and reduce it to its lowest terms, and, if it proved to be mean, why then to get the whole and genuine meanness of it, and publish its meanness to the world; or if it were sublime, to know it by experience, and be able to give a true account of it in my next excursion.'"

She glanced up cautiously and was a little relieved to find she still had his attention. "Wouldn't that be sad, to die without ever having lived?" she asked thoughtfully.

Cole nodded. "There's a lot of folks who do, though," he said.

"What do you think? About life, I mean. Is it mean, like he said, or is it good?" Rachel put down the book and tilted her head expectantly.

Cole considered and decided the answer was obvious. "It's both. Sometimes good, sometimes bad. Sometimes it's even both together."

Rachel pretended not to understand. "How can it be both together? Like right now, for instance. Our life is good, isn't it?"

Cole shook his head. "Not exactly. For one thing, your father's not here anymore. That makes it a little bit bad." He could think of some other things, too. The fact that Statler might still be alive, for one, but he didn't have to mention it. Rachel seemed to get the point.

She sat in quiet thought for a long moment, regretting for the hundredth time that her father had not lived to see his grandchild. Then she pulled her attention back to her husband. "It seems a little silly that someone had to move out into the woods for years to come to the same conclusion you came to in about five seconds," she said. Then she narrowed her eyes shrewdly. "I'm going to test you again. See what you think about this." She flipped to another page and read another passage.

Cole listened tolerantly. He didn't really mind her reading to him. He had always loved the sound of her voice. Hearing it still reminded him of music boxes. The sight of her lips moving bothered him a little, making him want to kiss her, so he had to keep working on the hobble and not look at her when she read. That, of course, made him think of one other bad thing about their life, which was the fact that he couldn't make love to her. He forced himself to listen to what she was reading, hoping this Thoreau fellow would help take his mind off his troubles.

"Well?" she asked expectantly when she had finished.

She had been reading about how people get all caught up in living and forget about life. Or at least that's what he thought it had been about. He made some comment. It wasn't very profound, but she seemed very pleased.

She was. He was at least listening. She chose another passage and read it aloud. This time he frowned. He did not agree and said so. Rachel played devil's advocate, and they argued briefly. He put the hobble aside.

"What else does he say?" Cole asked, more interested than he would have thought possible.

Rachel read on, pausing wherever Thoreau made a point she thought worthy of discussion. When, much later, Colleen began to cry, they both were astounded to discover the baby's bedtime had long since passed.

"Oh, dear," Rachel said in feigned distress, very carefully laying the book facedown so it was still open to the page they had been discussing. "It was all Papa's fault," she explained to the baby, picking her up. "He likes to argue too much." Then she moved toward the bedroom, taking Colleen with her, but she stopped beside Cole's chair. "He's fun to argue with, though," she added with a twinkle and bent down to give him a good-night kiss.

Her lips touched his lightly, but the taste of him drew her. His hand came up to cup the back of her head and she opened to him, welcoming the sweet invasion on his tongue. For long moments they explored, savoring taste and texture, and the world narrowed down to hold just the two of them. Rachel's blood was rushing in her veins and pounding in her ears so that Colleen's cry came from someplace very far away. Only when the baby grabbed a lock of her mother's hair and pulled did Rachel return to consciousness.

"Ouch!" Rachel yelped against Cole's startled mouth.

Cole's head snapped back in surprise, but as soon as he saw what had happened, he couldn't help chuckling in spite of his frustration. "Here, I'll get it," he said, helpfully reaching up to pry the baby fingers loose. If his breath came a little quickly and his hands were none too steady, Rachel pretended not to notice.

Cole couldn't help but notice the way Rachel's dark eyes glittered, mirroring his own desire, and he needed all his willpower to keep from pulling her down onto the floor and taking her right there. When he had freed Rachel's hair, he made his hands drop to his sides and drew a somewhat ragged breath.

Echoing his breath, Rachel stepped back from him. "Thank you," she whispered, her eyes saying other things entirely. And then, "Good night."

"Good night." Cole watched them go with regret and then sank back down into his chair, swearing softly. How much longer was this going to go on? he wondered irritably. Reaching to retrieve the hobble he had dropped when

Rachel distracted him with her kiss, his eyes strayed of their own accord over to the book she had been reading. He studied it carefully from across the room. Then, after checking to be sure Rachel wasn't coming back out, he rose slowly from his chair and reached for it.

Rachel could hardly wait until the next morning. Sure enough, when she came out into the parlor again, the book had been moved. He had been careful to put it back just the way she had left it, open to exactly the same page, but she could see it wasn't in exactly the same spot on the table. She had purposely lined it up with the edge so she would know if it had been moved. Grinning triumphantly, she acknowledged that he might not have read very much, but at least he had looked at the book. That was a start.

If Miles had been right and Cole was ashamed of his lack of education, she would cure him of that. She would simply educate him. Before he knew it, he would have studied Thoreau and Emerson and Jefferson. She would read him stories, too, Poe and Hawthorne and maybe even Shakespeare, when he was ready. She might even get him to sit still for some poetry some day. The thought made her smile.

"You're sure about this?" Cole asked the Kid, frowning.

The Kid nodded. "Lettie told me first, and then I went and checked it out. Somebody drove off every last head of Statler's cattle. They did it in small bunches, like rustlers would have. Some men from some of the other ranches remember seeing strange riders around, but didn't think anything about it at the time, especially because none of their own cattle were missing."

Cole nodded and leaned back in his chair. They were seated across from each other in the ranch office. He drummed his fingers on the arm of his chair while he mulled over this new information. It could mean anything, of course. It could also mean nothing, but Cole didn't think so. Then something else occurred to him. "You've been seeing a lot of Lettie lately, haven't you?" he asked.

The Kid flushed to the roots of his hair. This was the first time Cole had mentioned the subject, although the Kid had a pretty good idea he had suspected all along. Why else would Cole have let the Kid stay behind when they went on the trail drive? "She's my girl now," he said, uncertain exactly how Cole would take the news. He didn't have any right to be jealous, of course, but that didn't mean he had to like the idea, either.

Cole grinned, genuinely pleased. "She's a lucky girl, then," he said. Cole wasn't simply being polite. He really was glad Lettie had found someone else, even though a small part of his pride couldn't help but wish she'd gone to her grave loving Cole Elliot. Far better for her to forget about him and get on with her life, and Cole knew a measure of relief that she had chosen a good man. The fact that the Kid adored her, and probably always had, didn't hurt either. "You'll be wanting to get back to town, then, and spend some time with her. You'd better get along."

The Kid rose gratefully. It was Christmas Eve, and he had ridden out to the ranch to tell Cole as soon as he had heard the news. But Cole was right, he did want to get back to Lettie, the sooner the better.

"But don't forget to come back for the celebration tomorrow," Cole called after him. "Rachel's got a real wing-ding planned."

She did, too. They roasted a steer and there were pies and cakes and cookies and doughnuts, more food than a man could shake a stick at. But that was all for the public celebration. On Christmas morning the Elliot family had a very private celebration first.

Cole pretended to be annoyed when he opened his largest present and discovered that Rachel had, finally, bought him the coat he had insisted almost a year earlier he didn't need. His smaller package turned out to be a new pair of leather gauntlets with the Circle M brand burned into the cuffs.

"You made these!" Cole exclaimed, discovering as he slipped on the finely stitched leather that they fit, well, like a glove. "When did you have the time?" And how, he wondered, had she done it without his knowledge?

Rachel gave him a long-suffering look. "I had the whole summer, remember?" she reminded him, making him wince. Then she opened her own present.

For a long moment Rachel could only stare. It was, she decided, the most beautiful thing she had ever seen. Gently she ran her finger over the inlaid mother-of-pearl covering the top of the finely polished mahogany box, and then she blinked back tears.

"Open it," Cole urged.

Rachel would have thought nothing could equal the beauty of the outside of the box, but when she opened it, she discovered she was wrong. Inside, nestled in the red velvet, was a tiny lady dressed in even tinier ruffles and lace. When the box opened, she stood up and turned in time to the music that began when the lid was raised.

"It's a music box!" Rachel cried in delight, no longer bothering to hide her tears. She wasn't certain what had pleased her more, the beauty of the gift or knowing Cole had chosen it especially for her. A lot of love had gone into the selection, a love he had never yet expressed to her in words but which he continued to show her over and over again in many other ways.

Cole frowned at her reaction. He had expected smiles and maybe even some hugs and kisses. "Why are you crying? Don't you like it?" he demanded.

That question, of course, destroyed her completely, turning her into a blubbering mess, but she set the box carefully aside and threw herself into his arms. "Of course I like it, you idiot!" she told him between sniffles. "I *love* it! Women cry sometimes when they're happy, too, you know."

He hadn't known, and he still didn't like to see her crying, but after she kissed him a few times, he felt a lot better.

Colleen seemed unimpressed with the toy horses and cows her father had carved for her and the baby doll her mother had fashioned from a sock. She even had the bad manners to fall asleep while her father was explaining to her about how the three wise men had started the custom of giving gifts at Christmastime. Her parents didn't mind too much, though.

Later the public festivities began, and when everyone had eaten himself into misery, Cole passed out the presents to the crew. Each man got a scarf Rachel had knitted over the long summer months, but the Kid got two packages. Amid the good-natured complaints of favoritism, he opened his second gift. It was a hatband made of tiny silver conchos that matched the ones which adorned his vest. Engraved on each one was a cow. He stared at it for a long moment, not quite understanding the significance.

Rachel rose from where she had been sitting by the fire, and moved toward him. The only sound in the room now was the rustle of her skirts. "That," she told him, pointing to the hatband, "is to thank you for what you did for Colleen, and so is this." She leaned over and kissed him on the cheek.

For a minute, the Kid just blushed and tried to stammer something in reply. Then the rest of the men came to his rescue and began to issue teasing remarks about how if they had only known what the reward was going to be, they would have milked the goldarn cow themselves and on and on. Cole clapped him on the back and pumped his hand, and he soon regained his composure and grinned hugely.

Shortly afterward, the party broke up. "Hey, Cole, why don't you come on down to the bunkhouse and have a drink with us? It'll be just like old times, before you got to be the boss," the Kid invited cheerfully.

Cole obviously wanted to accept the invitation, but he also

did not want to leave his family alone on Christmas. He cast Rachel a questioning glance.

"You go ahead," she told him. "I have to get Colleen to bed soon anyway. I might even turn in myself," she added, lying through her teeth. She had one more thing to do before she went to sleep tonight, and it would be the best Christmas present Cole Elliot would ever have.

Chapter XII

Cole didn't stay at the bunkhouse long. In spite of the fact that Rachel had said she didn't mind, he still didn't like being away from her. To his disappointment, however, he returned to find she had already gone to bed. Without even bothering to say good night, either.

Feeling a little irritated, he went straight to his own room, not noticing someone had left a lamp burning low on the bedside table for him until he had already crossed the threshold. That was when he finally did notice something: Rachel was in his bed. Grinning at him. The sight of her sitting there propped up on the pillows with her hair all loose around her like a black velvet curtain took his breath away. How many times had he imagined her here like this? How many nights had he dreamed about what he would do to her the next time she came to his bed? He felt his body quickening in response, but he made no move toward her, knowing if he did, he could not possibly control his impulses. Instead, he simply watched her. She was twisting a lock of her hair and looking like butter wouldn't melt in her mouth.

"What are you doing in here?" he asked warily. When she had that expression on her face, he knew she was up to something.

Rachel continued to curl her hair around her finger, and

she let her gaze drift slowly over the length of his body. Standing there with his eyes narrowed to two suspicious slits and his hands planted on his lean hips, he didn't look as if he could possibly have the slightest idea why she was here. "We're moving in with you," she told him, nodding slightly in the direction of the cradle Colleen occupied. Silently, she hoped the baby would be all right down there for a little while. Lupe had already warned her that babies had to sleep with their parents until they were a year old or else they would die. But a few hours in the cradle wouldn't hurt Colleen, Rachel thought, not when Colleen's parents so badly needed those few hours alone.

Cole considered Rachel's statement. Rachel and the baby had moved in with him. He should have been happy. This was what he'd wanted since the day he'd first married her. This was what he had decided was going to happen as soon as he got back from Kansas, before he knew about Rachel's pregnancy. This was what he still wanted more than anything. The problem was he was having a hard enough time keeping his hands off her when she slept in the next room. How was he going to control himself when she was in the bed beside him?

When he didn't respond to her statement, Rachel's confidence began to sag. "Do you mind?" she asked, a little chagrined. She had expected a lot more enthusiasm from him.

"Oh, no, I don't mind a bit," he assured her, still frowning. He walked slowly over to the chair and sat down to remove his boots, trying not to think about how hard it was going to be to climb into bed with her and not do anything.

Rachel watched him in puzzled silence. What was the matter with him? He looked almost glum! She would have thought that her news . . . Suddenly, she realized what it was: he didn't know her news. Yet.

"Cole?" she said, stretching out his name provocatively. His head snapped up. She had his complete attention.

"I have another Christmas present for you," she said, barely able to hold back the smile trembling on her lips.

The hairs on the back of his neck prickled in warning. She was definitely up to something. He cast a quick look around the room, searching for something that might be this "other" Christmas present. "What is it?" he asked, still wary, his gaze returning to her when he found nothing.

Rachel felt a prickling, too, only this prickling was much lower than her neck and much more exciting. Gooseflesh puckered on her inner thighs, and she drew her legs more tightly together beneath the bedclothes to contain the excitement. "Well," she drawled, "If you want to, we can make love tonight."

Cole stared, hardly able to believe his ears. "Are you sure? You were awful sick."

But she was nodding. "I'm sure. I'm fine now." She didn't bother to hide her smile while she watched him jerk off his shirt and then his undershirt.

His hands were on the buttons of his pants when another possibility occurred to him. "What if you get pregnant again?" It was a logical question. She had gotten pregnant practically the first time before, and this time . . . The thought stopped him cold, and he glanced over at the cradle where Colleen was sleeping. "It's so soon . . ."

But Rachel was still smiling at him. "I won't get pregnant as long as I'm nursing Colleen. Lupe explained it to me," she lied. What Lupe had actually explained was that women hardly ever got pregnant while they were nursing, but that was good enough for Rachel. Besides, she didn't care if she had ten children, as long as they were all Cole's.

"Lupe did, huh?" he repeated, a slow smile splitting his face. "Good old Lupe." He would have to add this to the long list of things he owed the old woman for. "Well now, let's find out if she's right."

Rachel laughed delightedly as Cole leaned over and blew out the lamp. He really wanted to leave it burning, but he didn't want her to see just how eager he was, something that would be painfully obvious as soon as he removed his pants. When he slipped beneath the covers, Rachel was waiting for him. Just Rachel, with no nightdress and no holding back.

Rachel had forgotten how strong he was and how warm and how wonderful. She held him close and let him smother her with drugging kisses while she stroked herself against the length of him and relearned the differences between them. Hands touched and explored and molded and urged, smooth hands on sinewy flesh, rough hands on silken flesh. Her need was as great as his and flared as quickly.

"I don't want to hurt you," he gasped, using all his strength to hold back.

"You couldn't," she whispered against his ear, destroying his tenuous control.

Spurring him on with ravenous mouth and demanding hands and churning hips, she drove him to the fever pitch of passion. He rode her through that lonely place where the world narrows down to hold only two, faster and faster, until they broke through to the ultimate freedom, sobbing out their release in gasps of ecstasy.

When he could move again, Cole rolled off of Rachel, but she came with him, still clinging to his love-dampened body. He cradled her against him, marveling at how imperfect a thing memory was. How could he have forgotten what Rachel—the real Rachel—was like? For too long he had seen her all prim and proper and fully clothed, the perfect lady, or else with only her milk-laden breasts exposed as, Madonna-like, she suckled their child. He had all but forgotten that this Rachel, his Rachel, existed, the one who turned the darkness into an enchanted land of wanton delights. He was finding it difficult to believe all three of these Rachels could be the same person.

Rachel sighed with contentment. She was exactly where she had longed to be for so many months, feeling exactly the way she had longed to feel. Now she had changed her mind about having ten babies, at least for a while. She hoped Colleen would nurse for years so she could enjoy this part of being married to Cole for a good long time. She nuzzled her face into the comfortable curve of Cole's shoulder. "That was so nice," she breathed. "I've missed you." As proof, she let her hand stray provocatively low.

Her contentment evaporated as she felt him go completely still at her remark. Even his breathing ceased. Lifting her head in alarm, she squinted, trying to make out his expression in the darkness. "What is it? What's wrong?"

"Nothing," he lied, forcing out his breath and trying to sound normal. It really was nothing, too, he knew it was, and it certainly wasn't anything he could explain to her. How could he tell her she had shocked him? Just a little, of course, but shocked him nevertheless. Rachel the lady would never have said a thing like that, would never have done a thing like that. He was going to have to get used to this other Rachel all over again. That, and the way she liked sex. He thought he had accepted that, but he'd forgotten just how *much* she liked it. It was a little disconcerting, but he would get everything sorted out in a little while.

Rachel knew he was lying, knew he was hiding something from her, and she had a very good idea what that something was. Lupe had warned her it might not be good between them at first after so long a time. As far as Rachel was concerned, it had been perfect, but she wanted him to be pleased, too. "You can tell me," she coaxed, propping herself on one elbow. "If I didn't please you . . ."

"Rachel!" he cried in dismay. Where on God's earth had she gotten an idea like that? "Of course you please me," he assured her.

But she knew something was still wrong. "Then what is it? What's the matter? Did I do something wrong?"

"Stop it," he commanded. He couldn't stand hearing Rachel's sweet, music-box, parlor voice talking about things that sweet, music-box, parlor Rachel shouldn't know anything about. He just couldn't reconcile the two in his mind, not in the dark, not right now, not when he'd just felt her writing beneath him the way he'd always thought no lady would do.

Rachel didn't like his tone. Her alarm melted into irritation. It was bad enough he was upset, but now he wouldn't even tell her why. "Cole, I'm your wife. If there's something wrong, you have to talk to me about it. This is our life, and it's not just the two of us anymore. We have Colleen now, and if we have problems, we have to work them out."

She was right, he knew, only this wasn't their problem, it was his problem. How could he explain what was bothering him without hurting her? Hadn't he just said a few moments ago he didn't want to hurt her? But, he recalled suddenly, she had said he couldn't hurt her. Maybe, if he was careful, he could make her understand. He tried. "It's just . . . no lady would . . ." No, that wasn't right. He stopped, searching for the right words.

"No lady would what?" she demanded, jerking away as if he'd slapped her. She didn't really want to hear his answer, though. She had a very good idea what it was he thought no lady would have done. So that was it. All this time, she had thought she could win his love by sharing his bed, but all she had succeeded in doing was losing his respect. Obviously, her passionate responses to him had repelled him even as he held her close for his own satisfaction. She should have known, should have guessed. This was why he had never wanted to share a bedroom with her before. Her face burned in humiliation as she threw back the bedclothes and began searching in the darkness for her nightdress.

"Rachel, what are you doing?" Cole demanded, even though he knew very well she was getting out of bed. "Wait a minute. I didn't mean . . . listen to me, Rachel . . ." But he could tell she wasn't. He, too, threw back the bedclothes and swiftly tugged on the pants he had so hastily discarded earlier. "Where are you going?" he asked, blindly fastening buttons.

"Back to my own room, where I won't offend you," she replied.

Oh, God, she sounded like she was crying. In an agony of fumbling, he found a match on the bedside table and struck it. She was standing with her back to him, and she had just settled her nightdress over her head. He watched one moment while she reached and pulled the length of her hair free of the neckline and began to do up her own buttons. Then, swiftly, he jerked the glass chimney off the lamp and lit it. "Rachel, listen to me, I didn't mean . . ."

But she wasn't listening. She was heading for the cradle so she could take the baby and go. Cole raced around the bed and caught her just in time. "You aren't going anywhere until you listen," he told her roughly, holding her fast in spite of her struggles.

"Let me go, you son of a bitch," she cried, tears streaming down her face.

"Rachel!" Cole stared at her.

"I know," she informed him acidly, "ladies don't swear either. Well, you'd better let me go or I'll say something that will make you faint dead away!"

When he didn't let her go, or even loosen his grip, she punched at him, landing a blow on his bare chest that bounced harmlessly off. It felt good to lash out at him, though, so she did it again and again while she told him off.

"You bastard! Do you think I'd do that with just anyone? Well, you're wrong! I'd die before I'd let another man touch me! The only reason . . . it's because . . . I love you . . . so much . . ." Sobs wracked her, weakening her. Her blows came more slowly, more feebly, until her hands fell harmlessly to her sides and only Cole's grip held her upright.

When he felt her sag, he pulled her to him, crushing her against the heart that ached for the hurt he had caused her. "Don't cry," he begged. "Please, Rachel, don't cry. I didn't think that. I never thought that." Instinctively, he stroked her hair, her back, her shoulders, silently willing her to believe him. "It's not you. It's not anything you did. It's me."

He had to say it a few times before he finally got through to her. Rachel's weeping came to a sniffling halt. She reached up and scrubbed the sleeve of her nightdress across her face before lifting her head to look at him. He still held her close and he wasn't about to let her go, but he loosed his grip slightly, allowing a small space between them. Rachel was suddenly aware of the expanse of bare chest she had been wailing against. It stretched before her temptingly, so she raised her hands and laid them gently against it, propping herself away to help her resist the urge to seek the solace it still offered. The curling hairs tickled her fingertips, and she could feel the heart drumming beneath the sinewy strength of his ribs. He was still too thin, she thought irrelevantly.

Forcing herself to meet his eyes, she said, "All right, I'm listening now." She waited several heartbeats for his reply.

"I never thought what you said," he began. "It's just, I always thought that ladies . . ." He stopped, seeing her expression harden.

"Go on," she ordered, angry all over again.

"I'm saying this all wrong," he complained.

"Try," she demanded.

He closed his eyes for a moment, hoping he could get it right, say it so she would understand, but when he opened them again, he didn't feel any wiser. "I always thought ladies didn't . . . enjoy things like that. Oh, I know different, now," he hastened to explain, seeing her eyes spark. "But it's still hard to . . ." His voice trailed off again, but not because he could not think of the right words this time. This time it was because he was examining a new thought.

"It's hard to what?" she asked impatiently.

But he could not answer, not just yet. He was still examining that thought, still coming to grips with what the real problem was. He was right, it really had nothing to do with how passionate Rachel was or wasn't. It had to do with him, with him accepting that for what it was, her love for him. That was the thing he couldn't quite believe and that was what really bothered him about Rachel.

Now if he could just explain it to her. "I know you like going to bed with me because you . . . you love me." He hesitated over the words, because he still had difficulty accepting the fact. "It's just almighty hard for me to believe you *can* love me."

Rachel's dark eyes grew wide and her mouth dropped open in a very unladylike fashion. "Why?"

Now Cole looked amazed. "Why?" he echoed, dropping his arms and stepping away from her. "Just look at you. You're perfect, that's why!"

"I'm not perfect!" she insisted, still incredulous. He couldn't really believe she was.

"The hell you're not! You're beautiful, you're smart, you're educated, you're . . . you're *perfect,"* he concluded, throwing up his hands.

"And what are you?" she asked, wondering how he might characterize himself if he thought her faultless.

That was a good question, one Cole had rarely allowed himself to even consider because he knew any answer would only accentuate the differences between them. "I'm a lot less than perfect, that's for damn sure," he hedged.

Rachel's eyes narrowed suspiciously. Finally, after almost a year, she felt she was getting close, very, very, close, to understanding Cole Elliot. "And why do you think I married you, then?" she inquired thoughtfully.

Was she kidding? "You needed my gun."

Rachel laughed mirthlessly. It was not a pretty sound. "Let me tell you something, Cole Elliot. If all I'd wanted was a fast gun, I could have picked any man on this place. Miles would have been a logical choice. He's seen a lot more trouble than you'll ever know, and he's older and more mature, and he's a good leader, and he's good company, too."

"He's too old for you." Cole tried to object, feeling unaccountably jealous.

But Rachel wasn't about to be interrupted. "And then there's the Kid. He's better looking and a lot more cheerful and he's even better with a gun than you are."

"Now wait a minute," Cole said, planting his hands on his hips. What made her think the Kid was faster than he was?

"No, you wait a minute. Why do you think I picked you when I could have chosen anyone? I'll tell you," she said, not letting him reply. "I picked you because underneath all that bluff and bluster and cold-eyed-man-with-a-gun business, I thought I saw a gentleman. Get that? A *gentle-man*, a man I could love, a man who could love me, a man I could make a life with long after all the fighting was over. Do you understand? I picked you because I wanted you, not just somebody who was handy with a gun. You, Cole Elliot."

She had been punctuating her speech by poking her forefinger into his chest, and now he grabbed it and hauled her into his arms. He knew he should have said something. He knew he should have acknowledged the tribute she had just paid him, but he didn't have any words. Instead, he found her mouth with his own and said it with his body.

It was all there, all the things he felt for her. Rachel was having none of it, though. She wanted the words. She wrenched herself loose from the kiss and glared up into his startled face.

"Oh, no, you don't, Cole Elliot. You're not starting that stuff again. I'm still mad at you for saying I'm not a lady," she said, trying unsuccessfully to break out of his grasp.

He scowled down at her in exasperation. "I never said you weren't a lady," he informed her.

"You did, too," she informed him right back.

He frowned. "I never thought that," he said very quietly.

Rachel felt her anger melting, but somehow managed to maintain her belligerent expression. She waited, silently willing him to tell her the rest of it.

The words came hard, dredged up from someplace deep inside of him. "I didn't mean to hurt you, Rachel. I'd cut off my arm before I'd hurt you."

She believed him. Oh, how she believed him, and she threw her arms around him with a happy little cry. This time she let him kiss her, and this time he kissed her with tiny, hungry little kisses that left her breathless. He hadn't exactly said he loved her, not yet, but she knew he did. Now she was certain of it. After a few minutes, she pushed away from him again. "If you're through fighting with me, can we go back to bed now? My feet are freezing!"

Cole made a funny little sound in his chest that was part exasperation and part laughter. Then he scooped her up in his arms and carried her over to the bed. "I'll warm up your feet and the rest of you, too, little girl," he promised ominously. Then he tucked her down under the covers.

He straightened up slowly and stood there for a moment. Then, just as slowly, he began to release the buttons of his jeans. Rachel watched in fascination as each one slipped free, and her eyes grew wide when he pushed the pants down over his hips and let them fall to the floor.

"Oh, my" was all she could think of to say when she saw the very obvious evidence of his renewed desire. Pleasure rippled over her.

"You were the one who wanted to come back to bed," he reminded her as he climbed in next to her. This time he didn't put out the light. This time he was going to watch her.

But Rachel wasn't quite finished with him yet. "I'm not sure a lady should do this twice in one night," she said, primly clutching the covers to her bosom and trying desperately not to giggle. "I mean, it doesn't seem . . . well, ladylike." She batted her eyes innocently at him.

"Don't worry," he countered, reaching for her. "I think I've decided I like you much better when you're not acting like a lady."

"Oh, good." She sighed in mock relief. "Then you won't be

shocked if I do this." She put her icy cold hand on what was, at that moment, the warmest spot on his body.

Cole yelped a string of words Rachel's tender ears had never heard before and grabbed both her hands, pinning them safely above her head.

"You little . . . I ought to turn you over my knee and spank your pretty little behind," he threatened, trying to look dangerous.

Rachel wasn't fooled. "Oh, my," she said again, her delighted smile clearly conveying the fact that she found such a prospect far from frightening.

Cole groaned in exasperation and rolled away from her, onto his back, and threw an arm across his eyes in an imitation of despair.

Rachel turned onto her side to watch him. She longed to reach out and run her fingers through the curling hairs on his chest, but she resisted, remembering her hands were still cold and that she probably wouldn't get the proper response if she touched him just now. Crossing her arms, she tucked her hands under her armpits to warm them, and while she was waiting, she considered all the things her husband had said to her this night.

"Cole?" she asked a little timidly.

Cole lifted his arm cautiously until he could peer out at her. "What?"

Rachel bit her lip, a little embarrassed to ask. "Do you . . . do you really think I'm . . ." She paused. He had used two different words to describe her. Modestly, she chose, "Pretty?"

He bit back a smile. "No," he said quite honestly. He waited a beat, savoring her crestfallen look and the satisfaction he got from knowing how important his opinion was to her. "No," he repeated thoughtfully. "I never did think you were pretty. I used to think you were handsome, but that was when I didn't know you very well," he continued, explaining it very matter-of-factly. "Now that I do know you, though," he added, lifting his arm completely away so he could leer at her, "I think you're beautiful."

She watched him a minute, judging his sincerity. Then, convinced, she squealed, "Oh, Cole," and hurled herself at him. He caught her and settled her on top of him. "I think you're beautiful, too," she said, smiling down into his face, her dark hair falling around them in a silken cloud.

His surprise was comic. "Rachel," he chided. "Ladies shouldn't tell lies, either."

"I'm not lying," she said indignantly. "I think your eyes are the most beautiful blue I've ever seen and I love the way your hair falls down across your forehead and I just adore your smile, especially that little dimple." She poked her finger gently into the spot where it would appear, trying to encourage it. She succeeded.

"I like your dimples, too," he said, grinning wickedly.

"I don't have dimples in my cheeks," she informed him.

"Not those cheeks, these cheeks," he replied, giving her bottom a gentle squeeze and alerting her to the fact that he had been busily working her nightdress up the whole time they had been talking.

"Oh!" she cried in mock outrage, but Cole was too quick for her. He flipped her over so she was on her back, lying helplessly beneath him. Before she could make another sound, his lips skillfully silenced her, and she surrendered willingly, eagerly.

She noticed immediately that he had completely recovered from her cold hand, and now she continued to warm her hands on the heat of his body, rubbing and stroking and kneading while he drank the sweetness of her mouth. His hands, too, were busy, but he was encountering a lot more barriers than she.

"Can we get rid of this thing?" he asked hoarsely, lifting his mouth from hers and gesturing toward her nightdress.

Rachel made a shocked sound. "Mr. Elliot! A lady would never . . ."

403

"Shut up," he rasped, tearing at the buttons. But he had to smile. The little vixen was never going to let him forget what he had said. Awkwardly, because she wasn't helping one little bit, he tugged off her nightdress and tossed it over the side of the bed.

Rachel lay, limp and martyr-like, fully intending to keep up the teasing until she saw the expression in his eyes. He had not seen her like this in a long time, and he took several minutes just to look at her. His gaze moved over her, warming her like the touch of a loving hand, and she felt the heat gather and settle into her center. She shifted restlessly.

Cole could not seem to get enough of looking at her. He had seen her body often enough in the days when she had been sick, but that had been different, and she had been different, too. Now her body had returned almost to its original slenderness, except for a few important differences. Her breasts, of course, were larger, the nipples darker, but it seemed all her curves had changed and softened. Her hips were fuller, accentuating the indentation of her waist more, and her stomach, which had been so flat it had been almost concave, was now gently rounded.

Rachel was aware of the changes in her body and wondered if he was pleased. When she again raised her eyes to her, she knew for certain.

"You're so beautiful," he whispered.

She didn't want to ask, but she needed to hear the words. "You love me, don't you?"

He gazed down at her in surprise. He saw the dark hair swirling around her, the sparkle of desire glittering in her equally dark eyes, the gentle softness of her cheek, the ruby moistness of her thoroughly kissed mouth. He saw it all, but the only thing that registered was his amazement that she could even ask him such a thing. Didn't she know? Hadn't he shown her in every possible way how much he adored her? "Yes. God, yes," he breathed.

He moved toward her, but she stopped him, placing one

small hand against his chest. "Then say it. Tell me."

She could see how difficult it was for him. Expressing such things in words would not come easily for a man like Cole. Another time, another place, and he might not have spoken them at all. This time was different, though. "I love you," he said.

Rachel absorbed the words into her soul, suspecting she might never hear them spoken again. She would know, though. She would always know he loved her, even if he could not tell her. Then she moved her hand, sliding it up and around his neck to draw him to her.

They made love slowly this time. Cole seemed determined to kiss every inch of her, and she lay back languorously and allowed him to try. He found a sensitive spot behind her knee and another on her ankle. Even her toes became centers for erotic stimulation under Cole's determined efforts. Then he worked on her arms, teasing the tender skin inside her elbows and wrists. By the time he had moved on to kiss her shoulders and throat, Rachel felt as if all her bones had completely dissolved and wondered vaguely how she would ever be able to rise from the bed again.

He saved the best for last, and now he began to feast on the breasts that he had jealously watched his child suckle for so many weeks. Rachel gasped at the tingling sensation his lips and teeth evoked as they tugged gently at her nipple, sending ripples of pleasure down and down to the core of her femininity. It was a new, yet familiar, feeling.

His hungry mouth moved lower, tasting the tiny cavern of her navel before sliding even lower where he could sample the nectar of her desire.

"Cole!" she protested feebly, knowing he shouldn't be kissing her there, but liking it all the same. In spite of her earlier teasing, Rachel did have a few inhibitions, but Cole seemed determined to break down even these now that he had broken down his own. "Cole," she said again, but this time it was a silken sigh as she surrendered to the insidious warmth.

Soon she was writhing, and he had to cup his hands to her hips to hold her in place for the exquisite torture. He ceased only when he heard her call his name yet again, this time pleading for the release she knew he could give her. He moved over her then, and sank into her depths with a sigh of contentment. "Rachel," he said, not even aware he had spoken aloud. It was Rachel, all around him, under him and over him and in him, too, in his heart and in his soul. God, how he loved her.

At the sound of her name, her eyes flickered open. His voice had come to her from a great distance, but his precious face was close, so close. She watched him, watched him watching her, part of her experiencing the luscious sensations below and part of her accepting the tribute of his eyes. He rocked her gently, gently. Each plunge brought him closer and closer still, and each plunge brought the hot waves higher until they were breaking over her heart and over her shoulders and then and then . . .

Rachel cried out when they came crashing down over her head, enveloping her in the blissful oblivion that trembled through her entire body.

Cole never took his eyes from her face, not even when he felt her spasms reverberating through him. He hadn't known before, hadn't realized it was really as good for her as it was for him. He knew, now, though. That was his last conscious thought before the sweet oblivion overtook him, too.

They clung to each other for a long time afterward, whispering secrets beneath the passion-scented cocoon of the bedclothes.

"When did you first fall in love with me?" Rachel asked against his lips, secure now in the knowledge that he did love her.

Cole considered, sampling those lips before replying. "God, I don't know. It must have been the very first time I ever saw you," he decided at last.

"At the train?" Rachel replied incredulously, rearing up on one elbow. "It couldn't have been! You didn't even like me!"

"Didn't like you?" he repeated, just as incredulously. "Whatever gave you an idea like that?"

"The way you never would look at me or talk to me. And at the party, you wouldn't even ask me to dance," she challenged.

"I can't dance," he defended himself.

Rachel made a rude noise. "That's what you said that night, too, if I remember correctly. You did just fine once I shamed you into it."

"You almost got more than you bargained for that night," he informed her ominously, pulling her back down to his side.

"Oh, yeah?" she goaded, moving sinuously against him.

"Yeah," he goaded right back. "You're just lucky I didn't drag you off somewhere and have my way with you."

Rachel shivered deliciously at the threat. "I wouldn't have minded," she confessed.

"What?" he demanded, thoroughly shocked.

"I said, I wouldn't have minded. I was madly in love with you then. I would have been thrilled if you had so much as spoken a civil word to me. If you had tried to kiss me, I would have . . ."

"Rachel," he chastened, certain she was lying to make him feel good. "You didn't even like me then."

"Whatever gave you an idea like that?" she mimicked.

He started to tell her but suddenly realized his reasons sounded suspiciously like hers. "All right, then, exactly when did you fall in love with me?" he inquired.

"Wellll," she said, provocatively swirling the hairs on his chest. "It wasn't at the train." At his I-told-you-so-grunt, she went on. "But I did think you were a very interesting man, and by the time I saw you breaking your stallion, Hundred Dollars, I was head over heels . . ."

Cole groaned, remembering that day. "Is that why you had such a funny look on your face?"

"I didn't have a funny look on my face," she contradicted him indignantly.

"Yes, you did," he informed her, shifting her onto his chest so he could see her expression.

"Well, if I did, it was only because that was the first time I ever saw your dimple," she teased, "and I thought it was the cutest thing . . ."

"Rachel," he said threateningly, but she kissed him into silence.

More kisses followed and so did more confessions. Reasons, real reasons, for their past behavior were revealed and probed and analyzed far into the night, until a baby's cry interrupted them.

Telling Rachel to say where she was, Cole rescued his daughter from her lonely cradle and carried her back to her mother. When Colleen had filled her tummy, the three of them cuddled together and fell into a contented sleep. It had been, just as Rachel had predicted, the best Christmas Cole Elliot had ever had.

After that night, Rachel noticed a definite change in her husband. Gone was the Cole Elliot who treated her with deference and in his place was a new man who recognized her as his equal. Sometimes, she knew, he still found it difficult to believe his good fortune that she loved him, but she reminded him often, and sometimes he even said the words back to her.

With the cold weather, the rumors of Will Statler slowed to a trickle, and sometimes Cole did not think of his old enemy for days at a time. He was able to reflect on how good his life had become. He even learned not to mind when Colleen woke up and demanded a midnight snack right when her parents were in the middle of something far more interesting.

Most of the winter slipped by in this idyllic fashion, and

then one night Cole reflected that it would soon be almost a year since he and Rachel had made their trip to Stillwater to tie the knot. At the moment the thought occurred to him, he was lying quite contentedly, holding his wife in his arms. They had just finished making love, without interruption for once, and had settled down to sleep.

"What are you thinking?" Rachel inquired sleepily.

"What makes you think I'm thinking anything?" he asked with great interest.

She sighed. "I can tell by the way you're breathing."

Cole smiled in the darkness. She surely was a caution. "I was just thinking you didn't have much of a wedding."

Rachel murmured her agreement. "But then, you didn't have much of a honeymoon, either," she added wickedly, tweaking his chest hair.

"Ouch!" He slapped her hand away affectionately. "Behave yourself or I won't tell you my idea."

She perked right up at that. "What idea?"

"Wellll," he drawled slowly, to torment her. "I was figuring maybe we should have a party. You know, to celebrate our anniversary. We cheated folks out of one when we ran off, so maybe this could make up for it."

Rachel was propped up on her elbow now. "What a wonderful idea! We could get some fiddlers and have dancing in the parlor and . . ." She paused, remembering one of the reasons she had originally thought it would not be a good idea to have a wedding celebration. "What about Statler?"

Cole caught his breath. "What about him?" he asked cautiously. Wanting to protect her, he had not told her about the rumors.

She knew about them, though. "What if he and his men show up at the party?"

Cole let his breath out in a long sigh. He should have known better than to think he could keep anything from her. "They wouldn't dare show their faces around here. Besides,

409

if they do, there'll be more than a hundred men to stand up to them. You don't need to worry about Statler anymore, honey."

Rachel wasn't too sure about that, but at least she believed what he had said about the party's being safe. She began to plan.

Cole was soon sorry he had suggested the party. Rachel's every waking hour for the next three weeks was devoted to preparations. First the whole house was turned upside down and cleaned within an inch of its life. Then Rachel and Lupe started cooking. Cole thought it was pure-dee torture to come in every night to the delicious aromas only to be told he could not have even so much as a taste until the party.

He told Colleen all about his problems, and she sympathized very sweetly. To Cole's great delight, she was learning to smile, and she practiced on him quite regularly. She even seemed to recognize him now, grinning and waving her hands whenever he appeared.

The day of the party dawned bright and clear and unseasonably warm. The first guests began to arrive along about noon, and by sundown the ranch house was crammed to the rafters. That was when the dancing started. All day Cole had been the perfect host, encouraging his company to enjoy themselves to the fullest. Now he simply stood back and watched his wife become the belle of the ball. He was reminded of the party her father had given for Rachel when she first came back from school, the party at which he had stood watching her just like this. That time he had been jealous as she danced and flirted with partner after partner. This time, he watched indulgently, knowing that although she might be smiling at this man or that, it was he whom she loved. Secure in his knowledge, he simply enjoyed the lovely picture she made as she swirled around the floor.

She was simply lovely. She was wearing the same dress she had worn to their wedding, the blue one with the lace on it. He hadn't ever seen her wear it for any other occasion, and he had concluded she considered the dress very special. When she put it on earlier in the day, he'd even made a remark to that effect.

She had turned on him, saying, "This is my wedding dress! Of course it's special!" Then she had grinned at him, flirting, and said, "Besides, it's exactly the same color as my husband's eyes, so that makes it my favorite."

He had grabbed her and kissed her soundly as a reward for her compliment, and he had wished very fervently they didn't have over a hundred guests due any minute so he could carry her off and remove that very special dress. Still, he didn't mind too much sharing her today, not when he so thoroughly enjoyed having all the other men seeing her and envying him.

"Cole?"

Startled from his reverie, Cole glanced up. It was Miles, but his expression showed he had not been enjoying himself.

"What is it?" Cole asked, coming instantly to attention. He suspected trouble. Perhaps some cowboy had had a little too much of the Elliots' whiskey and started a fight.

"There's somebody out here I think you need to talk to" was all he said. He motioned for Cole to follow him outside.

A brisk wind had picked up just after sunset, and the men had moved the whiskey barrel inside the bunkhouse. What had been until a few minutes earlier a lively group of cowboys were gathered there. Now they all stood silently, waiting for Cole to arrive.

Miles and Cole stepped inside, and Cole looked around, his sense of unease growing with every second. Miles gestured to one of the cowboys. "You know Pinto, don't you?" he asked unnecessarily.

Cole looked at the small rider who went by the name Pinto, and nodded. The man had worked at a neighboring ranch. "Haven't seen you around in a while," he remarked.

Pinto nodded in return. "I been working up north." He glanced at Miles as if for approval, and then went on. "I seen

Statler, Mr. Elliot."

Cole felt himself go cold, as if all his blood had ceased to flow and retreated into some secret recess deep in his body. "You're sure it was him?" he asked calmly.

Pinto shifted in his dusty boots. "Yes, sir. It was him, all right. I hardly knew him at first. He was awful gaunted up, like he'd maybe been real sick or something . . ." His voice trailed off as the men exchanged glances, remembering Cole had wounded him badly, maybe even fatally, or so they had then thought.

"It was in a saloon, up in Mason," he went on, naming a town far north of Stillwater. "I might not of recognized him, but then I heard him talk and somebody with him called him 'Will.' It was him, Mr. Elliot, sure as I'm standing here."

Cole nodded, glancing at Miles. Miles obviously believed the story, too. Pinto had no loyalties to the Circle M, but he would have no reason to lie about such a thing, either. Cole gave Pinto a small grin. "I appreciate you coming here to tell me, Pinto. You looking for a job?"

Pinto shrugged. "I sure am. I been riding the grubline, drifting down this way so's I could tell you the news before I head on south."

"Well, you don't have to head anywhere. You've got a job here as long as you want one. Miles," he turned to his foreman, "put him to work. Tomorrow," he added with what he hoped was a jovial laugh to break the tension. "Tonight we're having a party. How about some of that whiskey?"

The other men responded slowly, but they did respond. One by one they each forced a smile and refilled their cups. Cole joined them in a toast, and by the time he left again, their festive mood had almost been restored.

Miles walked back with him to the house. "It's nothing we didn't already know," he pointed out.

Cole slanted him a wry grin. "Yeah, but hearing rumors second and third hand that somebody thought he might of seen Statler is a little different than talking to somebody

412

who's actually seen him."

"You think he'll be back here?" Miles asked.

Cole lifted his eyebrows in surprise that Miles would even ask. "The only question is *when* he'll be back. You heard Pinto. Statler looks like he's been sick. I hurt him bad. He won't forget. I'm just surprised he hasn't come before this."

"Maybe it's like we figured, he's waiting until he's strong enough to beat us," Miles suggested.

Cole nodded. "He probably found out we didn't let any of our men go for the winter, so he's biding his time." Cole paused at the foot of the ranch house stairs. The sound of laughter spilled out the partially opened door. "I've had just about enough of Will Statler for tonight, though," he declared. "Like I said, this is a party, and I for one am going in there and dance with my wife. Come on, Miles," he said, slapping his friend on the back. "Let's see if we can't find you somebody to dance with, too." The two men went inside.

At that moment, back in Canaan, two other people who had not attended the party were consoling each other. Or at least they had been.

Lettie glanced up from her pillow in irritation. She wished Hank Oliver would put out the light. It was bad enough that he was sitting there grumbling to himself. At least if he would put out the light, she could plug her ears and go on to sleep. She was beginning to regret her decision to let him spend the night.

She hadn't wanted to be alone tonight, though. Everyone—or at least all the respectable people in town—had gone to the Elliots' party, and the saloon had been nearly empty all evening. The tomblike silence had irked her, reminding her she was an outsider and would never be invited to parties. Cole Elliot had cheated her out of her chance to become respectable when he had married someone else.

Even the Kid had earned his share of her wrath when she remembered that he, too, would be at the party and would probably be dancing and flirting with all the young girls. The way her luck was running, he would decide to marry one of them, and then he'd dump Lettie, just like his pal Cole Elliot had done.

She had been a little surprised when Hank Oliver had come into the saloon earlier in the evening. She knew he would have been invited to the Elliots', so he must have decided not to attend. Both of them had scrupulously avoided mentioning the party all evening, but they each knew the other had been thinking of little else. When Sam closed the saloon early, Hank walked her home.

They did not speak all the way to her house, but Hank followed her inside the way he always did when he walked with her. Lettie lighted a fire and then slipped behind the screen to undress. Hank was the only man she had ever known who didn't like to watch the process, but she was more than willing to spare his delicate sensibilities. When she came out, clad in the wrapper which she would not remove until the room was completely dark, Hank was already in bed, safely under the covers.

Lettie blew out the light and joined him. He did not speak. He never spoke when they were in bed together. He simply moved over her and did it.

When he finished, something that rarely took very long and which took even less time tonight, he rolled off her. This time, though, instead of getting up and putting his clothes back on as he usually did, he lay there for a while. Finally, he said, "Could I . . . I mean, would it be all right if . . . if I stayed . . . here . . . all night?"

Lettie could have laughed at his hesitancy. Any other man would have coaxed or teased or even demanded. But she didn't laugh. Instead, she sighed. Her sigh had disturbed him.

"I'll pay you extra," he offered almost in desperation.

She might have thrown him out then, so annoyed was she by his offer, except that she, too, had no desire to be alone on

414

this of all nights. "You don't have to pay me at all, Hank," she had said wearily. "Just stay."

At that moment, her decision had seemed wise. Now, she was having second thoughts. First he had tossed and turned for a while as if trying to get comfortable, and finally she had suggested he get himself a drink to help him sleep. He had, and now he was sitting on the edge of her bed with his back to her, muttering to himself. He was wearing his longjohns—he never undressed completely in her presence—and puffing furiously on a cigar, something she had rarely seen him do.

"Hank, are you coming to bed or not? I can't sleep with you making all that racket," she said irritably.

He jumped guiltily and stubbed out the cigar in a plate sitting on the bedside table. "I'm sorry. I didn't realize you were still awake," he said, turning to face her.

Lettie was surprised at the strange gleam in his eye. It was an expression she had never seen on him before. He looked almost excited. Lettie had discovered that nothing, not even sex excited him. She thought at first that he might be drunk.

"We'll get even with him, Lettie. You'll see. For what he did to her and what he did to you. We'll fix him," Hank said in a strangely agitated voice.

Lettie frowned. He was certainly talking crazy but he couldn't be drunk. When she thought back, she remembered he had only had two drinks all evening. Counting the one he had just gotten from her bottle, that only made three. A man didn't get this crazy on three drinks. "Get even with who?" she asked, genuinely puzzled.

He seemed a little surprised at her question. "Why, Elliot, of course," he said.

Lettie sighed wearily. Couldn't he think about anything or anyone else? She was, however, a little touched that Hank wanted to get even on her behalf as well as to avenge poor little Rachel McKinsey. She smiled indulgently. "And just how do you plan to get even with him?"

Hank's handsome face twisted into a smug grin, another

415

expression Lettie had never seen. "*I* am not going to do anything," he explained triumphantly, "but Will Statler is. He and I are partners now."

Lettie gasped. "Is Statler still alive?" she asked, struggling to a sitting position.

Hank averted his eyes until she had pulled the bedclothes up over her breasts. He didn't like to look at her naked body. When she was decently covered, he turned back to her and said, "Of course he's still alive. Everybody's been talking about it for months. Haven't you heard?"

Of course she had heard, but she wanted proof. "Have you actually seen him?"

Hank nodded, that look of pious smugness again distorting his fine features. "I sent word I wanted to meet with him. We got together a little over a week ago, and I told him I'd do anything to help him get even with Elliot. We're partners," he repeated.

Lettie felt a chill. Will Statler didn't need a partner. If he had agreed to anything, it would be because he saw a way to get something from Hank Oliver. What that might be, she had no idea and didn't really care. What she did care about was what they planned to do to Cole. "Do you have a plan?" she asked, hoping she sounded only curious and not desperate.

"Not yet. Statler has to work out a few things first. It won't be long, though," he said reassuringly, as if such information should bring her comfort. "Then you can spit on Elliot's grave."

Lettie shuddered, but Hank didn't notice. He was blowing out the lamp. She sat stock-still while he climbed cautiously into the bed, being careful not to touch her.

"Good night, Lettie," he said when he had settled himself with his back to her.

"Good night," she murmured absently. Spit on Elliot's grave! Was that what she wanted? Oh, she had been angry and hurt, but the anger had cooled and the hurt had settled

416

down into a sort of plaguing bitterness. In truth, she hadn't even wanted revenge way back when she really had been angry. Oliver had misjudged her there, but it was lucky he had. Now he would trust her, give her information about Statler's plans.

Lettie lay down stiffly beside Oliver who had already begun to snore softly. She knew she didn't owe Cole Elliot anything and certainly not her loyalty. She also knew he had that loyalty, whether he deserved it or not. It was a humbling thing to admit, but Lettie admitted it. She just wouldn't examine her motives too closely. If she did, she might have to admit she was in love with the man.

Cole Elliot smiled in amusement as the latest dance ended and Rachel's partner led her back to her chair where she was once more surrounded by eager potential partners. Cole did not intend for any of them to be victorious, so he elbowed his way through the crowd, tossing good-natured insults to anyone who complained.

"Mrs. Elliot will be dancing with her husband this time," he announced to all and sundry when he had succeeded in reaching her side.

Rachel rewarded him with a dazzling smile, and she laid her hand willingly in his and rose gracefully to her feet. She looked him over from head to toe, her eyes glinting her approval. He was wearing the same outfit he had worn to their wedding. She would, she decided, be more than happy to marry him all over again.

Her smile never wavered while they walked out to the floor, but when she turned and stepped into his arms, he saw the mischievous glitter in her eyes. "Mrs. Elliot will indeed be dancing with her husband," she remarked. "It's a shame, however, that Mr. Elliot will not be dancing with his wife, since he *still* can't dance.!"

Cole rolled his eyes. She had nagged him and nagged him

417

to let her teach him, but he knew it was hopeless and hadn't even let her try. In retaliation, he hauled her into his arms and held her indecently close as the music began. "I didn't really want to dance with you anyway," he countered, grinning broadly. "I just wanted an excuse to hold you."

Rachel made a disgusted noise, but she was still smiling. She didn't mind being held as long as he didn't step on her feet, and said so.

He laughed and promised to be careful. Then he pulled her head against his chest and laid his cheek on her temple. For a few blissful moments they stood like that, swaying in a gentle imitation of the dance. Then she heard him sigh with what she guessed was melodramatic intensity.

"You know, sometimes I just can't quite believe you really love me," he said, and sighed again.

Suddenly suspicious, Rachel tried to look up to read his expression, but he was holding her too tightly.

"You do love me, don't you, darlin'?" he asked, sounding remarkably insecure.

"Of course," she said into his shirtfront, struggling to lift her head but failing because he was still hugging her face to his chest.

He leaned over slightly so his lips were level with her ear and whispered provocatively, "Would you like to go off somewhere with me and prove it?"

Rachel gasped and finally succeeded in breaking loose and rearing back in his arms. "Cole!" she chastened, her cheeks burning. Then she looked around to see if anyone had heard his outrageous suggestion. Satisfied that no one had, she raised her eyes to his, only to blush all over again at his expression. Anyone looking at him would have known exactly what was on his mind. "Behave yourself," she admonished primly, even though those deliciously familiar shivers were dancing up her legs. She couldn't help but remember that this was exactly what he had told her he had wanted to do the very first time they had danced together.

"We're married. There's nothing wrong with it," he complained comically. He was still moving as if they were dancing although she had stopped stock-still at his suggestion. He gave her a little nudge to set her in motion again, and then pulled her back into his arms.

"Cole, there's a time and a place . . ." she whispered.

"I know just the place . . ." he whispered back.

"We have guests! We can't just . . ."

"They won't miss us," he predicted. "Besides, it won't take very long." He pressed himself against her so she could feel the truth of his statement.

"Cole!" Rachel glanced around once again, but no one seemed to be paying any attention to them.

It just wasn't fair. How could she feel this excited from just talking about it? "Where could we go?" Rachel asked reluctantly, not looking up so she would not have to see the gloating smile she knew would be on his lips.

Rachel knew she had him with that question, though. The truth was there was noplace on the entire ranch that wasn't swarming with people. Their bedroom was where the older ladies had gathered to gossip, and Colleen and the other babies were all sleeping in the other bedroom. The rest of the guests were either dancing in the parlor or eating in the dining room where all the food had been spread, and people would be bustling back and forth in the kitchen. It was too cold to go outside.

"Come on, I'll show you," he said mysteriously. Pulling her by the hand, he led her from the room, into the dining room where they spoke to several people briefly before hurrying on past into the kitchen.

The kitchen was dark, but when they entered, they heard a startled cry and saw the silhouettes of two people breaking from an embrace. "Don't mind us," Cole informed them cheerfully, heading straight for the storeroom. He went on in, pulling Rachel in behind him and closing the door.

"Cole!" Rachel cried in an urgent whisper. "We can't! Not

in here! Those people, whoever they were, saw us come in here. They'll know!"

But Cole wasn't concerned. He had already taken her in his arms and begun kissing her throat. "They won't care. They're probably mad because they didn't think of it first," he said against her skin. "I'll bet you a gold eagle they'll be in here as soon as we're gone."

"Cole!" she tried again, but he wasn't paying much attention. "What if Colleen wakes up and wants to be fed?" she argued, even though his lips were already working their magic and melting her resistance.

"Lupe'll take care of her. Now shut up," he commanded, claiming her lips with his own to insure she did. One large hand closed over the mound of her breast while the other urged her hips into closer contact with his.

When he lowered her to the floor, she did not resist. Her legs had turned to jelly and would no longer have supported her anyway. "My dress," she mumbled, remembering her fancy attire and the dirty floor.

But it was all right. He was going to be on the bottom. He pulled her down on top of him.

Rachel delved her fingers into his hair, holding his head captive while she devoured his willing mouth. He tasted of tobacco and whiskey and Cole, a delicious combination she consumed greedily.

He accepted her kisses with a deceptive passivity. Just when she began to wonder why he wasn't even hugging her, she realized he had been busy with her skirts and now was tugging on her pantalettes. They gave with a slither of the drawstring, and Rachel gasped as the cool air struck her warm center.

"Cole! This is wicked!" she complained, but she was already much too breathless to expect him to take her seriously.

"I know," he agreed, equally breathless as he struggled with the buttons of his pants. Then he grasped her hips and lifted her to him.

Rachel sheathed him, moaning softly as she settled herself around him. "Oh, Cole," she whispered, marveling anew at his strength.

"Oh, Rachel," he groaned back in tender mockery, and she could hear the joyous smile in his voice.

She rocked gently, teasing him and herself, sending little shivers of pleasure careening through her body. But he was much too impatient for such nonsense, and urged her with hands and hips, bucking against her like an eager stallion. She responded with equal urgency, riding him harder and harder still. The storeroom muffled the sounds of their impassioned gasps and the rustle of their clothing, closing them into a secret world where sight and sound ceased and only sensation remained.

The sensation was enough, swirling around them and through them, binding them closer and closer still into the sacred unity, until with one searing flash they melded into one.

Rachel collapsed onto his chest, sobbing in the breath that her corset was restricting and vowing never again to try making love while she was trussed up like this. She listened to Cole's breathing slow to normal, too, and savored the way his hands lovingly caressed her. A small smile curved her lips.

"Now do you believe I love you?" she asked, a teasing lilt in her voice.

He considered a long moment. "I'm starting to," he allowed, and then yelped as Rachel pinched him in an unmentionable spot. "Be careful," he warned, capturing her hands, "or I'll never ask you to do this again."

Rachel chose not to dignify such a remark with a reply and contented herself with biting the tip of his nose before scrambling to her feet. "You're a wicked man, Cole Elliot," she decreed. "Now what did you do with my drawers?"

Cole fished in his pocket for a match so they could have

some light by which to put themselves back together again. The process took several matches and quite a bit of doing. Rachel discovered that Cole hadn't bothered to untie the drawstring before removing her drawers, which meant she had to tie it together where he had broken it. Then she had to fight Cole off when he wanted to help her put the drawers back on.

"Watch that match!" she cautioned once. "You'll catch us both on fire!"

He shook his head regretfully. "I think you've put out all my fires for the time being," he complained in comic distress, making her laugh.

At last Rachel thought she might be presentable, and she proceeded to brush the dust off Cole's back so he would be, too. Even when she was finished, though, she had the uncomfortable feeling that everyone would still be able to tell what they had just done simply by looking at them. One glance at Cole's face when they finally reached the lamplit dining room confirmed her suspicions.

"Wipe that grin off your face," she whispered urgently.

Cole choked down his laughter and managed to strike a fairly respectable pose. "How's this?" he asked innocently.

Rachel glared at him.

He grinned again. "You'd better get that glint out of your eye, or I'm going to carry you back off to the storeroom again," he warned, making her blush furiously, but before she could reply, a baby's wail distracted her.

They both looked up to see tiny Lupe pushing her way through the crowd toward them holding a squalling baby in her arms. "Where you go?" she demanded when she reached them, allowing Rachel to take the baby from her.

Rachel, conscious of the way her cheeks were still burning, did not even dare meet the old woman's eyes, but Cole said, "We were checking out the storeroom, to see if we're going to have enough food to feed this crowd breakfast."

Lupe scowled up at him a moment, trying to make sense

422

out of what he had just said. Then she noticed something about the relaxed way he was standing and let her tiny dark eyes skim first over him and then over Rachel. All of a sudden Rachel's blush began to make sense. Lupe grinned her toothless grin and nodded sagely. "Do we?" she teased.

Cole looked mildly astonished. "You know, we couldn't tell. It's mighty dark in there."

"Cole!" Rachel gasped and scurried off with the baby. Lupe's knowing laugh followed her.

As Rachel sat nursing Colleen in the privacy of the spare bedroom, surrounded by the other sleeping infants, she considered the many ways in which her husband had changed. A bare year ago, he had consented to sleep in a different room because he thought that was what she wanted. Now he was dragging her off to make love in a closet when they had a houseful of guests. The change was incredible, and wonderful, and for some reason Rachel could not stop smiling.

Later, Cole saw her come out of the bedroom when she had put Colleen back down to sleep. She was, he readily admitted, the most beautiful woman in the room and quite possibly the most beautiful woman alive. He still felt warm and loose from their encounter in the kitchen, and he could tell from the smile she flashed him before she was surrounded by would-be dance partners, that she was remembering, too.

Yes, he thought to himself, his life was just about perfect. Or it would be if Will Statler were out of the way. The worst part was in not knowing what Statler had up his sleeve, not knowing when and where he was going to strike. Cole would, he decided, get the Kid to ask Lettie to keep her ears open. She had been good about that so far, and Cole had no reason to doubt that she would let them know anything she heard. He never asked himself why he could feel so certain.

Chapter XIII

"Don't undress."

Lettie glanced up at Hank Oliver in surprise. He had been acting strangely all evening, and on the way over to her house from the saloon he had continually kept looking back over his shoulder as if he suspected someone of following them. Who that someone might have been, Lettie had no idea. The Kid wasn't even in town. Now Oliver was standing by her window, peeking out the curtain, and he didn't want her to take her clothes off. The first prickle of unease crawled up her neck.

"What's going on?" she demanded, not certain she really wanted to know and more than certain she didn't want to be involved. Only a few days had passed since Oliver had told her about his "partnership" with Statler, and she hadn't even had a chance to tell the Kid about it. Now something else was brewing.

Oliver did not answer her, though. Instead he said, "There he is," and moved to the door. He opened it quickly and another man stepped inside.

Lettie frowned, not recognizing the newcomer. The visitor was a spindly scarecrow of a man who walked slightly bent over. His clothes were of good quality but considerably worn and his boots were down at the heel. His restless eyes glanced around the room, as if checking for intruders, and then those eyes lighted on Lettie. That was when she knew him.

"Statler!" she breathed, hardly daring to believe the change in him. He had lost at least thirty pounds since she had last seen him, and he had experienced a lot of pain, if the new lines in his face were any indication. One thing that hadn't changed were his eyes, and Lettie shivered with apprehension as she looked into them.

Statler's mouth twisted into a parody of a smile. "Lettie," he acknowledged, "I'm surprised you recognized me."

"Oh, I knew you right away," she lied, forcing a pleasant smile in return. There was no sense in reminding him how badly he looked. He must be all too aware of his appearance, and Lettie knew he would be remembering who was responsible, too. "I'm glad to see you're still alive. I'd heard you were," she added quickly, "but I was afraid it was just rumors."

"I'm alive all right, just barely," he confirmed bitterly, "and no thanks to Cole Elliot. I heard he thought he'd pulled my cork, but it takes more than a two-bit gunslinger to get rid of Will Statler." He laughed then, an unpleasant sound that made Lettie shudder.

"Sit down, Will," Hank invited, indicating the one easy chair in the room.

Statler crossed to it slowly, moving carefully like an old man might. Lettie wondered fleetingly if he were still in pain but thought it unwise to ask. Instead she said, "I'll make some coffee."

"Put something stronger in mine," Statler ordered, sinking into the chair.

As Lettie went over to the stove to start the coffee, Hank pulled out a straight-backed chair from Lettie's table and sat down in front of Statler. "Have you figured out a plan, yet?" he asked with almost boyish eagerness. Lettie thought he sounded as if they were planning a picnic instead of what she guessed would be murder.

Lettie had her back to them, but she could imagine Statler tossing a questioning look her way.

"It's all right to talk in front of Lettie," Oliver assured him. "She hates that bunch as much as we do."

"Do you, Lettie?" Statler inquired with elaborate casualness.

Lettie clenched her hands so they would not shake and took a deep breath. "Of course," she replied with what she hoped was convincing assurance. She did not turn around.

"Well, then," Statler murmured, "here's what we're going to do." He began to outline the strategy of the attack on Cole Elliot and his men. The plan was remarkably simple, Lettie realized. They would wait until the spring roundup began in a few weeks, and then, one night while most of the men were sound asleep and not expecting any trouble, Statler's men would attack. Since their object this time was not to steal the cattle but merely to wipe out Elliot and his crew, they would strike early in the roundup so the cowboys would not yet be expecting trouble.

Lettie soon realized from Hank's comments that he thought he was to have an important role in the proceedings.

"And you still want me to . . . to do what we talked about?" Hank asked anxiously.

"Yes, and don't worry," Statler assured him, "You'll get exactly what I promised you."

Lettie could not imagine what Statler wanted Hank to do, but she simply could not imagine Hank riding on a midnight raid.

"Tell me, Hank," she asked with forced lightness as she served the men their coffee with hands that trembled only slightly, "exactly what is your part in all this?"

Hank blushed scarlet and looked nonplussed, not daring to meet her eyes, but Statler stepped in and answered for him. "Didn't he tell you? He's bankrolling the whole thing," he told her. "An operation like this calls for men with special talents. They don't come cheap."

427

Lettie felt certain that was true. Now she also understood Statler's willingness to become "partners" with Hank. Although she did not know what Statler had promised Hank as his reward, she had a pretty fair idea he would never receive it. She even felt a little sorry for Hank until she reminded herself he was paying to have Cole Elliot murdered. Fortunately, Lettie was well practiced in hiding her true feelings, and now she hid her revulsion. "Where have you been keeping yourself, Mr. Statler?" she asked cheerfully. "I've heard stories that had you as far off as Indian Territory and New Mexico and as close as Mason."

"Oh, Mason is about right," he told her, sipping his coffee thoughtfully. "I've got a camp a little ways north of there."

Lettie did not like those pale gray eyes watching her, studying her, trying to read her face, but she felt compelled to get as much information out of him as she could. "Was that where you went after . . . after you had the fight with Elliot?" she asked.

Statler did not answer right away. He only kept on looking at her for a long moment. "Yeah," he said softly when it seemed he had seen enough.

"You must have a lot of men working for you now," she guessed, still smiling although her face was beginning to feel stiff. "You'd have to if you're ready to face Elliot again."

This time he only nodded, his eyes never leaving her face. An awkward silence fell as Lettie realized with a slight panic that she had aroused his suspicions.

Hank forced a hearty laugh and threw his arm around Lettie, pulling her close to his side. "Lettie wants to be sure you can beat Elliot this time, don't you, honey?"

"Yes, I do," she agreed with phony enthusiasm, but she had a hunch Statler was not fooled. Her hands were still trembling, and she clasped them together in front of her to hide it.

Statler watched the gesture and then rose carefully to his feet, setting his empty cup on the floor. "I reckon I'll be going now. I want to be far away come sunup," he said, and started for the door. Lettie breathed a silent sigh of relief, even allowing herself to believe she might have been mistaken when she thought Statler saw through her. He wouldn't be leaving now if he thought she was going to betray their plan, would he? She watched, still smiling her false smile, while Hank went with Statler to the door and checked to make certain the street was empty before allowing Statler to leave.

"What's the matter?" Hank asked, turning back to her when Statler had gone. "You're white as a ghost."

Lettie shuddered, no longer bothering to hide it. "Statler makes my skin crawl," she said.

"Yes," Hank agreed, "he does look awful. I hate to think what he's been through. They say he very nearly died when Elliot shot him, and looking at him now, I can readily believe it."

Lettie's shoulders slumped in defeat. Hank didn't understand that her revulsion had little to do with Statler's appearance, and she knew she was better off not trying to explain it to him. "Why did you meet him here?" she asked instead, suddenly angry at the way Hank had dragged her into his ugly plans.

Hank was a little taken aback. "Because I thought you'd want to know what's going to happen, that it won't be long until Elliot is taken care of."

"Just don't bring Statler here again," she snapped, turning to pick up the empty coffee cups.

Hank watched her in puzzled silence, but then he shrugged off his confusion and began to concentrate on Statler's magnificent plan. To Lettie's relief, Hank was entirely too excited for sex. Instead, he spent the evening talking about how much he hated Elliot and how good it would be when the man had finally been put in his place. Lettie was only too glad to see him leave when he had at last run out of things to say. Once alone, she barely had time to draw a calming breath, when someone knocked on the door again.

Thinking it was Hank returning to get in one last word, she threw the door open in dusgust. Before she could register who her visitor really was, Statler had pushed past her into the room.

"Surprised to see me, Lettie?" he asked malevolently, closing the door behind him.

"Hank's gone," she said, twisting her hands nervously in front of her and hoping to direct him away from her house and after Oliver.

"I know. I've been waiting for him to leave so we could be alone," he said, taking one slow, careful step toward her.

"Whatever for?" she asked, smiling with false brightness in a desperate bid to distract him.

Statler smiled his evil smile back at her. "Well, I could pretend I just wanted to go to bed with you. We both know I've wanted that a long time. You've always been too busy for me, though, haven't you? First with Elliot and now with Oliver. I've even heard you've got Kid Collins sniffing around, too. You've been a mighty busy lady, Miss Lettie."

"I've never been too busy for you, Mr. Statler," she lied frantically. "All you ever had to do was say the word. Even now . . ." she offered with a strained smile, more than willing to make a deal. She didn't like the way Statler's eyes were glittering, and she thought maybe if she went to bed with him, afterward she could get away and find Cole. She had to find Cole and warn him.

Statler was nodding at her suggestion. "Yes, now," he agreed, "but first, I've got to teach you a little lesson."

The blow was swift, too swift for her to avoid, and it knocked her to the floor. Momentarily stunned, half blinded by the lights glittering before her eyes, she had no chance of avoiding the second blow. Or the third. Or the fourth. Vaguely, she wondered how his frail, twisted body could muster such strength while she tried vainly to ward off the blows. Soon, however, she slipped into unconsciousness.

Later, although she never knew how much later, Lettie

roused to a world dominated by pain. For a long time she lay there, unable even to sort out the many sources of that pain, but at last she managed to force her eyes open. One of them opened fairly well, but the other was little more than a slit. She knew without even touching it that it would be black and swollen.

From the absolute silence around her, she knew she was now alone. Slowly, she became aware of other details about her condition and the fact that she was laying sprawled, spread-eagled, on the floor with her skirts bunched up around her waist. The cool air on her legs told her she was completely exposed, and the searing agony between those legs reminded her of the last indignity Statler had performed.

He had said something, too. She could remember it vaguely, as if she'd heard it through a thick fog. He had warned her, told her this was only a sample of what she'd get if she even thought about warning Elliot. Statler knew. He had seen through her even if Hank had not. The thought made her smile, but she discovered Statler had also split her lips and that smiling was too costly to even consider.

So Statler had thought to scare her, had he? Well, if Hank had misjudged her, then Statler had equally misjudged her. Lettie didn't scare easily. In fact, she didn't scare at all, she decided, flexing her arms and legs tentatively to make sure she had no broken bones. If anything, Statler had only made her more determined to warn Cole. She must warn him. She knew she must. She couldn't quite remember what she had to warn him about, but it would come to her. When she saw him, she would remember. But first she had to see him.

Cautiously, she pushed herself up on one elbow, gasping at the pain. She would rest a moment, and then she would move again. It would take a long time, she knew, but she would get there. She would find Cole. She would warn him.

*　　*　　*

Rachel came around the corner into the parlor and stopped dead at the sight of her husband having a conversation with their daughter. Of course, that wasn't such an unusual sight. It was what he was saying that shocked her.

"Paaaa-paaaa," he pronounced very carefully into the tiny, fascinated face.

"Ahh-gooo," Colleen replied, grinning broadly and flailing her arms.

Cole was holding the baby up so her face was level with his, and he shook his head in disapproval. "No, no, no," he chastened gently. "Paaa-paaa."

"That's not fair!" Rachel informed him indignantly and marched over to rescue her offspring from such treachery. "Everybody knows a baby's first word is supposed to be 'mama.'"

Cole had the grace to look abashed but he was still unrepentant. "Is that a rule?" he inquired, reluctantly relinquishing possession of the baby.

"Of course it's a rule," she replied haughtily, turning away slightly as if to shield Colleen from her father's evil influence. "Eve made it a long time ago."

"A mother! I should have known!" He made a playful lunge for the baby and succeeded in capturing both mother and daughter and pulling them both onto the settee with him. After a few hasty adjustments, he had them securely in his lap, and then he leaned over until he was nose to nose with the baby. "Paaa-paaa," he tried again.

"Cole!" Rachel squealed, laughing uncontrollably.

He scowled up at her. "Well, it's not fair! You get to be with her all day . . ."

"And half the night," Rachel added.

"And I only get her for a few hours. How is she ever going to figure out who I am?" he demanded.

"I explain it to her when she's old enough to understand," Rachel offered generously, whooping with delight when

Colleen grabbed Cole's nose in a death grip.

"You women are all alike," he complained, prying the baby fingers loose. "Always grabbing hold of something you shouldn't." He flashed Rachel a wicked grin that made her blush.

"If you mind so much, I won't do it anymore," Rachel informed him with mock indignation and feigned a struggle to get free of his embrace.

He only held her tighter and made a valiant attempt to kiss her.

"Cole! Cole, come quick!"

The alarm in the Kid's voice broke them apart instantly. He was calling from out in front of the house. Cole wasted a moment wondering why he hadn't just come on in if something was so very wrong, and then the voice came again.

"Cole! For God's sake!"

Rachel scrambled up, allowing his to rise. He moved swiftly, a premonition of disaster prickling at his nerve endings. He threw open the front door and stepped out onto the porch, squinting in the bright morning sunlight. The Kid was sitting his horse at the bottom of the steps holding what Cole at first took to be a bundle of filthy, bloody rags. Then he noticed the Kid was crying.

"Good heavens! It's a woman!" Rachel's voice behind him startled him into recognition. It really was a woman. Before he could react, Rachel, who had come out right behind him after taking a moment to put the baby in her cradle, rushed past him down the stairs. "Who is she? What happened?" she asked.

The Kid did not reply immediately. Instead he continued to look at Cole. "It's Lettie," he said at last.

"My God!" Cole charged down the stairs then, frantically searching the battered face for any hint that what the Kid had said was true. After several agonizing moments, he finally recognized her. He lifted horror-filled eyes to the Kid.

433

"Who did this to her?"

"Statler." He spit out the word as if it were a curse.

Cole did curse and Rachel gasped. Her eyes went first to the pathetic creature named Lettie and then to the Kid and finally to her husband. "Who is she?" Rachel asked.

Cole started slightly, as if he had momentarily forgotten she was there. "She's . . . she's a girl who works at the saloon," he hedged, not really certain how else to identify her.

Rachel watched his face, knowing this Lettie was far more than just a girl who worked in the saloon. A dozen different emotions warred within her, jealousy being a major one, but she was much too practical to let it conquer her now. Swallowing her feelings, she looked up to the Kid and was startled to discover he was weeping. "Is she alive?" she asked gently.

The Kid nodded. "Barely," he said.

"Then let's get her inside."

Cole hesitated only an instant, until he had searched Rachel's eyes to make certain she really intended for him to bring a saloon girl into her home. Then he reached for Lettie's broken body.

"Be careful," Rachel and the Kid warned in unison, but Cole was being very careful. When he had her securely, he started up the stairs. Rachel darted in front of him, rushing ahead to make preparations. "Lupe!" she called needlessly. The old woman met them at the door.

"You didn't bring her all the way from town like this, did you?" Cole asked over his shoulder. The Kid had dismounted and was following close behind.

"No, I found her a couple of miles from here, just laying in the middle of the road," he said, scrubbing a sleeve across his face. The Kid had left that morning to spend the day in town and see what gossip he could pick up and to tell Lettie what the cowboy Pinto had reported. "From the tracks, it looked like she'd been on a horse, but she must've fallen off. I guess

434

she was too weak to hold on anymore."

"Did she tell you anything?"

The Kid sniffed loudly. "I asked her who did it, and she said Statler did. Then she mumbled something about how she had to see you or tell you something. I couldn't quite make it out."

Cole cursed softly and looked down into the once-familiar face. At least she was unconscious now and wouldn't be feeling any of this, he thought. He hoped she was only unconscious.

"Bring her in here," Rachel called from her old bedroom. She had already turned back the bed. Cole laid his burden gently down and stepped back, feeling suddenly uncomfortable. Somebody had to do for Lettie, but he couldn't ask his wife to take care of a saloon girl.

Rachel sensed his distress and shared it. She shouldn't even have a woman like this in her house, but then Lettie, too, was one of Statler's victims. Rachel might have ended up the same way if it hadn't been for Cole. And Lettie was obviously Cole's friend.

Or something.

"You and the Kid go on out," she told him. "Lupe and I will take care of her."

Cole cast her a grateful glance and then retreated, gently leading the Kid back into the parlor. He paused before closing the door. "If she wakes up or says anything, call me," he requested, and Rachel nodded her agreement.

When he had gone, Rachel looked down at the broken body on the bed and for a moment shared Lettie's pain. Tears stung Rachel's eyes. "How could anyone do something like this?" she asked Lupe who had already begun to cut Lettie's clothes off.

Lupe muttered something incomprehensible, and then said, "Help me." Rachel did.

A while later, when Lettie had been bathed and bandaged and dressed in one of Rachel's nightdresses, Rachel went out to give the men a report on her condition. She found them in the parlor. The Kid was slumped in the wing chair, nursing a glass of whiskey, and Cole was pacing, smoking what most certainly was not his first cigarette. Both of them came to attention as soon as Rachel opened the door.

"How is she?" they asked in unison.

Rachel studied both their faces, comparing. The Kid was in love with the woman, she judged, and his concern came from that. Cole was a little harder to figure. He was sincerely concerned, but exactly why, Rachel was afraid to guess and equally afraid she already knew. Still, she was reluctant to give them the news. "Not good. Lupe doesn't think she'll make it. She's bleeding inside from the beating she took."

Rachel barely had time to register Cole's reaction to her words when the Kid's anguished cry distracted her. He surged to his feet. "Can I see her?" he asked.

Rachel did not have the heart to deny him, and besides, what could it possibly hurt? "She's still unconscious," Rachel warned, knowing that would not deter him. Hastily setting down his whiskey glass, he hurried into the bedroom.

When they were alone, Rachel moved closer to Cole, watching his face. He had been disturbed by her news but not nearly as disturbed as the Kid. She tried in vain to judge his true feelings. When she was no more than arm's length away from him, she stopped. "Who is she?" Rachel asked again.

Cole blinked, a little startled at the question. "She's . . . I told you, she's a girl who works in the Silver Dollar Saloon," he said.

"Who is she to you?" Rachel insisted.

Cole rubbed the back of his neck wearily. "She's an old friend. She's been helping us keep track of Statler. She hears all sorts of rumors at the saloon and she tells the Kid." He made an apologetic gesture with his hand. "She's his girl."

"Oh," Rachel replied, thinking this over carefully. "I thought she might be your girl." The words left a sour taste in her mouth but she had to say them. She had to know for certain.

Cole's blue eyes narrowed as he tried to read her thoughts. "No," he said after a minute. "She's not my girl."

"She was, though, wasn't she?" Rachel maintained. "She was the one you went to . . . that night."

At first Cole genuinely did not know what she was talking about, but the stricken look in her eyes jogged his memory. It was the same look he had seen that night, and he could almost hear her voice accusing him: "You've been with a woman!"

He wished he could deny it. He would have given anything to be able to swear an oath that he had never done such a thing. At least there was something he could truthfully tell her. "Nothing happened. I swear to you, nothing happened. As soon as I got there, I knew I'd made a terrible mistake. I left right away."

She knew he was lying. "You reeked of her perfume," she accused, hating the tears that sprang to her eyes at the pain of this ancient betrayal. The smell of Lettie's perfume just now in the bedroom had triggered Rachel's memories and made her aware of the truth. But as painful as the memories were, she felt compelled to probe the wound.

Cole sighed. "She . . . she tried to get me interested. But it just didn't work, Rachel," he explained, reaching out to her with an imploring gesture. Then he gave her a sad smile. "You've ruined me. I haven't been able to enjoy looking at another woman since the day we got married."

She watched him, her dark eyes large in her pale face. She wanted to believe him, and she searched in vain for any sign of deceit on his craggy face. Then, quite suddenly, she knew he was telling the truth. With a small cry, she threw herself into his arms, and he caught her gratefully.

Weeping tears of joy and relief, she clung to him and allowed him to soothe her with fervently whispered endearments. After a few moments, she regained her control and pushed far enough away so she could see his face. "You

437

haven't even looked at another woman since we got married?" she asked in watery challenge.

He shook his head. "I didn't say I haven't looked. I said I haven't *enjoyed* it."

"Not even in Kansas?" she insisted.

"Not even in Kansas," he vowed. "Although," he added, gently teasing, "if I'd known how pregnant you'd be when I got back, I might have been a little more tempted."

"Oh, you," she chided, punching him lightly on the chest.

He looked down at her with an adoration that slowly sobered her. "You're not the only woman I've ever gone to bed with, Rachel," he told her with regret. "There've been more of those than I care to remember, but you're the only woman I've ever really made love to and the only woman I've ever loved. You believe me, don't you?"

Rachel nodded and then laid her head back against the solid comfort of his chest. "I'm sorry I wasn't your first woman, but I'll settle for being your last. Your *very* last," she added, giving him a warning squeeze.

He replied with a bear hug that almost cracked her ribs, but before he could kiss her, the bedroom door flew open.

"Cole, come quick. She's calling for you," the Kid's frantic voice interrupted them.

In spite of all he had just told her, Rachel could not help the pang of jealousy that stabbed her at the alacrity with which Cole answered the summons. She took comfort in the way he grabbed her hand and dragged her right along with him. Once inside the bedroom, Cole dropped her hand and approached the bed with caution.

Looking down at Lettie, he wasn't at first certain her eyes were really open, but she must have seen him. "Cole?" she whispered, her voice a slender thread of sound.

"Yes, I'm here," he assured her, leaning over so she could see him and so he could hear her. "We'll get him, Lettie. Statler will pay for what he's done to you."

"He'll get you," she warned, her swollen lips forming

438

awkwardly around the words.

"No, he won't," Cole assured her. "We'll be ready for him." He made his promise lightly, in an effort to comfort her. But she would not be comforted.

"No . . ." she gasped, frantically grasping his hand with surprising strength. "He has . . . plan . . . when you . . . round up . . . attack your camp . . . at night, when you . . . sleep . . ."

Coe frowned. This sounded like a genuine plan. It also sounded suspiciously like the last time Statler's men had attacked them. "Does he want to steal our cattle?"

"No . . . just kill . . . you."

Rachel gasped, but no one paid any attention to her. They were all straining to catch every one of Lettie's words.

"Hank Oliver . . . in on it . . . too . . ."

"Hank Oliver? How on earth did he get mixed up with Statler?" Cole wondered aloud, not really meaning for Lettie to answer him.

She did, though, her battered face twisting into the grimace of a knowing smile. "Revenge . . ." she whispered, ". . . for Rachel."

Rachel made a small sound of protest, and Cole's expression hardened. He had misjudged the little store-keeper. The man had more gravel in his gizzard than Cole had given him credit for. He hardly noticed the way Lettie had suddenly lost interest in her story. Her gaze left his face and stared off somewhere, as if she were looking at something distant.

"Is that . . . baby?" she asked.

For the first time, the rest of them noticed Colleen's fussing at having been abandoned. She was still lying in her cradle in the front room. When no one else answered Lettie's question, Rachel finally admitted, "Yes, that's our daughter."

Lettie's gaze found Rachel where she hovered at Cole's shoulder. "Can I . . . see . . . it?" The request touched

439

Rachel's heart, making her forget she had once been jealous of this poor, broken creature.

"Of course. I'll fetch her," she said, hurrying off to do so.

Colleen's fussing ceased the instant her mother picked her up, and she bestowed a beatific smile on her benefactor. Rachel returned the smile automatically even as she rushed back into the sickroom. Cole, she noticed immediately, had stepped away from the bed, and the Kid had taken his place. The Kid knelt near Lettie's head, holding her limp hand as if it were a precious jewel.

Rachel stepped up beside him and held the baby down for Lettie to see. "This is Colleen."

Lettie just looked at the child for a long moment, and then she lifted her free hand and lightly, reverently, stroked one baby cheek. "I'll never . . . have one . . . now . . ." she murmured with regret.

"Lettie!" the Kid protested with strained enthusiasm. "Yes you will! You'll get better, you'll see. We'll get married, you and me, and we'll have a dozen kids, as many as you want, whatever you want."

Rachel could have wept at the despair in the Kid's voice, and she wished fervently that she might spare him the pain he was experiencing. Lettie, it seemed, felt the same. For just a moment, she turned her glance away from the gurgling infant and cast the Kid a pitying look. With those awful, swollen eyes, she told him how sorry she was his dream would never come true. Then she lifted her gaze to Rachel.

"My name . . . not . . . Lettie . . ."

"What is it?" Rachel asked, not certain why her true name could matter now.

"Leah."

Lettie's eyes held hers until the realization set in. Slowly, Rachel recalled the Bible story of the two sisters, Rachel and Leah, who had both loved the same man. That man, of course, had loved only Rachel in return.

"Put 'Leah' . . . on my grave . . ." Lettie whispered when

440

she was certain Rachel understood.

Rachel nodded, and then, clutching Colleen's small body to her, she breathed, "I'm sorry." For the first time in her life, Rachel felt greedy and selfish and extremely blessed in the knowledge of all she possessed in comparison with this poor, ravaged woman.

Lettie sighed, a sigh of surrender, and those awful eyes closed one last time.

Several minutes ticked by before the Kid realized the truth. "Lettie?" he asked in sudden panic.

Cole laid a comforting hand on his shoulder. "She's gone, Kid."

"No," he insisted, "she can't be. *Lettie!*"

But she did not respond, not even when he lightly stroked her cooling cheek. "Lettie, don't die!" he begged, tears streaming down his face again. But she couldn't hear him.

They dressed her in one of Rachel's gowns and put her in the plain pine coffin the men built for her and buried her in the tiny, fenced plot where Rachel had buried her father only a scant year earlier. The Kid fashioned a wooden cross and burned the letters of her name—her real name—into it. It wouldn't last long, he knew, but it would do until the marble headstone he was going to order arrived.

That night Rachel and Cole did not speak as they prepared for bed. Both of them were lost in their own somber thoughts. Once more death had touched someone close to them, reminding them how fragile life really was. Rachel could not forget Lettie's warning that Statler intended to kill Cole. The knowledge chilled her to the marrow. When Cole at last blew out the lamp and slipped into the bed beside her, she reached for him with a desperation that had nothing to do with physical desire.

Understanding only too well, Cole held her fiercely. "I love you," he whispered. He no longer had any trouble saying the words. Or believing that she returned his love. Without waiting for her to speak her love back to him, he

441

kissed her, sealing anew the commitment he had made to her.

Rachel returned the kiss, accepting his silent pledge and returning one of her own. They came together in a fury of need, as if their coupling could mystically protect them from the forces that would part them. Even when the blaze of passion had burned to embers, they clung together, as if to break their physical bond would endanger the emotional one.

But for once their lovemaking did not bring them the blissful oblivion of sleep afterward. Neither of them could forget Lettie's pathetic face and her useless death, or what all that meant to their future. For a long time they simply lay together in the darkness, awake and only too aware of the dangers that surrounded them.

"What are you going to do now?" Rachel asked finally.

Cole sighed. "I've got two choices. I can go after Statler. We've got a pretty good idea where he's holed up, but we don't know exactly. That makes it hard. Our other choice is to let him come to us. That's bad because he picks the time and we won't know when he's coming, but at least we'll be expecting him."

Rachel raised up on one elbow. She couldn't see his face in the darkness, but she could still judge his mood. "You're going to wait for him, aren't you?" she asked.

"Think you know me pretty well, don't you, Miss Smarty Pants?" he teased, but Rachel could hear the strain in his voice. He did not want to discuss these things with her, to worry her, and now he was trying to distract her. In his male wisdom, he would think she was better off not knowing all the gruesome details. He simply could not seem to understand she needed to know and that not knowing only gave her one more thing to worry about.

Colleen whimpered tentatively a few times before working

442

to a full-fledged squall. Both her parents groaned in unison.

"At least she waited till we were finished," Cole remarked. Rachel was wondering from where she would gather the energy to even move, much less get out of bed to get the child when Cole eased her off him. "Stay put. I'll get her," he said, reminding her of the way he had fetched the baby for her on Christmas night.

Rachel waited while he sat up and struck a match to light a candle. Then she watched as he walked the few steps to the cradle and picked up his daughter. They made quite a picture, the baby in her pink nightdress and the father in nothing at all. Rachel gave them both a sleepy smile as Cole slipped back into bed and tucked the baby in between them.

Colleen's cries had ceased the moment her father picked her up, and now she was gurgling happily. She didn't refuse the breast her mother offered her, but she kept pausing to look back and flirt with her father.

"Now she thinks it's playtime, Papa," Rachel said with a tired smile. "You shouldn't have lit the candle."

"I'll play with her," he said, smiling back and stroking first one baby cheek and then the curving breast it nestled against. Each was equally soft and warm. Tempted beyond his ability to bear it, he leaned over and kissed them both.

"Hurry up, Colleen," he whispered into the baby's ear. "I want to play with your mama some more, too."

Rachel groaned dramatically, certain he must be teasing. Speaking for herself, she would be lucky if she had the stamina to find her nightdress and put it back on. She wasn't too tired to ask a question, though.

"While you're waiting, you can tell me what your plans are for dealing with Statler," she said with an anticipatory smile.

Cole scowled at her, but her smile did not waiver, so he tried the direct approach. "You don't have to worry about it, Sweetheart. That's my look-out."

"But it's my look-out, too. I'll be sitting here at home and worrying, whether you tell me or not, so you'd better tell me . . . *If* you want to 'play' any more tonight," she added, giving him a provocative look.

He was still scowling, so she squinched her face into a scowl, too, and said, "I'm not made of glass, Cole Elliot. Tell me or I'll beat it out of you."

Not made of glass. Now where had he heard that before? Ignoring her threat, he sighed in resignation and said, "All right, you were right when you guessed I'd wait for Statler to come to us. I know just the place . . ." And so he told her the plan. It was a good one, too, even better than the last one. She only prayed this one would work. And that once again, Cole would return safely to her.

When Colleen finally drifted off to sleep again, Cole blew out the candle and hauled Rachel back into his arms.

"I'm too tired to 'play,'" she protested, smiling in spite of herself.

"I thought that was your bribe," he said, pretending to be offended. "You don't have to 'play,' though," he added wickedly. "You just lay there like a good girl, and I'll take care of you."

He did, too.

Cole remembered that night during the long, lonely ones that followed. He wasted no time getting started on the roundup, and he and the men pitched a camp the very next day. It was a little early in the year. Ordinarily, he wouldn't have started the spring branding for another few weeks, but Cole figured there was no point in waiting. Just to make certain word spread to all interested parties, Cole himself went to town that morning to stock up on supplies.

He needed great restraint to walk into the Mercantile and hand his list to Oliver without betraying any signs of anger. Rachel, he thought with some amusement, could never have done it. Every time she even thought about Oliver's treachery, she started ranting and yelling and behaving in what Cole reminded her was a very unladylike fashion. She, of course, would tell him to mind his own business and keep on ranting. Cole was glad she had the excuse of the baby to keep her away from town for the time being. Given half a chance, she'd probably punch Hank Oliver right in the nose.

Smiling at that picture, Cole walked up to the counter and handed Oliver his list. As usual, Oliver treated him coldly, but for the first time, Cole detected a slight smugness about the storekeeper, as if he thought he knew something Cole didn't. Cole had to bite his lip to keep from smirking right back.

"Looks like you're going to start your roundup soon," Oliver commented after reading the order.

"Yeah, I sent the men out this morning, as a matter of fact," Cole remarked casually while pretending to be very interested in a pristine white Stetson displayed on the counter. Oliver betrayed himself with an indrawn breath, but Cole pretended not to notice.

Then Oliver cleared his throat. "I . . . uh . . . I heard a rumor that Statler's been seen around these parts," he ventured.

Cole could have laughed out loud, so delighted was he for the opportunity to throw his enemy off guard. He snorted derisively instead. "Rumors! That's all it is. Statler's dead. We've seen the last of him."

"You're sure? What about all the stories?" Oliver insisted.

"I'm sure," Cole said with a disgust that was only partly feigned. Oliver was so excited that Cole was afraid the little storekeeper might wet himself. He almost hated to do this to him. He could see Oliver was satisfied—and delighted—at this information, but he wasn't quite through yet. "By the way, have you heard about Lettie?"

Oliver was instantly wary. "I know she didn't show up for work last night," he admitted.

Cole judged Oliver really did not know what had happened. For a while, he had thought perhaps Oliver had been in on Lettie's beating, too, but no guilt clouded the storekeeper's handsome face. "She's dead," he said bluntly, gratified to see Oliver's horrified disbelief.

"She can't be!" he insisted. "I mean, I just saw her night before last. She was fine then."

Cole's eyes narrowed down to dangerous slits. "For your sake, that better be true," he warned. "Somebody beat her to death sometime that night. One of my men found her body on the road." This was the story they had decided to give out so no one would guess Lettie had warned them.

"Oh, my God!" Oliver moaned, blanching.

Cole pressed his advantage. "You got any idea who might've done it?" he demanded.

"No, oh, no," Oliver assured him quickly, and then added, "She was a whore, you know. She knew lots of men. Any one of them . . ."

Cole snatched up the storekeeper by the front of his shirt and dragged him halfway across the counter. "Lettie wasn't a whore," he hissed into Oliver's terrified face.

"No, of course she wasn't," Oliver agreed in a high, nervous voice.

Cole knew an almost overwhelming urge to shake the little rat until his neck snapped, but unfortunately they still needed him. There would be plenty of time later to find out exactly what part he had played in Lettie's death and to exact the appropriate revenge. Reluctantly, he released Oliver, letting him slide back to his own side of the counter.

Cole had glared at Oliver as the storekeeper had straightened his clothes and tried to resume his previous dignity. "If you hear anything about who killed Lettie, you let me know," Cole had said, and Oliver had readily agreed before scurrying off to fill Cole's order.

Recalling that scene now as he stood guard over the phony roundup camp, Cole smiled grimly. Yes, he still had a little score to settle with Oliver. He only hoped the storekeeper would be riding in the raid. It would make things a lot easier.

The camp looked fine, Cole judged, squinting into the midnight darkness. If anyone had happened by, they would have thought it completely ordinary. The bedrolls were spread in the usual haphazard manner, and the fire had burned down to coals. The two men riding night herd around the small bunch of cattle they had managed to collect so far were singing lazily to lull the animals and keep them together.

Suddenly, the hairs on the back of Cole's neck prickled. Nothing had happened, at least nothing any innocent bystander would have noticed, but Cole had gotten the signal. It was a clever one, if he did say so himself. No one would ever guess that when the singer had switched to the ballad "The Streets of Laredo," he had alerted the entire camp.

This time there would be no stampede, or at least not one over the camp. Cole had chosen a spot with enough natural barriers between the herd and the camp so such a thing was simply not feasible. He suspected any stampede would be merely for distraction, but he also suspected this attack would come much more quietly than the last because this time Statler hoped to catch them all napping.

He did, too. In the dark, Statler's men had surrounded the camp, and on a prearranged signal, they all opened fire, pumping bullets into the sleeping forms clustered around the fire. Not one of them even had a chance to escape.

In the distance, Cole heard the familiar rumble of running cattle, and the shouts and shots of the men who would be chasing the two cowboys on night watch. When that noise had died away, an eerie silence settled on the camp as Statler and his men waited for any retaliation.

There was none.

"Come on, men," Cole heard a familiar voice shout. "Looks like we got 'em all!"

447

The waiting was agony, but Cole waited, crouching in his hiding place and gritting his teeth at the urge to fire off a shot in the direction of Statler's voice. Shadows moved cautiously in the darkness, approaching the still forms on the ground. Someone threw some kindling on the fire and it flared up brightly.

"Hey, what the hell . . ." someone said in alarm, and Cole knew it was time. They had discovered the bedrolls were filled only with straw.

He pulled back the hammer of his gun, and the click sounded unnaturally loud to his ears. "You didn't get us all, Statler," he shouted. This was the other signal, and the rest of the Circle M men, hidden at strategic points around the camp, cocked their guns, too. "We've got you surrounded. Throw down your weapons."

"No!" Statler's voice boomed above the blast of his pistol as he fired in the direction of Cole's voice.

The ensuing battle was bloody but brief. It was, to Cole's disgust, like shooting fish in a barrel, and even though the victims had fully intended to murder him and his men the same way, he hated it. That was what had prompted him to give them a warning, and that was what prompted him to call out, "Hold your fire, men!" after only a few minutes.

When the shooting stopped, he called again, "If any of you are still alive, throw down your guns and put up your hands. We won't shoot if you surrender."

"The hell he won't!" Statler yelled. "Don't listen to him!"

Cole knew a small regret that Statler had survived, but consoled himself that the man would have to stand trial for his crimes. Before Cole could think how to override Statler's objections and get the ambushers to surrender, however, he heard sounds of a small scuffle, and then a strange voice called out from where Statler's voice had last been heard.

"I got Statler's gun, Elliot. He's shot to hell. He won't be causing any more trouble. The rest of us are giving up.

Don't shoot."

"Throw down your guns and stand up real slow with your hands over your heads," Cole commanded.

The surrender was accomplished with surprising ease. A few of the men were dead or dying, but most were not even seriously wounded. Only two of Cole's men had been hurt in the firing, and their wounds were not serious. In short order, the Circle M cowboys had trussed up their surviving enemies and begun loading them onto the chuck wagon for transportation to jail in town. It would, Cole reflected, be a humdinger of a trial. Too bad Statler wouldn't live to see it.

Cole walked over to where his nemesis lay dying. The stories he had heard were true. He might never have even recognized Statler under other circumstances. The man's gaunted face glared up at him in the flickering firelight, full of all the hate Cole knew he must feel. Seeing the man soaked in his own blood, Cole could almost feel sorry for him.

Almost.

"Looks like your number's about up, Statler," he said.

Statler smiled a knowing smile but said nothing.

Cole had no desire to torture a dying man, not even a man like Statler who well deserved it, but he did want a little information. "Was it you who killed Mr. McKinsey?" he asked. He already knew the answer, of course, but he was hoping to make certain the right man had been punished for the crime.

Statler grimaced. "I wasn't even with them."

"It was your men, though, wasn't it?" Cole insisted. "Which one did it?"

His smile never wavering, Statler said, "Remember the two men who ambushed you and Miles?"

"Kirk and his partner?" Cole asked.

Statler nodded. "They were the ones. I sent them out to get you, too. I guess they just weren't as good when the odds were even." He shrugged fatalistically.

449

Cole knew a moment of satisfaction. One score, at least, had been settled. Still, he did have another murder to solve. "I heard Hank Oliver was in on this little adventure. Where is he?"

Statler's smile faded. "Who told you that?"

Cole's blue eyes narrowed down to slits. "Lettie told me . . . just before she died."

"She died?" Statler echoed faintly. "Too bad. I had plans for her . . ."

Impatiently, fighting an urge to hurry Statler along on his journey to meet his Maker, Cole squatted down next to the dying man. He had to remind himself there was nothing he could do for Lettie and that Statler was already paying the price for what he had done to her. Cole wasn't going to let the last member of this little farce get away though. "What about Oliver? Was he part of this or not? There's no use in letting him get off scott-free, not when you'll have to die for it," he pointed out impatiently.

Statler thought this over and his lips stretched into a smile again. "Yeah," he agreed. "Oliver was my partner. He paid these men to kill you." He laughed weakly at Cole's furious reaction to this information and then grimaced with pain.

"Where is he then?" Cole demanded. "Was he with you?" Cole couldn't wait to get his hands on the storekeeper.

But Statler was shaking his head. "No, he . . ." Statler's voice was growing fainter and Cole had to lean closer to hear. "He's not tough enough for this. He's . . . more of a . . . *lady* killer. He's . . . at your ranch."

Cole cursed at his own stupidity. He had been so sure of his plan, so sure that he was the only intended victim, he hadn't even left a guard at the ranch. He had been a fool! Rachel was there all alone with only Lupe and the baby, and now Oliver . . .

What would Oliver do to her? Frantically, he tried not to imagine, but he could hear Rachel's words echoing in his head: "I'd die before I'd let another man touch me!"

He breathed her name, and then he saw the gun. Some distant part of his brain had noticed it one second earlier, had registered the fact that Statler should not have a gun, not even a tiny gun like this one. In that second he thought to reach for it, to turn it away, but he was one second too late. Just as his hand moved, the gun exploded in his face.

Chapter XIV

Rachel went to the window and looked out at the setting sun. Drawing her shawl around her against the late evening chill, she wondered how many evenings like this would pass before it would be all over. Recalling she had once thought it *was* all over, she frowned slightly. This time would be different, she knew. This time Cole would not rest until he had Statler, one way or another. Or Statler had him. Rachel shivered at the thought, a shiver that had nothing whatsoever to do with the coolness of the evening.

She was so lost in her thoughts that at first she did not notice the lone rider. Even when she did, she did not at first realize he could not be one of her own men since he was coming from town. Watching him carefully, every nerve suddenly alert, she soon recognized him, and swore under her breath in what Cole would have told her was a very unladylike manner. "Lupe!" she called.

Sensing more than hearing the old woman enter the room, Rachel kept her eyes on the rider and said, "Hank Oliver is coming to pay us a visit."

"Madre de Dios," Lupe muttered, moving silently over to stand beside Rachel at the window. "He is alone," she observed.

"What could he want?" Rachel wondered aloud, but

before Lupe could reply, the truth dawned on her. "Lupe, it must be tonight!"

The old woman nodded. "He has confidence, that one. He does not even think what will happen to him when your man comes back here."

If he comes back, a tiny voice in Rachel's head taunted. No! She would not think about that. Cole would win. He had to. Still, Oliver's presence indicated the same sort of certainty existed on the other side, too.

Lupe glanced up at Rachel. "Do we shoot him now?" she inquired dryly.

Rachel smiled in spite of herself, dearly wishing they could but knowing such an action would be a little difficult to explain. She was also fairly certain she would not be able to bring herself to pull the trigger in such a cold-blooded murder. Not that Hank Oliver didn't deserve such a fate, she reminded herself. Still, she went over and checked the loads in the pistol Cole had left her, but she hid it in her sewing bag instead of taking aim at Oliver's head. Then she sat down on the settee and waited.

Oliver did not take long to make his appearance. As she had expected he would, he actually knocked on the front door. Lupe let him in, condemning him silently with her dark eyes, but saying nothing.

"Good evening, Rachel," he said, stepping into the parlor. Apparently, he did not notice Lupe's disapproval.

Rachel glared at him with barely suppressed revulsion. "Hank, what a surprise," she said without expression. "What brings you here?" She did not bother to rise. She didn't want to get too far from her sewing bag and its contents.

He gave her what she took to be a pitying smile. "It's all over, Rachel," he said, moving toward her.

A small tendril of fear curled in her stomach but her face revealed nothing. It couldn't be over, she told herself sternly. Lettie had said Statler was going to attack at night, when they were all asleep. If the attack had come last night, she would have heard something about it by now. That meant the attack would come tonight. Hank was a trifle premature in his pronouncement.

"What is all over?" she asked, feigning ignorance. As far as Hank knew, they were completely oblivious to Statler's plans, and she would be wise to maintain the fiction.

Hank sat down beside her on the settee, and she fought the urge to shrink away from his nearness. He was still smiling that condescending smile, and she was having a difficult time controlling her rage.

"Everything," he explained cryptically. "Your marriage, everything. Statler is back."

Rachel lifted her eyebrows in pretended surprise. "Statler is dead," she told him, clenching her fists in her lap to keep from slapping the smirk off his face.

Hank shook his head, still smiling. "He's very much alive, and this time he has a plan that won't fail. Very soon he's going to be . . . uh . . . taking care of your . . . of Elliot and your men."

"What do you mean, 'taking care'?" she asked, unable to keep the edge from her voice any longer. Oliver was acting as if he were doing her a favor by telling her Statler intended to murder her husband.

His smile never wavered. "In a few short hours you're going to be a widow, Rachel. You'll be free."

Rachel couldn't help the gasp that escaped her. He had said it so matter-of-factly, almost as if he had expected her to be relieved. For one horrible moment, she even believed him, but then she got hold of herself. "Hank, how can you say such a thing?" she demanded.

Hank's guileless blue eyes turned tender. "You don't have to pretend anymore, Rachel. I know how you feel. You don't have to honor any conventions with me. You must be very happy to know you'll be free of him."

Rachel didn't know what was more shocking, his words or the fact that he so very obviously believed them. "I don't

455

want to be free of him!" she insisted angrily.

Hank, still wearing his vapid grin, nodded his understanding. "Under the circumstances, your loyalty is commendable."

"Hank!" Rachel cried, surging to her feet. "He's my husband! I love him! And he's not . . ."

She had intended to say he was not going to lose the fight with Statler, but Hank had risen, too, and suddenly grasped her shoulders. His grip was hard and fierce and so was his expression. "Don't say that, Rachel. Don't *ever* say that," he warned.

Rachel knew instantly she had misjudged Hank. He was not nearly so calm as he had seemed at first, nor even as rational. Underneath his courteous exterior, he was a raw bundle of nerves. Like her, he was thinking of the coming fight, and he was not nearly as certain about the outcome as he would have her believe.

"All right, Hank," she said, trying to soothe him and wishing she had the gun in her pocket instead of in the sewing bag. She would have liked nothing better than to tell him Cole knew all about his plot and would be waiting for Statler, but she guessed such a confession would be foolish in the extreme. From the look in Hank's eye, he'd be very likely to ride out and warn Statler and ruin everything. No, Rachel would have to play along with him and try to keep him calm. "Let's sit down," she suggested, forcing a placating smile and making a desperate effort to control the quivering of her voice. "Maybe you'd like some coffee or something."

Hank blinked a few times and then, as if suddenly realizing he was still holding her, he let his hands drop. "I . . . I'm sorry, I . . . Yes, I would like some coffee," he said, sitting back down on the settee.

Rachel flashed Lupe a look, and the older woman nodded and crept silently from the room. "Now tell me what's supposed to happen tonight," Rachel said, keeping her false smile in place as she sat down beside him.

Oliver cleared his throat importantly. "Statler has a plan. He's going to sneak up and surround the camp late tonight when all the men are asleep. It will . . ." Hank paused as he pictured the scene in his mind. To his credit, he seemed a little disturbed that Statler would be shooting sleeping, defenseless men. Not disturbed enough to stop it, though, Rachel noted bitterly. "It will all be over before they know what hit them," Oliver concluded, as if such swiftness were a form of mercy.

Rachel shuddered in revulsion.

"What's the matter?" Hank asked solicitously. "Are you cold?"

"Yes," she lied, drawing her shawl more closely around her. She knew she should hide her true feelings but she could not help pointing out, "That's murder, Hank."

Hank looked a little offended. "They deserve it, Rachel. They're the ones who killed your father, you know."

For the second time Rachel gasped in outrage, but before she could speak, he said, "I can see you didn't know. I'm sorry to be the one to tell you, but it can't be helped. Statler told me the whole story. Elliot wanted your ranch for himself, so he and his men murdered your father. When you were all alone and unprotected, he forced you to marry him, and then started all that talk about Statler being responsible in order to cover his tracks." Hank wore the righteous expression of a man forced to tell an ugly truth that must be told.

Rachel hardly glanced up when Lupe came back carrying a tray with two cups of coffee. She was staring transfixed at Oliver's face, unable even to believe her own ears. He believed it, though, the whole crazy story. He really believed it. Rachel felt a hysterical urge to laugh, except she was afraid once she started, she would not be able to stop.

Not certain she really wanted to know anymore, she still asked the question that was next in logical progress. "What happens after . . . after Statler is finished?"

Hank smiled again, the same smile that had often charmed her in the past. Now his smile repelled her, and she suppressed another shudder. "Well, as I said, you'll be free then. It will be just the way it was before all this happened, and you and I can get married, the way we planned. You'll be mine then, Rachel. All mine."

Rachel thought he could say nothing to appall her more than his description of how Statler intended to murder Cole, but she was wrong. Hank seemed intent on deluding himself, justifying his actions with half-truths and outright false-hoods, but she was only beginning to learn how deep the delusion went. She and Hank had never planned to be married, and yet he had convinced himself they had. That, combined with the fact he also believed Cole had forced her into marriage against her will, made him certain she would be only too grateful for this "rescue."

Watching him sip his coffee, Rachel sat frozen in her horror, wondering what on earth she should do. "When is the . . . attack supposed to take place?" she asked in a strangely calm voice.

"Sometime after midnight," Hank said helpfully.

Midnight. Rachel glanced longingly out the window. It was barely sundown. She had hours until the attack actually took place. If only she could get to Cole, warn him. But she could do nothing as long as Oliver was here watching every move she made. Surely, she could think of some way to get rid of him.

She was turning several possibilities over in her mind when she heard the baby start to fuss. Until now, Colleen had been playing happily in her cradle near the fire, out of Oliver's direct line of sight. His head came up in alarm.

"What's that?" he demanded, jumping to his feet and clumsily pulling a revolver from his coat pocket.

"It's the baby," Rachel explained, jumping up, too, and backing cautiously away from him and toward the cradle. "Put that gun away!" she commanded.

458

"The baby?" he asked, looking around until he saw the cradle. His gaze hardened immediately, and Rachel quickly picked the child up and cradled her protectively. "Elliot's whelp," Oliver muttered, jamming the gun back into his coat pocket. Reading Rachel's expression, he misinterpreted her fear. "Don't worry, darling. I don't hold it against you," he assured her in a voice meant to soothe but which sent clammy chills up her spine. "I know he forced you to . . . to submit to him." Hank's handsome face curled into a mask of disgust, and he spit out the word "submit" as if it had left a bad taste in his mouth. "I'd never treat you that way," he promised.

Which was, Rachel told herself, something to be thankful for. What was wrong with a man who could look at a tiny innocent baby with offense and could speak with disgust of the act of love that had created her?

Colleen twisted in her mother's arms, rooting for the breast that had not yet been bared to her. When Rachel made no move to appease her, she howled her protest.

"What's the matter with it?" Oliver asked, his alarm returning.

"She's hungry," Rachel said, wondering how she could have so greatly misjudged him in all the months she had known him. How could she have let him court her for so long? How could she ever have even considered marrying him? He was looking at Colleen as if the baby were some obnoxious creature that had crawled out from under a rock.

"Then feed it," he snapped impatiently.

"I . . . I need some privacy," Rachel forced herself to say. The thought of exposing herself in front of Oliver was gagging her, but she couldn't very well let the baby continue to scream in hunger.

Oliver's face creased in puzzlement as he sorted out the meaning of her request. Then he noticed how the baby was nuzzling Rachel's bodice. "Oh," he said in a strangled voice. "Of course . . . I . . . of course." He made a vague gesture

459

with his hand as if to motion her away and out of his sight.

She had been afraid he would want to leer at her while she fed the baby, but apparently he found the idea as unpleasant as she did. This would be one more oddity to add to her list when she had the time to think about it. Right now she was simply grateful. Fleeing to her bedroom, she closed the door, wishing it had a lock, and carried Colleen over to the rocking chair. Awkwardly juggling the baby in one arm, she turned the chair to face away from the door, just in case Oliver decided to pay them a visit after all. By the time she had settled in and unbuttoned her dress, Colleen was in a rage, a rage that ended abruptly when Rachel thrust the nipple into her tiny mouth.

Her milk letting down brought a surge of calmness, and Rachel could feel the tension draining from her body. Closing her eyes, she leaned back in the rocking chair and tried to think rationally about her situation. She had to get rid of Oliver some way so she would be free to warn Cole. If only Oliver would go to sleep, she thought frantically, and then she remembered a way in which she could insure he would fall asleep. She smiled as she mentally worked out all the details.

"Rachel?" Hank's voice interrupted her musings. "How long does that take?"

"I'm coming," she replied quickly, surprised to see that Colleen had long since dozed off while her mother made her plans. Jumping up, Rachel carried the baby over to the bed and tucked her in carefully, placing a pillow on each side of her to prevent her from rolling. Then, drawing in a fortifying breath, Rachel fastened up her dress and returned to the front room.

Oliver was pacing when she came out. From the look of him, he had been pacing the entire time she had been gone, too. His usually-well-groomed hair was tousled from his having run his fingers through it repeatedly, and he had removed his coat. The gun, she noticed, had been transferred from his coat pocket to the waistband of his pants.

"How about if I make us a fresh pot of coffee? It's going to be a long night," she suggested with stiff cheerfulness. From the corner of her eye she caught Lupe's sudden movement. The old woman had been hovering in the corner of the room keeping an eye on their visitor the whole time Rachel had been gone, and Rachel flashed her a quelling look when she would have offered to make the coffee. Rachel had to do this herself.

"I'd like some coffee," Oliver agreed, but to Rachel's dismay he followed her out into the kitchen.

With hands that shook slightly, she emptied the coffeepot and began her preparations. Inside, her mind was racing. She needed an excuse to get Oliver out of the room for a few minutes while she carried out the next step in her plan. "You know, Hank, I shouldn't drink any more coffee," she said in a voice that sounded false even to her own ears but which she prayed would fool Hank. "What I'd really like is some cold, fresh milk. I think there's a pitcher down in the well. Would you fetch it for me?"

Fortunately, Hank did not seem to find anything unusual in the request. "Of course," he agreed with a spark of the old, courteous Hank.

Rachel gritted her teeth as the door slammed behind him, and she forced herself to count to ten before she ran to the cupboard where she knew the small brown bottle was stored. Yes, there it was. Breathing a prayer of thanks as her fingers closed around it, she rushed back to the simmering coffeepot flicked off the lid and emptied the contents of the bottle into the black brew.

"What are you doing?" Hank demanded.

Rachel whirled to face him. The brown bottle slipped from her suddenly nerveless fingers and clattered to the floor. He was standing in the doorway and Rachel realized from his expression that he had not been fooled by her ruse at all. He had simply pretended to leave and then come

461

sneaking back to catch her in the act. "Hank, I . . ." she began but she could think of no words to placate him.

He strode purposely up to her, outrage at her betrayal glittering in his eyes. "What is this?" he asked bitterly, stooping quickly to retrieve the bottle she had dropped. "Some kind of poison?"

"It's only laudanum," she explained, laying a hand over her clamoring heart. "I only wanted to put you to sleep so I could warn Cole . . ."

"Warn him?" Hank raged, flinging the bottle away and grasping her by both arms.

But Rachel was unmoved by the horror and disbelief on his handsome face. "Yes, warn him," she replied, lifting her chin in defiance, oblivious to the way his fingers were brushing her flesh. "I told you, he's my husband and I love him. But it doesn't matter whether I warn him or not, Hank. Cole already knows about the attack, and he's ready for it."

"Knows? How could he know?" Hank demanded, tightening his hold until Rachel winced.

"Lettie told us everything," Rachel said through gritted teeth.

Hank blinked as if absorbing this information were difficult. Slowly, his hands relaxed and Rachel was able to pull free of him. "Lettie is dead," he said after a full minute of puzzled silence.

"She died after she got here, but she was alive when we first found her. She told Cole all about Statler's plan," Rachel informed him, rubbing her upper arms to ease the discomfort Hank had caused her.

"He knows all about it," Hank repeated, his voice small and lost and still a little puzzled.

Taking advantage of his inattention, Rachel began to sidle away from him, but she was not quick enough.

"It won't do him any good," Hank announced triumphantly, grabbing Rachel's arm again. "He doesn't know that the attack will come tonight and Statler has more men and the element of surprise . . ."

"Let her go, *señor*."

Both Hank and Rachel were startled at the note of command in the raspy voice. When Rachel looked up, she had to suppress an almost hysterical urge to laugh at the sight of Lupe holding a pistol that was practically as big as she was. "Let her go," Lupe repeated, using both thumbs to pull back the hammer of the revolver. The click was loud in the silent room. Hank obediently released Rachel's arm and once more she stepped away from him.

"Sit down, *señor,* and put your gun on the table. Very careful," Lupe said as Rachel moved to stand beside her.

Hank sank down into the chair he had vacated earlier, still looking slightly dazed. "It won't matter," he said faintly, "Statler will win. Elliot doesn't even stand a chance." Rachel thought he sounded as if he were trying to convince himself.

"You, go to your man," Lupe told her.

Rachel needed another moment to realize the import of Lupe's command. Things were happening so quickly that she had not yet realized she was now free to go to Cole. "Oh, thank you, Lupe," she said, giving the old woman a grateful glance. Then, turning on her heel, she raced for the front room.

There was still some daylight left, she noticed, snatching a jacket from a hook by the door. She knew the area in which Cole had planned to camp and a herd of cattle should not be too difficult to spot. Please, God, let her be in time.

Moving swiftly, Rachel coaxed a horse from the corral and took in into the barn to saddle. She had just tightened the cinch strap when she heard the muffled pop of a gunshot. For one minute, she could not move, not daring to trust her own ears, her blood frozen in her veins in terror at what such a sound might signify. Several heartbeats passed and no other sound came from the house. "Oh, dear God," Rachel breathed, and then she cried, "Lupe! Colleen!"

Panicked, she raced toward the house which now looked

ominous in the growing twilight. "Lupe!" she called again, but when the front door opened, it was Hank Oliver whom she saw.

"No!" she shrieked in protest, and then once more screamed Lupe's name in desperation, but it was no use. No one came except Oliver, and he came quickly, catching her and holding her when she would have run from him to the house. "What have you done?" she cried. "Where's Lupe? Where's my baby?"

But Hank did not answer her. Instead, he half carried, half dragged her to the barn in spite of her frantic struggles. "Let me go! I want my baby!" she begged when she realized she was no match for him physically.

"Stop it! Stop it right now!" he commanded, pulling her up short and shaking her viciously until she thought her teeth might rattle. When she was finally still, he hauled her up against him until her eyes were level with his. "I killed the old woman and if you don't come along with me quietly, I'll go back and kill that damned baby, too."

Rachel stared at him in horror. The Hank Oliver she had known, the civilized gentleman, was gone. In his place was a demented stranger whose eyes glittered dangerously. She could easily believe that he had killed Lupe and would murder her child, also, if provoked. For a long moment Rachel heard no sound except the blood thundering in her ears and her own breath rasping in her throat. With great effort she fought off the hysteria that threatened. Poor, dear Lupe was past help, and Rachel could not allow herself the luxury of feeling the pain of loss. Now she had to think of Colleen. Looking into Hank's eyes, she could easily believe him capable of murdering a defenseless infant. She would have to get Hank as far away from her child as she could, even if it meant leaving that child alone. "All right, Hank," she said, proud that her voice quivered only slightly. "I'll go with you."

Oliver stared at her for a long time as if judging her

sincerity. Then, satisfied with what he saw, he released her and looked around to get his bearings. Seeing the horse she had saddled, he pointed to it. "Get on. We'll ride double. That way I won't have to worry about you getting away."

Rachel drew a shaky breath and did as he instructed, vaguely aware that he had already eliminated one possibility of escape. She would worry about that later. For the moment all she could think about was getting Hank away from her baby. She settled herself awkwardly in the saddle, adjusting her skirts as best she could to cover her legs. Then she looked back down at Hank and a brand-new fear shivered over her.

He was staring at the exposed length of her calf, his face a mask of naked longing. The promise he had spoken earlier echoed in her mind, "I'd never treat you that way," but it brought her small comfort. Plainly, this new Hank *would* treat her that way. For the first time she realized with horror that in going with Hank, she was putting herself in danger. "Hank . . ." she said, not really knowing what she was going to say, certain only that she must convince him not to do what he was so obviously thinking.

At the sound of her voice, he jumped, startled out of his staring. For a second he closed his eyes and a shudder passed through his body. When he opened his eyes again, the expression that had frightened her was gone and she wondered briefly if she had imagined it. Hank had never looked at her that way before, and her logical mind still could not quite accept such a drastic change in him.

As she wondered, he mounted the horse, seating himself behind her, and she stiffened in revulsion at the nearness of his body. Dear God, what had she gotten herself into? she thought frantically as his arm came around to clasp her waist and draw her back against him. The heat of his body and the rancid odor of his own tension enveloped her in a suffocating cloud and for a moment she thought she might faint.

Then he took up the reins and kicked the horse into

motion. The bite of the chill evening breeze as they left the barn revived her somewhat, enough so that she noticed the way Hank's hands were trembling. In fact, she realized with surprise, his whole body was trembling. Could he possibly be as frightened as she? Swallowing the terror that was trying to choke her, Rachel forced herself to remain calm. She would never get away from him, would never be able to protect herself, if she panicked.

Consciously, she drew several deep breaths and let them out slowly. She would act as if nothing were wrong, as if they were simply going for a little ride. If she could convince Hank that she was not afraid of him, he would be calmer, too, and easier to control. When she felt her voice would be steady enough, she asked, "Where are we going?"

Hank took his time answering and Rachel realized that he really did not know himself. "We're going where no one will ever think of looking for us," he said at last.

Hank repeated the words over again to himself, convinced that he was right. It was a brilliant move, he decided. They would be safe there, and he would have Rachel all alone, all to himself. The thought sent a hot shaft of longing through his body, the same longing he had felt moments ago when he had glimpsed the shapely curve of Rachel's ankle. No! he thought fiercely. Rachel wasn't like that. Rachel was good and pure. She was the woman he loved, and he would never use her in that way, never degrade her. Such a thing would be unspeakably wrong.

But, a tiny voice inside his head argued, Elliot had already degraded her. Elliot had used her and gotten her with child. She was no longer pure and good. The wind carried a wisp of her hair across his face and with it her scent, light and sweet and floral. His body hardened with desire. No, she was no longer his perfect Rachel, and she should be punished for her betrayal . . .

Rachel twisted around for one last look at the house. She saw no sign of life, and her heart throbbed with the raw pain of losing Lupe so senselessly and the terror of leaving her helpless baby behind. If only she had taken that one extra minute to tie Oliver up before she left. She should have known that Lupe was no match for him, gun or no gun.

Once she started berating herself, Rachel could not seem to stop her torturous thoughts. What if Lupe were not really dead but only wounded? What if even now she were suffering? Rachel should have insisted that Hank take her back to the house to see for herself. And what about Colleen? What if she woke up, hungry and frightened and no one came for her? What if she fell off the big bed? What if . . . ?

Rachel stifled a sob as a dozen horrible possibilities tormented her and panic surged through her once more. And then there was Hank and the lust she had seen flickering in his eyes. Why had she agreed to go with him? Why hadn't she fought him? She could have made him promises, she could have . . . Then she remembered his threat to kill Colleen and his contempt when he had called the baby "Elliot's whelp."

Rachel closed her eyes over the tears that blinded her and she could quite clearly picture her baby lying snug and safe on the big bed, just as she had last seen her. The dangers Colleen faced alone in the house were small compared to the danger she faced from Hank Oliver. Rachel knew she had to keep on protecting her baby, even if that meant going with Hank. Even if that meant enduring . . . No, she would not think of it. If she did, she would not be able to bear it. Straightening her spine in resolve, Rachel blinked away her tears.

She would be brave. She would not mourn now. She would not dwell on what might have been or what might be. She would instead, concentrate on getting away from Oliver as soon as possible and going back to rescue her baby.

When she had cleared the tears from her eyes, Rachel noticed that they were on the road to town. Hank had said he was taking her someplace where no one would think to look for them, but surely there was no such place in Canaan. She decided not to point that out to him, however. In town lay her greatest chance of attracting attention and winning her escape. So she rode quietly, never letting him suspect the rebellious thoughts fermenting in her brain.

When they reached the outskirts of town, Hank fumbled in his coat and drew out the gun he had flashed earlier in the evening. Rachel stiffened in renewed terror when she felt the barrel pressed into her side.

"I don't want to hurt you, Rachel, but I've already killed once tonight and I don't want to be caught. Just be quiet and everything will be fine," he promised.

Rachel drew a ragged breath, knowing everything was far from fine. Her logical mind was arguing that the Hank she knew would not kill her, but she did not trust the note of panic in his voice. This was not the Hank she knew. If he shot her, he might regret it later, but his regret would not help her a bit. Painfully aware of the cold metal, she decided to be very quiet.

To her complete surprise, he rode right up to the town. She was beginning to think he was crazy enough to take her to the boardinghouse where he lived, but then he circled off the main street and into a back alley. Rachel frantically searched the darkness for someone who might see them and recognize the oddness of her situation, but she saw no one. The hour was late, and the streets were deserted. She could have screamed, of course. That scream was very close, rising up like a bubble in her constricted throat, but as if sensing her impulse, Hank prodded her with the barrel of the gun. Terrified anew, Rachel swallowed down hard and concentrated on controlling her trembling.

Hank pulled up in front of a small cabin sitting alone at the end of the alley. It looked deserted.

"Whose house is this?" she asked through lips stiff with fear.

"Shhh!" Hank cautioned, giving her a warning shake that silenced her immediately. He swung down from the horse

468

and stepped away, keeping his pistol trained on her. "Get down."

Nearly paralyzed with fear and the stiffness of riding, Rachel did so with difficulty. The moment her feet touched the ground, Hank grabbed her, wrapping his gun hand around her throat and dragging her with him as he led the horse into the lean-to beside the cabin. While he secured the animal, a difficult business considering the way he was holding Rachel, Rachel tried to regain her control, tried to plan, but her brain could not seem to function. Simply breathing became a conscious effort as his arm cut into her windpipe and her own agitation belabored her lungs.

When he finished with the horse, Hank dragged her back outside and toward the door of the cabin. The door was unlocked, and Rachel stumbled inside beside Hank. "There's a lamp and some matches on the table. Light it," he commanded, shoving her against the table she could only barely make out in the darkness. With trembling hands she found the matches and struck one. In another moment she had lit the lamp and replaced the glass chimney.

Conscious that Hank still held the gun on her, Rachel took a moment to compose herself, and then she looked around carefully, hoping to find a means of escape or at least a weapon of some sort. All she saw was what was obviously a woman's one-room dwelling. The bed in the corner was carefully made up and everything was neatly kept, but Rachel saw definite signs that a struggle had taken place: an overturned chair; a dresser scarf pulled halfway off, taking several knicknacks with it; dresser drawers partially opened as if the piece of furniture had been violently jarred. Horror slithered over her.

"Whose house is this?" she asked again, her voice hoarse with the suspicion that she already knew.

"Lettie's," he said, confirming that suspicion.

Rachel closed her eyes against the vision of Will Statler beating and violating the poor, pitiful girl whom she had known only briefly. Was that what Hank had planned for her?

Hank watched her straighten away from the table, letting his gaze drift slowly over her. He took in the way her dark hair glinted in the lamplight, the way the curves of her body were appealing even beneath the jacket she wore.

The room was still warm from the heat of the day. "Take off your jacket, Rachel," he said.

Rachel turned to face him, clasping both her hands against her churning stomach. "I'm still cold . . ." she began.

But he cut her off. "Take it off," he commanded, waving the gun at her menacingly.

Rachel obeyed, fumbling with the buttons in her haste. When she had at last slipped the coat from her shoulders and laid it on the table, she allowed herself to meet his gaze once more. She shuddered at the expression in his pale eyes. "Hank . . ." she tried in an appeal to whatever reason he might have left.

"Over there," Hank ordered, motioning her toward the bed. When she did not move, he went to her, clutching her arm and dragging her.

"No, Hank! Don't do this!" Rachel pleaded even as she struggled, heedless now of the gun.

But Hank was unmoved. Rachel had betrayed him. She was no better than Lettie now, no better than a common whore. He'd never been able to bring himself to touch Rachel before, but now things were different. Now he could do whatever he wanted with her.

Dimly, Rachel heard Hank's gun clatter to the floor, but still she could not wrench loose from his grasp. Then he threw her down onto the bed and fell on top of her, driving the air from her lungs and leaving her gasping and unable to fight. His mouth came down on hers, wet and revolting, and Rachel felt her stomach turn. Bile rose in her throat as she twisted frantically to avoid his kiss.

His fingers dug painfully into her hair, holding her still for his assault. Unable to move her head, she twisted her body, violently trying to buck off his weight, but her movements only seemed to arouse him more. His hips churned against hers through the layers of their clothing in a frenzy of need.

At last she managed to grab a handful of hair and yank, forcing his mouth from hers. "Stop it!" she gasped.

"No, Lettie, you can't stop me," he said, his voice almost shrill.

"I'm not Lettie!" Rachel cried, thrashing even more furiously until her knee worked free and she lifted it swiftly in an attempt to disable him.

Her blow missed, catching him in the hip, but the combination of the impact and her words startled him enough so that she was finally able to push him off her and lunge to safety. And the gun.

Her fingers were on it when Hank caught her and batted her aside, sending her sprawling across the floor. By the time she scrambled to her knees, he had picked up the weapon and had it pointed, however unsteadily, in her direction.

"Don't move, Rachel. Don't make me hurt you," he begged as his chest heaved in reviving breaths.

Rachel, too, was fighting for breath and her heart was pounding in her chest as if it might burst free at any moment. She did not move as she reassessed her situation. Would Hank resume his rape now that he had the gun again? Or had he only tried to rape her because he had confused her and Lettie for just a moment? And would he confuse them again?

She forced herself to calm down. "Hank, I'm not Lettie," she said very slowly. She did not want to antagonize him or startle him, but she had to know his current mental state.

Hank nodded, still panting. "No," he agreed, "you're Rachel. My Rachel."

Rachel grasped at this straw. "That's right, Hank. I'm your Rachel. You don't want to hurt me, do you? You promised that you wouldn't." She tried a small smile, although her body was still trembling violently.

471

His brow creased in puzzlement as he thought this over. At long last, he shook his head. "No, I don't want to hurt you."

Rachel breathed a silent prayer of thanks. "Then put the gun away, Hank," she said softly, coaxingly.

He stiffened at this. He was not that far gone. "No, not until I know he's dead. Not until I know you're really mine."

Fear clutched at her heart at the reminder of the danger Cole was still in, but she had to concentrate on getting out of her current situation before she could help Cole. "I won't try to get away as long as you don't try to hurt me," she tried, still forcing herself to smile.

Hank looked at her in astonishment. "I'd never hurt you, Rachel," he said, straightening and using his free hand to adjust his clothes and smooth his hair. He was turning back into the old Hank right before her eyes. She felt some of her panic abating.

"I'm glad, Hank," she said quite truthfully. "Now put the gun away so we can . . ."

"No," he said abruptly. "I can't do that, not yet. Go back over to the bed."

Rachel gasped in horror, all her panic returning in a rush.

Seeing her terror, Hank hastened to reassure her. "Oh, no, not for that," he said, blushing furiously. "It's only . . . I just want you to be comfortable. It's going to be a long night. I'm afraid I'll have to tie you, just to be sure you don't try to get away. But I won't . . . I promise . . ." His voice trailed away helplessly. He couldn't even say it, and Rachel believed that he would not be able to do it, either, at least for the moment. She would have to be careful, though. His mood was very fragile. If she said or did the slightest thing to upset him, there was no telling what he might do.

Forcing herself to remain outwardly calm, she rose carefully to her feet. "All right, Hank. I'll lie down, but you don't need to tie me." She moved cautiously over to the bed.

Hank watched her. "When Statler goes to the ranch and

472

doesn't find me, he'll come to town. We'll hear him and his men, and then we'll know for certain that they've won. Then you'll be free, Rachel." As he spoke he glanced around and finally spotted some stockings sticking out of one of the partially open dresser drawers. Jamming his gun into the waistband of his pants, he drew out the stockings and began to tie them together to form a rope.

Rachel tried to protest when he began to wrap one end of this rope around her wrists, but her protests agitated Hank and she began to fear he would grow hysterical again. At last, she let him tie her hands to the bedpost. The rope was loose. If she really needed to get free, she felt certain she could easily do so.

"This may be a little uncomfortable, but at least you'll be able to lie down and get some rest," he told her when he had finished. "I'm afraid I'll have to gag you, too, but this is only temporary. I know when you see that I've won, you'll realize that you love me."

Rachel nodded dumbly, knowing she must play along. "I'm starting to realize it already," she lied, even though the words tried to stick in her throat.

But he was not convinced enough to forgo the gag. "I'm sorry about this," he apologized as he slipped a clean strip of fabric between her lips and tied it securely behind her head. "It's only for tonight. By tomorrow everything will be different," he said, pressing her to lay back against the pillow.

Yes, Rachel thought, by tomorrow everything would be different. For right now, all she could do was pray, pray that Lupe would be alive when someone found her, pray that Colleen would be safe, pray that Cole would survive the fight with Statler . . . and pray that Hank would keep his promise through the long night to come.

Rachel's eyes snapped open as she awakened from the

473

light doze into which she had slipped. She must truly have been exhausted to fall asleep when she was so thoroughly terrified. Even though she herself was momentarily safe, she could not forget that everyone she loved was in mortal danger. All she could think about was Lupe lying in a pool of blood, of Cole fighting off Statler's men amid a hale of bullets, and of Colleen crying, alone in the night. And hadn't Hank said something about Statler going to the ranch? What if he found the baby? Would he harm her? But no, she chastened herself, Statler would not find her because he would not be going to the ranch. Cole was going to win the fight, and it would be Cole who went to the ranch and found Colleen. Then he would come for Rachel. Rachel closed her eyes in despair. Would anyone even think to look for her in Lettie's cabin?

Fighting off that ugly thought, she forced her eyes back open and glanced around. She found Hank seated at the table on the other side of the room. He was slumped forward, his head resting on his arms, apparently asleep. The lamp had long since burned out, and the fact that she could see him clearly made her realized that it must be daylight, or close to it.

She turned her gaze to the window, verifying her suspicions. Dawn was making feeble headway into the darkness, but it would soon be morning. Then, before her startled eyes, a shadow cut off the light. The silhouette of a man's head appeared at the window, rising cautiously above the sill. The face was shadowed, but she would have known that hair anywhere. The Kid! They had found her!

Before she could stop herself, a joyous cry slipped past her gag. The noise woke Hank and his alarmed grunt terrified her. She could not let Hank know they had been found.

"What is it? What's the matter?" he demanded, running a hand over his face to wipe away the fog. He quickly surveyed the room, and finding nothing amiss glanced out the window.

Rachel held her breath, but when she let her own gaze follow his she saw nothing except the morning sunlight. The Kid was gone. She barely had time to feel relieved when she looked up to find Hank looming over her. "What's the matter?" he repeated, and then realized the folly of his question. He quickly moved to untie her gag.

As his fingers fumbled with the knot, Rachel's mind raced. What would she say? She did not dare tell Hank that the Kid and probably Cole and the rest of her men were outside. She knew from experience that if he panicked, he might do something crazy. No, she couldn't tell him, and she knew her men would not rush the house with her inside. The best thing to do would be to get Hank outside somehow.

Very carefully, Hank removed the gag from Rachel's mouth. She worked her jaw and tried to speak, but found her tongue would not cooperate. "Water," she managed to croak.

Hank stared stupidly for a moment and then, as if finally understanding her request, moved quickly to the bucket sitting beside the stove. Rachel closed her eyes in frustration. She had hoped he would go outside to the pump. In another second, he brought her a cup of warm, brackish water and helped her sit up so she could drink it.

As she swallowed the water, another of her needs became apparent. The perfect excuse. Why hadn't she thought of it sooner? She knew an hysterical urge to laugh at her own cleverness. "Hank, I . . ." she stammered, feigning embarrassment. "I need to go outside."

Hank's embarrassment was not feigned. He turned scarlet. "Of course," he muttered, hastily untying her hands. "I'm sorry, I should have known, I mean . . ." he rattled on, but Rachel paid him no attention. She was too busy making her plans.

If she were in the way, Hank might use her as a shield. She

475

would have to get out of the way very quickly. She stood, testing her legs. Everything seemed to be in working order, although her hands and arms were stiff and clumsy. Hopefully, she would not need to use them.

They started for the door, but Hank stopped her for one last warning. "Don't try to run or scream, Rachel," he said, patting the gun that still rested at his waist.

Rachel nodded her understanding. She had no intention of doing either.

Hank took her arm in a secure grip as he opened the door and they stepped out onto the small stoop.

"Hank, you're hurting my arm," she said loudly, so her men would know exactly who had come out the door.

"Stay right there, Oliver!" The Kid's voice cut through the morning stillness. "Not one more step."

Startled, Oliver released his hold on Rachel and she threw herself off the porch, scrambling to safety while staying close to the ground.

From a different direction she heard another very familiar, very welcome voice. "Don't draw your gun," Miles warned.

But Hank wasn't listening to any more commands. Roaring an incomprehensible curse, he finally managed to pull his gun free. Waving it wildly, he charged down the steps and fired off a shot in the general direction of Miles's voice.

Rachel cringed, drawing herself into a protective ball, as other shots answered his. Hank ran a few more steps and then, as if he had collided with an invisible wall, he stopped short and slumped to the ground.

The gunfire ceased abruptly, and Rachel watched the Kid hurry out from his hiding place behind a barrel and over to where Hank lay sprawled on the ground.

"Rachel, are you all right?" Miles's voice so close startled her and she looked up into his concerned face.

"Yes, I'm fine but where's . . ."

"He's not hurt bad," the Kid reported loudly after examining Oliver's wound. "He'll live to hang."

"Hang!" Oliver screeched. "I didn't do anything!" He continued to protest violently as some of her men bound him.

With Miles's assistance, Rachel finally stumbled to her feet. "Did he hurt you?" Miles asked anxiously.

Rachel did not even hear the question. She had seen the Kid and she had seen Miles and she had seen the others. She had not seen Cole. Something was very wrong. "Cole? Where's Cole?" she demanded, grasping Miles by his shirt.

"He's . . ." Miles started to explain, but he was cut off.

"Rachel!"

Rachel turned at the sound of her name. "Cole!" she cried and ran to him.

Something was still wrong. She registered that fact in the few seconds it took to reach him, but then his arms closed around her and his mouth came down to hers, and she forgot all about it. She clung to him for long minutes, savoring the bliss of simply touching him, of knowing he was safe. Then the thought or the impression that had disturbed her before disturbed her again. Reluctantly, she broke the kiss, pulling back to look at him again.

"You're hurt!" she cried in alarm at the sight of the bloody bandage peeking out from under his hat. Pulling back farther, she caught sight of the bloodstains on his shirt and fought off a wave of dizziness. "Cole," she whispered faintly.

"It's nothing," he assured her, alarmed at the way the color had suddenly drained from her face and cursing himself for not having changed his shirt. It hadn't seemed very important before, in the rush to find her.

"What happened?" she asked, not wanting him to know how very frightened she was but unable to keep the fear out of her voice.

Before he could find the words to make light of his injury,

Miles spoke up.

"It's just a scratch, Rachel. Nothing to worry about. Statler took a potshot at him, but luckily he hit him where it would do the least damage . . . in his head."

Miles's jest fell flat. Rachel really did feel faint now. "He shot you in the head?" she demanded tearfully, reaching up to remove his hat so she could get a better look.

"He missed," Cole insisted, ducking to avoid her ministrations, but when he did, her hand bumped his wound and drew an involuntary moan from him. "Well, he almost missed," Cole corrected in the face of her accusatory look.

"How bad is it?" she asked Miles, no longer trusting Cole's evaluation.

"It's just a scratch," Miles repeated. "Cole was leaning over talking to Statler when the old bas—the old buzzard pulled a gun. He had a derringer up his sleeve. I reckon he meant to blow Cole's brains out. 'Course, if Cole had any brains to start with, he wouldn't have been leaning over Statler in the first place . . ."

"Shut up, Miles," Cole growled, seeing the growing horror on Rachel's face. He drew her aside, away from Miles and the rest of the men, away from where Hank still shrilled his protestations of innocence. "How about you?" he asked anxiously when they were alone. "Are you hurt? Did he . . . ?"

Rachel shook her head. "No, he didn't touch me," she lied. There was no use telling him what had almost happened, not now. She went willingly when he drew her back into his arms.

"Thank God," he breathed into her hair. "When I got back to the ranch, and Lupe told me what happened, I almost lost my mind . . ."

"Lupe?" Rachel repeated, pulling away. "Lupe told you?" she asked, almost afraid of the answer, afraid she had misunderstood.

Cole looked a little puzzled at her question. "Yes, she told us that Oliver had taken you and . . ."

"Lupe is alive!" Rachel almost shouted, grabbing Cole's arms as if by doing so she could make it be true.

Now Cole really was puzzled. "Yes, she's alive," he verified cautiously.

"Oh, thank heaven," Rachel murmured. "How badly is she hurt? I should go to her right now. Oh, Cole . . ."

"She's fine," Cole assured her. "She's got a bump on her head from where she fell, but other than that . . ."

"Fell? A bump?" Rachel echoed incredulously. "Cole, Hank told me he'd killed her! I heard the gunshot!"

Cole's eyes widened in understanding. No wonder Rachel was so upset. "He tried to overpower her. The gun went off, I guess, and he knocked Lupe over. She hit her head, and she must have been stunned for a minute. By the time she came to, you and Oliver were riding away."

Rachel's eyes blurred with tears of relief. "He told me he'd killed Lupe and if I didn't go with him, he would go back and kill Colleen . . ."

Cole crushed her to him, unwilling to hear any more. "Lupe's fine," he whispered soothingly.

"And Colleen?" Rachel asked, no longer afraid to hear the answer because if Lupe was alive and almost well, she would have taken perfect care of the baby.

"Last time I saw her she was mad as a wet hen because her mama wasn't there to feed her," Cole said.

Rachel gave him a watery smile, suddenly conscious of her overfull breasts and an overwhelming longing to see her child. "I want to go home. Please take me home, right now," she begged.

There was nothing he wanted to do more.

Leaving Oliver in Miles's capable hands, Cole rented a buggy at the livery. By the time the hired horse had been hitched to it, however, Rachel had begun to notice that her

479

husband was not nearly as unaffected by his head wound as he wanted her to believe. His hands were far from steady, and once he sat down abruptly as if afraid he might fall down.

Cole protested when she announced that the Kid would drive them back, but the fact that he gave in with only a token argument convinced Rachel that he really was ill.

"When we get home, we'll have Lupe look at your head," Rachel decided, "And on the way, you can explain to me how you happened to get shot in the first place."

Since that was the very last subject Cole wanted to discuss, he decided to play on her sympathy. Feigning fatigue, he leaned back against the seat, propped his hat over his face, and pretended to doze.

Unwilling to disturb him, Rachel kept silent for a while until she began to remember all the questions she had about her rescue.

To the Kid, in a low voice so she would not awaken Cole, she said, "I saw you looking in the window."

The Kid glanced up and gave her a lopsided grin. "I know you did. That's why I ducked. It was pretty smart of you to get Oliver outside like that."

Rachel returned his grin. "He's a pretty easy man to fool." Then she frowned. "How did you ever find me, though? He thought that was the last place anyone would look."

The Kid shrugged modestly. "We'd managed to figure out from the tracks that he was taking you someplace in town. We'd looked every place else we would think of. That was the only place left."

"The Kid thought of it," Cole said from under his hat. Rachel threw him a curious look which he did not see, and then turned back to find the Kid blushing.

"Thank you," she said simply, giving his arm a squeeze. She darted another look at her husband who was still hiding under his hat as the buggy rattled along on its way toward the Circle M. She gave the Kid a conspiratorial wink. "Now maybe you'll tell me where my husband was hiding while the rest of you men were taking care of Oliver."

"I was not hiding," Cole asserted indignantly, snatching the hat away from his face.

Rachel ignored him, listening intently to the Kid's overly earnest explanation. "The fact is, ma'am, that Cole was so peaked from being shot up that we made him lay down while we went after Oliver."

"Damn you," Cole blustered, "I was not laying down!"

Rachel was giving him a considering look, as if she were trying to judge the severity of his injury. Torn between needing her sympathy in order to escape some other, very embarrassing explanations, and not wanting to appear cowardly, he hesitated a minute. He decided the truth was a good compromise. "They made me stay in the background. They didn't think my gun hand was steady enough to trust my shooting so close to where you were. And neither did I," he admitted grudgingly.

"That's the truth, Mrs. Elliot," the Kid said. "Cole, he thought of the whole plan, told us not to go busting in there with you inside but to wait until Oliver came out, the whole thing. It was all his idea. We practically had to tie him up to keep him back, though," he added loyally.

Rachel glanced thoughtfully at the men seated on either side of her. "Do you have any idea how frightened I was when I saw the Kid and Miles and all the others and you were nowhere to be seen?" she inquired of Cole. "I was afraid you'd been hurt, maybe even killed, and it looks like I had a lot to worry about," she said, eyeing his bandaged head.

Cole winced. So far, he'd managed to remain the hero in her eyes, but she would be really disgusted when she found out how stupid he had been where Statler was concerned. He decided now would be a good time to distract her, so he groaned and pretended to be in pain. He did not have to pretend very much.

"Oh, I'm sorry," Rachel said, instantly repentant. "I never should have started on you. Lay back and rest. We'll be home soon."

Cole did as instructed.

When they reached the ranch, a very relieved Lupe greeted them on the porch. She was holding a very outraged baby in her arms who lunged the moment she recognized her mother. Rachel captured them both in her embrace, tears of joy and relief streaming down her face. When she was certain that Lupe was none the worse for her experience, she said, "Would you look at Cole's head? He's in a lot of pain."

"Really, it's nothing," he insisted, but he had convinced Rachel too thoroughly, so he had to submit to Lupe's examination. Lupe ordered him into the kitchen where she had all her medicines already laid out. Rachel followed, carrying the baby. She took a seat opposite Cole at the table and began to nurse the demanding child while she watched Lupe minister to Cole.

Lupe pushed him down into one of the kitchen chairs and got to work unpeeling the crude bandage. Rachel gasped when she saw the groove the bullet had made on the side of his head, and when she thought of how close it had come to killing him, she had to close her eyes for a moment.

Cole grumbled while Lupe clipped the hair away from the wound. "I can see I'll have to keep my hat on from now on if I want to look respectable," he remarked in a feeble effort to lighten the mood. He failed. Reaching over, he covered Rachel's hand with his own where it rested on the kitchen table. "It's only a scratch," he said, repeating Miles's earlier assessment.

Rachel scowled at him. She wondered what these men would consider a serious wound. "That's an awful lot of blood for a scratch," she judged, indicating his stained clothing.

"Yeah," he agreed, glancing down at his shirt. "I bled like a stuck pig, all right, but the bullet just barely broke the skin. Tell her, Lupe," he ordered, appealing to a higher authority.

Lupe grunted. "He will live," she announced grudgingly. "Maybe he even get some sense knocked into him. Hold still," she added when he tried to glare up at her.

"And speaking of sense," Rachel said, feeling a sudden surge of anger, "why were you so close to Statler in the first place if he had a gun?"

Cole winced again at the memory of his foolishness, but he knew he could no longer keep the truth from Rachel. "I didn't know he had a gun," he defended himself. "And he was dying, Rachel. He got gutshot in the fight. I was asking him about who killed your father, just to be sure we'd gotten the right ones last year. We did. It was those two men who ambushed me and Miles last spring, just like we thought."

Rachel nodded. Who had been responsible seemed almost unimportant now. Nothing would ever bring her father back and the thought of revenge seemed slightly ridiculous in light of everything else that had happened lately. Still she was relieved to know that her father's murderers were not still running around loose somewhere. But Cole was going on with his story.

"And then he started telling me that . . ." Cole had to pause as he almost choked on renewed fury. ". . . that Oliver had come here after you."

Rachel squeezed his hand. "I'm safe now. We're all safe. There's nothing more to worry about."

Cole opened his mouth to say something in reply, but his words turned into a very outraged "Hey!" which he directed at Lupe.

His protest didn't stop Lupe from continuing to clean his wound, however, and when he glanced back at Rachel, he noticed she no longer seemed inclined to give him any sympathy. In fact, she looked almost mad.

"I hope you did get some sense knocked into you, Cole Elliot," she said as Lupe finished bandaging his head. "If you ever do a fool thing like that again, I'll . . ."

"Kill me?" he supplied helpfully. Then he grinned at her.

Rachel fought hard not to grin back, but she just couldn't seem to help it. She loved him so much, and she was so very glad he was still alive in spite of his foolishness. "No, I won't kill you, but you'll wish I had," she threatened, scowling with mock fierceness.

What Cole was really starting to wish was that Lupe was about a thousand miles away or at least in the next room so he could do to Rachel what he very much wanted to do. "Are you finished?" he asked the old woman when she started cleaning up her mess.

"*Sí,*" she said, giving him a knowing look.

He acknowledged the look. "Thanks," he said, a twinkle in his eye. "Maybe you'll take care of Colleen for a couple of hours while her parents get a little rest."

"I don't need any rest," Rachel protested. She also did not want to be separated from her baby just yet. Unfortunately, Colleen was not being very accommodating. She had already fallen asleep.

Lupe took the child from her arms.

"She'll be fine," Cole assured Rachel, trying to look weak and sickly. "I need you to help put me to bed."

"Oh, dear, are you feeling bad?" Rachel asked, suddenly remembering that she had earlier been very concerned about Cole. She felt awfully guilty about berating him when he was so obviously hurt. "Come on, you're going right to bed and no arguments." Arguing was, of course, the farthest thing from Cole's mind. "Can you walk? Are you dizzy? Do you need some help?"

Cole allowed as how he did and draped his arm across her shoulders. Rachel gave him a suspicious look when his fingers brushed her breast, but he groaned dramatically and distracted her. As they made their way through the house, Cole contented himself with the feel of her body next to his and the delicate scent of roses that emanated from her. God, she was delectable. He only hoped he could wait until they were in the bedroom.

Awkwardly, Rachel managed to close the bedroom door behind them, and then she led Cole over to the bed where he sank down with a moan. "Will you help me get my clothes off?" he asked, hoping he didn't sound too eager.

"Of course," she said, moving immediately to unbutton his shirt. "This thing will have to be burned," she remarked, noting the bloodstains once more and shuddering slightly. Death had come frightfully close.

"Fine," he murmured, not really hearing what she said. He was too busy noticing how cute she looked with her hair all mussed and her clothes all wrinkled from her ordeal. He rarely got to see her looking less than perfect. She made an enchanting picture.

"Stick your foot up here, and I'll pull your boot off," she said.

He lifted his right foot, and Rachel turned around and straddled it. She gave a few tugs but nothing happened. "Cole, you have to help," she prompted.

"What? Oh, yeah," he replied absently. He'd been so busy looking at the way Rachel's dress curved over her bottom that he'd completely forgotten why she was in that position. In another second his foot slid free. Then he raised the other one and Rachel repeated the process. When she had peeled off his socks, she straightened again and grimaced.

"You really could use a bath," she observed, tossing the socks across the room.

"I'll let you give me one after," he offered.

"After what?" she inquired, a little puzzled.

Opps, he'd almost ruined it. "Nothing. Ohhhh." He feigned an attack of dizziness.

"You'd better lie down," she said, her beautiful dark eyes alive with worry.

"Help me get my shirt off first," he said, pretending to struggle with the garment. Naturally, she came to his rescue, sliding it from his shoulders. He groaned when her hands brushed against his bare skin, and she murmured, "Poor baby." Then she laid him very gently back on the bed, and went to work on the intricate process of removing his leather leggings.

"You never did say for sure," she remembered suddenly, tugging on the metal clasps. "Is Statler . . . dead?"

"He is now. He'll never bother anybody again," Cole reported, closing his eyes against the luxury of her hands on his body. "The rest of his men are locked up along with Oliver now."

Rachel paused in her task, frowning at the thought of Oliver. "Will he really hang? I mean, he didn't actually kill anyone."

Both of Cole's eyes flew open. Was that regret he heard in her voice? Had he misjudged her feelings for Oliver? Could she still care for him, in spite of everything that had happened? Something very like jealousy burned in his chest like gall. "Rachel, we . . . we don't have to keep Oliver. We can let him go."

It wasn't exactly a generous offer. If she did have feelings for the man, Cole didn't want him around, standing trial and all, where he'd be right under their noses. Where Rachel would see him and think about him every day. It would be better all around if Oliver took off, and they never had to see him again.

"Let him go!" she repeated incredulously. "Not on your life! He paid those men to kill you! He hurt Lupe and he threatened our baby. Do you think I could let him go? I'd like to hang him myself!" She wouldn't even mention what he had almost done to her. That was something Cole need

486

never know.

Cole blinked at the sight of her fury. A few moments ago she had been all soft with concern, but now her face was flushed, her lovely mouth set in an angry line, her dark eyes glittering dangerously, and her hands curled into fists and planted belligerently on her shapely hips. His jealousy evaporated in the heat of his desire, and he smiled slightly. "Are you going to get rid of those leggings or not?" he asked in a slightly husky voice.

Recalling herself, Rachel set to work again, not realizing exactly why Cole was so anxious to get his clothes off until she had tossed the leggings away and started on the buttons of his pants. Noticing at last the telltale bulge beneath the buttons, she raised suspicious eyes to his face. "Cole Elliot, shame on you," she chided, fighting a smile.

He looked up from where he still lay across the bed. "I can't help it," he complained, trying to look innocent. "It happens every time a beautiful woman takes my clothes off."

Rachel straightened in mock indignation. "And just how often do you have beautiful women taking your clothes off?" she demanded.

He grinned up at her. "I didn't say 'women,' I said 'a woman.' That's you."

"It had better be," she warned, ruthlessly tugging off his jeans.

"Hey, take it easy," he cautioned, not quite certain from her actions whether she were really angry or just pretending.

She was just pretending, of course, and she had to bite her lips to keep from letting on. When she had tossed his jeans on top of where the leggings already lay on the floor, she reached up to turn back the bed. "Now crawl in here and get some sleep. You look like you could use some."

"Aren't you going to take these off?" he asked, plucking the cotton drawers that was the only garment he still wore.

Rachel eyed them suspiciously, paying close attention to

what the thin fabric could not conceal. "I don't think so. They'll keep you warm."

"*You* could keep me warm," he supposed, and before she could guess his intention, he had grabbed her wrist and pulled her down onto the bed beside him.

"Cole!" she protested, struggling but not too hard.

"Come on, Rachel, you need some sleep, too. You can sleep with me," he explained, nuzzling her neck.

She just barely stifled a moan of pleasure. "Somehow, I think that if I get in this bed with you, neither of us will get much sleep," she remarked.

"I won't mind," he said into the hollow below her ear.

Rachel fought the weakness that shivered through her. "I just couldn't take advantage of you in your weakened condition," she protested. "It wouldn't be . . ."

Cole reared back as if she'd stung him and stared into her face, noticing for the first time the mischief dancing in her eyes. "You little . . . one of these days I really will turn you over my knee," he threatened.

"Promises, promises," she murmured against his lips.

After a little while she did help him take off his drawers, but only after he had helped her remove her clothing, too.

"I always forget just how beautiful you are," he whispered as he drew the sheet up over them both.

"It's for you. It's all for you," she whispered back, slipping her arms around him to pull him close again.

For the first time they made love without the threat of danger hanging over them, and when they touched, it was with a wondrous sense of freedom. Cole's fingers grazed her lightly, almost too lightly, touching here and there, lingering where that touch brought her pleasure and then gliding on to find and reexplore the miracle that was Rachel.

She melted under his hands, chanting his name over and over as she offered herself to him, holding nothing back. Lost in her world of sensation, she could still hear his ragged breathing and the love words he murmured against her skin, and she knew immediately when he had reached the limit of his self-control. She drew him to her then, guiding his strength into the haven of her softness.

He entered her slowly, savoring the moment of possession, worshiping her with his body as he had long worshiped her with his mind. She was everything beautiful and wonderful and good in his life, and he showed her how he felt, loving her until she cried out his name in mindless abandon and clung to him with a fierceness that marked his flesh.

Only when she lay quivering with aftershocks did he take his own pleasure, sobbing her beloved name into the rose-scented cloud of her hair.

A long time later he rolled off her, taking her with him. "Don't go to sleep," he cautioned in a slightly raspy voice. "I want to make love to you again in a minute or two."

Rachel settled into the crook of his arm, draping her leg over his and tunneling the fingers of one hand into the hair of his chest. "A minute or two?" she asked skeptically.

"Well, maybe three or four," he acknowledged.

"Oh," she said, smiling delightedly, and then added, "While we're waiting . . . I mean, for the next three or four minutes, you can tell me what happened last night with Statler."

Cole frowned, twisting his head around to better see her face. "I already told you."

"No, you didn't. I want you to tell me everything that happened, step by step, all the gory details, starting right from the very beginning. I'm especially interested in how you almost let him murder you." The look on her face told him she would brook no arguments, either.

His frown deepened. It was his duty to shield her from the unpleasantness. He knew it was. "You don't need to know all that . . ."

"Yes, I do," she insisted, rearing up again. "I told you before, I'm not made of glass. You don't have to protect me."

"I have to take care of you," he protested.

"We take care of each other," she corrected, "but that doesn't include keeping secrets about important things. Now are you going to tell me or do I have to beat it out of you?"

This was not the first time she had made such a threat, but at the moment she actually looked as if she might try to. Cole didn't know whether he should laugh or run for his life. He didn't really feel much like fighting about it, though, and when he thought about it, maybe she was right. They shouldn't keep secrets from each other. And he knew Rachel could take it. He knew she was strong, a lot stronger than she looked from the outside. Anybody who could give birth to a baby had to be strong. More than that, she was mentally strong. Just look at the way she had stood up through this whole thing, for over a year. Just look at the way she had taken care of Oliver, for pity sakes!

A year ago he would have predicted that sweet little Rachel McKinsey would fold up at the first sign of trouble, would turn into a weeping, hysterical creature. But she hadn't. Instead she had proposed marriage to a virtual stranger and made him a happy man into the bargain, in spite of all the stupid things he'd done to botch things up. She'd stood by him through everything, even though they'd both almost died, and she'd even come to love him. That was the part he found most amazing, but faced with the proof she had given him over and over, he could not doubt it.

No, he had been wrong all the way around. Wrong about Rachel, and probably wrong about ladies in general, too. He guessed maybe she did have a right to know everything that had happened, and so, with a weary sigh, he told her. He did omit some of the gore, but he gave her all the details.

When he had finished, they lay in silence for a while. Cole was fingering a silken lock of her hair, and almost without thinking he whispered, "I love you."

She sighed contentedly. "I love you, too."

Cole grinned. It had been more than three or four minutes. "Want to prove it?"

Rachel grinned back. "Yes."

And she did.

SIZZLING ROMANCE
from Zebra Books

REBEL PLEASURE (1672, $3.95)
by Mary Martin
Union agent Jason Woods knew Christina was a brazen flirt, but his dangerous mission had no room for a clinging vixen. Then he caressed every luscious contour of her body and realized he could never go too far with this confederate tigress.

PASSION'S PARADISE (1618, $3.75)
by Sonya T. Pelton
Angel was certain that Captain Ty would treat her only as a slave. She plotted to use her body to trick the handsome devil into freeing her, but before she knew what happened to her resolve, she was planning to keep him by her side forever.

TEXAS TIGRESS (1714, $3.95)
by Sonya T. Pelton
As the bold ranger swaggered back into town, Tanya couldn't stop the flush of desire that scorched her from head to toe. But all she could think of was how to break his heart like he had shattered hers—and show him only love could tame a wild TEXAS TIGRESS.

WILD EMBRACE (1713, $3.95)
by Myra Rowe
Marisa was a young innocent, but she had to follow Nicholas into the Louisiana wilderness to spend all of her days by his side and her nights in his bed. . . . He didn't want her as his bride until she surrendered to his WILD EMBRACE.

TENDER TORMENT (1550, $3.95)
by Joyce Myrus
From their first meeting, Caitlin knew Quinn would be a fearsome enemy, a powerful ally and a magnificent lover. Together they'd risk danger and defy convention by stealing away to his isolated Canadian castle to share the magic of the Northern lights.

Available wherever paperbacks are sold, or order direct from the Publisher. Send cover price plus 50¢ per copy for mailing and handling to Zebra Books, Dept. 2009, 475 Park Avenue South, New York, N.Y. 10016. Residents of New York, New Jersey and Pennsylvania must include sales tax. DO NOT SEND CASH.

THE BESTSELLING ECSTASY SERIES
by Janelle Taylor

SAVAGE ECSTASY   (824, $3.50)

It was like lightning striking, the first time the Indian brave Gray Eagle looked into the eyes of the beautiful young settler Alisha. And from the moment he saw her, he knew that he must possess her — and make her his slave!

DEFIANT ECSTASY   (931, $3.50)

When Gray Eagle returned to Fort Pierre's gate with his hundred warriors behind him, Alisha's heart skipped a beat: Would Gray Eagle destroy her — or make his destiny her own?

FORBIDDEN ECSTASY   (1014, $3.50)

Gray Eagle had promised Alisha his heart forever — nothing could keep him from her. But when Alisha woke to find her red-skinned lover gone, she felt abandoned and alone. Lost between two worlds, desperate and fearful of betrayal, Alisha, hungered for the return of her FORBIDDEN ECSTASY.

BRAZEN ECSTASY   (1133, $3.50)

When Alisha is swept down a raging river and out of her savage brave's life, Gray Eagle must rescue his love again. But Alisha has no memory of him at all. And as she fights to recall a past love, another white slave woman in their camp is fighting for Gray Eagle.

TENDER ECSTACY   (1212, $3.75)

Bright Arrow is committed to kill every white he sees — until he sets his eyes on ravishing Rebecca. And fate demands that he capture her, torment . . . and soar with her to the dizzying heights of TENDER ECSTASY.

STOLEN ECSTASY   (1621, $3.95)

In this long-awaited sixth volume of the SAVAGE ECSTASY series, lovely Rebecca Kenny defies all for her true love, Bright Arrow. She fights with all her passion to be his lover — never his slave. Share in Rebecca and Bright Arrow's savage pleasure as they entwine in moments of STOLEN ECSTASY.

Available wherever paperbacks are sold, or order direct from the Publisher. Send cover price plus 50¢ per copy for mailing and handling to Zebra Books, Dept. 2009, 475 Park Avenue South, New York, N.Y. 10016. Residents of New York, New Jersey and Pennsylvania must include sales tax. DO NOT SEND CASH.

ROMANCE IN THE OLD WEST
by Cassie Edwards

SAVAGE PARADISE   (1985, $3.95)
When a virile Chippewa brave saved Mariana's life, she
never wanted to leave the wilderness of the unsettled Min-
nesota Territory which she had once detested. Lone Hawk
cursed his weakness for the hated paleface, but for now he
would take her time and again to glory in their *Savage Paradise*.

EUGENIA'S EMBRACE   (1880, $3.95)
At sixteen, Eugenia Marie Scott was ill prepared for the
harsh life she was thrust into: the rough, coarse gold min-
ing town of Cripple Creek. There she was drawn to Drew,
an exciting man of adventure. Drew made Eugenia a
woman, and she fell under a spell she would never break
for the rest of her life.

PASSION'S FIRE   (1872, $3.95)
At first sight, Samantha thought Troy was a cad, but after
one brief kiss, one tender caress, he awakened an unfamiliar stirring from deep within her soul. Troy knew he would
be the one to unleash her passions, and he swore to find
her again . . . to make her burn with *Passion's Fire*.

SAVAGE TORMENT   (1739, $3.95)
Judith should have been afraid of the red-skinned warrior,
but those fears turned to desire as her blue eyes travelled
upward to meet his. She had found her destiny—bound by
his forbidden kiss.

*Available wherever paperbacks are sold, or order direct from the
Publisher. Send cover price plus 50¢ per copy for mailing and
handling to Zebra Books, Dept. 2009, 475 Park Avenue South,
New York, N.Y. 10016. Residents of New York, New Jersey and
Pennsylvania must include sales tax. DO NOT SEND CASH.*

ROMANCE FOR ALL SEASONS
from Zebra Books

ARIZONA TEMPTRESS (1785, $3.95)
by Bobbi Smith
Rick Peralta found the freedom he craved only in his disguise as
El Cazador. Then he saw the exquisitely alluring Jennie among
his compadres and the hotblooded male swore she'd belong just
to him.

RAPTURE'S TEMPEST (1624, $3.95)
by Bobbi Smith
Terrified of her stepfather, innocent Delight de Vries disguised
herself as a lad and hired on as a riverboat cabin boy. But when
her gaze locked with Captain James Westlake's, all she knew was
that she would forfeit her new-found freedom to be bound in his
arms for a night.

WANTON SPLENDOR (1461, $3.50)
by Bobbi Smith
Kathleen had every intention of keeping her distance from the
dangerously handsome Christopher Fletcher. But when a hurri-
cane devastated the Island, she crept into Chris's arms for comfort, wondering what it would be like to kiss those cynical lips.

GOLDEN GYPSY (2025, $3.95)
by Wanda Owen
When Domonique consented to be the hostess for the high stakes
poker game, she didn't know that her lush body would be the
prize—or that the winner would by the impossibly handsome
Jared Barlow whose fortune was to forever crave the *Golden
Gypsy*.

GOLDEN ECSTASY (1688, $3.95)
by Wanda Owen
Nothing could match Andrea's rage when Gil thoroughly kissed
her full trembling lips. She was of his enemy's family, but they
were forever enslaved by their precious *Golden Ecstasy*.

*Available wherever paperbacks are sold, or order direct from the
Publisher. Send cover price plus 50¢ per copy for mailing and
handling to Zebra Books, Dept. 2009, 475 Park Avenue South,
New York, N.Y. 10016. Residents of New York, New Jersey and
Pennsylvania must include sales tax. DO NOT SEND CASH.*

BESTSELLING HISTORICAL ROMANCE
from Zebra Books

PASSION'S GAMBLE   (1477, $3.50)
by Linda Benjamin
Jessica was shocked when she was offered as the stakes in a poker
game, but soon she found herself wishing that Luke Garrett, her
handsome, muscular opponent, would hold the winning hand.
For only his touch could release the rapturous torment trapped
within her innocence.

YANKEE'S LADY   (1784, $3.95)
by Kay McMahon
Rachel lashed at the Union officer and fought to flee the dangerous fire he ignited in her. But soon Rachel touched him with a
bold fiery caress that told him—despite the war—that she
yearned to be the YANKEE'S LADY

SEPTEMBER MOON   (1838, $3.95)
by Constance O'Banyon
Ever since she was a little girl Cameron had dreamed of getting
even with the Kingstons. But the extremely handsome Hunter
Kingston caught her off guard and all she could think of was his
lips crushing hers in feverish rapture beneath the SEPTEMBER
MOON.

MIDNIGHT THUNDER   (1873, $3.95)
by Casey Stuart
The last thing Gabrielle remembered before slipping into unconsciousness was a pair of the deepest blue eyes she'd ever seen. Instead of stopping her crime, Alexander wanted to imprison her in
his arms and embrace her with the fury of MIDNIGHT THUN-
DER.

*Available wherever paperbacks are sold, or order direct from the
Publisher. Send cover price plus 50¢ per copy for mailing and
handling to Zebra Books, Dept. 2009, 475 Park Avenue South,
New York, N.Y. 10016. Residents of New York, New Jersey and
Pennsylvania must include sales tax. DO NOT SEND CASH.*